Cecil Headlam

Selections from the British satirists

With an introductory essay

Cecil Headlam

Selections from the British satirists
With an introductory essay

ISBN/EAN: 9783337275532

Printed in Europe, USA, Canada, Australia, Japan

Cover: Foto ©Andreas Hilbeck / pixelio.de

More available books at **www.hansebooks.com**

SELECTIONS

FROM THE

BRITISH SATIRISTS

With an Introductory Essay

BY

CECIL HEADLAM

Late Demy of Magdalen College, Oxford

LONDON
F. E. ROBINSON
20 GREAT RUSSELL STREET
1897

PREFACE.

I SHARE with many people a holy horror of ' Selections,' but the British satirists are so little known that I am not without hope that specimens from their works may prove both useful and interesting to the ordinary reader.

It is, indeed, due to the same causes that the satirists are little read and that they lend themselves to this treatment of selection. In the first place, especially in the case of the earlier authors, their good things are buried in a mass of writing, partly satiric, partly not, which is dreary and obscure, now that its interest has evaporated with the ephemeral occasion of its production. In the second place, the works of these earlier writers are often quite beyond the reach of the man in the street. In some cases they have never been reprinted, in many cases they have only been reprinted in elaborate and expensive editions, intended solely for scholars and connoisseurs. In the third place, the frank filth and savage coarseness which disfigure so much of our satire have rendered it revolting to modern taste. But there are pearls to be found in almost all these dunghills, and I have endeavoured to present to the reader as many jewels of pure wit and sarcasm and irony as space would allow.

With the object of selecting, where desirable, more copiously from less available writers, I have denied myself the pleasure of giving extracts from the novelists of this century.

Jane Austen, Peacock, Thackeray, Beaconsfield, may, after all, be left to speak for themselves without this adventitious aid of snippets.

Again, with a view to saving space for pieces more generally interesting and more genuinely amusing, I have been as sparing as possible in my selections from authors who require to be read dictionary in hand. I have aimed merely at giving extracts representative of the early English school, not of each early English satirist.

As to the Introduction, I have tried to give a bird's-eye view rather than an exhaustive account or a dull and confusing systematized classification of our satirists, and, whilst noting what seem to me the distinguishing characteristics of them, I have tried, also, in dealing with so many writers in so short a space, to avoid the perhaps unavoidable dulness of a catalogue.

It remains to remind the reader that my criticisms deal almost exclusively with the satirical work—in many cases but a small part of the whole—of the writers reviewed.

4, SMITH SQUARE,
    WESTMINSTER.

SELECTIONS FROM
THE BRITISH SATIRISTS

INTRODUCTION.

I T is useful, in considering a subject of so large
and so vague a character as satiric writing, to
attempt a definition of it. A definition is always
the best introduction to a discussion. But satire is
so elastic a term—it is used to denote a form of
literature which at one time includes, and at another
excludes, so many different elements—that it is impossible to define it accurately.

Satire may be frankly personal, with no other
object than that of private revenge, or professedly
general, with the avowed object of improving public
morals. For all satire is not moral, any more than
all moralizing is satire. Though we are apt to look
for an air of moral superiority and of moral intention
in the satirists, we do not always find these qualities.
Wit, humour, sarcasm, irony, invective, ridicule,
burlesque—all these find a place in satiric writing, but
it is difficult to determine how far any one of them is
necessary to this species of literature; so that it is
perhaps best to be content with saying that satirical

I

writers are the censorious critics of life, literature, and manners—critics, in fact, of everything and of everybody except themselves—and that they use one or more of the above-mentioned weapons. Satire itself, it will then follow, is a matter of critical intelligence. It is founded on intellect and wit rather than on imagination; but when wit and intellect are combined with the creative faculty, there we find the most effective, because the most pleasing, the most ironic, and the most subtle form of satire.

This kind of composition will naturally be most popular, and attract the greatest writers during those periods of literature when men's thoughts turn from the passions to politics, from sentiment to a study of social phenomena; when, in fact, the critical predominates over the imaginative faculty. The triumph of reason and the stir of politics at the time of the Reformation are reflected in the writings of Skelton, and a hundred years later an age of argument and criticism finds expression in such writers as Marvell, Butler, Dryden, Swift, Pope, and Addison.

From the middle of the seventeenth to the middle of the eighteenth century all the world wrote satires,[1] whether against satirists, politics, brandy, coffee, or man.

The reaction in favour of the romantic type of literature begun by Thomson and others, encouraged by Bishop Percy, and established by Sir Walter Scott, left little room for cold and clear-cut criticism, as it had been formulated in the classical satires of Pop But in an advancing civilization the occasion c satire can never wholly be wanting. Byron, Peacock, Beaconsfield, Carlyle, Thackeray, all modulated in different keys on the scale of satire, which criticises or condemns the existing state of literature, society and politics. Till we are all Houyhnhnms,

---

[1] *Vide* the collections of Poems relating to State Affairs.

till the millennium has arrived, when vice and affectation have vanished off the face of the earth, there
will always be scope for the satirist. *Dum civitas
erit, judicia fient*,[1] is true in more ways than one.
Law cannot deal with the offences of bad taste.
Satire was introduced into the world to supply the
defects of law. The satirist should be the watch-
dog of society.[2] This is the ideal. But we have to
admit that the modes of satire are as various as the
motives of satirists. The motive may be the pleasure of laughing in a corner, of reforming mankind,
of making a hit, or of taking revenge. The mode
may be that of denunciation, of irony, or, most useful and least offensive, that which, instead of lashing,
laughs men out of their follies and vices.[3] Of all
these we shall find in the present review examples
that will bear comparison with any that the literature of Greece or Rome or France can afford.

Up to the middle of the fourteenth century the
English satirical spirit expressed itself in the form
of Latin verse,[4] or of imitation and translation of
the prevailing French models.[5] Popular ballads,[6]
satirical and political lays there were, dealing with
the evils that provoked the Lancastrian Revolution ;
but as poems these have little but an antiquarian

---

[1] Cicero, pro Sex. Roscio.
[2] Hor., Sat. II. i. 85 : Si quis opprobriis dignum latraverit.
[3] Swift, *Intelligencer*, No. 111.
[4] *E. g.*, Apocalypsis Goliæ, and the various poems attributed
to Walter Mapes.
[5] *E. g.*, ' The Land of Cockayne.'
[6] This country has always at periods of excitement been
prolific in the production of political squibs, 'libels,' lampoons.
I must refer the curious reader to Mr. Wright's collections of
political poems. Among the chief writers of these ballad-satires
in later days may be mentioned Cleveland, Brome, Buckingham,
Rochester, Dorset, Congreve, Swift, Gay, Sir Charles Hanbury
Williams, Wolcot and the writers in the *Anti-Jacobin*, Hook,
Moore and Burns.

interest, and as satires they are sufficiently illustrated by the extracts given from them and from Langland.

William Langland, the author of 'The Vision of Piers the Plowman,' may claim to be the first great English satirist, and he has the additional interest of being almost the last writer to compose in that native, unrhymed, alliterative verse which his contemporary Chaucer was sending for ever out of fashion. Chaucer himself, who had learned to handle his weapons by translating the 'Roman de la Rose,' wrote, incidentally, brilliant satire, with that sly but genial humour and keen observation which are his. But he wrote it as a poet and a realist, as a transcriber of life, a teller of tales.

His stories are not written with a didactic purpose, but they occasionally give rise to ironical descriptions. In his 'Sir Thopas' he anticipated that sphere of literary criticism in which so much satire has since been centred; whilst, in his carefully-studied portraits of men and manners, he may be said to have foreshadowed the methods of the poets of the seventeenth and eighteenth centuries.[1] The humorous realism with which in the 'Canterbury Tales' he delineates men as he saw them, instead of mere abstract virtues and vices in the allegorical fashion of the day, shows how great a satirist he might have been if he had had any motive for devoting himself to satire; if, in place of a large-hearted interest in men as they were, he had been possessed of a burning zeal to improve them.

Chaucer, however, only grew didactic in his decline. Otherwise, he lacked the moral purpose which we look for in the deliberate satirist. This purpose inspired Langland as truly as it inspired Wycliffe.

[1] Professor Courthope's 'History of English Poetry,' vol. i.

The chief merit of 'Piers Plowman' lies in its being a democratic document, an exact expression, in a homely guise, of the popular sentiment. It gives voice, in the language of the people, to the indignation roused by the corruption it exposes in the nobility, in the Government, and in the Church. Unfortunately, it was necessary for the author to veil his attacks under an allegory, and to resort to the personification of vices and virtues to avoid personalities. To make a long-drawn allegory at all palatable is one of the most difficult of undertakings, and one of the most rarely successful. It says much for Langland's genius that he succeeded in this almost impossible task. For 'Piers Plowman' is still readable, and it is so because the author has known how to relieve the tedium of his allegory by diversions, by sarcastic and ironical wit, by the vigour of his descriptions, and by his minute and vivid drawing of domestic scenes. Langland knew low life as well as Skelton or Crabbe, and he painted it with all the skill of a Dutch master.

But neither this attention to detail nor his allegorical method obscures the earnestness which inspired the humble country priest, who, like Wycliffe, saw in the abuse of wealth by the rich and in the possession of wealth by the Church and Mendicant Friars the root of all the evils he deplored. 'It is in his intense, absorbing moral feeling,' Dean Milman has well observed,[1] 'that he is beyond his age: with him outward observances are but hollow shows, mockeries, hypocrisies without the inward power of religion. It is not so much in his keen cutting satire on all matters of the Church, as his solemn installation of Reason and Conscience as the guides of the self-directed soul, that he is break-

[1] 'History of Latin Christianity,' quoted by Dr. Skeat, to whose admirable edition of Langland I am much indebted.

ing the yoke of sacerdotal domination ; in his constant appeal to the plainest, simplest Scriptural
truths, as in themselves the whole of religion, he is
a stern reformer. The sad, serious satirist, in his
contemplation of the world around him, the wealth
of the world and the woe, sees no hope but in a new
order of things in which, if the hierarchy shall subsist, it shall subsist in a form, with powers, in a
spirit totally opposite to that which now rules mankind. The mysterious Piers the Plowman seems to
designate from what quarter that Reformer is to arise.'

After Chaucer and Langland a long interval
elapses before we come across any English satirist
of worth. Lydgate's satirical work is too insignificant to give us pause, and John Gower, to whom
Chaucer and Lydgate apply the epithet of ' moral,'
is a moralist indeed in whom there is no humour.
He has no individuality and no power of creation.
Thomas Occleve has a distinct humour of his own,
but his verses have hardly any claim to be considered
literature. For fifty years after the death of Lydgate
(? 1440), England, torn as she was by civil wars,
produced neither satirist nor poet. But during this
period the lamp of literature was kept burning
across the Border. A group of Scottish writers, with
James I. of Scotland at their head, kept alive the
tradition of Chaucer. Of this group, Henryson,
Dunbar and Lyndesay concern us, and chiefly
Dunbar. All three were afflicted with the prevailing
disease of allegory. Robert Henryson in his ' Moral
Fables' adapted the Æsopian 'Fables' to the manners
of the day in order to show

> ' How many men in operation
> Are lyke to bestis in condition,'

and is so singularly successful that he may even bear
comparison with La Fontaine. For he has the gift

of easy narration and the power of satiric comment to a remarkable degree. But in spite of his wit and humour—and he has both—he is over-prone to moralize and too ready to preach.

William Dunbar, the foremost and most versatile poet of this Scottish school, has two manners of satire. He can be mild or vindictive, subtle or violent in his attacks. At one time he uses the allegorical style to lash with a wild and burlesque humour personified vices, at another he deluges with furious outbursts of abuse his personal enemies at the Court of King James. In 'The Dance of the Deadly Sins' he has come near to equalling Langland in those passages of 'Piers Plowman' which suggested it. In his railing mood he is a Scottish Skelton, and displays in his satirical ballads just that quality of extremely coarse wit which in later times distinguished Burns. No great amount of originality either in matter or in manner can be justly claimed for Dunbar. But in his verse, as in that of Henryson, there is a music which is seldom to be found in that of Skelton or Barclay, their English contemporaries. Sir David Lyndesay, however, though a daring and trenchant satirist, is so unpolished and uncouth that he can hardly rank as a poet at all. His life was one of action. His writings are those of a man who is, above all things, an earnest reformer, a would-be corrector of all abuses. He was sincere in his convictions and courageous in expressing them. The volume of his work is large. 'The Complaint of Papingo' is perhaps his best political satire. The allegorical method of this piece does not blunt its edge. His full-blooded humour and trenchant invective against corrupt priests and vicious Court favourites are best exemplified in his 'Satyre of the Threi Estates'—a Morality or Interlude acted before the Court and

having the additional interest of being the first
approach to regular dramatic composition in Scotland. But Lyndesay wrote so much during a life
busied with the stormy politics of the time that his
work is in execution far below the level of his pre-
decessors. His aim is practical, but he has no
mastery over his machinery. Moreover, the very
sincerity which inspired him to write at all leads
him too readily, for a satirist, into political moralizing and somewhat prosy preaching.

At the beginning of the sixteenth century we can
return once more to England, and there, in the comic
and satirical part of the 'pithy, pleasaunt and profitable works of John Skelton,' we recognise a writer
truly original in his own special line. In him, however, we need look for no refinement of style, and
little trace of Chaucer's influence. Gifted with a
rude but caustic humour and considerable force of
imagination, he added to these qualities a profound
knowledge of life both high and low. Even apart
from the fascinating originality of his matter and
manner, his almost exhaustless vocabulary of popular
English renders him well worth reading.

Laureate of both Universities and perhaps Court
Poet[1] to Henry VIII., Skelton became Rector of
Diss about 1500, and continued to pour forth invectives in the metre which is called after his name.[2]
The verses rattle on one rhyme till they can no
more.[3] 'The chimes ring in the ear and the thoughts
are flung about like coruscations.'[4] There is in these

---

[1] Certainly he was tutor to Prince Henry.
    'Yt cometh the wele me to remorde
    That creaunser [tutor] was to thy sofreyne lord,'
he says in a poem against lusty Garnyshe.
[2] Skeltonics.
[3] Cf. the metre of Ingoldsby Legends.
[4] I. D'Israeli.

quick-returning rhymes a stirring spirit which is heightened by the playfulness of the diction. His new words are not 'new words with little or no wit,'[1] but pungent, ludicrous and expressive. He used slang knowingly, in the manner of a scholar. His chief satirical productions are 'The Bowge of Courte,' 'The Boke of Colyn Cloute,' and 'Why Come Ye Nat To Courte.' In the first of these he gives us a gallery of characters painted with a boldness and discrimination unknown since the days of Chaucer, and displayed by none of his contemporaries, save, perhaps, the brilliant Dunbar.[2]

Here, however, there is little of the sincere native ring, none of the virulence and bitterness of the personal note which we find in 'Why Come Ye Nat To Courte.'

Colyn Cloute is a savage satirical philippic against the corruptions of the Church. Skelton attacks the bishops for their laziness, luxury, and ignorance, and does not spare the lower orders of the clergy. Like Langland, he based his attack on popular feeling. When he pronounces of this piece:

> ' For though my rhyme be ragged,
> Tattered and jagged,
> Rudely rayne beaten,
> Rusty and moughte eaten,
> If ye take well therwith
> It hath in it some pith' (ll. 53-58),

he is not over-rating its vigour and fearlessness. Yet good criticism of his own work was hardly to be expected from an author who wrote a poem of 1,600 lines in honour of himself.[3] None the less is he right with regard to the merits of Colyn Cloute. In all these satires, indeed, there is a moral earnestness underlying intemperate and scurrilous

---

[1] Hudibras.   [2] Dyce, Skelton's Works, 1843
[3] 'The Garlande of Laurell.'

buffoonery. His wrath is tremendous. He hits straight from the shoulder, and indulges in none of Juvenal's sly backhanders. He writes in a scurry of rhymes which leaves us breathless with righteous indignation.

In 'Why Come Ye Nat To Courte' the satire is entirely personal, and is aimed at Wolsey. The causes which turned 'Skelton Laureate obsequious and loyall' into the bitter assailant of his former powerful patron are unknown. We only know that he attacked the full-blown pride of Wolsey[1] with a boldness that made it necessary for him to flee to Westminster for sanctuary, and with a fierceness of invective almost unparalleled. In Colyn Cloute he had indulged in a few hits at the Cardinal, but in 'Speke, Parrot,' and in 'Why Come Ye Nat To Courte' he gives free rein to the bitterness of his satiric genius. He wields the weapon of his satire with tremendous force and skill, though perhaps a little more generosity would have made the on-slaught more effective. Hardly ever since Catullus attacked Cæsar had a powerful living statesman been so abused. Skelton, indeed, lacks none of the impetuous virulence of Catullus, but he falls short in neatness and finish. There is, however, nothing in this sincere and decent poem to bring the blush to the cheek of 'the young person,' nothing to justify Pope's epithets.[2] These, indeed, are true of the torrents of Billingsgate poured on the head of

[1] Cf. Dyce, Skelton's Works, 1843.
[2]   'Chaucer's worst ribaldry is learned by rote,
        And beastly Skelton heads of houses quote.'
           Pope, 'Imitations of Horace,' Bk. II., Ep. i. 38.

His note is even more unfair: 'Skelton, poet laureat to Henry VIII., a volume of whose verses has been lately re-printed, consisting almost wholly of ribaldry, obscenity, and Billingsgate language.'

'Gaudy, Gresy, Garnyshe,' who apparently challenged the poet

> ' Thus to contaminate
> And to violate
> The dygnyte laureate,'

but they are most untrue of the bulk of his work.

We have not to consider the justice of this attack on Wolsey;[1] only the quality of the satire. The merit of this is in some ways first-rate. The picture Skelton draws will bear comparison for simplicity and bitterness with the passages in Juvenal which suggested it. It was, he tells us, ' at Juuynal's request ' that he was ' forcibly constrayned to wryght of this glorious gest.' But, we feel, he needed no urging. He wrote ' quia difficile est Satiram non scribere,' and his work is stamped with the spirit of a spontaneous outburst. His qualities, in fine, are vivacious fancy and humorous originality tinged by moral earnestness. In this, as in his jubilant freedom, he is truly Rabelaisian before Rabelais.

Alexander Barclay lived and wrote in Skelton's time, but he shared but little in Skelton's views and still less in his originality. Though he also claims to be a follower of Juvenal, he is really the last of the purely mediæval English allegorists.[2] Like Gower, he moralizes incessantly. His ' Ship of Fools ' is a translation, though not a slavish one, of Brandt's ' Stultifera Navis,' but he is more original in being the first to adapt Virgil's Eclogues to the English tongue, with the view of satirizing the manners of the Court. In this line he was followed at intervals by Barnabe Googe and Spenser.

---

[1] *E.g.*, ll. 396 *et seq.*
[2] Cf. Professor Courthope's chapter on the Progress of Allegory, ' History of English Poetry,' vol. i.

1528. 'Rede me and be nott wrothe' is a curious work written by William Roy and Jerome Barlow. It is really a reformation pamphlet, attacking, chiefly in the form of a dialogue between 'two prestes servauntes,' the hierarchy and priesthood of England, especially as represented by Wolsey. It is none too timid, even when tried by the standard of Skelton. The spirit is excellent; the satire is more salt than bitter, and what bitterness there may be is due rather to the facts than to the expression.

1503-1542. Sir Thomas Wyatt may claim the distinction of being our first classical satirist. He gives us the mellowed moralizing of one who has found himself out of place at Courts, and being unable to 'frame his tongue to feign, to cloak the truth,' retires from the world without regret, without bitterness. This feeling at any rate was perfectly genuine; his disdain for the meanness which frequents high places was entirely unaffected. But to express these views, being conscious of the incompleteness of his own language and of the forms of poetry then in use as vehicles of thought, he deliberately imitated foreign and classical models. It is not by this imitation that the vigour and individuality of his thought is impaired, but by the inability of the pioneer to master the technique of these new forms. Still Wyatt's three pieces are terse and smooth in comparison with his contemporary satirists. The first and third of his satires are imitated from Horace and written in the terza rima of Alamanni; the second is imitated from that Italian author.

It is hardly within the scope of this essay to point out how Wyatt and Surrey brought about a revolution in English versification by introducing a metrical in place of a rhythmical structure, nor how these two poets, by setting the example of admitting the influence of the Italian school of the Renaissance, gave a death-blow to the mediævalism which had for so long haunted our literature. In so doing they prepared the way for the freedom and harmony of the Elizabethan writers. However, in satire, Wyatt's example was not immediately followed, nor when, after an interval of over half a century, the Elizabethan classical satirists arose, did they, like Wyatt, imitate the polished irony and witty ridicule of Horace, but rather the vehement denunciations, the coarse and rugged virulence, of Juvenal, Persius and Martial. It is probably in no small degree due to this fact that English satire has almost always been distinguished by two disfigurements—an excessive personal bitterness and an unnecessary coarseness combined with an exaggerated air of moral indignation.

Meantime, Robert Crowley, whose dreary epigrams exhibit him as a 'censor morum,' handed on the flickering torch of native satire to George Gascoigne. This versatile author 'invented,'[1] to quote his own words, 'a morall and godly Satyre called the Steele Glasse, written without rime, but I trust not without reason.' The Steele Glasse, or Mirror, typifies the plain manners of England as opposed to the Crystal Glass—the foreign luxury and corruption of Venice. Though his metres show that he has felt the Italian influence, Gascoigne does not follow Wyatt in imitating classical models, but rather inclines to that allegorical treatment which Spenser frankly adopts. Spenser and Gascoigne, in fact, are, as satirists, nearer to the spirit of Dante and Langland than to that of the era which was now beginning. Spenser, not to mention the incidental satire in the 'Faery Queen,' uses this allegorical method of

1550.

1576.

[1] Epistle Dedicatory, and Dedication of 'Delicate Diet for Daintie Mouthde Drunkards.'

satire in the fifth Eclogue of the 'Shepheard's Calendar' to gird at 'the colourable and fained goodwill
of Protestant and Catholic,' and openly attacks the
loose living of popish prelates in Eclogue IX.
'Prosopopoia, or Mother Hubberd's Tale,' again, is
in the shape of a fable, published in 1591, but
composed, as Spenser tells us, in the raw conceit of
his youth. It is a satire of some heat and choler,
but the point of it is blunted by the allegory. None
the less it contains some fine and famous passages.
Whilst Spenser wrote this fable in over-fluent
heroics, Gascoigne used still less polished blank
verse. The latter, a man of the world and a soldier
of experience, devoted, as he himself put it, ' tam
Marti quam Mercurio,' as much to the God of War
as to the God of Learning, is a shrewd critic of man's
vices and follies, and he preserves for us a curious
picture of the manners and morality of the age. In
spite of his imperfect mastery of blank verse
rhythm, and his tendency towards the prosaic, he
can boast an ease and harmony rare at that date.
His style, which is clear and, except in his prose
works, unaffected, shows him to be a master of the
English language. Without any great fertility of
fancy, he has masculine energy and an undoubted
gift of satirical description.

The work of Edward Hake[1] has some little
recommendation beyond its rarity, and

> ' Intent good living to erect,
> And sin rescinde which rifely raignes abroade.'

He boldly attacked not only bawds, lawyers, and
physicians, but also vice in high places, at a time
when the Star Chamber was not idle. His hatred
of Papists is quite rabid. If his easy black-letter
rhymes are not poetry, they deserve, at any rate,

[1] M.P. for Windsor, *circa* 1579.

some mention as a collection of professedly serious satires.

We now find ourselves on the threshold of the Elizabethan era. Robert Greene and Thomas Nashe may be taken as representing the prose satire of that period. They availed themselves of the pamphlet, which at this time supplied the place of journalism, to carry on personal controversies, or to amuse the public by ridiculing the affectations and vices of the age—but always with the object of putting money in their own pockets.

The rollicking humour and fertile genius of the Elizabethans were not favourable to satire. Men were not, in those days, sufficiently out of temper with themselves and the world to be critical. The spirit of romanticism—of emotional imagination, rather than the critical spirit, was abroad. So that in the satiric compositions of the day, wit unpruned, wild burlesque, and exuberant horse-play take the place of that acid intellectual aloofness, that restrained inward revolt, which have marked the greatest satirists.

As it was the direct impulse of classical studies acquired at the Universities which at this time inspired Lodge, Donne, Marston, and Hall to write satiric verse, so Greene and Nashe also were 'University wits.' But their biting pamphlets owe nothing to the classics. They are the outcome of their life in London. They are pasquinades thrown off in a fever heat of personal resentment, or satiric romances, confessions, exposures written under pressure of want. Wild and unrestrained in their lives, these writers were equally wild and unrestrained in their prose. Their touch is uncertain, their style diffuse, their sarcasm often pointless, their satire frequently degenerates into the absurdest buffoonery, but, in spite of all those defects, the wit, and warmth, and life of the Elizabethans was in them, and these are imperishable qualities.

1560-1592. Robert Greene, as dramatist or euphuistic romancer, lampooner or moralist, lyricist or pamphleteer, blackguard or repentant, offers one of the most interesting character-studies in Elizabethan literature. But we have only to consider him in the one capacity of satirist; we must not even stay to moralize over his unfortunate surfeit of Rhenish and pickled herrings.

Greene spent his life in passing from violent fits of debauchery to equally violent fits of remorse, which found voice in confessions and culminated in the **1591.** 'Groat's-worth of Wit,' an autobiography in the form of a novel, written on his death-bed. In the 'Conny-catching' series he uses his unrivalled knowledge of knavery to expose the ways of the London sharpers. It is very probable that, with characteristic irony, he also wrote the 'Defence of Conny-catching,' in which he is himself roundly abused, with the view of advertising his previous pamphlets. Here, and in 'The Life and Death of Mourton and Ned Browne, two notable Conny-catchers,' he shows great skill in wielding the weapon of irony. The latter work is, indeed, a faint foreshadowing of 'Jonathan Wild,' though it lacks the strength and consistent irony of that masterpiece.

Greene's best satiric work, however, is 'A Quip for an Upstart Courtier,' wherein he ridicules the whole race of *parvenus* in the person of Gabriel Harvey, whose brother Richard, an astrologer given to indulging in troublesome prophecies, had caused offence by calling Greene's circle 'piperly make-plaies and make-bates.' The description of the jury, who decide the 'Quaint Dispute' as to the social value of foreign luxuries between Velvet-breeches and Cloth-breeches in favour of the latter, gives occasion for a whole gallery of contemporary portraits drawn from members of the various professions. Besides the historical interest of these portraits there is much satiric humour to be found in the delineation of them.

In his best satiric work, we may note, there is little trace of that pedantic, affected, euphuistic style which Greene exhibited in his love-stories. The sentences, indeed, are straggling and unframed, but the style becomes simple and natural. The chief fault of his prose, dramatic or other, is that there is no air of repose, but a continual straining after wit, which signifies a lack of art and self-criticism, and results in the tedious quality attending so much Elizabethan wit. The 'Quip for an Upstart Courtier,' however, is comparatively free from this fault. The unity of plan makes this piece a more artistic whole than is usually the case in the pamphlets of the time.

Greene's attack upon Harvey gave rise to a literary warfare, which was carried on for five years by Harvey and Nashe. So virulent and rancorous was this war, and so much did it excite popular feeling, that it became necessary at last for the authorities to interfere and put a stop to it. 1597.

Thomas Nashe, like Greene, was a University 1567-1601. man, and, like him, was a dramatist, romancer, pamphleteer—everything by starts and nothing long. His work is marred conspicuously by the lack of form and self-restraint which distinguish all the Elizabethan prose writers; but his brilliant mother-wit, his gift for irony and burlesque, and his power of scathing sarcasm to a large extent redeem these faults. He is not, however, so dexterous in the use of irony as Greene, and he is more boisterous. His share in the Martin-Marprelate controversy[1]—

[1] For the history of the Martin Marprelate controversy and tracts see Dexter's 'The Congregationalism of the last Three

2

a controversy in which there was little real humour displayed on either side—and his literary quarrel with Gabriel Harvey, begun in defence of Greene, made him famous. His controversial severity led him to great lengths of caricature and violence, but he is now and again extremely happy, as, for instance, in his criticism of Harvey's craze for English hexameters. 'Have with you to Saffron Walden,' the last and best known of his attacks on Harvey, is full of scornful ridicule wrapped in a whirl of wit, and is written in his most characteristic 'yerking, firking, jerking veine.' There are many good things, too, in the 'Anatomie of Absurditie,' a shapeless collection of shrewd observations.

We must be content with the bare mention of 1596-1601. other writers in the native school. The 'Kinde friendly snippinge' and the moral disquisitions of Breton,[1] the truths shadowed forth by strong-phrased Gilpin,[2] and the fantastic verses of silver-tongued Sylvester,[3] do not indeed call for any lengthy notice; but Thomas Lodge, though he cannot compare with Greene and Nashe for vigour, originality, and wit, demands some attention.

1556-1625. He was one of the least boisterous, but by no means the least interesting, of the University wits who came up to London at the end of the sixteenth century. He tried his hand at every sort of com-

---

Hundred Years,' and for that of the quarrel with Gabriel Harvey see Nashe's Works, ed. Grosart (Huth Library), pp. liii-lviii.

[1] Nicholas Breton's 'No Whippinge, nor Trippinge, but a kinde friendly Snippinge,' is the last of a trilogy arising out of an attack on Ben Jonson: 'The Whippinge of the Satyre by W. I[ngram?]', and 'The Whipper of the Satyre—his Penance in a White Sheet,' etc., the reply of some friend of Marston's with more zeal than wit.

[2] 'Skialetheia.'

[3] 'Tobacco Battered and Pipes Shattered about their Eares that Idlely Idolize so Base and Barbarous a Weed.'

position, and succeeded in rivalling, if not in surpassing, 'Lilly the famous for facility' in his own
line of euphuistic romance. As a satirist he is, it
may be, somewhat tame and lacking in force, but his
writings have a certain distinction which recommends
them. For when Hall boasted in the 'Virgidemiarum'   1597.

> 'Follow me who list,
> And be the second English satirist,'

he did an injustice to Lodge, who had anticipated
him in his own particular line of heroic satire; for
the rare British Museum copy of 'A Fig for Momus'
bears the date of 1595. 'Would God our realme
could light upon a Lucilius!' Lodge had exclaimed
in his reply to Stephen Gosson's 'School of Abuse.'[1]
We now find him coming forward with a modest
attempt to supply that deficiency in the realm.

In the preface 'To the Gentlemen Readers whatsoever'—a preface, be it noted, of supreme interest
in the history of English satire—the title of the
volume 'Fig for Momus' is explained. The explana-
tion is, 'In despight of the detractor who, worthily
deserving the name of Momus, shall ... at my hands
have a figge to choake him.' 'The satyres,' he goes
on to say, 'included in this volume are by pleasures,
rather placed here to prepare and trie the ear then
to feede it: because, if they passe well, the whole
centon of them, alreadie in my hands, shall sodainly
be published.'[2] It does not seem that he met with

---

[1] The 'School of Abuse' was a foolish invective against the
stage. It was afterwards honoured by calling forth Sir Philip
Sidney's beautiful reply, 'The Defence of Poesie.'

[2] 'In them, under the name of certaine Romaines, where I
reprehend vice I purposely wrong no man, but observe the laws
of that kind of poeme. If any repine thereat, I am sure he is
guilty, because he bewrayeth himselfe.' He shows that he is
not of the compromising sort: 'If any man reprove let him
looke to it; I will lip him. As I am ready to satisfy the
reasonable, so I have a gird in store for a railer.'

the needed encouragement. There is no trace of that centon. As to the five satires contained in the 'Fig for Momus,' the preface quoted leaves little to be added. The importance of them lies in their form rather than in their matter or intrinsic merit. Lodge takes Juvenal for his model, and in the fifth satire follows the tenth satire of Juvenal closely. But his denunciations are of too general a character to have much interest, and his style is too much steeped in euphuism to redeem that defect.[1]

Of his other works in this line, 'Truth's complaint over England' is a fairly vigorous satirical poem, the exact meaning of which is concealed under an allegory, a course dictated alike by prudence and fashion, but which, it must be admitted, somewhat spoils the satire.

'Catharos—a Nettle for Nice Noses' is a rabid and pedantic prose-dialogue of no merit. It abounds in this sort of stuff, put in the mouth of Diogenes: 'My friend, sayth the shoemaker, your shooe is good on the last, but whoso puts it on shall find small peniworth in the lasting.' The 'Alarum against Usurers' is a tedious moral story of no merit.

Lodge, as we have hinted, dabbled in almost every style of literature, and was too anxious to 'have his oar in every paper boat' to achieve very great success; but we must give him the credit he deserves for being the introducer into English of the satire in heroics, which passed from him, through Hall and Donne, to Dryden, Pope, Churchill, and Byron.

1593. The MSS. of two of Donne's satires are, indeed, dated 1593, earlier, that is, than the publication of Lodge's 'Momus.' Donne is the chief of that meta-

---

[1] It is worth noting that in the same volume Lodge published some Epistles to various friends in heroic verse—also the first of their kind in English.

physical school which delighted in 'the irregular and eccentric violence of wit.'[1]

His satire is fresh, but too often, like the elegies, extremely coarse. The see-saw style of reading does not suit his lines, which have 'a deep and subtle music of their own.'[2] This, however, is often spoilt by the metrical roughness deliberately affected by classical satirists of this period.[3] The Romans allowed licences in this branch of literature; their object was to preserve the free, open-air character of the satiric muse. But the satires of Horace, Persius, and Juvenal are only harsh when compared, not with the crude vigour of Ennius, but with the correctness of Virgil's Epic and the *curiosa felicitas* of Horace's 'Odes.'[4] Donne and his fellows, on the other hand, are uncouth, even in comparison with the imperfect precisians of their own day. This slavish copying of Roman models—especially of Persius, the most crabbed of them all—is responsible also for the deliberate obscurity of allusion and the air of imitation which mar the poetical satirists of the Elizabethan period. But the gain is greater than the loss; for without these classical models English satiric poetry would not so readily have found the proper form in which to express itself, or a canon by which to test its material.

Donne, however, is not so wilfully obscure as Hall. In his matter he is pungent, but never angry. He knows how to proportion his criticism. Vices he treats not too gently, but he deals lightly with vanities. Sometimes he laughs out joyously, some-

---

[1] Johnson, 'Life of Cowley.'

[2] Cf. Craik's 'History of English Literature.'

[3] *E.g.*, 'As prone to ill, and of good as forget-
　　Full, as proud, lustfull, and as much in debt.'
　　　　　　　　　　　　　　　　　　　Sat. iv. 13.

[4] Petronius, Satyr. 118: 'Horatii curiosa felicitas.'

times you catch a sob of unutterable sorrow and remorse;[1] but you will not find in him that extravagant exaggeration and only half-sincere denunciation of contemporary vice and folly which Marston and Hall borrowed from Juvenal.[2] The cry *Omne in præcipiti vitium stetit*[3]—'The world is worse than ever it was'[4]—disfigures many English satirists, and not least the learned and voluminous Bishop Hall.

Like Donne, Hall thought it necessary for a satire to be 'hard of conceit and harsh of style';[5] but, for all that, he lets us see that he is a master of style, and the fabric of the couplets in 'Virgidemiarum' approaches much nearer to the standard of Pope. Unlike Donne, he can raise a laugh without the aid of quibbles and conceits. But, though his felicitous phrases, racy humour, and intrepid invective are pleasing for a while, the author's too obvious delight in laying bare the frailty of mankind soon nauseates the reader. Saturnine is the epithet to be applied to his wit. The real value of his work lies in the realistic portraiture of men and manners. In 'Mundus Alter et Idem' he ventures not unsuccessfully into the domain of satirical fiction. There he proves himself more akin to the author of 'Gulliver' than to the author of 'Rasselas.' Unfortunately, it is written in Latin—the language of More's 'Utopia,' and of Erasmus' 'Encomium Moriæ.' Hall, in his 'Vertus and Vices,' also set the example of writing character studies, after the manner of Theophrastus —an example quickly followed by Dr. Earle, and later by Sir Thomas Overbury. These 'characters'

1608.

---

[1] See his sermons *passim*.
[2] Their contemporary Regnier could have taught them to avoid this fault in moral preaching.
[3] Juvenal, i. 149.
[4] 'Rede Me and be nott Wroth.'
[5] Postscript to 'Virgidemiarum.'

gave plenty of scope for satire and epigrammatic description.

Hall comes nearest of any at that period to the classical prototypes. The influence of Persius is reflected in occasional crabbed obscurities and ellipses; there are reminiscences also of Horace, but Juvenal is the great master whom he imitates at every turn,[1] both in his view of life and his tricks of style, especially in that artifice of making his illustrations and allusions themselves satirical. Taking pleasure in detecting faults, Hall was indiscriminate in his literary criticism; thus he was led into conflict with Milton[2] on the one hand and Marston on the other.

John Marston's[3] castigation of living characters 1598. was but thinly disguised, and brought upon him rebukes from Ben Jonson,[4] who ridiculed his somewhat absurd vocabulary, from Hall, and from anonymous writers. Of these, the author of 'The Whipping of the Satyre' says truly enough,

> ' He scourgeth villainies in young and old
> As boys scourge tops for sport on Lenten day.'

Decidedly, the author of the licentious 'Pigmalion's Image' was not likely to prove a sincere satirist. Marston, however, had a considerable power of ridicule and of incisive description. More facile than Hall, he is less pedantic. Hall thinks deeper, and is more obscure; Marston is clear, but less acute and less epigrammatic. Hall is more humorous and forced; Marston more acrimonious, but also more natural.

---

[1]   ' Renowned Aquine, now I follow thee
            Farre as I may for feare of jeopardie.'
                                        Lib. v., Sat. i. 8.
[2] Milton, ' Apology for Smectymnus.'
[3] ' Pigmalion's Image and Certain Satyres ' and ' Scourge of Villainie.'
[4] Crispinus in the ' Poetaster.'

Marston, indeed, was more of a satirist in his dramatic work than in his avowed satires, where he rails in a harsh and disconnected fashion at the affectations and effeminacies of his time. But his railing is that of a boisterous buffoon, and the 'Scourge of Villainie' proves him the foulest writer of his time.

In the great era of dramatic writing on which we have now entered, criticism of life and manners naturally found its chief expression on the stage. The 'Histrio-mastix,' the 'Poetaster,' and the 'Satiro-mastix'[1] are examples of this tendency, which needs no further illustration.

In the region of pure satire, the 'Abuses Stript and Whipt' of George Wither earned for its author a long imprisonment in the Marshalsea. It is a vague and somewhat profuse condemnation of the vices of the time, lacking both vigour and wit, and we cannot help sharing Lamb's wonder that these perfectly general denunciations of gluttony, and so forth, should have seemed worthy of such punishment. He meant, no doubt, *Qui capit, ille facit*, but it seems hard to imprison a man for meaning more than he says. With the exception of the 'Canterbury Tale'—too long for insertion in our extracts—there is little that is amusing in these satires, which have, truth to say, a smack of priggishness about them.

From the Marshalsea Wither addressed 'A Satire to the King,' in justification of himself, with the

1610.

1613.

---

[1] The 'Satiro-mastix' was a retort to Ben Jonson's 'Poetaster' by Thomas Dekker on behalf of himself, Marston, and others. Dekker wrote, besides his plays, a large quantity of prose, some of it satirical. Another dramatist whose satirical gifts call for notice is John Day. His 'Parliament of Bees' would come under the heading of dramatic satire, a subject too large to enter on here, but I give an extract from the delightful ramblings of his 'Peregrinatio Scholastica.'

characteristic motto, *Quid tu si pereo.* Here he refers to his offence with bold sincerity. 'All my griefe,' he declares, 'is that I was so sparing.' He complains that 'Want of power and friends be my confusion,' and that

> 'My foe unto particulars would tie
> What I intended universally.'

The poem, which shows great command of rhyme and metre, is lacking in polish; but in his satires generally, as in his later poems, we miss the happiness of touch and finished freshness, and above all the melody, of 'Faire Virtue, Mistress of Philarete.' Wither fell a victim to his fatal facility. But, though we may prefer his 'affable Looke to encourage Honesty'[1] to his wearing of the 'sterne Frowne to cast on Villainie,' we cannot but admire the unflinching bravery of his petition for release,[2] and the charm of that other note, almost unsounded hitherto in English poetry:

> 'Here can I live and play with miserie . . .
> Here have I learned to make my greatest wrongs
> Matter for mirth and subjects for my songs.'

Sir John Denham does not owe his position 1615-1688. in English literature to his satires. He had at the best but a thin vein of cynical wit, which was soon exhausted. He affects to be a humorous writer, but when he attempts the ludicrous he generally fails. When he tries to be witty, he usually succeeds only in being dull, coarse, or disgusting. His 'Directions to a Painter,' an imitation of Waller's 'Instructions,' is said by Pepys[3] to have 'made my heart ache, being too sharp and so true'; but both this and the 'Petition to the Five Members'

---

[1] Preface to 'Epithalamion.'
[2]   'And need I now thus to apologize
        Only because I scourged villainies ?'
[3] 'Diary,' September 14, 1667.

set the modern reader wondering, between his yawns, at the esteem in which Denham's comic vein was held by his contemporaries. His satires are, in fact, merely coarse squibs and bad lampoons.

1582-1635. Bishop Corbet is a more interesting figure in the history of English satire. He writes in the light Horatian vein, and in his longest piece imitates Horace's 'Journey to Brundusium.' Corbet wrote, without elaboration, for the amusement of the moment. His rough ballads aim at no smoothness of versification. They are obviously trifles thrown off in the intervals of more serious business. In spite of this carelessness, Corbet is of some importance, because in adopting as he does the ballad metres for his light-hearted rebukes of the follies of the age, he stands out as the forerunner of those other writers of witty *vers de société*, in whom satire finds its least serious and its gentlest exponents.

1618-1667. Abraham Cowley gave promise of much satiric power in the play 'Love's Riddle,' written while still a 'King's Scholler in Westminster Schoole'; and from the boy poet who could ask to be preserved

> 'From singing men's religion, who are
> Always at church, just like the crows, cause there
> They build themselves a nest,'[1]

we expect much. But, though we find in his other works a gentle Elian humour and grave-faced fun, in satire proper he loses his delicate felicity. In the 'Puritan and the Papist'—if he is really the author of that piece—he is truculent, heartless, and dull. He discovers all the faults of the fantastic school. He runs an idea to death, and is ingenious to the degree of extravagance. The *motif* of the piece is a comparison between the tenets of Puritans and Priests, with the deduction that 'You [Puritans] into the

[1] Cp. the passage on 'Justification by Works.'

same error deeper slide.' This becomes intensely wearisome when worked out through the whole Roman Catholic Creed. His touch is not sure; but his versification, though often lame, occasionally approaches the perfection of a Popian couplet.[1] Our verdict on him may perhaps be rendered in the Tacitean formula : *Capax saturæ, nisi scripsisset.*

Lord Herbert of Cherbury is one of Donne's 1581-1648. earliest disciples, and in his two satires, more than elsewhere, he betrays the influence of his master. Mr. Churton Collins[2] has recently vindicated Lord Herbert's claim to the rank of poet, but of his satiric works he can only find heart to say that ' the second would disgrace Taylor the waterpoet ; the first, though intolerably harsh and barbarous in style and rhythm, contains some interesting remarks.' There is little more to be said. His versification, distinguished in his other poems for sweetness and originality, in his satires is uncouth in the extreme. The matter is both obscure and trivial.

John Cleveland shares with Donne the charge of 1613-1658. being fanciful and obscure. Like Brome an ardent Royalist,[3] he ' followed the fates of distressed loyalty,' his biographers tell us. His love poems are marked by wearisome conceits and absurd exaggerations. The cynical note is never absent. As a satirist, he carried on a kind of guerilla

---

[1] ' Character of an Holy Sister ' :

> ' She that will sit in shop for five hours' space,
> And register the sins of all that pass,
> Damn at first sight, and proudly dare to say
> That none can possibly be saved but they
> That hang religion in a naked ear,
> And judge men's hearts according to their hair.'

[2] See his edition of the poet.

[3] Alexander Brome fought manfully for the royal cause with his rough but effective political songs throughout the Protectorship.

warfare with the enemies of his king and party. His poems relating to State affairs are coarse and profane, and are only saved from insincerity by his fine loathing of Puritans, Rebels and Scotchmen.

His prose, as, for instance, in the ' Character of a London Diurnal,' is in the style of wit affected by Mercutio, and, like his verse, it is overcrowded with images.[1] Rough and careless though his work is, it yet has many of the qualities of ' Hudibras.' But even when we come across phrases that are final, needles of wit in bundles of failures, these seem to be the offspring of accident, rather than of care. When he exclaims in ' The Rebel Scot ':

> ' Lord ! what a godly thing is want of shirts !
> How a Scotch stomach and no meat converts !'

we recognise the origin of that manner which was developed by Butler's patience and laborious persistency. But Cleveland, lacking the application which made Butler an artist in raillery, remained merely a witty roysterer, a clever amateur.

1620-1678. Lord Beaconsfield maintained that Lord Shelburne was one of the suppressed characters of history.[2] If we admit that there are suppressed characters in literature, as in politics, Andrew Marvell may be called the Shelburne of English letters. In the days of Charles II. two men, Butler and Marvell, made satiric writing once more a powerful weapon. But the satires of the Puritan writer, though admired and feared in their day, have met with unjust oblivion. ' The liveliest droll of the age,' as Burnet[3] calls him, a man of pleasing and festive wit, Marvell excelled in the use of that

---

[1] Cleveland was also the author of ' The Rustick Rampant '— a long pamphlet on the Insurrection of Wat Tyler, full of obvious satiric references to the Civil Wars of his own day.

[2] Cf. ' Sybil,' ch. iii.

[3] Burnet's ' History of his Own Time.'

ironical banter in which Swift and Junius were his most apt pupils ; but in him, for reasons not altogether unconnected, perhaps, with politics, the lyric poet has survived the satiric writer. He fought on the losing side.

'Fleckno,' his earliest satire, droll if unpolished, is a revolt against the Jesuits ; and his later poems are all in the character of the Puritan, attacking, as became the friend and assistant of Milton, tyranny and wickedness in Church and State. The strength and dignity of his position as an incorruptible member of the Opposition in the corrupt and servile Parliament of Charles II. are reflected alike in his fearless poems and in his more perfect pamphlets.

In 1653 was produced 'The Character of Holland' —'that scarce deserves the name of land.' The irresponsible frivolity, the unpremeditated style, the ludicrous exaggerations of this piece remind us of the 'excellent wit' of Butler, of which he himself speaks so generously.[1] But beneath these qualities there is also a feeling of true patriotism, which raises the tone above that of 'Hudibras.' His point of view, we feel, is not that of Cleveland, of Oldham, or, to say truth, of Dryden.

On the fall of Clarendon,[2] Marvell, who, whilst aiming at the King's evil counsellors, always maintained his loyalty to the King, produced a long and weighty impeachment of those who led the King astray. His 'Last Instructions to a Painter' is modelled, indeed, upon the pieces by Denham and Waller, but is vastly superior to them, although the interest it arouses is now mainly historical. If the attack on the Duchess of York[3] be something too fierce, the lines describing the King[4] must be admitted to rise to a great height of solemn poetry, full of im-

---

[1] 'The Rehearsal Transprosed.' [2] September, 1667.
[3] 'Last Instructions,' ll. 49 *et seq.* [4] *Ibid.*, ll. 837-880.

pressive warning. This note is repeated in 'Britannia and Raleigh.' It required no little courage, be it remembered, to write thus of the King, or of Lauderdale as Marvell wrote of him in the 'Historical Poem.'[1]

Passing over 'The Dialogue between Two Horses,' which has been praised beyond its deserts, we come to his prose satires. In these he relies both on argument and ridicule. His play is light, lively, and effective. 'Mr. Smirke' is a very witty and learned piece of argumentative work, but inferior to 'The Rehearsal Transprosed.' Few dramas have given rise to so vast and so unceasing a succession of works, good and bad, as Buckingham's brilliant skit, 'The Rehearsal';[2] and never, one may add, has a popular success been more skilfully turned to the account of an earnest pamphleteer.

It was in a Church controversy that Marvell produced the elaborate essay, 'The Rehearsal Transprosed,' answering in a burlesque strain 'to shame by dint of wit' the extravagant doctrine of Dr. Parker, one of the most detestable of the Restoration Prelates. He would not 'commit such an absurdity as to be grave with a buffoon.' Swift justly praises this book,[3] and Burnet tells us that 'from the King down to the tradesman it was read with great pleasure.' Anthony Wood speaks of the author as 'hugely well vers'd and experienced in the then but newly refined art of Sporting and Jeering Buffoonery.' Wit and raillery had, in fact, long been strangers in the land, and the Court hailed with delight any sign of their return. Nor has the pleasure to be derived therefrom evaporated. If, in

---

[1] 'Historical Poem,' ll. 114-125.
[2] The forerunner of Fielding's 'Pasquin' and Sheridan's 'Critic' and 'Rehearsal.'
[3] Swift, 'Tale of a Tub.'

this conflict, Marvell had no foeman worthy of his
steel, yet was he attacking one in authority at the
time; whilst, from a literary point of view, he has
preserved from oblivion a lump of religious controversy by the plentiful salt of his light raillery or
grave wit, sarcastic humour or brilliant repartee.
Here alone perhaps he has, like all great satirists,
triumphed over the ephemeral interest of the subject.

His satires have been described as obscene and
filthy; but the grossness is of the things, and not of
the writer. He was honestly performing the watch-
dog function of the satirist. The critic of such
a Court could hardly fail to introduce gross expressions; but even where he is most brutal and indiscriminate and merciless—and Marvell can be all of
these — you feel that he is impelled by a lofty
motive.

It was far otherwise with such poetical courtiers 1647-1630
as the Earl of Rochester and the Earl of Dorset.
Violence without sincerity, and coarseness with
little real wit, are the qualities of their writings.
It takes a deal of salt to make scurrility sweet, and
though Rochester does now and then show great
strength of expression and considerable happiness
of thought, yet his verses are too often halting, and
his pen is too often dipped in dirt—merely for dirt's
sake—for us to admire his work.

His 'History of Insipids,' a lampoon published in
1676, is, indeed, a seemingly fearless, if unpolished,
attack on Charles, not devoid of sly hits and crushing blows. But one can hardly credit with sincerity
the satirist who tried to cure the King of his weaknesses, either by winning his mistresses from him, or
severely lampooning him and them. Rochester
imitated Boileau in his 'Satire against Mankind,'
and, in 'The Trial of the Poets,' he adapted with

neatness and vigour Horace on Lucilius to a review of the poets of his own time. Considering his unceasing debauchery, however, it is hardly surprising that Rochester's great reputation for colloquial wit is not borne out by his writings.

Dorset's foul and violent lampoons, also, bear the character of the Court. He, too, has a schoolboy delight in using naughty words, which to our modern notions are simply offensive. Praised beyond measure by his contemporaries,[1] by Rochester,[2] by Dryden,[3] and by Pope,[4] he has now sunk into the obscurity he deserves.[5]

1662.

While Marvell and Wither stood forth as the critics of the Court, Butler, taking his cue from Cleveland, appeared as the champion of the cavaliers, and the literary persecutor of the Puritans. The first part of 'Hudibras' was published in 1662. The object of this poem is simple and definite—to render the party represented by the lay figure of Hudibras vile and ridiculous. The method is more or less that of the 'Satyre Ménippée,' which, beyond doubt, taught Butler the mystery of his noble trade.[6]

The phrase on his monument in Westminster

---

[1] 'State Poems,' vol. i., p. 200.

[2] Rochester calls him 'The best good man with the worst-natured Muse.'

[3] Dryden instanced ' Your lordship in satire and Shakespeare in tragedy' as superior to the authors of antiquity.

[4]   'Dorset, the grace of courts, the Muses pride,
          Patron of arts, and judge of nature, died.'—Pope.

[5] The lines in 'An Essay upon Satire,' 255-265, though severe, are not too severe a criticism on this school of courtly satirists.

[6] Dryden, 'Essay on the Origin and Progress of Satire':
'How easy it is to call rogue and villain, and that wittily ! but how hard to make a man appear a fool, a blockhead or a knave, without using any of those opprobrious terms. . . . This is the mystery of that noble trade.'

Abbey describes the accomplishment of his purpose :
' Perduellium scelera liberrime exagitavit.' It is
important to bear this in mind, because we praise
him to-day, it will be found, only or almost only in
so far as he rises superior to his purpose. Where
he achieves that purpose most successfully his satire
is most ephemeral in its interest; it loses for us
much of its point through lacking even the semblance
of truth. To render Hudibras completely contemptible, Butler does not shrink from being trivial
and flagrantly unjust. Certainly ' Experience had
shown the swords of the Presbyterians were not to
be despised,'[1] yet this typical strict Presbyterian is
represented as a coward, as a Jack Falstaff in the
presence of rogues in buckram. Hypocrisy, however,
and pedantry, and the other vices which Butler represents as the monopolies of the hated Puritan, are
qualities to be found in every society. There is
a Hudibras in every camp, and in every party.
Therefore, in spite of his partisanship, Butler's
satire is as applicable and salutary to-day as when
it was first written, and in spite of the specific aim
of his lampoon, the universality of many of his
portraitures is established.

' C'est Don Quichotte, c'est notre Satyre Ménippée
fondus ensemble,' says M. Voltaire of ' Hudibras ';
' c'est de tous les livres que j'aie jamais lus celui où
j'ai trouvé le plus d'esprit.' It is in this quality of
pure wit that Butler stands pre-eminent. If as a
satirist he lacks the indignation of Juvenal, in wit
he excels him. Isaac Barrow's searching list of the
different forms that wit may assume is but an
enumeration of the varieties to be found in ' Hudibras.'[2]

[1] Johnson's ' Life of Butler.'
[2] ' The pat allusion to a known story, the seasonable application of a trivial saying ; the playing in words and phrases, taking

3

We cannot say of Butler as he says of his hero :

'Although he had much wit,
H' was very shy of using it.'[1]

His very rhymes are often witty, so that some of his couplets are remembered for the humour of their rhyme rather than for the excellence of their matter. The metre, too, is singularly happy, and in this connection fundamentally humorous. In Butler's hands it is almost as rattling as Skeltonics. It gives him ample scope for his power of easy yet fantastic rhyme. As poetry, it is open to Horace's objection : 'Neque enim concludere versum Dixeris esse satis ; neque si qui scribat uti nos, Sermoni propiora, putes hunc esse poetam.'[2]

We are continually struck by Butler's wealth of comic simile, and by his fecundity of witty illustration. Here we have no 'dry desert of a thousand lines ' to traverse ere we come upon a solitary shining simile. For the number of lines which begin with adverbs of comparison is remarkable, and the strange analogies thus introduced startle us with their excellence.

---

advantage from the ambiguity of their sense, or the affinity of their sound. Sometimes it is wrapt in a dress of humorous expression ; sometimes it lurks under an odd similitude ; sometimes it is lodged in a sly question, in a smart answer, in a quirkish reason, in a shrewd imitation, in cunningly diverting or cleverly retorting an objection ; sometimes it is couched in a bold scheme of speech, in a tart irony, in a lusty hyperbole, in a startling metaphor, in a plausible reconciling of contradictions, or in acute nonsense ; sometimes an affected simplicity, sometimes a presumptuous bluntness giveth it being ; sometimes it riseth only from a lucky hitting upon what is strange, sometimes from a crafty wresting obvious matter to the purpose.'

[1] Part i., Canto i.
[2]   '"Tis not enough to close the flowing line,
         And in *eight* syllables your sense confine,
         Or write in mere prosaic rhymes like me,
         That can deserve the name of poetry.'
              Hor., Sat. I., iv. 40 (translated by Francis).

If true wit lies, as has been said, in seeing unexpected, extraordinary analogies, then surely there
never was a wittier writer !

There was, we have noted, a unity of purpose in
Butler's vast lampoon; but in the wanderings of this
caricature of a Quixote, with his burlesque Sancho
Panza, there is no unity of interest. This is, indeed,
not altogether a disadvantage. The irregular and
undecided march of the poem displays the fertility of
the author's invention, and, incidentally, discovers
opportunities for satirizing almost every side of
human frailty. A more carefully constructed plot
would not have offered the same free scope. The
poem becomes more picaresque as it progresses; and
in this way Butler rises more and more above mere
partisanship, and finds occasion to aim his shafts
of wit at so many of the persistent shams of life.

Of his method we know something. His note-
book was filled with gibes jotted down from his
observation of life and of people. These notes were
worked up and inserted in the body of his rambling
poem. The felicity and finality of his descriptions,
which form his chief claim to our notice, are the
outcome of unwearied observation and learned persistency. But the poem has the defects of the
qualities of such a method. Regarded as a whole,
'Hudibras' is both fragmentary and diffuse, failing
to hold our attention. The luxuriant wit is straggling
and unpruned. The tendency to diffuseness is never
checked.

That he took a lesson in the use of his material
from the Satyre Ménippée; that he found something
of his manner in the rough work of Cleveland, and
the idea of his fable in the romance of Cervantes, in
no way impairs his originality. His object, let it be
repeated, is simply to scourge the Roundheads. No
alleviating stroke is allowed to interfere with this

purpose, even though such strokes would add to the effectiveness of the satire, by introducing that element of illusion which is so entirely lacking in his grotesque monsters. Accordingly, we find him sometimes tedious, sometimes over-spiteful. But he is ever redeemed from dulness by the abundance of his wit and by the acuteness of his wide observation.

Not that mere brilliancy of wit is sufficient to prevent a long poem from becoming tedious. The stimulus if too often applied loses its efficacy. 'Though all the parts are forcible, and every line kindles new rapture, the reader, if not relieved by the interposition of something that soothes the fancy, grows weary of admiration, and defers the rest.'[1] This remark applies to ' Hudibras ' even more fitly than to ' Absalom and Achitophel.' Uniformity must tire at last, though it be uniformity of excellence ; and here there is little to soothe the reader's fancy. Poetical imagery rarely relieves the attention from the strain of surprised admiration. Such a couplet as

> ' True as the dial to the sun,
> Although it be not shined upon,'

is quite exceptional.

We conclude, then, that if Butler had troubled himself to polish and prune ' Hudibras,' and to make it a more perfect whole ; if there were more in it of poetry and less of burlesque, it would take an even higher rank among the masterpieces of literature. As it is, in spite of, or even because of, its excellences, the poem palls. It falls off in the continuation ; it owes its immortality to the first canto. For the rest, we find the author too voluble, relying, in Swift's phrase, too much on ' the embroidery of sheer wit.' But for happiness of expression, for

---

[1] Johnson, ' Life of Dryden.'

sound sense and robust English, for acute criticism
of life, for satire delivered in lines each vigorous like
the crack of a whip and cutting like a sharp razor—
for these qualities, too, apart from mere wit, Butler
will always be read and justly admired.

John Oldham, once regarded as the 'darling of
the Muses,' 'the Marcellus of our tongue,' claims our
attention chiefly as the immediate predecessor of
Dryden in satire. Dryden, indeed, recognised in
him a kindred spirit, and in his generous memorial
verses grudges no praise, admitting that he was 'by
too much force betrayed,' but maintaining that
'satire needs not smoothness,' and

> 'Wit will shine
> Through the harsh cadence of a rugged line.'

Son of a Nonconformist minister, from whom it is
said he drew his 'Character of an ugly old Priest,'
Oldham was usher of a school at Croydon when he
wrote the 'Satires against the Jesuits.' These were
occasioned by the Popish Plot, and inspired by
popular fanaticism. The usher was visited, on **1678.**
the strength of the reputation of his poems, by
Rochester, Dorset, and Sedley,[1] whom he presently
followed to town. A fine, manly independence
distinguishes his intercourse with these salacious
wits, and lends point and dignity to the satire
addressed to a friend about to leave the University.
He warns him to follow his own example, and refuse
to become chaplain to any nobleman, and so lay
himself open to unpolite treatment. In his attack
on the Jesuits he plied the 'vile brood of Loyola'
with 'pointed satire and the sharps of wit.' He
meant his stabbing pen to draw blood, and lashed
himself into a frenzy of indignation, the violence of
which left no room for chastity of rhyme, language,
or grammar.

[1] To whom he dedicated his 'Bion.'

Pope, who was not above borrowing a hint from Oldham now and again, considered the fourth satire the best ;[1] in the first, his rank envenomed spleen, excited imagination and fluent pen led him into mere vulgar abuse and exaggerated invective, redeemed only by the grim sincerity of his convictions. In the second he is less violent and more successful. The piece contains many legitimate hits, somewhat too carelessly expressed. His imitations of Juvenal, Boileau, and Horace, are by no means lacking in felicity. The adaptation of Juvenal's third satire to the London of his own day is especially interesting in view of Johnson's similar but more noble effort ; whilst the fact of his imitating Boileau prepares us for that change in style which the new school of French criticism aided, if it did not inaugurate. But in general the lack of harmony in his numbers is scarcely outweighed by the keenness of his satire and the clearness of his wit.[2] His grossness, too, is beyond all bounds, and intolerable.

1681-1683. We come now to consider the three greatest masters of English satirical writing—Dryden, Pope, and Swift, the first of whom excels in breadth and vigour, the second in point and elegance of phrase, the last in mordant sarcasm and savage irony. Two peculiarities distinguish the literature of this epoch from that which preceded it. When, at the age of fifty, Dryden was led, almost without any wish of his own, to work at that vein of verse, which under his hands was to prove so rich in ore, a change had come over the mechanism of writing. This is not the place to discuss the causes or to describe the history of that change.[3] Suffice it to say that, largely owing to the French influence

[1] It is based on an imitation of Horace's ' Olim truncus eram.'
[2] ' So keen in satire and so clear in wit.'—Waller.
[3] See De Quincey, Works, vol. ix.

introduced by the Court at the Restoration, a lighter and more direct style was coming into fashion. The fantastic conceits, the long-drawn subtleties, the verbal quibbles of the so-called metaphysical school were dropped. Correctness, as Pope puts it, began to be our care.[1]

Signs of the coming change can, indeed, be traced throughout the seventeenth century. Waller and his fellow-poets had long been improving the heroic verse, making correctness, terseness, smoothness their object, and in prose, before the civil wars, Bishop Hall, Sir Thomas Overbury, and John Earle, inspired with the keen interest in men as they are which began to distinguish the prose-writers of that period, prepared the way, by their character studies, for that school whose chief tenet was to be, ' The proper study of mankind is man.' It is as painters, or etchers of portraits, that Pope and Dryden excel.

Spread over a literary career of more than forty years, the various and voluminous works of John Dryden exhibit the growth of that tendency towards literary neatness, towards a nimbler style of wit and a more incisive manner of talk and expression, which culminated in the technical perfection of the Popian couplet. A change had taken place also in the tone of moral sentiment. The revolt against Puritanism, which appears in the Royalist poets, and finally triumphant in Butler, had been accompanied by an intellectual movement ' which was on the whole a downward one, from faith to scepticism, from enthusiasm to cynicism, from the imagination to the understanding.'[2] Such a tendency, it has already been suggested, is eminently favourable to satire.

Although it was not till the publication of the first part of 'Absalom and Achitophel' that Dryden sprang

---

[1] Pope, Ep. ii. 271.   [2] Lowell, ' My Study Windows.'

into fame as a writer of satirical verse, he had already given ample proof of his capacity in this direction. His satirical power had, in fact, been slowly but surely developed. As a boy at Westminster he had translated the third satire of Persius; as a poet he seems to have helped the Earl of Mulgrave in the composition of 'An Essay upon Satire'; as a writer for the stage his happiest efforts were felt to be those prologues and epilogues in which he used his gift of didactic declamation to deal satirically with the manners and opinions of the day. The fact that the prologue and epilogue to 'Amboyna' consist almost entirely of lines transferred from ' The Satire on the Dutch' illustrates the satirical tendency of these 'sallies of badinage occasionally intermixed with a grain of salt satire, or doing duty as acid invectives or patriotic bluster,'[1] wherein we can trace surely enough the same qualities which, in their perfection, distinguished 'Absalom,' 'The Medal,' ' MacFlecknoe,' and still flavour 'The Hind and the Panther,' and the Preface to the ' Fables.'

If satire is the product of the intellect rather than of the imagination, the power of reasoning in verse is akin to it. In his plays Dryden had shown a delight in this exercise, and had been laughed at in the ' Rehearsal' for the habit.[2] In 'Absalom and Achitophel' he gave Buckingham a Zimri for his Bayes. Vigour and finish, directness and stinging invective, but, above all, discrimination and self-restraint, render this the greatest, as it was the most effective, of English political satires. Polished in detail and irresistibly fluent, it loses none of its edge through the simple, allegorical form under which the political state of England was represented by the

1679.

1673.
1662.

[1] Ward, 'English Poets.'
[2] 'Reasoning? I'gad I love reasoning in verse.'—Buckingham's 'Rehearsal' (1671).

courtly Laureate. The simplicity of aim makes Absalom effective as Hudibras could never be. Felicity of language and pleasing harmony of numbers heighten the skilful characterization. Almost alone among satirists Dryden is a master of light and shade. Refusing to deal his blows indiscriminately, he increases the severity of his attack. Further, the tone and quality of the satire is excellently adapted to the persons satirized. The manner in which Oates is held up to scorn differs rightly from that in which Shaftesbury is gibbeted. The character of Shimei is drawn after Butler's manner, but that of Absalom is tender and noble. Following the example of Shadwell, Settle, and the other Whig scribblers, Dryden gladly applies 'personal satire to the support of public principles,'[1] and takes ample revenge on Zimri. This character, however, as he himself declares, is ' not bloody, but ridiculous enough,'[2] whilst even Achitophel receives praise where praise is deserved. He tells us that he purposely rebated the satire from carrying too sharp an edge. This moderation, due, no doubt, in some degree to the peculiar political circumstances, is the most remarkable feature of this wonderful poem, which comprised, in Johnson's words, all the excellences of which the subject is capable. It is a feature which is lacking in 'The Medal,' for the situation had changed. The idea of taking as a subject the medal struck by the Whigs to celebrate the liberation of Shaftesbury is said to have originated with Charles himself. The execution is perfect in vehemence and vigour. With over-whelming directness, with poignant and unsparing personality, Dryden ridiculed 'this piece of notorious impudence.'[3] In ' the representation of the Whigs'

[1] Johnson, ' Life of Dryden.'
[2] ' Essay on the Origin and Progress of Satire.'
[3] Preface to the ' Medal.'

own hero,' every point in Shaftesbury's character is damned so exhaustively that the words of 'my Uncle Toby' leap to our lips: 'I declare my heart would not let me curse the devil himself with so much bitterness.'[1] So terrible was the severity of this attack that it probably hastened Shaftesbury's end. But such severity reflects on the author. It lays him open to the charge of profanity and cruelty, and does credit rather to his head than to his heart.

This note is repeated in 'MacFlecknoe,' one of the best as well as one of the severest of our purely literary satires. The occasion of it rose directly out of the publication of 'The Medal'; the object was the castigation of Thomas Shadwell, who, besides being a better dramatist than Dryden, had dared to reply on behalf of the Whigs in a scurrilous skit entitled 'The Medal of John Bayes.' He therefore is the hero of the piece, chosen by Flecknoe to inherit the throne of dulness. Exquisitely satirical, the matter of 'MacFlecknoe' is keen, vigorous, and crushing, the versification finished and skilful. In the qualities of spite and polish it must yield perhaps to its literary offspring, the 'Dunciad'; but 'MacFlecknoe' still excels by virtue of its blistering simplicity. Shadwell was lashed yet again, and with tenfold severity, in the second part of 'Absalom and Achitophel.' Of this, Dryden's 200 lines are as powerful as ever, and the characters of Shadwell and Settle, as Og and Doeg, are 'painted in the liveliest colours that his poignant satire could afford.'[2] Nahum Tate's work is by no means bad; but Tate was nearer to Brady than to Dryden, and his rushlight burns dimly in the brilliant blaze of Dryden's genius.

Once again Dryden broke out against his critics,

---

[1] 'Tristram Shandy,' Book III., chap. ii.
[2] Hooper.

and handled Sir Richard Blackmore[1] satirically in the Preface to the 'Fables,' and still more severely in the last lines he ever wrote.[2] His translation of Juvenal we may dismiss with Johnson's dictum that it 'preserves the wit, but wants the dignity of the original.'[3]

Virgilium vidi tantum, Alexander Pope used to say; but though he was only a precocious lad of twelve years when Dryden died, his work as a satirist may best be gauged by comparing his qualities with those of the older poet, whose versification he had distinguished as the model to be copied.[4]

By this time the influence of the critical school founded by Boileau dominated Europe. Imagination had been well-nigh driven from the land; antithesis and precision, elegance of diction and technical skill reigned supreme. The last flicker of idealism seemed extinguished. The age of criticism and reason was at hand. Good sense expressed in epigrammatic verse took the place of emotional poetry, and found its most successful exponents in those moral poets whose satire was addressed to good society rather than to human nature, chastening manners rather than the source of them in the soul. Pope's position in literature is that in this province he is perfect in execution and pre-eminent in wit. His success was the apotheosis of point and polish. This success he first achieved with the 'Essay on Criticism,' which displays a ripeness of judgment, firmness of touch, and excel-

---

[1] He had written a 'Satire upon Wit,' suggesting 'a bank for wit,' and in this was very severe upon Dryden.

[2] Prologue to Fletcher's 'Pilgrim,' 1700.

[3] Johnson, 'Life of Dryden.'

[4] Wycherley is worth mentioning here for his friendship with Pope, rather than for the obscene doggerel of which his satires are composed.

lence of craftsmanship little short of marvellous for a boy of twenty-one.

In the ' Rape of the Lock,' the poet of society, the delineator of manners, first declares himself, laughing at the ' little unguarded follies of the female sex.'[1] In this poem, in which the ' heroic style is set in satirical juxtaposition with cares, events, and modes of thought with which it is in comical antipathy,'[2] the satire is of the most pleasing and smiling sort. But, however much we may admire the bright fancy and ' merum sal ' of this ' delicious little thing,'[3] we cannot choose but feel that the edge of the satire is somewhat blunted by the essential triviality of the incidents in a triumph of insignificance.

The 'Dunciad '[4] suffers from something of the same defect ; where Pope rages against contemptible persons his vehemence is superfluous, where he attacks great men the libel reflects chiefly on himself. It was in 1728 that Pope, following Atterbury's advice,[5] showed his satirical power in the ' Dunciad.' The object of this mock heroic poem, ' styled heroic as being doubly so,'[6] was, under the pretence of deifying dulness, to ' manifest the dulness of those who have only malice to recommend them.' Every vile scribbler of dull and dead scurrilities finds a niche in this temple of infamy ; all the ' momentary monsters ' and ' industrious bugs,'[7] all the Dunces of the day are preserved like flies in the amber of this fierce and brilliant work. Satire ' spreads its

---

[1] Introduction to the ' Rape of the Lock.'

[2] Lowell.

[3] Addison.

[4] Pope in his dedication to Lord Middlesex gives a history of the ' Dunciad ' from its rise in the ' Treatise on Bathos.'

[5] Advice founded on the first sketch of his satire on Addison.

[6] Note to Preface.   [7] ' Dunciad.'

broad wing and souses on all '¹ the knaves and fools
who displease the author. There is something fine
in Pope's scorn of folly, except when it leads him
into too bitter a hatred of fools. His belief, as Mr.
Leslie Stephen has observed, that stupidity could be
cured by satire is splendid if over-sanguine. We
cannot indeed defend the 'grossness of the images,'²
nor clear the poem of the charge of nastiness, yet,
though it breathes all the savageness of Swift and
reeks of the filth in which he delighted, it recalls
some of the imagination displayed in the 'Rape of
the Lock.' Pope was not so ungenerous as he is
painted. Most of the good writers of the day³ are
praised freely and fully. On the other hand, if we
confess that Pope has suffered, in accordance with
Swift's prophecy, from the insignificance of his
enemies, we must also admit that he was justified
by the correctness of his judgment. Satirical criticism serves a useful and legitimate end when it improves public taste, saving it from admiration of bad
models, and ridiculing the dulness that boasts itself
to be somewhat. So far as it performs this duty it
is saved from the fate of dying with the writers it
destroys. Public taste is ever in need of a corrective,
and the types that Curll and Theobald represent in
the Dunciad are still with us.

The 'Essay on Man' might almost stand for a
satire on man, 'the glory, jest and riddle of the
world.'⁴ It is, really, a commentary on 'Gulliver's
Travels,' obscured by an alien philosophy, an un-
historical account of society and an optimism at
once intellectually false and morally callous. It
is a farrago of inconsistent doctrines relieved by

---

¹ 'Epilogue to the Satires,' Dialogue ii. 15.
² Johnson.
³ Dryden, Congreve, Addison, Locke. Bentley was attacked
as the editor and mutilator of Milton, not as a classical scholar.
⁴ 'Essay on Man,' ii. 18.

epigrammatic pungency and true wit as the author defined it.[1]

The classical strain which was never long absent from the 'Dunciad,' suggesting Juvenal, Horace, and Persius, recurs again in the 'Moral Essays,' the 'grave epistles bringing vice to light,' and in the 'Imitations of Horace.' Here Pope is at his best. As in the 'Rape of the Lock,' so here, he has once more in describing 'the one thing which he knew, the Court and Town of his time, the proper material on which to lay out his elaborate workmanship.'[2] Wit and epigrams sparkle on every page. Most of all, in these half-satirical, half-familiar epistles, where 'satire heals with morals what it hurts with wit,'[3] has he deserved the praise he desired.[4] In the 'Characters of Women,' for instance, his powers of terse and finished portraiture, of brilliant wit and epigram, of exquisite flattery, are admirably displayed. Sweeping denunciation, ruthless vivisection of many types in the persons of Flavia, Narcissa and Atossa, only serve to heighten the effect of the delicate compliment and courtly exception.

The 'Imitations of Horace' are written in accordance with the dictum previously expressed in the preface to the edition of his works published in 1716: 'All that is left us is to recommend our productions by imitation of the Ancients.' No man's spirit was ever less Horatian than that of

---

[1] ' Essay on Criticism' :

> 'True wit is Nature to advantage dressed ;
>   What oft was thought, but ne'er so well expressed.'

[2] Mark Pattison.   [3] Ep. II., i. 261.
> ' Happily to steer
> From grave to gay, from lively to severe,
> Correct with spirit, eloquent with ease,
> Intent to reason or polite to please.'

this jealous, waspish rhymer. None the less, Pope shows marvellous cleverness and admirable pungency when he adapts the satires of Horace. He improves, indeed, on the point and wit of individual lines, though he loses the flavour and inner unity of thought. Nothing can exceed the skill with which, by bitter and pointed sarcasms, he turned the courtly flattery of Horace to Augustus into a stinging satire on George II.[1] In these Imitations, the pleasure of unexpected analogies compensates for the violence done to history and for the extreme artificiality of the method.

Dryden observes in his essay that 'fineness of raillery, the best manner of satire, is not offensive ; a witty man is tickled while he is hurt : a fool feels it not.'[2] If, despite his delicate theory, he is sometimes rough, he is always straightforward. He deals a knock-down blow, but does not stab in the dark. If he is coarse, it is usually in reply to a coarse and scurrilous attack. He does not descend to the nastiness of Pope. Not so sly as Chaucer, nor so insinuating as Addison, he is without malice. The consciousness of easy superiority which never left him saves him from mere pettiness and spite. The underhand malice of Pope is alien to his manly character. Though he was not one of the 'gentle bosoms,' he was not venomous. 'Spiteful he is not, though he wrote a satire.'[3] Quick to anger, he was also quick to forgive and forget. But of Pope, Bentley said with good reason, ' The portentous cub never forgives.'

Where Pope's satire is most stinging, his motives

---

[1] Ep. II. i.

[2] 'On the Origin and Progress of Satire,' prefixed to his translation of Juvenal. Cf. ' No creature smarts so little as a fool.'— Pope, ' Prologue to the Satires,' 84.

[3] 'Abs. and Ach.,' Part II.

are frequently mean. His laurels are entwined with the thorns of hatred. There is as much gall and wormwood in his composition as in that of Archilochus himself, the father of satire. As with the Greek, his motives are mainly personal. His virulent prose satire, 'The Frenzy of John Dennis,' was written to please Addison, though it failed in its object. His attacks on Theobald were dictated by literary jealousy, on Addison by wounded self-love, on Lady Mary by the savage vindictiveness of rejected admiration. His treatment of women, even his praise of women, is degrading. He had, in fact, like Boileau, a bad heart, and cannot be acquitted of the charge, *Lædere gaudes . . . et hoc studio pravus facis.*[1] Partisan poetry had been severe enough in Dryden's hands, but in the hands of Pope, it became still more personal and bitter. In Dryden we find strong sense, command of the happy word, and wit marked by a certain breadth ; in Pope sense as strong, if narrower, a more 'curious felicity,' wit unrivalled in keenness and point. A certain colloquial familiarity lends an air of easy strength to Dryden's satire. His comparisons are usually happy. His work abounds with knowledge, and sparkles with pithy sentences which drop from his pen as if unawares. Pope's art is always peeping out ; his comparisons lack grandeur, and often truth also, whilst his expressions are sometimes less accurate than he supposes.

As a delineator of character, as a describer of personal weaknesses, Pope stands unrivalled. Although he boasts that he 'praises a courtier where he can, and even in a bishop can spy desert,'[2] he lacks as a rule the discrimination of Dryden.[3] Hence

---

[1] Hor., Sat. I., iv., 78, 79. 'You delight to hurt, and do so with zeal by reason of your bad heart.'

[2] Dialogue ii., 63, 70.

[3] An exception to this is the portrait of Addison.

his detached passages are superior to the complete poems.

Unequalled as a satirist of individuals, and as an observer within a limited compass, he is invaluable as a critic of the social life of his own day. His particular portraits are as excellent as his philosophy and his theories are ridiculous. He has no gift for general moralizing. When he declares that the proper study of mankind is man, man means with him Bolingbroke, Walpole, Swift, Curll, and Theobald.[1] Dryden is pre-eminent in the reflective vein of satire. Pope, without Dryden's gift of reasoning in verse, displays more than his love of it.[2] He has no consecutive power of argument. His precision of thought is not able to cope with the fascination of a brilliant phrase, and is sacrificed to his method of composition. His epigrams are the quintessence of a volume of reflection ; his couplets are the product of incredible toil. To make verses was his first labour ; to mend them was his last. He suffered the tumult of imagination to subside, and was never tired of polishing his mosaics until they were finally inserted, too often without due regard to the consistency of the whole.

Dryden, on the other hand, wrote, he says, with very little consideration, to please others, and to make a living. Pope, being independent of money, wrote, without haste, to please himself. Whilst Pope's satire deals only with externals, Dryden's goes to the root of the matter. When Dryden is describing a character satirically, every line adds to or modifies it, but Pope's verses amplify and spin upon the same idea. Dryden excels in comprehension, Pope in minuteness; Dryden in breadth, Pope in compression; Dryden in rugged strength and

---

[1] Leslie Stephen, ' Hours in a Library.'
[2] *E.g.*, ' Essay on Man.'

nervous majesty, Pope in smooth uniformity and pungent epigram. We quote, it will be found, the phrases of Pope, and we apply the satire of Dryden. It is possible to love Dryden through his works, but Pope can only compel our admiration. Both alike found the 'life of a wit a warfare upon earth,'[1] and both might justly feel with Horace—*sunt quibus in satura vidcar nimis acer*. But while much may be forgiven to the poet whose 'life was one long disease,' we respect the greater self-restraint of him who, 'being naturally vindictive, often suffered in silence, and possessed his soul in quiet.'[2]

1667-1745. 'Cousin Swift,' said Dryden, 'you will never be a poet'—a verdict which gained him the dislike of that furious and gifted man. The prophecy was correct. But the verses of so striking and original a genius could not be dull or insignificant. Swift had a gift of fluent rhyme : his poems are distinguished by their ease, if not by their elegance ; often harsh and uncouth, they are never laboured. Some of his poetical lampoons show an extreme virulence of invective. 'The Legion Club,' in which every line has the sting of a hornet, will serve as an example. 'The Rhapsody on Poetry,' though it suffers from the inevitable comparison with the 'Dunciad,' yet displays in a high degree that quality of irony in which Swift is pre-eminent. The trenchant bitterness of the 'Beasts' Confession' likewise betrays the hand of the author of 'Gulliver's Travels.'

Whatever the merit or interest of his poetry, it is as the prince of prose satirists that Swift claims our attention. He ranks with Lucian and Voltaire, rivalling the former in irony, and surpassing the latter in originality. His power was tremendous.

[1] Pope, Preface.
[2] 'Essay on Origin and Progress of Satire,' Dryden's Works, vol. iii., p. 171 (Malone's edition).

Even to-day his writings affect us as, sometimes, his presence affected Vanessa.[1] No satirist ever scored such exquisite triumphs. Concerning 'Gulliver's Travels,' we have it on his own authority—whatever that is worth—that 'a bishop here said that book was full of improbable lies, and for his part he hardly believed a word of it; and so much for Gulliver.'[2] Mr. Isaac Bickerstaff's 'Predictions' were burnt in all seriousness by the Inquisition in Portugal. In the 'Rhapsody on Poetry' the irony of his censure is so perfect and so admirably sustained that he received, at the hands of the Royal Family he had satirized, thanks for the passages of praise. No political writer ever had such power. Each pamphlet was worth hundreds of votes to the Tories, and the author of the 'Drapier Letters' could boast that he had but to raise his hand to bring about an Irish rebellion. His political and personal satire has much of the freedom and point of Junius;[3] but he is not a mere carper. Since he lived in an epoch of party literature and unbridled slander, when all the best writers were retained for the purpose of exalting or defaming the Whig or Tory leaders, his writings are necessarily to a certain extent bound up with the politics of his time, but they touch none the less the wider human interests of all ages. His suggestions are often eminently practical, and much in advance of his day.[4]

---

[1] 'There is something in your look so awful that it strikes me dumb.' 'You strike me with that prodigious awe I tremble with fear.'—Letters of Miss Vanhomrigh to Swift.
Cf. the story of the barber who besought him on his knees not to put him into print, for that he was a poor barber, and had a large family to maintain (vol. i., p. 415).

[2] Letter to Pope, November 17, 1726, written from Ireland.

[3] *E.g.*, 'A short character of Thomas, Earl of Wharton.'

[4] Cf. the very remarkable passage on the early closing of public-houses and the serving of intoxicated persons : 'Project

It was in the Bentley-Boyle quarrel—a quarrel
which was soon developed into a violent dispute as
to the relative superiority of the Ancients or Moderns
—that Swift, with his 'Battle of the Books,' made
his reputation as the wittiest of controversialists,
a reputation he confirmed in the following year
by the 'Tale of a Tub,' a sort of 'Hudibras' in
prose, in which he shows the happy gift of satirical
allegory, which was brought to perfection in 'Gulliver's Travels.' The 'Tale of a Tub' ridicules,
'with all the rash dexterity of wit,'[1] superstition and
fanaticism, but not the essentials of religion.
Though pleading for charity in argument, Swift's
own strong feeling for 'Martin' renders him somewhat uncharitable to 'Peter' and 'Jack.'[2] Voltaire
recommended this work as a masterly satire against
religion in general, and Thackeray denies Swift's
belief in that Christian religion which he had de-
fended with such perfect irony in his 'Argument
against abolishing Christianity.' But neither in the
'Tale' nor in the politico-religious pamphlets is any
reason to be found for a charge which reduces Swift
to the level of the hypocrites he satirized. His
hatred of cant and his dread of the imputation of
cant have caused his attitude to be misconstrued
into that of mere irreligion. His loathing of hypocrisy was so intense that he ran into the opposite
extreme, and exhibited the vice which Bolingbroke
termed hypocrisy reversed. Like Plato, he has often
fallen a victim to his own irony.

1704.

---

for the Advancement of Religion,' vol. iii., pp. 297, 298. Cf.
also his views on the education of women, which he put into
practice with Stella. 'G. T.,' IV., chap. viii., 'My master thought
it monstrous in us to give the females a different kind of education from the males.'

[1] Pope, 'Essay on Man,' ii. 83.
[2] Church of England, Church of Rome, Dissenters.

'The Tale of a Tub,' it is said, cost Swift a
bishopric. Twenty years later, when, like some
world-weary Timon, embittered by the fall of his
party and the failure of his own ambitions, he
had 'commenced Irishman for ever,' he produced
'Gulliver's Travels,' in which he satirized the
politics, manners, and philosophy of Europe, and
analyzed the corruptions of human nature. This
'formal grave lie'[1] is so simple in the narration,
so apparently artless and sincere, that it imposed
upon many people at the time, and still delights
the child who does not penetrate the satire.[2] Swift
is more realistic, if less exuberant, than Rabelais.
The story of Gulliver's preposterous adventures is
more completely a satirical allegory than is that of
the wanderings of Gargantua. The satire itself
is the most bitter and overwhelming Swift ever
wrote. Its province is the mortification of human
pride.[3] Light and amusing at first, it becomes more
severe as it progresses, till in the description of the
Yahoos it reaches a pitch of savage intensity. The
author strips the rags from shivering humanity.
Beneath the resolvent acid of his satire our miserable covering of shams crumbles and disappears.
Sometimes he gazes on the naked imposture with
that cold, hard grin which still lingers on the marble
lips of Voltaire, but often with the kindly firmness
of a reformer. He wishes to prevent people from
winking at their own faults, as Gulliver winked at
his own littleness.

Critics have been too ready to assume that Swift
really regarded all his fellow-creatures as Yahoos, and
to charge him with misanthropy. The description

margin note: 1726.

---

[1] Journal to Stella.

[2] 'From the highest to the lowest it is universally read, from
the Cabinet Council to the nursery.'—Gay, letter to Swift,
Nov. 17, 1726.

[3] 'Gulliver's Travels,' Part IV., pp. 392, 393.

of the Yahoos is not a mere libel on the human race. It teaches a very definite and moral lesson—that the greatness of humanity lies in mind, mind that is set on righteousness. Without it we are as the beasts that perish; with it, even horses are more excellent than we. Man is not man by virtue of his form, but by virtue of his right reason.[1] St. Paul—or are we to say Apollos?—teaches that each time a man does wrong he sins against the divine nature within him, and crucifies Christ afresh. Swift, using the point of his pen and not the feather, puts it, that so man becomes more of a Yahoo and less of a Houyhnhnm. The more odious and vile the Yahoo is represented, the more effective therefore is the lesson. The only proof of Swift's misanthropy is his desire to reform mankind by displaying their vices in the most hateful light.

Against this charge we have the evidence of his journal, of his charities, of his sermons, of his humanitarian suggestions, of his legacies, of those tracts relating to Ireland, which do honour, in Burke's phrase, to his heart as well as to his head. His friends[2] also—they were many and distinguished—speak of him as really good-natured and tender-hearted, though from his excessive hatred of cant he strove to conceal the fact. When he boasts in a letter to Pope, ' I hate and detest that animal called man,' he has to add, ' although I heartily love John, Peter, Thomas, and so forth.' We need not, indeed, go so far as this to seek to disprove this charge. His humour is too deep and genuine to admit of his being a misanthrope.

[1] ' Gulliver's Travels,' Part IV., chap. iii.
[2] *E.g.*, Addison, who wrote in a copy of his ' Travels ' presented to Swift, ' To Dr. Jonathan Swift, the most agreeable companion, the truest friend, and the greatest genius of the day.'

Swift's style consists of 'proper words in proper places.'[1]   Clearness was his chief aim, and his very simplicity, combined with his inventive genius, made the sarcasm and irony keener.   Johnson says, ' He always understands himself, and his readers always understand him.'   This is true enough of his style, but so successfully does the artist conceal his art that it is not, as we have seen, equally true of his intention.   For complete and consistent irony is the chief characteristic of his work.   His best and most constant method is to take some absurd proposition, to adopt some paradoxical idea, and to pursue and develop it with inimitable gravity and relentless logic.   His grammar is often faulty, but his diction is always clear.   He rivals Voltaire in lucidity of thought and style.   The satire of Voltaire is seldom veiled ; but that of Swift frequently lurks beneath much excellent fooling.[2]   His attacks are often coarse, sometimes disguised by subtle irony, sometimes breaking out into furious volleys of abuse ; but they are sincere.   He has command alike of vituperation and of sarcasm.   His gross wit and grotesque invention can always present his opponents in an ignominious or contemptible light.   Never commonplace, he ridicules what is trite, even at the risk of being dirty, and then he seems to sit like one of his own Yahoos, squirting filth on all mankind.   In his ' Polite Conversation and Directions to Servants ' he discovers great power of minute observation ; and in his ' Journal to Stella,' a child-like tenderness, which his sardonic humour and wounding satire have elsewhere obscured.   At the back of all his work there lurks the hidden tragedy of that horrid fear of approaching madness, which embittered his life, and

---

[1] ' Proper words in proper places make the true definition of a style.'—Letter to a Young Clergyman.
[2] Cf. ' Candide ' with the introduction to the ' Tale of a Tub.'

proved in the end only too well founded. We cannot 'take his book and laugh our spleen away,'[1] for that *sæva indignatio*,[2] that cruel indignation with life, vexed him even as a thing that is raw. But we can say of him, in the words of Pope, ' One there is 'who charms us with his spleen,' and, charming us, we may add, fills us with the profoundest pity by the outpourings of his troubled heart, and the tragic silence of his miserable end.

1717.　It is a relief to turn from the malice and personal bitterness, 'the spleen and sour disdain'[3] which lie at the heart of so much English satirical writing, to the hinting, gentlemanly satire of Joseph Addison. His was the criticism that only half says what it means, but is none the less effective. The most graceful of our social satirists does not sit in the seat of the scornful. *Hic tibi comis et urbanus liberque videtur.*[4] This line, written by Horace, equally with that line written of Horace—*admissus circum præcordia ludit*[5]—applies to Addison. It is in these gentle prose satires that the truest representation of the Horatian spirit is to be found. These essays correspond, far more really than Pope's ' Imitations,' to Horace's Causeries,[6] his talks on the art of living, his sketches of life as he saw it. As with Horace, the purpose of his satire is general. The aim is not to gibbet individuals. He assails the follies, not the fools of the age. He tries to go to the

---

[1] Dryden, Ep. ix.
[2] Cf. his epitaph, written by himself : 'Ubi sæva indignatio ulterius cor lacerare nequit'—' Where fierce indignation can no longer lacerate his heart.'
[3] ' Essay on Criticism,' l. 530.
[4] Horace, Sat. I., iv. 90 : ' He seems to you a courteous, well-bred gentleman.'
[5] Persius, i. 118 : ' He finds his way to our inmost feelings and plays round them.'
[6] ' Sermones.'

root of the matter. He will not, he says, be 'very satirical upon the little muff that is now in fashion,'[1] but he applies his remedies to the seeds of every social evil. When he attacks the vicious, he sets upon them in a body, and will not make an example of any particular criminal. He passes over a single foe to charge whole armies, and lashes not Lais or Silenus, but the harlot and the drunkard. Gifted with observation that is acute but not profound, and with a peculiar humour blended with wit, he depicts, without offence, by playful and subtle strokes of irony, the manners and habits, the faults and foibles of various classes of men. He never descends to mere caricature ; as a critic he is tolerant, and never wounds by severity of sarcasm. Judging with coolness, he is, we feel, ' not dully prepossessed nor blindly right ' ;[2] rather he shows himself ' modestly bold, and humanly severe.'

His delicate humour, the urbanity of his manner, and the gentleness of his rebuke lead almost un- awares those whom he criticises to condemn what is ridiculous or unworthy. A more tolerant censor, a more genial and useful satirist never wrote. He is an exception to the rule one is too ready to frame, that the lash of the satirist only serves to please him who cracks it ; for he and his colleague Steele made the *Spectator* an instrument of education and social reform. Steele, however, had none of the sly malice and satirical bent of Addison.

Of the latter's inimitable prose style it is impos- sible to treat adequately in this place. It is impos- sible here to show forth all its praise. This style, to the sober grace of which we owe our love of Addison, is full of varied cadence and subtle charm. The

---

[1] Cf. *Spectator*, No. 16.
[2] Pope, ' Essay on Criticism,' 634, 658.

influence of Dryden's prose and the influence of the best French models are indeed plain, but here also are reflected the ease of Cowley, the purity of Tillotson, the melody and naïveté of Temple.

1738. The 'London' of Samuel Johnson was published on the same morning as Pope's '1738,'[1] and surpassed it in popularity. It is an adaptation of the third satire of Juvenal to the neglect of letters in London, and to those humiliations of the honest native which Johnson the dinnerless[2] knew only too well. London, that London which he was to love so fondly, he calls 'the needy villains' gen'ral home,' which 'sucks in the dregs of each corrupted state.' We trace here something of the vehemence and contemptuous indignation of Juvenal. *Facit indignatio versum.* Like Pope, the author was not without the inspiration of personal motives. The bitter experience of poverty prompted that majestic line, 'Slow rises worth by poverty depressed.' There is in 'London' much of the liveliness of manner and allusion, much, too, of the personal satire of Pope. But in 'Rasselas' and 'The Vanity of Human Wishes' Johnson represents the didactic school when freed from those qualities. With advancing years he becomes grave and sonorous ; bitterness softens into composed moralizing, and satire deteriorates into learned dulness of declamation. Mention should also be made of that most galling offspring of his 'defensive pride,' his letter to Lord Chesterfield.

Of the members of the famous Scriblerus Club, which included Pope, Swift, Gay, Prior, Parnell, and Arbuthnot, and produced the volume of ' Mis-

---

[1] Pope said at once, 'Whoever be the author, he will soon be *déterré.*'

[2] He signed himself on one occasion, 'Yours impransus, S. JOHNSON.'

cellanies' edited by Swift and Pope, John Arbuthnot is, of the minor lights, the most important. His 'History of John Bull' is perhaps responsible for that national character which we enjoy abroad, and on which we pride ourselves at home. The History otherwise loses interest from being a mere burlesque of the politics of the time. But the 'Art of Political Lying,' by the same author, a 'pretty discourse,' as Swift called it, deals wittily enough with an expedient which has not yet gone out of fashion.

Matthew Prior used more than one manner of satire. In the appalling, didactic piece 'Solomon on the Vanity of the World,' and in the pleasant skit on Boileau's abject ode *Sur la Prise de Namur*, it is hard to recognise the same hand. The wit and whimsical nature of 'Alma'[1] are entirely in the manner of Butler. In conjunction with the Earl of Halifax Prior also caricatured Dryden's 'Hind and the Panther'—transversed it to the story of the 'Country Mouse and the City Mouse'; but his most characteristic work is to be found in those minor pieces and satiric epigrams on which his fame chiefly rests. Here he is, as a satirist, working essentially the same vein as the Elizabethan epigrammatists and Corbet, as Rochester and his fellows, as Swift and Pope, in the 'Rape of the Lock,' had worked before him. Prior has much both of the careful ease of Horace and of the point of Martial. The light ridicule of Anstey's 'New Bath Guide,' the polished, well-bred wit of William Praed, and the neatly humorous political lyrics or *vers de société* of a host of other writers, have down to the present day continued the tradition of this light form of laughing satire.

The work of John Gay also takes various 1688-1722.

---

[1] A discursive dialogue on the seat of the mind.

forms.   Less witty than Prior, he is less cynical.
He follows Horace rather than Martial in spirit.
His criticisms are usually amiable, his bur-
lesques not bitter except when he remembers
how he has been disappointed of Court favour and
public office.   In his mock-didactic ' Trivia,' in his
epistolary verses, and in his ' Shepherd's Week '—
written to ridicule the sham pastorals of Philips—he
shows that ' native humour tempering virtuous rage '
with which Pope credits him in his epitaph.   He is,
however, perhaps at his best as a satirist, as he is
certainly at his best as a poet of original merit, and
as a tuneful singer, in the ' What d'ye Call,' a
farcical burlesque after the manner of the ' Rehearsal,'
and in the ' Beggar's Opera,' and its continuation,
' Polly.'   The ' Beggar's Opera ' originated from
Swift's suggestion that ' a Newgate pastoral might
be an odd, pretty sort of thing.'   It was the first
English light opera, and one of the most successful.
In addition to side-glances of burlesque on the
newly-imported and popular Italian opera, it contained many general satirical allusions.   In ' Polly '
there was more personal satire, for Sir Robert
Walpole was severely ridiculed in the piece, and
had it prohibited for that reason.

   Gay is, however, chiefly remembered for his
' Moral Fables.'   He is distinguished here by the
good-humoured sense which is essentially his, and
by an easy fluency of narration in the familiar, colloquial style which we know was the product of much
toil.   Prior, too, had written Tales, and imitated
the *Contes* of La Fontaine.   But these tales, like
the *Contes*, are disfigured by immorality both of
subject and of treatment.   Gay, in his ' Fables,'
shows himself less witty than Prior and far below
the standard of La Fontaine, but he is at any rate
free from any imputation of modesty.   As a mode

of satire the Fable is open to the objection that the
morals must often be far-fetched, and hang like
tails on the body of the narrative. In the adoption
of the lighter form of satire, and the use of the
short fable to convey it, Swift, Prior, and Gay, and,
later, Smart and Wilkie, may be regarded as representing the reaction against classical models, in
matter and style, which already, even in the days of
Pope's supremacy, was beginning to set in.

There is some feeble satire buried in Blair's dull
'Grave.' The interest of Garth's 'Dispensary' 1699.
has faded with the dispute which gave rise to it,
but Matthew Green's little poem on the 'Spleen' 1696-1737.
deals with a more enduring subject in a vein of
pleasing originality. It is spiced with touches of
humorous ridicule which are, however, not too
splenetic.

The other contemporaries and imitators of Pope
produced much satiric and abusive verse, of which
the enumeration would be tedious, and criticism of
which is unnecessary. The mere Goodes and
Ralphs of the 'Dunciad' have achieved, by being
mentioned there, an immortality they did not
deserve. Pope, however, had little right to speak of
Bernard Mandeville so contemptuously as he does
in that poem, except in so far as execution is con-
cerned. For he has embodied much of the philosophy of the 'Fable of the Bees' in his third 'Moral
Essay.' In this fable and the accompanying remarks
Mandeville maintains with considerable ingenuity,
in prose and in verse, which is not poetry, the half-
truth of the paradox that private vices are public
benefits—that the interests of society are served by
the play of human passions, or, as Pope puts it,
'Extremes in man concur to general use.'

As for 'The Author to Let' of Savage and
Whitehead's 'State Dunces,' Armstrong's 'Taste,'

Christopher Smart's dull lampoon the 'Hilliad,' Owen Cambridge's feeble 'Scribleriad,' and the solemn and fatuous expositions of Akenside, they hardly deserve to be mentioned.

The satires of Edward Young have not that epigrammatic felicity which sometimes illumined his 'Night Thoughts.' The author of the 'Love of
1725. Fame' and 'Epistles' is content, as a rule, to keep on a dull level of commonplace epigram. It is interesting to observe that he professes to follow Horace and Boileau, but he lacks the humour of the one and the style of the other, and without these qualities even didactic moralizing, unrelieved by personalities, is apt to pall. Swift's criticism of these satires, that they should either have been more angry or more merry, holds good. Young is most successful where he is least didactic—in his two
1728. 'Satires on Women.' These suggest a comparison with Pope's 'Characters of Women,' and they do not suffer in the process so much as might have been expected. Defoe's 'Short Way with the Dissenters' is an amazingly clever burlesque. Tobias
1721-1771. Smollett began his literary career with two satires in verse—'Advice' and 'Reproof.' They are acrimonious attacks on well-known individuals, and as vigorous as we should expect from his genius, temper, and command of language. We find in them the same propensity to personal satire and rank indecency which he indulged to a less extent as a novelist.

In prose, Fielding, through the medium of the novel,[1] of the essay, of witty parody and dramatic satire,[2] shows a power of mischievous wit and pure irony second only to that of Swift and Lucian. Fielding declared war on affectation and hypocrisy. His massive common-sense shines through every line,

---

[1] 'Joseph Andrews.'   [2] 'Pasquin.'

and nowhere more brightly than in ' Jonathan Wild,' of which the peculiar and excellent irony is but faintly reflected in Thackeray's ' Barry Lyndon.' Goldsmith, as an artist, was the pupil of Fielding, though he knew it not, but, as a satirist, he was akin to Addison. 'The Haunch of Venison' is indeed ' a miniature farce,' but ' The Retaliation' is an exquisite *jeu d'esprit*, as playful and witty as it is free from gall, whilst in the ' Citizen of the World ' Goldsmith comments, after the manner of Addison, on Georgian England and the Republic of Letters. In these papers and in ' The Bee,' he anticipates much of the matter of the ' Traveller ' and ' Deserted Village,' poems in which the didactic school may be said to have culminated. Here, as in all his work, kindly satire, softened by the witching simplicity of his style, lurks beneath gentle humour and genuine pathos. It was not for him to follow in the footsteps of that boisterous literary bully, Churchill.

The success of Lloyd's 'Actor ' induced Churchill to try his powers in the same line, though on a ⁕ more personal plan. The result was the ' Rosciad,' wherein he ridiculed with absurd violence the actors of his day. It was the most successful, as it was the most finished, of his coarse and impudent lampoons. In heroics his versification represents an unsuccessful reaction against the smoothness of the school of Pope. His octosyllabics, when he adopts that metre, have neither the wit of Butler nor the keenness of Swift. As a moralist his impudent assumption of superiority harmonizes but poorly with the facts of his life. As a political satirist he was a friend of Wilkes, and indulged in an indiscriminate use of the bludgeon. Though he invariably writes at the top of his voice, he is always fighting for mean causes, scourging small fools and

1761.

unimportant villains. Nor does his style atone for the lack of sympathy aroused by his subjects. When taste was almost at its lowest in England, a certain gift of observation and imitation, a thin vein of humour eked out by rough vehemence, and occasionally an undeniable force and felicity of expression, gained Churchill an unmerited reputation, the glow of which still tinges the judgments of those who do not read him.

1769-1772. We may pass over the pointless invectives of the inexperienced Chatterton, but some of the letters of Junius, that shadow of a name, give the author a clear title to be noticed, for although they are on the whole to be classed as mere political invectives, they contain many passages of bitter and powerful satire, salted with the irony which redeems vituperation.

1786-1795. We may pause also to give a word of praise to Cowper's satirical sketches, and to the whimsical and sarcastic mock-heroic 'Lousiad' of Wolcot,[1] who was also responsible for a mock pastoral 'Bozzy and Piozzi,' in which he ridiculed those recorders of every trifling incident in Johnson's life. The perennial freshness of this subject gives him a distinct advantage over Churchill, who dealt with ephemeral incidents and conditions. Cowper, when he is serious, too often proses and rants. But in his lighter moments, when he is just sketching in a character, he shows much humour and happiness of touch. But at the end of the century two greater satirists than these appeared. Both as a translator of Juvenal,[2] and as the author of the 'Baviad' and 'Mæviad,' Gifford is entitled to distinction. The latter poems are very bitter and

[1] Peter Pindar. The 'Lousiad' is unfortunately, like the rough political poems of the author, very coarse.
[2] Of which the preface is perhaps the most valuable part.

very powerful literary satires, cast in the classic mould. Gifford, it must be confessed, is somewhat heavy-handed and deficient in humour, but his fine command of language and admirable sincerity atone to a certain extent for any faults of taste and style.

The satire of Crabbe, on the other hand, was 1754-1832. sad rather than savage. Surgeon and priest, he was also the poet of the poor. He was the first to give the lie to the false ideals of rustic happiness and virtue that had hitherto pervaded poetry. ' I paint the cot,' he says, 'as Truth will paint it and as bards will not.' Byron calls him ' Nature's sternest painter, yet the best ';[1] but if we pass that, we must at least take exception to his description of Crabbe as the saviour of the school of Pope. For Crabbe was a realist; it was about the truth of his pictures that he cared. Like most realists, he is lacking in the sense of beauty. He often errs, therefore, in giving us vulgar details unrefined by selection. His studies are like Hogarth's in minuteness, but he has not Hogarth's gift of finding matter for comedy in the sin and sorrow he has observed. For he is less of a satirist and more of a humanitarian than Hogarth. His pathos is deep and unaffected, his style, except in accidental points, decidedly his own. His feeling is too sincere to allow him to waste time over polish ; he relies on the general human interest of his characters rather than on epigrammatic felicity of language. He paints the pride of the rich and the misery of the poor with unrelenting acuteness, and possesses to a remarkable extent the quick intuitive power of exposing us to ourselves, and tearing the veil which human self-love draws over human frailty. We cannot resist the searching keenness of his satire;

[1] ' English Bards and Scotch Reviewers.'

it penetrates into what Rochefoucauld[1] has called
'the unknown land of self-love.'

1759-1796. As a poet Burns did for Scotland the same
work as Blake and Crabbe and Cowper were doing
for England. He, too, sings the song of the manhood of man, whether rich or poor. But his coarse
1786. epigrams and political songs cannot be said to
have placed him among the great satirical writers.
His fun as a rule is boisterous, his wit of the
broadest. He has too much joy in living, and too
much compassion for the sorrow and sin of life to
be other than a gentle critic of vices. But he was
a satirist with something to say, a moralist after
the manner of Fielding, when he revolted against
the hypocrisy and worship of appearances marking
the 'unco guid' who condemned the open excesses
into which his own strong passions had led him
against his will. This note recurs continually in
his poems. It is struck most firmly in 'The Holy
Fair,' and most bitterly in 'Holy Willie's Prayer.'
It will be sufficiently exemplified by the address to
the Rigidly Righteous. Of his epistles and other
satires, it is enough to add that the form and spirit
are those of Alan Ramsay and Robert Fergusson,
but the genius that inspires them is the fitfully
burning genius of Robert Burns.

1798. A new era of journalism was begun when the
political satires of George Canning were published
in the *Anti-Jacobin.* Under the title of the ' New
Morality,' he poured forth, with a fine air of moral
indignation and elegant fluency of verse, a general
denunciation of the prevailing tendency to push
every principle in politics and morals to excess.
The piece has much vigour and point, and contains

---

[1] 'Maximes du Duc de la Rochefoucauld,' No. 111 : ' Quelque
découverte que l'on ait faite dans le pays de l'amour-propre
il y reste encore bien des terres inconnues.'

at least one line which has passed into the common stock of quotations. 'The Needy Knife-Grinder,' in another style, is a brilliant little piece of condensed sarcasm.

The influence of Gifford can be clearly traced   1808.
in Byron, who at the beginning and the end of
his career dealt in satire. 'English Bards and
Scotch Reviewers'[1] was the product of mere rage at
that critique of 'Hours in Idleness' which he
described as 'a masterpiece of low wit and a tissue
of scurrilous abuse.' This reply teems with powerful
and indiscriminate invective. It differs in two
important respects from the 'Dunciad.' On the
one hand, most of Byron's heroes were on a level
with their satirist, but on the other, Byron is not
justified by the correctness of his judgment as Pope
may claim to be. Though worthless as literary
criticism, 'English Bards and Scotch Reviewers' is
remarkable as the most powerful expression of that
spleen which is always breaking out in Byron's
poems. The 'Vision of Judgment' is another ebulli-
tion of spite, wherein humour and common-sense
are aided by imaginative invention.

But Byron's best satire is to be found in his best
and most original work, 'Don Juan.' This wonderful record of passing fancies and fleeting humours is
regaining, there is reason to hope, some of its former
popularity. The same fervour and elastic strength,
the same lack of critical insight, are to be found here
as in 'English Bards and Scotch Reviewers,' but
there is also a melancholy undertone which, in
company with perpetual contrasts of sarcasm, flip-
pancy, and warm feeling, improve the effect of the
sudden outbursts of spleen.

Shelley's satirical poems form about one-twelfth   1820.

---

[1] With this piece satire in heroic verse would seem to have died.

of the bulk of his work; but they are not important. There was not in him the stuff of which
satirists are made. With him imagination pre-
ponderated over judgment and reason. 'Peter Bell'
is inspired by a Byronic contempt for one side of
Wordsworth and part of his works; whilst ' Swellfoot
the Tyrant' strikes us rather as an amusing extrava-
ganza than as a serious or convincing satire. Though
it contains some excellent strokes, it does not at all
persuade us that Shelley's genius lay in that direction.

1831.   ' Sartor Resartus ' is one of the few great purely
satiric prose works of our century. In describing the clothes-philosophy oɪ Teufelsdröckh, to
whom 'the Upholsterer is no Pontiff, neither is
any drawing-room a temple,'[1] Carlyle displays a
style and sincerity all his own, and an ironic humour
akin to that of Swift, to whom he owes many a hint.
Essentially Swiftian indeed is Carlyle's deep hatred
of shams, his paradoxical choice of subject, and
much of his method.

Thomas Moore is the last of the considerable
poets who wrote much satire.[2] The levity of his
Irish wit rendered his brisk pasquinades highly
popular at the time, but they have since fallen into
oblivion, due partly to their occasional character,
and partly to the waves of a literary revolution
which have passed over all Moore's works.

The age of the novel had now arrived. The
fashion set by Fielding was at length adopted. In
the novels of Miss Burney, Miss Ferrier, and
Theodore Hook we find satire of a crude and
inferior sort. But Miss Austen stands alone and
supreme in the art of delicate and humorous satiric
writing in fiction of this kind.

[1] 'Sartor Resartus,' ch. iv.
[2] 'Fudge Family in Paris,' 'Twopenny Post-Bag,' 'Fables
for the Holy Alliance.'

The qualities of Thomas Love Peacock betray themselves in the caustic irony of his songs, as well as in the genial extravagance of his 'little publications.'[1] In all his novels the wine is the same, but improved by keeping.[2] Plot he ignores, his characters are types, and dialogue is the essence of his books, which, in their sprightly humour and satiric fancy have not a little of the salt of Aristophanes, of Rabelais, and of Petronius.

Dickens, in his social and political satire, is vulgar and overstrained, but 'Ixion in Heaven,' 'Popanilla,' and 'The Infernal Marriage,' proved that a portion of the mantle of Lucian had fallen on Lord Beaconsfield, who, a few years later, in a trilogy of political novels, with a brilliant, good-humoured wit all his own, laughed at 'the fussy and impotent intrigues of great ladies, the agitation of hungry office-seekers, the manœuvres of political wire-pullers, and the disappointment of pompous grandees.'[3]

No writer of this century has indulged the satiric vein more frequently than Thackeray. Before all things he is a novelist—a novelist who possesses the rare art of endowing his characters with life. It is in the portrayal of men, especially of bad men, that he excels. His women, when they are not insipid, are impossible, but they are never incredible; for we can believe in the impossible, but in the improbable never. But there are in his books both men and women who live in the mind as types or examples of folly, weakness, or vice. Barnes Newcombe, Becky Sharp, Lord Steyne, Sir Pitt Crawley, and the rest, have more substance in them than Achitophel or Lord Fanny. The George IV. of Thackeray is almost as famous a portrait as Juvenal's Domitian. Thackeray, in fact, could create. Imagination, even

---

[1] Preface to 'Headlong Hall,' 1837.
[2] Dr. Richard Garnett.   [3] H. D. Traill.

more than indignation, guided his pen. The strange diffuseness of his style is an index of the author's mind, and of his limitations as a satirist. The 'Book of Snobs' is an instance: it is far too discursive. The author is attacking a noted failing of his countrymen. He does so wittily, forcibly, happily; but he pursues his theme along devious paths, pausing to illustrate or to moralize. He is apt to go that other stage[1] which makes a journey of a progress, and turns delight into fatigue. When satire attacks, every line should go home with the full strength of the striker behind it. If the writer lengthens his pages, he should also broaden his charity. Thackeray is more long-winded than Horace, and bitterer than Juvenal. His manner would be admirable if he wished us to smile, to be tolerant and good-humoured with the personages of his work. It is ill-fitted either to rouse or to sustain the detestation which he evidently wishes to excite.

It is not in complete narratives, but in the portraiture of individuals that Thackeray proves himself a great satirist; but in satire, it may be said, this is a great part of the whole.

Thackeray's example has been followed. We live in the era of the novel, and it is among the novelists that we look nowadays for the censorious critics of life. Satire, however, has not been altogether engrossed by novels. For on the stage, too, criticism of life has of late years been attempted by the dramatists, and, in a lighter and more successful manner, W. S. Gilbert, the successor of Gay,[2] on the one hand, and Molière on the other, with his paradoxical wit, gift of rhyme, and lyrical ability, has

---

[1] Cf. Dryden's Essay.
[2] It would be entertaining to work out a comparison between 'Patience,' 'The Beggar's Opera,' and 'Les Précieuses Ridicules.'

ridiculed with exquisite humour the follies and excesses of society. The temptation to discuss the qualities of living satirical writers is almost irresistible ; but we must be content to glance at the tendencies of the present age.

As civilization has grown more complex, there has been a corresponding growth in the complexity of character. A more delicate method of analysis is required, and the psychological studies of Browning have taken the place of the satirical portraits of Pope.

Though the thunder of Carlyle still rolls in our ears, general denunciation of shams has gone out of fashion. Humanity has learnt to pity rather than to condemn itself. We live in an age of excuses, when righteous indignation is felt to be a little out of place. We need not look nowadays for a Juvenal, in whose constant and ruthless declamation there are no lights and shades and no uncertainties. Indignation no longer makes verses. The school of Keats and Swinburne, which has nothing in common with satire, prevails in the poetry of the nineteenth century ;[1] whilst the analyzing and dissecting school of Browning finds the soul less simple and less black than did the followers of Juvenal. In these more charitable days denunciatory satire is a bruised reed, on which if a man lean, it will go into his hand and pierce him.

In prose, since the time of Canning, political spleen, deserting the pamphlet, has vented itself more and more in speeches and weekly reviews. Criticism of the sins of society has found a home in the pulpit or the novel. For when the novel, with all its opportunities of contrast and subtle characterization, came to be the prevailing form of litera-

[1] Mr. Alfred Austin, however, has written satires in heroic verse, *e.g.*, ' The Golden Age' and ' The Season.'

ture, the satiric spirit found a ready means of expressing itself with even greater effect than in verse. The great novelists present us with men, not with personified epigrams. From the nature of the case, in so doing they diffuse their satire and call in humour to take the place of bitterness. Now, the humour necessary for the best manner of satire is that peculiar humour which means, at bottom, the power of seeing things as they really are, undisguised by conventional trappings—the power of appreciating the ironical unfitness of things in this world. The best and finest form of satire, in the opinion both of Dryden and of Swift,[1] is the sharp, well-mannered way of laughing a folly out of countenance. Of this we have much—we cannot have too much—in the novels of the day.

The world will always need to be reminded, and we may rest assured that in one form or another it will not fail to be reminded, that in every path of life there is a limit set, beyond which it is not good to go. Satire will doubtless continue to concern itself with its traditional duty—the duty of enforcing by whatsoever means the ancient precept

> ' Est inter Tanain quiddam socerumque Viselli
> Est modus in rebus, sunt certi denique fines
> Quos ultra citraque nequit consistere rectum.'[2]

---

[1] Swift, ' Intelligencer,' No. 111.   Dryden, ' Origin and Progress of Satire.'

[2]
> ' Sure some difference lies
> Between the very fool and very wise ;
> Some certain mean in all things may be found
> To mark our virtues and our vices bound.'
>
> Hor., Sat. I., i. 105.

SONG AGAINST THE FRIARS [1375 ?].

PRESTE, ne monke, ne yit chanoun,
   Ne no man of religioun,
   Gyven hem so to devocioun,
    As done these holy frers.
For some gyven hem to chyvalry,
Somme to riote and ribauderey,
Bot frers gyven hem to grete study,
   And to grete prayers,
  Who so kepes thair reule al,
   Bothe in worde and dede;
I am ful siker[1] that he shal
   Have heaven bliss to mede.

Men may see by thair contynaunce
That thai are men of grete penaunce,
And also that thair sustynaunce
   Simple is and wayke.
I have lyved now fourty years,
And fatter men about the neres
Yit sawe I never then are these frers,
   In contreys ther thai rayke.
Meatless so meagre are thai made,
   And penaunce so puttes hem doun,
That each one is an horse-lade,
   When he shall trusse[2] of toun.

[1] Sure.   [2] Pack up and depart.

Alas! that ever it shuld be so,
Suche clerkes as thai about shuld go,
Fro toun to toun by two and two,
    To seke thair sustynaunce.
By God that al this world wan,[1]
He that that ordre first bygan,
Me thynk certes it was a man
    Of simple ordynaunce.
For thai have noght to lyve by,
    Thai wandren here and there
And dele with divers marcerye,
    Right as thai pedlers were.

Thai dele with purses, pynnes, and knyves,
With gyrdles, gloves, for wenches and wyves,
Bot ever bacward the husband thryves
    Ther thai are haunted tille.
For when the gode man is fro hame
And the frere comes to oure dame,
He spares nauther for synne ne shame,
    That he ne dos his wille.
If thai no helpe of housewyves had,
    When husbands are not inne,
The freres welfare were ful bad,
    For thai shuld brewe ful thynne. . . .

Trantes thai can[2] and many a jape,
For somme can with a pound of sape[3]
Gete him a kyrtelle and a cape,
    And somwhat else therto.
Wherto shuld I othes swere?
Ther is no pedler that pak can bere,
That half so dere can selle his gere,
    Then a frer can do.

---

[1] Redeemed.   [2] Know tricks.   [3] Soap.

For if he gife a wyfe a knyfe
    That cost but penys two,
Worthe ten knyves, so mot I thryfe,
    He wyl have ere he go. . . .

Thai say that thai distroye synne,
And thai mayntene men moste therinne ;
For had a man slayn all his kynne,
    Go shryve him at a frere,
And for lesse then a payre of shone
He wyl assoil him clene and sone,
And say the synne that he has done
    His saule shall never dere[1] . . .
Alle wyckednes that men can telle
    Reynes hem among ;
Ther shal no saule have rowme in helle,
    Of frers ther is suche throng. . . .

Ful wisely can thai preche and say ;
Bot as thai preche no thing do thai.
I was a frere ful many a day,
    Therfor the sothe I wate.[2]
But when I sawe that thair lyvyng
Acordyd not to thair prechyng,
Of I cast my frer clothing,
    And wyghtly went my gate.
Other leve ne toke I none,
    Fro ham when I went,
Bot toke ham to the devel eachone,
    The priour and the covent.

[1] Injure.   [2] Truth I know.

GEOFFREY CHAUCER [1340-1400].

From the Prologue to ' The Canterbury Tales.'

A FRERE[1] there was, a wantown and a merye,
A limitour,[2] a ful solempne[3] man.
In alle the ordres foure is noon that can[4]
So muche of daliaunce and fair langage.
He hadde maad ful many a mariage
Of yonge wommen, at his owne cost.
Un-to his ordre he was a noble post.[5]
Ful wel biloved and famulier was he
With frankeleyns[6] over-al in his contree,
And eek with worthy wommen of the toun :
For he had power of confessioun,
As seyde him-self, more than a curat,
For of his ordre he was a licentiat.
Ful swetely herde he confessioun,
And plesaunt was his absolucioun ;
He was an esy man to yeve[7] penaunce
Ther[8] as he wiste to han a good pitaunce :
For unto a povre ordre for to yive
Is signe that a man is wel y-shrive.
For if he yaf, he dorste make avaunt,
He wiste that a man was repentaunt.
For many a man so hard is of his herte,
He may nat[9] wepe al-thogh him sore smerte.
Therefore, in stede of weping and preyeres,
Men moot[10] yeve silver to the povre[11] freres.
His tipet was ay farsed ful of knyves
And pinnes, for to yeven faire wyves.
And certeinly he hadde a mery note ;
Wel coude he singe and pleyen on a rote.[12]

---

[1] Friar. [2] Beggar. [3] Cheerful. [4] Knows.
[5] Support. [6] Freeholders. [7] Give.
[8] Wherever he knew he would have a good pittance.
[9] Not. [10] Ought. [11] Poor. [12] Fiddle (kind of).

Of yeddinges[1] he bar[2] utterly the prys.
His nekke whyt was as the flour-de-lys.
Ther-to[3] he strong was as a champioun.
He knew the tavernes wel in every toun,
And everich hostiler and tappestere
Bet[4] than a lazar or a beggestere ;
For unto swich[5] a worthy man as he
Acorded nat, as by his facultee,
To have with seke[6] lazars aqueyntaunce.
It is nat honest, it may nat avaunce
For to delen with no swich poraille,[7]
But al with riche and sellers of vitaille.
And over-al, ther as profit sholde aryse,
Curteys he was, and lowly of servyse.
Ther nas no man no-wher so vertuous.
He was the beste beggere in his hous :
For thogh a widwe hadde noght a sho,[8]
So plesaunt was his ' In principio,'[9]
Yet wolde he have a ferthing, er he wente.
His purchas was wel bettre than his rente.
And rage he coude, as it were right a whelpe.
In love-dayes[10] ther coude he muchel helpe.
For there he was nat lyk a cloisterer,
With a thredbar cope, as is a povre scoler.
But he was lyk a maister or a pope.
Of double worsted was his semi-cope,
That rounded as a belle out of the presse.
Somwhat he lipsed, for his wantownesse,
To make his English swete up-on his tonge ;
And in his harping, whan that he had songe,
His eyen twinkled in his heed aright,
As doon the sterres in the frosty night.

---

[1] Songs.   [2] Carried.   [3] Moreover.   [4] Better.
[5] Such.   [6] Sick.   [7] Poor people.
[8] Though a widow had not any shoes.
[9] The ordinary greeting of a friar.
[10] Days for settling disputes by arbitration.

From 'The Prologue to the Pardoner's Tale.'

' LORDINGS,' quod he, ' in chirches whan I preche,
I peyne me to han an hauteyn[1] speche,
And ringe it out as round as gooth a belle,
For I can al by rote that I telle.
My theme is alwey oon, and ever was—
" Radix malorum est Cupiditas."[2]
First I pronounce whennes that I come,
And than my bulles[3] shewe I, alle and somme.
Our lige lordes seel on my patente,
That shewe I first, my body to warente,
That no man be so bold, ne preest ne clerk,
Me to destourbe of Cristes holy werk ;
And after that than telle I forth my tales,
Bulles of popes and of cardinales,
Of patriarkes, and bishoppes I shewe ;
And in Latyn I speke a wordes fewe,
To saffron[4] with my predicacioun,[5]
And for to stire men to devocioun.
Than shewe I forth my longe cristal stones,
Y-crammed ful of cloutes and of bones ;
Reliks been they, as wenen[6] they echoon.
Than have I in latoun[7] a sholder-boon
Which that was of an holy Jewes shepe.
" Good men," seye I, " tak of my wordes kepe ;
If that this boon be wasshe in any welle,
If cow, or calf, or sheep, or oxe swelle
That any worm hath ete, or worm y-stonge,
Tak water of that welle, and wash his tonge,
And it is hool[8] anon ; and forthermore,
Of pokkes and of scabbe, and every sore

[1] Loud.
[2] Avarice is the root of evil.
[3] Papal Bulls.
[4] Colour.
[5] Sermon.
[6] As they all suppose.
[7] Metal.
[8] Whole.

Shal every sheep be hool, that of this welle
Drinketh a draughte ; tak kepe eek what I telle.

  *   *   *   *   *

Good men and wommen, o thing[1] warne I yow,
If any wight be in this chirche now,
That hath doon sinne horrible, that he
Dar nat, for shame, of it y-shriven be,
Or any womman, be she yong or old,
That hath y-maad hir housbond cokewold,
Swich folk shul have no power ne no grace
To offren to my reliks in this place.
And who-so findeth him out of swich blame,
He wol com up and offre in goddes name,
And I assoille[2] him by the auctoritee
Which that by bulle y-graunted was to me."
By this gaude have I wonne, yeer by yeer,
An hundred mark sith I was Pardoner.
I stonde lyk a clerk in my pulpet,
And whan the lewed[3] peple is douny-set,
I preche, so as ye han herd bifore,
And telle an hundred false japes[4] more.
Than peyne I me to strecche forth the nekke,
And est and west upon the peple I bekke,
As doth a dowve sitting on a berne.[5]
Myn hondes and my tonge goon so yerne,[6]
That it is joye to see my bisinesse.
Of avaryce and of swich cursednesse
Is al my preching, for to make hem free
To yeve her pens, and namely un-to me.[7]
For my entente is nat but for to winne,
And no-thing for correccioun of sinne.
I rekke never, whan that they ben beried,
Though that her soules goon a-blake-beried ![8]

---

[1] One thing.   [2] Absolve.   [3] Common.
[4] Tricks, jests.   [5] Barn.   [6] Briskly.
[7] To give their money, and especially to me.
[8] Blackberrying = astray.

For certes, many a predicacioun
Comth ofte tyme of yvel entencioun;
Som for plesaunce of folk and flaterye,
To been avaunced by ipocrisye,
And som for veyne glorie, and som for hate.
For, whan I dar non other weyes debate,
Than wol I stinge him with my tonge smerte
In preching, so that he shal nat asterte[1]
To been defamed falsly, if that he
Hath trespased to my brethren or to me.
For, though I telle noght his propre name,
Men shal wel knowe that it is the same
By signes and by othere circumstances.
Thus quyte I folk that doon us displesances :
Thus spitte I out my venim under hewe
Of holynesse, to seme holy and trewe.
But shortly myn entente I wol devyse :
I preche of no-thing but for coveityse.
Therfor my theme is yet, and ever was—
'Radix malorum est Cupiditas.'
Thus can I preche agayn that same vyce
Which that I use, and that is avaryce.
But, though my-self be gilty in that sinne,
Yet can I maken other folk to twinne[2]
From avaryce, and sore to repente.
But that is nat my principal entente.
I preche no-thing but for coveityse ;
Of this matere it oughte y-nogh suffyse.
Than telle I hem ensamples many oon
Of olde stories, long tyme agoon :
For lewed peple loven tales olde ;
Swich thinges can they wel reporte and holde.
What ? trowe ye, the whyles I may preche,
And winne gold and silver for I teche,
That I wol live in povert wilfully ?
Nay, nay, I thoghte it never trewely !

[1] Escape.　　　　　　[2] To depart from.

For I wol preche and begge in sondry londes ;
I wol not do no labour with myn hondes,[1]
Ne make baskettes, and live therby,
Because I wol nat beggen ydelly.
I wol non of the apostles counterfete ;
I wol have money, wolle, chese, and whete,
Al were it yeven of the povrest page,[2]
Or of the povrest widwe in a village,
Al sholde hir children sterve for famine.
Nay ! I wol drinke licour of the vyne,
And have a joly wenche in every toun.

WILLIAM LANGLAND [1340-1400 ?].

*From ' The Vision of William concerning Piers the
Plowman.'*

In a somere seyson whan softe was the sonne,
Y shap me in-to shrobbis as y a shepherde were,
In abit as an ermite unholy of werkes ;
Ich wente forth in the world wonders to hure,
And saw meny cellis and selcouthe thynges.
Ac on a may morwenyng on Malverne hulles
Me byfel for to slepe for werynesse of wandryng ;
And in a launde as ich lay lenede ich and slepte,
And merveylously me mette as ich may yow telle ;
Al the welthe of this worlde and the woo bothe,

In a summer season, when the sun was warm,¡I betook me to
the shrubs (*i.e.*, to an out-of-door life) as if I were a shepherd,
dressed like a hermit of unholy works ; I went forth in the world
to hear wonders, and saw many cells (in religious houses) and
strange things. But on a May morning on Malvern hills I
happened to sleep, through weariness of wandering ; and as I
lay in a meadow I reclined and slept, and marvellously I dreamed,
as I may tell you. All the wealth of the world and the woe,

---

[1] Hands.   [2] Although it were given by.

Wynkyng as it were wyterly ich saw hyt,
Of tryuthe and of tricherye of tresoun and of gyle,
Al ich saw slepynge as ich shal yow telle.

      *   *   *   *   *

Somme putte hem to plow and pleiden ful seylde,
In settyng and in sowyng swonken ful harde,
And wonne that thuse wasters with glotenye
    destroyeth.

      *   *   *   *   *

And somme chosen cheffare they cheude the betere,
As hit semeth to oure syght that souche men
    thryveth.
And somme murthes to make as mynstrals conneth,
That wollen neyther swynke ne swete bote swery
    grete othes,
And fynde up foule fantesyes and foles hem maken,
And haven witte at wylle to worche yf they wolde.
That Paul prechith of hem proven hit ich myghte,
Qui turpiloquium loquitur ys Lucyfers knave.
Bydders and beggers faste a-boute yoden,
Tyl hure bagge and hure belly were bretful
    ycrammyd,
Faytynge for hure fode and fouhten atten ale,

---

sleeping as it were, I certainly saw it. Of truth and of
treachery, of treason and of guile, I saw all, sleeping, as I shall
tell you. . . . Some set themselves to plough, and amused
themselves very seldom ; with planting and sowing they worked
very hard and gained what these spendthrifts destroy with
gluttony. . . . And some chose merchandise ; they prospered
better, as it seems to our sight that such men thrive. And
some are skilled to make mirth as minstrels, that will neither
toil nor sweat, but swear great oaths, and invent foul fancies,
and make fools of themselves, and (yet) have their wit at
their will, (being able) to work if they wished. What Paul
preaches about them I might adduce here (2 Thess. iii. 10), (but
will not, for) he who speaks slander is Lucifer's servant. Beggars
went about quickly till their wallet and belly were crammed
brimful, telling lies for their food, and quarrelling at the ale-

In glotenye, god wot, goth they to bedde,
And aryseth with ribaudrie tho Roberdes knaves ;
Slep and synful sleuthe seweth suche evere.
Pylgrimis and palmeres plyghten hem to-gederes,
To seche seint Iame and seyntys of rome,
Wenten forthe in hure way with meny un-wyse tales,
And haven leve to lye al hure lyf-time.
Eremytes on an hep with hokede staves,
Wenten to Walsyngham, and hure wenches after ;
Grete lobies and longe that lothe were to swynke,
Clothede hem in copis to be knowe fro othere,
And made hem-selve eremytes hure eise to have.
Ich fond ther frerus alle the foure ordres,
Prechynge the peple for profit of the wombe,
And glosynge the godspel as hem good lykede ;
For covetise of copes contrariede some doctors.
Meny of this maistres of mendinant freres,
Hure monye and marchaundise marchen to-gederes-;
Ac sutth charite hath be chapman and chef to
    shryve lordes,
Many ferlies han fallen in a fewe yeres ;
Bote holy churche and charite choppe a-down swich
    shryvers,

---

house. In gluttony, God knows, they go to bed and arise with
ribaldry, those lawless vagabonds. Sleep and sinful sloth ever
pursue such men. Pilgrims and palmers agreed together to
visit the shrine of Saint James and of the saints of Rome. They
went forth in their way, with many unwise tales, and have leave
to lie all the rest of their lives. Hermits in a crowd, with
hooked staffs, went to (the shrine of our Lady of) Walsingham,
and their mistresses followed ; great tall lubbers that were unwilling to work clothed themselves in copes so as to be known
from others, and made themselves hermits in order to have their
ease. I found there friars—all the four orders—preaching to
the people for their stomachs' sake, and interpreting the gospel
as it pleased them from desire of copes. Many of these masters
of mendicant friars may clothe them as they will, for their money
and merchandise go together; but since Love (*i.e.*, the friars) has
turned pedlar, and chief confessor of lords, many miracles have

The moste myschif on molde mounteth up faste.
Ther preched a pardoner as he a prest were,
And brougte forth a bulle with bisshopis seles,
And seide that hym-selve mygte asoilie hem alle
Of falsnesse of fastinges, of vowes to-broke.
Lewede men lyvede hym wel, and likeden hus
    wordes,
Comen and kneleden to kyssen his bulles ;
He blessede hem with hus brevet, and blerede hure
    eyen ;
And raghte with hus rageman rynges and broches,
Thus ye geveth youre golde glotones to helpe,
And leneth it to loreles that lecherie haunten.
Were the bisshop blessid other worthe bothe hus
    eren,
Hus sele sholde nogt be sent in deceit of the puple.
Ac it is nogt by the bisshop that the loye precheth,
The parsheprest and the pardoner parten the selver,
That poore puple in parshes sholde have yf thei ne
    were.
Persones and parsheprestes pleynede to the bisshop,
That hure parshens ben poore sitthe the pestelence
    tyme,

---

happened in a few years ; but unless Holy Church and Love strike
down such shrivers the greatest mischief on earth will quickly
arise.   There preached a pardoner as if he were a priest and
brought forth a Bull with bishop's seals, and said that he himself
could pardon them all for breaking their fast and vows. The common people entirely believed him and liked his words and came
and kneeled to kiss his Bulls ; he blessed them with his letter
of indulgence and dimmed their eyes, and seized with his Papal
Bull rings and brooches.   Thus ye give your gold to help glut-
tons, and bestow it on the lawless.   Were the bishop truly
righteous or fit to have both his ears, his seal would not be sent
to deceive the people with.   But it is not against the bishop
that the young fellow preaches ; for often the parish priest and
the pardoner divide the silver, which poor people in the parishes
would have, if it were not for them.   Parsons and parish priests
complained to the bishop that their parishes are poor since the

To have licence and leve, in Londone to dwelle,
And synge ther for symonye for selver ys swete.
Bisshopes and bachilers bothe maisters and doctors,
That han cure under cryst and crownynge in tokne,
Ben chargid with holy churche charyte to tulie,
That is, leel love and lif among lered and lewed;
Thei lyen in londone in lentene and elles.
Somme serven the kynge, and hus selver tellen
In the chekkere and the chauncelrie chalengeynge
    hus dettes,
Of wardes and of wardemotes wayves and strayues,
Somme aren as seneschals and sarven othere lordes,
And ben in stede of stywardes and sitten and demen.

*　　*　　*　　*　　*

time of the pestilence, in order to have license and leave to
dwell in London and sing there (as Chantry priests) for simony,
for silver is sweet. Bishops and bachelors, both masters and
doctors, that have a cure under Christ, and tonsure in token,
are charged with Holy Church to cultivate charity, that is,
honest love and way of life among the learned and unlearned.
They dwell in London in Lent and at other times.   Some serve
the King and count his silver in the exchequer and the chancel-
lor's court, claiming his debts from wards and ward meetings,
waifs and strays. Some are as seneschals, and serve other lords,
and are instead of stewards and sit and pronounce judgment.

THE ALEHOUSE.

Now by-gynneth Gloton for to go to shryfte,
And kayres hym to-kirke-ward hus coupe to shewe.
Fastyng on a Fryday forth gan he wende
By Betone hous the brewstere that bad him good
    morwe,
And whederwarde he wolde the brew-wif hym
    asked.
    ' To holy churche,' quath he, ' for to hure masse,

And sitthen sitte and be yshriven and synwe
namore.'
  'Ich have good ale, godsyb Gloton, wolt thow
assaye ?'
'What havest thow,' quath he, ' eny hote spices ?'
  'Ich have piper and pionys and a pound of garlik,
A ferthyng-worth of fynkelsede for fastinge-daies.'
  Thenne goth Gloton yn and grete othes after.
Sesse the sywestere sat on the benche,
Watte the warynere and hus wif dronke,
Thomme the tynkere and tweye of hus knaves,
Hicke the hakeneyman and Houwe the neldere,
Claryce of Cockeslane the clerk of the churche,
Syre Peeres of Prydie and Purnel of Flaundres,
An haywarde and an heremyte the hangeman of
Tyborne,
Dauwe the dykere with a dosen harlotes
Of portours and of pykeporses and pylede toth-
drawers,
A rybibour and a ratoner a rakere and hus knave,
A ropere and a redyngkynge and Rose the disshere,

Now Glutton begins to go to shrift, and betakes him church-
ward to confess his sins. Fasting on a Friday, he began to go
forth by the house of Beton the brewster, who bade him ' Good-
morrow,' and the ale-wife asked whither he meant to go. ' To
holy church,' quoth he, 'to hear mass, and then sit and be
shriven and sin no more.' ' I have good ale, gossip Glutton ;
will you try it ?' ' What have you ?' quoth he, ' any hot spices ?'
' I have pepper and pæony seeds and a pound of garlic, a far-
thing's worth of fennel-seed for fasting-days.' Then Glutton
goes in, and great oaths after. Cis the sempstress sat on the
bench, Wat the gamekeeper and his drunken wife, Thomas the
tinker and two of his prentices, Hick the horse-jobber, and Hugh
the needle-seller, Clarice of Cock's Lane, the clerk of the church,
Sir Piers of Prie-dieu (a priest), and Purnel of Flanders, a
cattle-keeper and a hermit, the hangman of Tyburn, David the
ditcher, with a dozen rascally porters and pick-pockets and bald
drawers of teeth, a fiddler and a ratcatcher, a scavenger and his
prentice, a ropemaker and a lacquey, and Rose the dish-seller,

Godefray the garlek-mongere and Griffyn the
    Walish;
And of up-holders an hep erly by the morwe
Geven Gloton with glad chere good ale to hansele.
    Clemment the cobelere cast of hus cloke,
And to the newe fayre nempned hit to selle.
Hicke the hakeneyman hitte hus hod after,
And bad Bette the bouchere to be on hus syde.
Ther were chapmen y-chose the chaffare to preise;
That he that hadde the hod sholde nat habbe the
    cloke;
The betere thyng, by arbytours sholde bote the
    werse.
Two rysen rapliche and rounede to-geders,
And preysed the penyworthes apart by hem-selve,
And ther were othes an hepe for other sholde have
    the werse.
Thei couthe nouht by here conscience a-corde for
    treuthe,
Tyl Robyn the ropere aryse thei bysouhte,
And nempned hym a nompeyr that no debate were.
    Hicke the hakeneyman hadde the cloke
In covenaunt that Clemment sholde the coppe fylle,

Godfrey the garlick-seller, and Griffyn the Welshman, and a
heap of furniture-dealers, early in the morning gave Glutton, with
good cheer, good ale to propitiate him. Clement the cobbler
cast off his cloak and named it for sale at the new fair (an old
method of barter). Hick threw down his hood and bade Bette
the butcher be on his side. There were tradesmen chosen to
value the merchandise, that he that had the hood should not
have the cloak; the better thing by arbitration should give up
something so as to equal the worse. Two rose hastily and
whispered together, and appraised the pennyworths apart by
themselves, and there was a lot of swearing, for one or other
had to have the worse. They could not by their conscience
agree till they besought Robin the ropemaker to arise, and
named him umpire, whose decision was to be final.
    Hick got the cloak on the agreement that Clement should
fill his cup at the other's expense and have the horse-iobber's

And have the hakeneymannes hod and hold hym y-
   served ;
And who repentyde rathest shold aryse after,
And grete syre Gloton with a galon of ale.
   Ther was lauhyng and lakeryng and ' let go the
      coppe !'
Bargeynes and bevereges by-gunne to aryse,
And setyn so til evesong rang and songe umbwhyle,
Til Gloton hadde yglobbed a galon and a gylle.

   *   *   *   *   *

   With al the wo of the worlde hus wif and hus
      wenche
Bere hym to hus bedde and brouhte hym ther-ynne;
And after al this excesse he hadde an accidie,
He slep Saterday and Sonday tyl sonne yede to
   reste.
Thenne awakyde he wel wan and wolde have
   ydronke ;
The ferst word that he spak was 'ho halt the bolle?'

   *   *   *   *   *

---

hood. The first to repent of the bargain was to arise and pledge
Sir Glutton with a gallon of ale.   There was laughing and chid-
ing, and cries of 'Let go the cup!' Bargains and drinking
began to arise, and they sat so till evensong and sang occasionally till Glutton had swallowed a gallon and a gill. . . . With
all the sorrow in the world his wife and his daughter carried
him to his bed and put him therein. And after all this excess
he had a fit of sloth. He slept Saturday and Sunday, till sun-
down. Then he awoke very pale, and wanted to drink. The
first word that he spoke was, 'Who detains the bowl?'

SLOTH.

THO cam Sleuthe al by-slobered with two slymed
  eyen.
'Ich most sitte to be shryven,' quath he, 'or elles
  shal ich nappe.
Ich may nouht stonde ne stoupe ne with-oute stoule
  knele.
Benedicite' he by-gan with a bolke and hus brest
  knokede,
Rascled and remed and routte at the laste.
  'What a-wake, renk,' quath Repentaunce, 'rape
  the to shryfte!'
  'Sholde ich deye,' quath he, 'by this daye ich drede
  me sore,
Ich can nouht parfytliche my *pater-noster* as the prest
  hit seggeth.
Ich can rymes of Robin Hode and of Randolf, erl of
  Chestre,
Ac of oure lord ne of oure lady the lest that evere was
  maked.
Ich have a-vowed vowes fourty and for-got hem a
  morwe ;
Ich parfourned nevere penaunce that the preest me
  hihte,
Ne right sory for my synnes ich sey nevere the
  tyme.

Then came Sloth all slobbered over, with two dirty eyes. ' I
must sit to be shrived,' quoth he, ' or else I shall sleep. I may
not stand or stoop, or kneel without a stool. Benedicite,' he
began, with a belch, and beat his breast, stretched and groaned,
and snored at last. 'What! awake, man !' quoth Repentance ; ' haste thee to shrift.' 'If I die to-day,' quoth he, ' I
fear I know not perfectly my *Pater-noster* as the priest says
it. I know ballads of Robin Hood and of Randolph, Earl
of Chester, but of our Lord and of our Lady not the least
rime ever made. I have vowed forty vows, and forgot
them on the morrow. I never did penance ordered me by
the priest, nor was I ever right sorry for my sins. If I say

And ich bidde eny bedis bote hit be in wratthe,
That ich telle with my tunge ys ten myle fro my
herte.
Ich am ocupied eche day, haly day and other,
With ydel tales atte nale and other-whyle in
churches ;
Godes pyne and hus passion is pure selde in my
thouhte.
　Ich visited nevere feble man ne feterid man in
prisone ;
Ich hadde levere huyre of harlotrye other of a lesyng
to lauhen of,
Other lacke men, and lykne hem in unlykynge
manere,
Than al that evere Marc made Matheu, Iohan, other
Lucas.
Vigilies and fastyngdayes ich can for-gete hem alle.
Ich ligge a bedde in Lente my lemman in myn
armes,
Tyl matyns and messe be don then have ich a
memorie atte freres.
Ich am nought shryven som tyme bote syknesse hit
make,
Nouht twyes in ten yer yut tel ich nauht the halven-
dele.
　Ich have be prest and person passyng therty
wintere,

---

any prayers, unless it be in anger, what I say with my tongue is
ten miles from my heart.　I am occupied every day with idle
tales at the alehouse ; and at other times in church ; God's suffering and His passion are very seldom in my thoughts.　I
never visited the feeble, nor the fettered man in prison.　I had
rather hear a scurrilous tale or a lying story to laugh at, or
blame men, and liken them in a scandalous manner, than all that
ever Mark wrote, Matthew, John, or Luke.　Vigils or fasting-
days I can forget them all.　I lie abed in Lent till matins and
mass are done, and then I am mentioned at the convent.　I am
not shriven for a long time, unless sickness frightens me to it, not
twice in ten years, yet I tell not the half of my sins.　I have been

Yut can ich nother solfye ne synge ne a seyntes lyf
rede.
Ac ich can fynde in a felde and in a forlang an hare,
And holden a knyghtes court and a-counte with the
reyve ;
Ac ich can nouht constrye Catoun ne clergialliche
reden.
Yf ich bygge and borwe ouht bote hit be y-tayled,
Ich forgete hit as gerne and yf eny man hit
asketh,
Sixe sithe other sevene ich for-sake hit with othes ;
Thus have ich tened trewe men ten hondred tymes.
And som tyme my servauns here salarye is by-
hynde ;
Reuthe ys to huyre the rekenyng whenne we shul-
leth rede acountes,
That with so wicked wil my werkmen ich paye.
If eny man doth me a byn-fet other helpeth me at
nede,
Ich am unkynde ageyns courtesye ich can nat under-
stonde hit.
For ich have and have had somdel haukes maneres,
Ich am nat lured with love bote ouht lygge under
thombe.

---

priest and parson passing thirty years, yet I can neither sing
my notes nor read the life of a saint. But I can find a hare in
a field and in a furrow, and hold a knight's court and go through
accounts with the steward ; but I cannot construe Cato or read
like a scholar. If I buy and give a pledge for anything, unless
it be scored on a tally I forget it as soon, and if any man asks
for it, six or seven times I deny it with oaths. Thus have I
vexed true men a thousand times. And sometimes my servant's
wages are behindhand. 'Tis pity to hear the reckoning when we
must make up accounts, with so bad a will do I pay my workmen.
If any man does me a kindness or helps me at need, I am unkind
towards his courtesy, I cannot understand it, for I have and
have had in some measure the manners of a hawk ; I am not
lured with love unless something lie beneath the thumb. The

The kyndenesse that myn emcristene kydde me
fern yere,
Syxty sithe ich sleuthe have for-gute hit sitthe.
In speche and in sparyng of speche yspilt many
tymes
Both fleshe and eke fish and vitaile ich kepte so
longe,
Til eche lyf hit lothede to lokye ther-on, other smylle
hit ;
Bothe bred and ale, botere, melke, and chese
For-sleuthed in my service and sette hous a fuyre,
And gede a-bowte in my youthe and gaf me to no
thedom,
And sitthe a beggere have y-be for my foule sleuthe;
Heu michi, quod sterilem duxi uitam iuuenilem !

---

kindness that my fellow-Christians showed me long ago, sixty
times I, Sloth, have forgotten it since. By speech and by sparing
speech I have wasted many a time both flesh and fish. And
victuals I kept till every one loathed to look on it or smell it ;
both bread and ale, butter, milk, and cheese I wasted by idle
carelessness in my service, and I set the house on fire, and I
went about in my youth and devoted myself to no thrifty pursuit,
and have been a beggar since through my foul sloth. Alas
that I have passed my youth unprofitably !

From ' Richard the Redeless.'

THE PARLIAMENT.

AND whanne it drowe to the day of the dede-doynge,
That sovereynes were semblid and the schire-
knyghtis,
Than, as her fforme is, ffrist they beginne to declare
The cause of her comynge and than the kyngis will.

And when it came to the day of the deed, when lords and shire
knights were assembled, then, as their custom is, they begin
to declare the cause of their coming and then the King's will.

Comliche a clerk than comsid the wordis,
And pronouncid the poyntis aparte to hem alle,
And meved ffor money more than ffor out ellis,
In glosinge of grette lest greyves arise.
And whanne the tale was tolde anon to the ende,
A-morwe thei must, affore mete, mete to-gedir,
The knyghtis of the communete and carpe of the
     maters,
With citiseyns of shiris y-sent ffor the same,
To reherse the articlis and graunte all her askynge.
But yit ffor the manere to make men blynde,
Somme argued agein rith then a good while
And said, ' We beth servantis and sallere ffongen,
And y-sent ffro the shiris to shewe what hem
     greveth,
And to parle ffor her prophete and passe no fferthere,
And to graunte of her gold to the grett wattis
By no manere wronge way but if werre were ;
And if we ben ffalls to tho us here ffyndeth,
Evyll be we worthy to welden oure hire."
Than satte summe as siphre doth in awgrym,
That noteth a place and no-thing availith ;
And some had ysoupid with Symond overe even,

Eloquently a clerk then commenced the words, and pronounced
the points separately to them all, and moved for money more
than for anything else, deceiving the great lest grievances
arise ; and when the tale was told presently to the end, to-
morrow they must, before meat, meet together, the knights of
the community, and talk of the matters, with citizens of shires
sent for the same purpose, to rehearse the articles and grant all
they ask. But yet, as a blind, some argued against the king's
right of taxation a good while, and said, ' We are servants and
receive salaries, and are sent from the shires to show their
grievances and to speak for their advantage and go no farther,
and grant their gold to the great men in no wrong manner, but
if there were war. And if we are false to those who provide for
us here, evil are we worthy to receive as our hire.' Then some
sat like a cipher in arithmetic. that marks a place, though of no
value. And some had supped with Simon overnight, and

And schewed ffor the schire and here schew lost ;
And somme were tituleris and to the kyng wente,
And fformed him of foos that good ffrendis weren,
That bablid ffor the best and no blame served
Of kynge ne conceyll ne of the comunes nother,
Ho so toke good kepe to the *culorum.*
And somme slombrid and slepte and said but a lite :
And somme mafflid with the mouth and nyst what
    they mente ;
And somme had hire and helde ther-with evere,
And wolde no fforther affoot ffor ffer of her maistris ;
And some were so soleyne and sad of her wittis,
That er they come to the clos acombrid they were,
That thei the conclucioun than constrewe ne couthe.

---

showed for the shire and lost their show ; and some were tale-
bearers, and went to the King and informed him of foes that
were really good friends, who spoke for the best, and deserved
no blame from the King or Council or Commons either, whoever took good heed to the conclusion. And some slumbered
and slept and said but a little, and some mumbled and knew
not what they meant, and some were hired and would go no
farther for fear of their masters, and some were so sullen and
grave in their understandings that ere they came to the close
they were so encumbered that they could not explain the
conclusion.

WILLIAM DUNBAR [1459 ?-1513 ?].

From 'The Dance of the Sevin Deidly Synnis.

AND first of all in Dance was Pryd,
With hair wyld bak, and bonet on syd,
    Lyk to mak vaistie[1] wanis ;[2]
And round abowt him, as a wheill,[3]
Hang all in rumpillis[4] to the heill[5]

[1] Waste.   [2] Abodes.   [3] Wheel.
[4] Disorderly folds.   [5] Heel.

His kethat[1] for the nanis :
Mony prowd trumpour[2] with him trippit,
Throw skaldand[3] fyre, ay as they skippit
    Thay gyrnd[4] with hyddouss granis,[5]
Than Yre come in with sturt[6] and stryfe ;
His hand wes ay upoun his knyfe,
    He brandeist lyk a beir :
Bostaris,[7] braggaris, and barganeris,
Eftir him passit into pairis,
    All[8] bodin in feir of weir ;
In jakkis and scryppis and bonettis of steill,
Thair leggis wer chenyeit to the heill,
    Frawart wes thair affeir :
Sum upoun uder with brandis beft,[9]
Sum jagit utheris to the heft,
    With knyvis that scherp cowd scheir.[10]
Nixt in the Dance followit Invy,
Fild full of feid[11] and fellony,
    Hid malyce and dispyte :
For pryvie hatrent that traitour trymlit ;
Him followit mony freik[12] dissymlit,
    With fenyeit wordis quhyte :
And flattereris into menis facis ;
And bak-byttaris in secreit placis,
    To ley[13] that had delyte ;
And rownaris of fals lesingis,[14]
Allace ! that courtis of noble kingis
    Of thame can never be quyte.
Nixt him in Dans came Cuvatyce,
Rute of all evill, and grund of vyce,

---

[1] Robe.   [2] Deceiver.   [3] Scalding.   [4] Grinned.
[5] Hideous groans.   [6] Disturbance.
[7] Boasters, braggers, quarrellers.
[8] All arrayed in feature of war.
[9] Struck.   [10] Could cut sharply.   [11] Feud.
[12] Petulant fellow.   [13] Lie.
  Whisperers of falsehoods.

That nevir cowd be content :
Catyvis, wrechis, and ockeraris,
Hud-pykis, hurdaris, and gadderaris,[1]
All with that warlo[2] went ;
Out of thair throttis they schot on udder
Hett moltin gold, me thocht, a fudder[3]
As fyre-flawcht[4] maist fervent ;
Ay as they tumit[5] thame of schot
Feyndis fild thame new up to the thrott
With gold of allkin prent.[6]
Syne Sweirnes,[7] at the secound bidding,
Come lyk a sow out of a midding,
Full slepy was his grunyie.[8]
Mony sweir bumbard belly huddroun,[9]
Mony slute daw and slepy duddroun,[10]
Him servit ay with sounyie ![11]
He drew thame farth in till a chenyie[12]
And Belliall with a brydill renyie,[13]
Evir lascht thame on the lunyie :[14]
In Dance they war so slaw of feit,
They gaif thame in the fyre a heit,
And made them quicker of counyie.[15]
Than Lichery, that lathly corse,
Came berand[16] lyk a bagit horse,
And Ydilness did him leid ;
Thair wes with him ane ugly sort,
And mony stynkand fowll tramort,[17]
That had in syn bene deid :
When thay wer enterit in the Dance,
Thay wer full strenge of countenance,

---

[1] Usurers, misers, hoarders, gatherers. [2] Sorcerer.
[3] Load. [4] Lightning. [5] Emptied.
[6] All kinds of stamps. [7] Sloth. [8] Grunt.
[9] Many a lazy, tun-bellied sloven.
[10] Slovenly drab and sleepy slut. [11] Care.
[12] Into a chain. [13] With a bridle-rein. [14] Loins.
[15] Apprehension. [16] Snorting. [17] Dead body.

Lyke tortchis byrnand reid. . . .
Than the fowll monster Gluttony,
Off wame[1] unsasiable and gredy,
  To Dance he did him dress.
Him followit mony fowll drunckart,
With can and collep,[2] cop and quart,
  In surffet and excess ;
Full mony a waistless wally-drag,[3]
With wamis unweildable, did further wag,
  In creische[4] that did increase.
Drynk ! ay they cryit, with mony a gaip,
The feyndis gaif thame hait leid to laip,[5]
  Thair leveray[6] wes na less.

SIR DAVID LYNDESAY [1490-1553 ?].

*From 'The Complaint and Testament of the Papingo'[7]
(1530). The Raven ('ane blak monk') explains the
degeneracy of the clergy.*

LANG time efter the Kirk tuke property,
The prelatis leirt in greit perfectioun,
Unthral to riches or sensuality,
Under the halie Spreitis protectioun,
Ordourly chosin be electioun,
As Gregore, Jerome, Ambrose, and Augustyne,
Benedict, Bernard, Clement, Cleit, and Lyne.

Sic pacient prelatis enterit be the port,
Plesand the pepill by predicatioun ;
Now dyke-lowparis[8] dois in the Kirk resort,

---

[1] Belly.	[2] Drinking-cup.	[3] Spendthrift outcast.
[4] Fat.	[5] Hot lead to lap.	[6] Reward.
[7] Parrot.	[8] Thieves, interlopers.	

Be symonie and supplicatioun
Of princes, be thair presentatioun ;
Sa sillie saulis that bin the Christis sheip
Ar gevin to hungrie gormand wolfis to keip.

Na marvel is thoch we religious men
Degenrit be, and in our life confusit,
Bot sing and drink, nane uther craft we ken,
Our spiritual fatheris hes us sa abusit.
Aganis our will these trukouris[1] bene intrusit.
Lawit men hes now religious men in curis,
Profest virginis in keiping of strang huris.

Princes, princes, whair bin your heich prudence,
In dispositioun of your benefices ?
The guerdouning of your courticiens,
Is sum caus of thir greit enormiteis ;
Thair is ane sort waitand like hungry fleis
For spiritual cure, thoch thay be nathing abill,
Whose gredie thirstis bene insatiabill.

Princes, I pray yow, be na mair abusit,
To verteous men having sa small regaird ;
Why suld vertew throw flattery be refusit,
That men for cunning can get na rewaird ?
Allace ! that ane bragger or ane baird,
A hure-maister or common hazardure,
Suld in the Kirk get ony kinde of cure.

War I a man worthy to weir ane crown,
Ay when thair vaikit ony benefices,
I suld gar call ane congregatioun,
The principal of all the prelaceis ;
Maik cunning clarkis of universiteis,
Maist famous fatheris of religioun,
With thair avise mak dispositioun.

[1] Rogues.

I suld dispone all offices pastorallis
To doctouris of divinity or jure;
And caus dame Vertew pull up all the saillis,
When cunning men had in the Kirk maist cure,
Gar lords send their sonnis, I yow assure,
To seik science and famous sculis frequent,
Syne thame promove that war maist sapient.

Gret plesour war to heir ane bischop preiche
Ane dean or doctour of divinitie,
An abbot which culd weil the convent teiche,
Ane parsone flowing in philosophie.
I tyne my time to wis what will not be.
War not the preiching of the begging freiris
Tynt (extinct) war the faith amang the seculeiris.

JOHN SKELTON [1460—1528?].

From ' The Bowge of Courte.'

DISSIMULATION.

THAN in his hode[1] I sawe there faces tweyne ;
  That one was lene and lyke a pyned goost,
That other loked as he wolde me have slayne ;
  And to me warde as he gan for to coost,
  Whan that he was even at me almoost,
I sawe a knyfe hyd in his one sleve,
Wheron was wryten this worde, Myscheve.

And in his other sleve, me thought, I sawe
  A spone of golde, full of hony swete,
To fede a fole, and for to preve a dawe ;[2]
  And on that sleve these wordes were wrete,
  A false abstracte cometh from a fals concrete ;
His hode was syde,[3] his cope was roset graye ;
Thyse were the wordes that he to me dyde saye.

[1] Hood.   [2] Try a simpleton.   [3] Long.

7—2

Dyssymulation.

How do ye, mayster ? ye loke so soberly ;
  As I be saved at the dredefull daye,
It is a perylous vyce, this envy ;
Alas ! a connynge[1] man ne dwelle maye
  In no place well, but foles with hym fraye !
But as for that, connynge hath no foo
Save hym that nought[2] can, Scrypture sayth soo.

I knowe your vertu and your lytterature
  By that lytel connynge that I have ;
Ye be malygned sore, I you ensure ;
  But ye have crafte yourselfe alwaye to save :
  It is grete scorne to se a mysproude knave
With a clerke[3] that connynge is to prate ;
Lete theym go lowse theym, in the devylles date !

For all be it that this longe not to me,
  Yet on my backe I bere suche lewde delynge :
Ryghte now I spake with one, I trowe, I see ;
  But, what, a strawe ! I maye not tell all thynge.
  By God, I saye there is grete herte brennynge
Betwene the persone ye wote of, you ;
Alas, I coude not dele so with a Jew !

I wolde eche man were as playne as I ;
  It is a worlde, I saye, to here of some :
I hate this faynynge, fye vpon it, fye !
  A man can not wote where to be-come ;
  I wys I coude tell,—but humlery, home ;[4]
I dare not speke, we be so layde awayte,
For all our courte is full of dysceyte.

[1] A wise man may not dwell.   [2] Knows nothing.
[3] Scholar.   [4] Hum.

Now, by Saynte Fraunceys, that holy man and frere,
  I hate these wayes agayne you that they take :
Were I as you, I wolde ryde them full nere ;
  And, by my trouthe, but yf an ende they make,
  Yet wyll I saye some wordes for your sake,
That shall them angre, I holde thereon a throte.

I have a stoppynge oyster in my poke,
  Truste me, and yf it come to a nede :
But I am lothe for to reyse a smoke,
  Yf ye coude be otherwyse agrede ;
  And so I wolde it were, so God me spede,
For this maye brede to a confusyon,
Withoute God make a good conclusyon.

Naye, see where yonder stondeth the teder[1] man !
  A flaterynge knave and false he is, God wote ;
The drevyll[2] stondeth to herken, and he can :
  It were more thryft, he boughte him a newe cote ;
  It will not be, his purse is not on flote :[3]
All that he wereth, it is borowed ware ;
His wytte is thynne, his hode is threde-bare.

More coude I saye, but what this is ynowe :[4]
  Adewe tyll soone, we shall speke more of this :
Ye muste be ruled as I shall tell you howe ;
  Amendis maye be of that is now amys ;
  And I am your, syr ; so have I blys,
In every poynte that I can do or saye :
Gyve me your honde, farewell, and have good daye.

[1] The other.   [2] Low fellow.
[3] Flowing.   [4] But that this is enough.

From 'Colyn Cloute.'

AND if ye stande in doute
Who brought this ryme aboute,
My name is Colyn Cloute.
I purpose to shake oute
All my connyng bagge,
Lyke a clerkely hagge ;
For though my ryme be ragged,
Tattered and jagged,
Rudely rayne beaten,
Rusty and moughte eaten,
If ye take well therwith,
It hath in it some pyth.
For, as farre as I can se,
It is wronge with eche degre :
For the temporalte
Accuseth the spiritualte ;
The spirituall agayne
Dothe grudge and complayne
Upon the temporall men :
Thus eche of other blother
The tone agayng the tother :
Alas, they make me shoder !
For in hoder moder
The Churche is put in faute ;
The prelates ben so haut,
They say, and loke so hy,
As though they wolde fly
Above the sterry skye.
  Laye men say indede
How they take no hede
Theyr sely shepe to fede,
But plucke away and pull
The fleces of theyr wull,
Unethes[1] they leve a locke

---

[1] Scarcely.

Of wull amonges theyr flocke ;
And as for theyr connynge,
A glommynge and a mummynge,
And make thereof a jape ;
They gaspe and they gape
All to have promocyon,
There is theyr hole devocyon,
With money, if it wyll hap,
To catch the forked cap :[1]
Forsothe they are to lewd
To say so, all beshrewd ![2]

*　　*　　*　　*

And whyles the heedes do this,
The remenaunt is amys
Of the clergy all,
Bothe great and small.
I wot never how they warke,
But thus the people barke ;
And surely thus they say,
Bysshoppes, if they may,
Small houses wolde kepe,
But slumbre forth and slepe,
And assay to crepe
Within the noble walles
Of the kynges halles,
To fat theyr bodyes full,
Theyr soules lene and dull,
And have full lytell care
How evyll theyr shepe fare.
　　The temporalyte say playne,
Howe bysshoppes dysdayne
Sermons for to make,
Or suche laboure to take ;
And for to say trouth,
A great parte is for slouth,

[1] Mitre.　　　　[2] Altogether accursed.

But the greattest parte
Is for they have but small arte
And ryght sklender connyng
Within theyr heedes wonnyng. . . .[1]

*   *   *   *   *

 Thus I, Colyn Cloute,
As I go aboute,
And wandrynge as I walke,
I here the people talke.
Men say, for sylver and golde
Myters are bought and solde ;
There shall no clergy appose
A myter nor a crose,
But a full purse ;
A strawe for Goddes curse !
What are they the worse ?
For a symonyake
Is but a hermoniake ;[2]
And no more ye make
Of symony, men say,
But a chyldes play.
Over this, the foresayd laye[3]
Reporte howe the Pope may
An holy anker[4] call
Out of the stony wall,
And hym a bysshopp make,
If he on hym dare take
To kepe so harde a rule,
To ryde upon a mule
With golde all betrapped,
In purple and paule belapped ;
Some hatted and some capped,
Rychely and warme bewrapped,

---

[1] Dwelling. [2] Promoter of harmony (?) (Skeat).
[3] Aforesaid laity. [4] Anchorite.

God wot to theyr great paynes,
In rotchetts of fyne Raynes,
Whyte as morowes mylke ;
Theyr tabertes of fyne silke,
Theyr styrops of myxt gold begared ;[1]
There may no cost be spared ;
Theyr moyles[2] golde dothe eate,
Theyr neyghbours dye for meate.

From ' Speke, Parrot.'

So lytyll dyscressyon, and so myche reasonyng ;
So myche hardy dardy, and so lytell manlynes ;
So prodigall expence, and so shamfull reconyng ;
So gorgyous garmentes, and so myche wrechydnese;
So myche portlye pride, with pursys penyles ;
So myche spent before, and so myche unpayd
    behynde ;
Syns Dewcalyons flodde there can no clerkes fynde.

So myche forcastyng, and so farre an after dele ;
So myche poletyke pratyng ; and lytell stondythe
    in stede ;
So lytell secretnese, and so myche grete councell ;
So manye bolde barons, there hertes as dull as lede ;
So many nobyll bodyes undyr on dawys hedd ;
So royall a Kyng as reynythe uppon us all ;
Syns Dewcalions flodde was nevyr sene nor shall.

So many complayntes, and so smalle redresse ;
So myche callyng on, and so smalle takyng hede ;
So myche losse of merchaundyse, and so remedyles ;
So lytell care for the comyn weall, and so myche
    nede ;

---

[1] Adorned.   [2] Mules.

So myche dowgtfull[1] daunger, and so lytell drede ;
So myche pride of prelattes, so cruell and so kene ;
Syns Dewcalyons flodde, I trow, no man can tell.

So braynles calvys hedes, so many shepis taylys ;
So bolde a braggyng bocher,[2] and flesshe sold so
    dere ;
So many plucte partryches, and so fatte quaylles;
So mangye a mastyfe[3] curre, the grete greyhoundes[4]
    pere
So bygge a bulke of brow auntlers cabagyd[5] that
    yere ;
So many swannes dede, and so small revell ;
Syns Dewcalyons flodde, I trow no man can tell.

From ' Why come ye nat to Courte.'

WOLSEY.

HE is set so hye
In his ierarchy
Of frantycke frenesy
And folysshe fantasy,
That in the Chambre of Starres
All maters that he marres ;
Clapping his rod on the borde,
No man dare speke a worde ;
For he hathe all the sayenge,
Without any renayenge
He rolleth in his recordes,
He sayth, How saye ye, my lordes ?
Is nat my reason good ?

[1] Doubtful.
[2] Wolsey—said to be the son of a butcher. *Vide* p. 108.
[3] Wolsey.   [4] Henry VIII.   [5] Grown to a head.

Good evyn, good Robin Hood !
Some say yes, and some
Syt styll as they were dom :
Thus thwartyng over thom,
He ruleth all the roste
With braggyne and with bost ;
Borne up on every syde
With pompe and with pryde. . . .
Ones yet agayne
Of you I wolde frayne,
Why come ye nat to court ?
To whyche court ?
To the Kynges courte,
Or to Hampton Court ?
Nay, to the Kynges court :
The Kynges courte
Shulde have the excellence ;
But Hampton Court
Hath the preemynence,
And Yorkes Place,
With my lordes grace,
To whose magnifycence
Is all the conflewence,
Sutys and supplycacyons,
Embassades of all nacyons.
Strawe for lawe canon,
Or for the lawe common,
Or for lawe cyvyll !
It shall be as he wyll. . . .
But this medde Amalecke,
Lyke to a Mamelek,
He regardeth lordes
No more than potshordes ;
He is in suche elacyon
Of his exaltacyon,
And the supportacyon
Of our soverayne lorde,

That, God to recorde,
He ruleth all at wyll,
Without reason or skyll:
How be it the primordyall
Of his wretched originall,
And his base progeny,
And his gresy genealogy,
He came of the sank royall,
That was cast out of a bochers stall. . . .
No man dere come to the speche
Of this gentell Jacke breche,
Of what estate he be,
Of spirituall dygnyte,
Nor duke of hye degre,
Nor marques, erle, nor lorde;
Whiche shrewdly doth accorde,
Thus he borne so base
All noble men shulde out face,
His countynaunce lyke a kayser.
My lorde is not at layser;
Syr, ye must tary a stounde,
Tyll better layser be founde;
And, syr, ye must daunce attendaunce,
And take pacient sufferaunce,
For my lordes grace
Hath nowe no tyme nor space
To speke with you as yet
And thus they shall syt,
Chuse them syt or flyt,
Stande, walke, or ryde,
And his layser abide
Perchaunce halfe a yere,
And yet never the nere.

ALEXANDER BARCLAY [DIED 1552].

From 'Eclogue I.' [1517 ?].

WHAT is more foolish or liker to madnes
Then to spende the life for glory and riches ?
What thing is glory, laude, praysing or fame,
What honour, reporte, or what is noble name ?
Forsooth nought but voyce of artlesse commontie,
And vague opinion subject to vanitie,
Processe of yeares, revolving of reason,
Bringeth all these soone in oblivion.
When life is faded, all these be out of sight,
Like as with the Sun departeth the day-light ;
They all be fooles which meddle with the sea,
And otherwise might live in their owne country.
He is but a foole which runneth to tempest,
And might live on lande in suertie and in rest.
He is but a foole which hath of good plentie,
And it disdayneth to use and occupy.
And he which liveth in care and wretchednes
His heyre to promote to landes and riches
Is moste foole of all, to spare in misery,
With goodes and landes his heyre to magnify.
And he which leaveth that thing for to be done
Unto his daughter, executour or sonne
Which he himself might in his life fulfill,
He is but a foole, and hath but little skill.

WILLIAM ROY AND JEROME BARLOW,
1526, *circ.*

From ' Rede me, and be nott wrothe
For I saye no thynge but trothe.'

The Confessional and Cardinal Wolsey.

Wat. Dare they confessions to bewraye ?
Jeff. Confessions, catha ?   Ye, by my faye,
   They kepe no secretnes att all.
Though noble men have doctours
To be their private confessours,
   Yet they have one that is generall.
Wat. Besyde those which are particuler ?
Jeff. Ye, and that hath brought some to care
   Of whom I coulde make rehearceall.
Wat. His name wolde I very fayne here.
Jeff. It is the Englisshe Lucifer,
   Wotherwyse called—the Cardinall !
In all the londe there is no wyght,
Nether lorde, baron, nor knyght,
   To whom he hath eny hatred ;
But ether by sower speche, or swete,
Of their confessours he will wete [know]
   Howe they have themselves behaved.
What they saye, it is accepted,
In no poynte to be objected,
   Though they be as falce as Judas.
Wat. What authoritè do they allege ?
Jeff. It is their churches previlege,
   Falcely to fayne that never was.
Wat. Soche confessours are unjust,
Jeff. Yet nedes do it they must,
   Yf they will to honour ascende.
Wat. Promocions are of the Kyngis gift ?

Jeff. For all that, he maketh soche shyft,
    That in his pleasure they dependé.
  Though they have the Kyngis patent,
  Except they have also his assent,
    It tourneth to none avauntage ;
  His power he doth so extende,
  That the Kyngis letters to rende
    He will not forbeare in his rage.
Wat. This is a grett presumpcion,
    For a villayne bocher's sonne,
      His authorité so to avaunce ;
  But it is more to be marveyled,
  That noble-men wilbe confessed
    To these kaytives of miscreaunce.

SIR THOMAS WYATT [1503—1542].

‘ *Of the Courtier's Life.*’

MY Poins, I cannot frame my tungue to faine,
To cloke the truth, for praise without desert
Of them that list all vice for to retaine.
I cannot honour them, that set their part
With Venus and Bacchus all theyr life long.
Nor hold my peace of them, although I smart.
I cannot crouche nor knele to such a wronge ;
To worship them like God on earth alone,
That are as wolves these sely lambes among.
I cannot with my wordes complayne and mone,
And suffer nought ; nor smart without complaint:
Nor turne the word that from my mouth is gone.
I cannot speak and loke like as a saint ;
Use wyles for wit, and make desceit a pleasure,
Call craft counsaile, for lucre still to paint.
I cannot wrest the law to fill the coffer ;

With innocent bloud to fede myself fatte,
And do most hurt, where that most helpe I offer.
I am not he, that can allow the state
Of hie Ceaser, and damne Cato to dye,
That with his death did scape out of the gate
From Ceasers hands, if Livy doth not lie,
And would not live where liberty was lost ;
So did his hart the common wealth apply.
I am not he, such eloquence to bost,
To make the crow in singing, as the swanne ;
Nor call the lion of coward beastes the most ;
That can not take a mouse, as the cat can ;
And he that dyeth for honger of the golde,
Call him Alexander, and say that Pan
Passeth Apollo in musike manifolde,
Praise syr Topas for a noble tale,
And scorne the story that the knight tolde,
Praise him for counsell, that is dronke of ale ;
Grinne when he laughes, that beareth all the sway,
Frowne when he frownes, and grone when he is
        pale ;
On others lust to hang both night and day.
None of these pointes would ever frame in me :
My wit is nought, I can not learne the way.
And much the lesse of things that greater be,
That asken helpe of colours to devise,
To ioyne the meane with eche extremitie,
With nerest virtue ay to cloke the vice :
And, as to purpose likewise it shall fall,
To presse the vertue that it may not rise :
As dronkenness good felowship to call ;
The friendly foe with his faire double face,
Say he is gentle, and curties therewithall,
Affirme that Favel hath a goodly grace
In eloquence ; and cruelty to name,
Zeale of justice, and change in time and place :
And he that suffereth offence without blame,

Call him pitifull, and him true and plaine,
That rayleth rechless unto eche mans shame.
Say he is rude, that can not lye and fayne ;
The lecher a lover ; and tyranny
To be right of a princes raigne :
I can not I, no no, it wyll not be. . . .
I am not now in Fraunce, to judge the wine,
With savery sauce those delicates to fele,
Nor yet in Spaine, where one must him incline,
Rather then to be, outwardly to seme. . . .
But I am here in Kent and Christendome,
Among the Muses, where I reade and rime,
Where if thou list, mine own John Poins, to come,
Thou shalt be judge, how I do spende my time.

GEORGE GASCOIGNE [1525-1577].

From 'The Steele Glasse' [1576].

O KNIGHTS, O Squires, O Gentle blouds yborne,
You were not borne al onely for your selves :
Your countrie claymes some part of al your paines.
There should you live, and therein should you toyle,
To hold upright, and banish cruel wrong,
To helpe the pore, to bridle backe the riche,
To punish vice, and vertue to advance,
To see God servde, and Belzebub supprest.
You should not trust lieftenaunts in your rome,
And let them sway the sceptre of your charge,
Whiles you (meane while) know scarcely what is
        don,
Nor yet can yeld accompt if you were callde.

The stately lord, which woonted was to kepe
A courte at home, is now come up to courte,

8

And leaves the country for a common prey,
To pilling, polling, brybing, and deceit :
(Al which his presence might have pacified,
Or else have made offenders smel the smoke).
And now the youth which might have served him,
In comely wise, with countrey clothes yclad,
And yet thereby bin able to preferre
Unto the prince, and there to seek advance :
Is faine to sell his landes for courtly cloutes,
Or else sits still, and liveth like a loute. . . .
Lo these (my Lord) be my good praying priests,
Descended from Melchysedec by line
Cosens to Paule, to Peter, James, and John,
These be my priests, the seasning of the earth
Which wil not leese their savrinesse, I trowe,
Not one of these will reade the holy write
Which doth forbid all greedy usurie,
And yet receive a shilling for a pounde.
Not one of these wil preach of patience,
And yet be found as angry as a waspe.
Not one of these can be content to sit
In Taverns, Innes, or Alehouses all day,
But spends his time devoutly at his booke.
Not one of these wil rayle at rulers wrongs,
And yet be blotted with extortion.
Not one of these wil paint out worldly pride,
And he himselfe as gallaunt as he dare.
Not one of these rebuketh avarice,
And yet procureth ploude pluralities,
Not one of these reproveth vanitie
Whiles he himselfe, with hauke upon his fist
And houndes at heele, doth quite forget his text.
Not one of these corrects contentions,
For trifling things : and yet wil sue for tythes.
Not one of these (not one of these my Lord)
Wil be ashamde to do even as he teacheth. . . .
  I tell thee (priest) when shoomakers make shoes,

That are wel sowed, with never a stitch amisse,
And use no crafte, in uttring of the same:
When Taylours steale no stuffe from gentlemen,
When Tanners are with Corriers wel agreede,
And both so dresse their hydes that we go dry:
When Cutlers leave to sel old rustie blades,
And hide no crackes with soder nor deceit:
When tinkers make no more holes than they founde,
When thatchers thinke their wages worth their
    worke,
When colliers put no dust into their sacks,
When maltemen make us drink no fermentie,
When Davie Diker diggs, and dallies not,
When smithes shoo horses as they would be shod,
When millers toll not with a golden thumbe,
When bakers make not barme beare price of wheat,
When brewers put no bagage in their beere,
When butchers blowe not over al their fleshe,
When horsecorsers beguile no friendes with Jades,
When weavers weight is found in huswives web.
(But why dwel I so long among these lowts?)

When mercers make more bones to swere and
    lye,
When vintners mix no water with their wine,
When printers passe none errours in their bookes,
When hatters use to bye none olde cast robes,
When goldsmithes get no gains by sodred crownes,
When upholsters sel fethers without dust,
When pewterers infect no tin with leade,
When drapers draw no gaines by giving day,
When perchmentiers put in no ferret silke,
When Surgeons heale al wounds without delay.
Tush, these are toys, but yet my glas sheweth al. . . .
When al these things are ordred as they ought,
And see themselves within my glasse of steele,
Even then (my priests) may you make holyday

And pray no more but ordinarie prayers. . . .
Behold (my lord) what monsters muster here,
With Angels face and harmefull helish harts,
With smyling lookes and depe deceitfull thoughts,
With tender skinnes and stony cruel mindes,
With stealing steppes, yet forward feete to fraude.
Behold, behold, they never stand content,
With God, with kinde, with any help of Arte,
But curle their locks with bodkins and with braids,
But dye their heare with sundry subtill sleights,
But paint and slicke, til fayrest face be foule,
But bumbast, bolster, frisle, and perfume :
They marre with muske the balm which nature
    made,
And dig for death in delicatest dishes.
The yonger sorte come pyping on apace,
In whistles made of fine enticing wood,
Til they have caught the birds for whom they
    bryded.
The elder sorte go stately stalking on,
And on their backs they beare both land and fee,
Castles and towres, revenewes and receits,
Lordships, and manours, fines, yea farmes and al.
What should these be ? (Speake you, my lovely lord)
They be not men : for why ? they have no beards.
They be no boyes, which weare such side long
    gowns.
They be no Gods, for al their gallant glosse.
They be no divels (I trow) which seeme so saintish.
What be they? women ? masking in mens weedes ?
With dutchkin dublets, and with jerkins jaggde ?
With Spanish spangs, and ruffles fet out of France,
With high copt hattes, and fethers flaunt a flaunt ?
They be so sure even Wo to Men in dede.

EDMUND SPENSER [1552-1599 ?].

From ' Mother Hubberd's Tale.'

BESIDES all this, he us'd oft to beguile
Poore suters, that in Court did haunt some while :
For he would learne their business secretly,
And then informe his Master hastely,
That he by meanes might cast them to prevent,
And beg the sute, the which the other ment.
Or otherwise false Reynold would abuse
The simple suter, and wish him to chuse
His Master, being one of great regard
In Court, to compas anie sute not hard,
In case his paines were recompenst with reason :
So would he worke the silly man by treason
To buy his Masters frivolous good will,
That had not power to doo him good or ill.
So pitifull a thing is suters state !
Most miserable man, whom wicked fate
Hath brought to Court, to sue for had-ywist,
That few have found, and manie one hath mist !
Full little knowest thou, that hast not tride,
What hell it is, in suing long to bide :
To loose good dayes, that might be better spent ;
To wast long nights in pensive discontent ;
To speed to-day, to be put back to-morrow ;
To feed on hope, to pine with feare and sorrow ;
To have thy Princes grace, yet want her Peeres ;
To have thy asking, yet waite manie yeeres ;
To fret thy soul with crosses and with cares ;
To eate thy heart through comfortlesse dispaires ;
To fawne, to crowche, to waite, to ride, to ronne,
To spend, to give, to want, to be undonne.
Unhappie wight, borne to desastrous end,
That doth his life in so long tendance spend !

Who ever leaves sweete home, where meane estate
In safe assurance, without strife or hate,
Findes all things needfull for contentment meeke ;
And will to Court for shadowes vaine to seeke,
Or hope to gaine, himselfe will a daw trie :
That curse god send unto mine enemie !

EDWARD HAKE.

From ' News out of Powles Churchyarde,' Satire III.
(1579).

ONCE hapt it (through a fowle mischance)
　That great debate did ryse
Betweene a Doctor in the Law
　(For so th' example lyes)
And Doctor (eke) of Phisick, who
　Should have the upper hande
In each assembly where they met
　To walk, to syt or stande.
The Lawyer layed for himselfe
　And sayde well to the case,
Physition did full wisely to
　And with a goodly grace :
Alledging well (even both of them)
　Lyke handsome learned men.
But nought could be agreed upon.
　So fell the matter then,
That they unto the Pretor would
　For to decyde the same.
They made relation of the case
　And finely gan it frame.
The Pretor when he heard the dolts
　Contend about a straw
Was soone content to judge the same,
　And askte the man of Law

Who went unto the Gallowes first,
   The Hangman or the Thiefe ?
Who formost was of both them too
   And which was there the chiefe ?
The Hangman, quoth the Lawyer tho,
   For he doth kyll the man :
The Hangman he must go before,
   The Theefe must follow.   Than
Quoth Pretor harke :   This is my minde
   And judgement in the case.
Phisition he must go before,
   And Lawyer give him place.
Why then (quoth Bertulph) by your tale
   Phisitions men do kyll,
And Lawyers live by robbing men,
   And so their coffers fyll.

ROBERT GREENE [? 1560-1592].

From ' A Quippe for an Vpstart Courtier.'

I QUESTIONED them what they were, and the one
sayd hée was a barber, the other a surgion, and the
third an Apoticary. How like you of these (qd. I)
shall they be of your iury? Of the iury, quoth
Cloth-breeches never a one by my consent, for I
challenge them all : your reason qd. I, and then you
shall have my verdict. Mary (qd. Cloth-breeches)
first to the barber he cannot but be a partiall man
on Velvet-bréeches side, sith he gets more by one
time dressinge of him, than by ten times dressing of
me : I come plaine to be polde, and to have my
beard cut, and pay him two pence, Velvett-bréeches
he sittes downe in the chaire wrapt in fine cloathes, as
though the barber were about to make him a foot

cloth for the vicar of saint fooles: then begins he to
take his sissars in his hand and his combe, and so to
snap with them as if he meant to give a warning to
all the lice in his nittye lockes for to prepare themselves, for the day of their destruction was at hande,
then comes he out with his fustian eloquence, and
making a low conge, saith, Sir will you have your wor
haire cut after the Italian maner, shorte and round,
and then frounst with the curling yrons, to make it
looke like a halfe moone in a mist? or like a Span-
yard long at the eares, and curled like to the two
endes of an olde cast perriwig? or will you bée
Frenchefied with a love locke down to your shoulders,
wherein you may weare your mistresse favour? The
English cut is base, and gentlemen scorne it, novelty
is daintye. Speake the woord sir, and my sissars are
ready to execute your worships wil. His head being
once drest, which requires in combing and rubbing
some two howers, hée comes to the bason: then
béeing curiously washt with no woorse than a cam-
phire bal, he descends as low as his berd and asketh
whether he please to be shaven or no, whether he will
have his peak cut short and sharpe, amiable like an
inamorato or broad pendant like a spade, to be terrible
like a warrior and a Soldado, whether he wil have
his crates cut low like a Iuniperbush, or his suberches
taken away with a rasor, if it be his pleasure to have
his appendices primd, or his mustachios fostered to
turn about his eares like the branches of a vine, or
cut down to the lip with the Italian lash, to make
him look like a halfe faced bauby in bras? These
quaint tearmes, Barber, you greet maister Velvet-
breeches withall, and at every word a snap with your
sissors, and a cring with your knee, whereas when
you come to poore Cloth-breeches you either cutte
his beard at your owne pleasure, or else in disdaine
aske him if he wil be trimd with Christs cut, round

like the halfe of a holland cheese, mocking both
Christ and vs: for this your knauerie my wil is you
shall be none of the iurie.

VELVET-BREECHES OBJECTS TO AN HONEST KNIGHT.

WHY you may gesse the inwarde minde by the
outward apparell, and see how he is adicted by the
homely robes he is suted in. Why this knight is
mortall enimy to pride and so to me, he regardeth
hospitality and aimeth at honor with releeving the
poore: you may see although his landes and revenewes be great, and he able to maintain himself in
great bravery, yet he is content with home spun
cloth, and scorneth the pride that is now adaies used
amongst young upstarts: he holdeth not the worth
of his Gentry to be and consist in velvet breeches,
but valeweth true fame by the report of the common
sort, who praise him for his vertue, Iustice, liberality,
housekeeping and almesdeeds: *Vox populi vox Dei,*
his tenants and farmers would, if it might bee possible,
make him immortall with their praiers and praises.
He raiseth no rent, racketh no lands, taketh no in-
combs, imposeth no mercilesse fines, envies not
another, buyeth no house over his neighbours head,
but respecteth his country and the commodity thereof, as deere as his life. Hee regardeth more to have
the needy fed, to have his boord garnished with full
platters, then to famous himself with excessive furni-
ture in apparel. Since then he scorneth pride, he
must of force proclaime himselfe mine enimy, and
therfore he shal be none of my iury: and such as
himselfe I gesse the Squire and the Gentleman, and
therefore I challeng them all three. Why, quoth I,
this is strange, that a man should be drawne from a
quest for his goodnesse.

From ' *A Groats-worth of Wit bought with a Million of Repentance.*'[1]

AND thou[2] no lesse deserving than the other two,[3] in some things rarer, in nothing inferiour; driven (as my selfe) to extreame shifts, a little have I to say to thee: and were it not an idolatrous oth, I would sweare by sweet *S. George*, thou art unworthie better hap, sith thou dependest on so meane a stay. Base minded men al three of you, if by my miserie ye be not warned: for unto none of you (like me) sought those burres to cleave: those Puppits (I meane) that speake from our mouths, those Anticks garnisht in our colours. Is it not strange that I, to whom they al have beene beholding; is it not like that you, to whome they all have beene beholding, shall (were ye in that case that I am now) be both at once of them forsaken? Yes, trust them not: for there is an up-start Crow,[4] beautified with our feathers, that with his *Tygers heart wrapt in a Players hide*,[5] supposes he is as well able to bumbast out a blanke verse as the best of you: and being an absolute *Iohannes fac totum*, is in his owne conceit the onely Shake-scene in a countrie. O that I might intreate your rare wits to be imployed in more profitable courses: and let those Apes imitate your past excellence, and never more acquaint them with your admired inventions.

[1] Greene exhorts his fellow-dramatists to give up writing plays, and reflects on Shakespeare for borrowing without acknowledgment. (See Grosart's edition of Greene's works.)
[2] Peele.　[3] Marlowe and Nashe.　[4] Shakespeare.
[5] Parody of 'Henry III.,' Part III., Act I., Sc. 4:
　　'O tiger's heart wrapt in a woman's hide!'

THOMAS NASHE [1567-1601].

From ' The Anatomie of Absurditie' (1589).

IT fareth nowe a daies with unlearned Idiots as it doth with she Asses, who bring foorth all their life long: even so these brainlesse Buzzards are every quarter bigge wyth one pamphlet or other. But as an Egge that is full, beeing put into water sinketh to the bottome, whereas that which is emptie floateth above, so those that are more exquisitely furnished with learning shroude themselves in obscuritie, whereas they that are voide of all knowledge endevour continually to publish theyr follie.

Such and the very same are they that obtrude themselves unto us, as the Authors of eloquence, and fountains of our finer phrases, whenas they sette before us nought but a confused masse of wordes without matter, a Chaos of sentences without any profitable sence, resembling drummes, which beeing emptie within, sound big without. Were it that any Morall of greater moment might be fished out of their fabulous follie, leaving theyr words, we would cleave to their meaning, pretermitting theyr painted shewe, we would pry into their propounded sence, but when as lust is the tractate of so many leaves, and love passions the lavish dispense of so much paper, I must needes sende such idle wits to shrift to the vicar of S. Fooles, who in steede of a worser may be such a Gothamists ghostly father. Might *Ovids* exile admonish such Idlebies to betake them to a new trade, the Presse should be farre better employed, Histories of antiquitie not half so much belyed, minerals, stones and herbes should not have such cogged natures and names ascribed to them without cause, Englishmen shoulde not be halfe so much Italinated as they are, finallie, love woulde obtaine the name of lust, and vice no longer maske under the visard of vertue.

* * * * *

One requiring *Diogenes* judgment when it was best time to take a wife, he answered, for the young man not yet, and the olde man never. *Pythagoras* sayd, that there were three evils not to be suffered, fire, water, and a woman. And the fore named *Cinick* deemed them the wisest lyers in the world, which tell folke they will be married, and yet remaine single, accounting it the lesse inconvenience of two extremities to choose the lesse. . . . What shall I say of him that being askt, from what women a man should keepe himselfe, answered, from the quick and from the deade, adding moreover, that one evill ioynes with another when a woman is sicke. *Demosthenes* saide, that it was the greatest torment that a man could invent to his enemies vexation, to give him his daughter in marriage, as a domesticall Furie to disquiet him night and day. *Democritus* accounted a faire chaste woman a miracle of miracles, a degree of immortality, a crowne of tryumph, because shee is so harde to be founde. Another being asked, who was he that coulde not at any time be without a wife, answered, hee that was accurst: and what dooth thys common proverbc, he that marrieth late marrieth evill, insinuate to us, but that if a man meane to marry, he were as good begin betimes as tarry long, and beeing about to make a vertue of necessitie, and an arte of patience, they are to begin in theyr young and tender age. . . . There be two especiall troubles in this world, saith Seneca, a wife and ignorance. . . . For my part I meane to suspende my sentence and to let an Author of late memorie be my speaker, who affyrmeth that they carrie Angels in their faces to entangle men and devils in their devices. . . . I

omit to tell with what phrases of disgrace the ancient
fathers have defaced them, whereof one of them
saith *Quid aliud est mulier nisi amicitiæ*, etc. What
is a woman but an enemie to friendshippe, an un-
evitable paine, a necessary evill, a naturall temptation, a desired calamitie, a domesticall danger, a
delectable detriment the nature of which is evill
shadowed with the coloure of goodnes. . . . But
what I spend my yncke, waste my paper, stub my
penne, in painting forth theyr ugly imperfections,
and perverse peevishnesse, when as how many hayres
they have on theyr heads, so many snares they will
finde for a neede to snarle men in, how many voices
all of them have, so many vices each one of them hath,
how many tongues, so many tales, how many eyes,
so many allurements. . . . In *Rome* the bride was
wont to come in with her spyndle and her distaffe at
her side, at the day of her marriage, and her husband
crouned and compassed the Gates with her yarne,
but now a daies Towe is either too deere or too
daintie, so that if hee will maintaine the custome,
hee must crowne his Gates with their Scarfes, Peri-
wigs, Bracelets, and Ouches, which imports thus
much unto us, that Maydes and Matrons now adaies
be more charie of their store, so that they will be
sure they will not spend too much spittle with spyn-
ning, yea theyr needles are nettles, for they lay them
aside as needlesse, for feare of pricking their fingers
when they are painting theyr faces, nay, they will
abandon that trifling which may stay them at home,
but if the temperature of the wether will not per-
mitte them to pop into the open ayre, a payre of
cards better pleaseth her then a peece of cloth, her
beades then her booke, a bowle full of wine then a
hand full of wooll, delighting more in a daunce then
in *Davids Psalmes*, to play with her dogge then to
pray to her God: setting more by a love Letter, then

yᵉ lawe of the Lord, by one Pearle then twenty *Pater Nosters*. Shée had rather view her face a whole morning in a looking Glasse, then worke by the howre Glasse, shee is more sparing of her Spanish needle then her Spanish gloves, occupies oftner her setting sticke then sheeres, and ioyes more in her Jewels then in her Jesus.

A PROGNOSTICATION [1591].

(A Satire on the Astrology and Astronomy of Richard Harvey.)

WINTER being finished with the last grade of the watery signe Pisces, at the Suns joyful progresse into the first degree of Aries. The second quarter of our usuall yere commonly called the spring cometh next, which beginneth when grasse begins to sproute, and trees to bud. But to treat of this present season, forasmuch as I find the planets to be contradictorily disposed, in signs and mansions of diverse and repugnant qualities, I gather that this spring will be very il for schollers, for they shal studie much and gain litle, they shall have more wit in their heads then money in their purses, dunces shall prove more welthie than divers docters, insomuch that sundrie unlettered fooles should creep into the ministerie, if the provident care of good Bishops did not prevent them. And by the opinion of Proclus, women are like to grow wilful, and so variable, that they shall laugh and weepe and all with a winde : Butchers shall sell their meate as deare as they can, and if they be not carefull, horne beastes shall bee hurtfull unto them, and some shall bee so wedded to swines flesh, that they shall never be without a sowe in their house as long as they live. This spring, or vernall resolution, being naturally hot and moist, is like to be verie forwarde for sprouting fieldes and blooming trees; and because Saturne is in his proper mansion, olde men are like to bee froward, and craftie knaves shall neede no Brokers, usurie shalbe called good husbandrie, and men shalbe counted honest by their wealth, not by their virtues.

And because Aquarius has something to do with this quarter, it is to be doubted that divers springs of water will rise up in vintners sellers, to the great weakning of their Gascon wine, and the utter ruine of the ancient order of the redde noses. March Beere shalbe more esteemed than small Ale.

Cancer is busie in this spring-tide, and therefore it is like that florishing bloomes of yong gentlemens youth shalbe greatly anoide with caterpillers, who shall intangle them in such statutes and recognances, that they shall crie out against brokers, as Jeremy did against false prophets. Besides, thogh this last winter nipt up divers masterless men and cut purses, yet this spring is like to afford one every tearme this ten yere in Westminster hall : Barbers if they have no worke are like to grow poore, and for that Mercury is combust and many quarelles like to growe amongst men, lawyers shall prove rich and weare side gowns and large consciences, having theyr mouths open to call for fees, and theyr purses shut when they shoulde bestowe almes.

But take heed, O you generation of wicked ostlers, that steale haie in the night from gentlemens horses, and rub their teth with tallow that they may eate little when they stand at livery, this I prognosticate against you, that this spring, which so ever of you dies, shall leave a knaves carcasse in the grave behind him. . . .

Diseases incident to this quarter, as by astrologicall and philosophicall conjectures I can gather, are these following : Prentices that have been sore beaten shall be troubled with ach in their armes, and it shall be ill for such as have sore eies to looke against the sun. The plague shall raigne mortally amongst poore men, that diverse of them shal not be able to change a man a groate. Olde women that have taken great colde may perhaps be trobled with the cough, and such as have paine in their teeth shall bee grievouslie troubled with the tooth ach. Beside, sicke folke shall have worse stomaches then they which be whole, and men that cannot sleepe shall take verie little rest : with other accidentall infirmities, which I doe overpasse.

From 'Pierce Pennilesse his supplication to the Diuell'
[1592].

THE COMPLAYNT OF PRIDE.

O BUT a far greater enormite raigneth in the heart of the Court : Pride, perverter of all Vertue, sitteth appareled in the Merchants spoils, and ruine of yoong Citizens, and scorneth Learning, that gave their up-start Fathers titles of Gentry.

THE NATURE OF AN UPSTART.

All malcontent fits the greasie sonne of a Cloathier, and complaines (like a decaied Earle) of the ruine of ancient houses : whereas, the Weavers loomes first framed the web of his honour, and the locks of wool, that bushes and brambles have tooke for toule of insolent sheepe, that would needs strive for the wall of a fir-bush, have made him of the tenths of their tarre, a Squier of low degree : and of the collections of the scatterings, a Justice, *Tam Marti quam Mercurio,* of Peace and of Coram. Hee will bee humorous, forsoth, and have a broode of fashions by himselfe.

Sometimes (because Love commonly weares the liverey of Witte) hee will be an *Inamorato Poeta,* and sonnet a whole quire of paper in praise of Lady Swin-snout, his yeolow-fac'd Mistres, and weare a feather of her rain-beaten fanne for a favor, like a fore-horse.

Al *Italionato* is his talke, and his spade peake is as sharpe as if he had been a Pioner before the walles of *Roan.* Hee will despise the barbarisme of his owne Countrey, and tell a whole Legend of lyes of his travailes unto *Constantinople.* If he be challenged to fight, for his delaterye excuse, hee ob-jects that it is not the custome of the Spaniard, or the Germaine, to looke backe to every dog that barkes.

You shall see a dapper Jacke, that hath beene but over at *Deepe,* wring his face round about, as a man would stirre up a mustard pot, and talke English through the teeth, like *Jaques Scabd-Hams,* or *Monsieur Mingo de Moustrap :* when (poore slave) he hath but dipt his bread in wilde Boares grease and come home againe : or beene bitten by the shinnes by a Wolfe : and saith, he hath adventured upon the Barricadoes of *Gurney,* or *Guingan,* and fought with the yoong Guise hand to hand.

From ' *Christ's Teares over Jerusalem* ' [1593].

USURERS.

IF the stealing of one Apple in Paradise brought
such a universal plague to the worlde, what a plague
to one soul will the robbing of a hundred Orphans
of theyr possessions and fruite-yards bring ? In the
Country the Gentleman takes in the Commons,
racketh his Tennaunts, undoeth the Farmer. In
London the Usurer snatcheth up the Gentleman,
gyves him Rattles and Babies for his over-rackt
rent, and the Commons he tooke in, he makes him
take out in Commodities. None but the Usurer is
ordained for a scourge to Pride and Ambition.
Therefore it is that Bees hate Sheepe more then
anie thing, for that when they are once in theyr
wooll, they are so intangled that they can never get
out. Therfore it is that Courtiers hate Merchants
more then any men, for that being once in their
bookes, they can never get out. Many of them
carry the countenaunces of Sheep, looke simple, goe
plain, weare their haire short; but they are no
Sheepe, but Sheep-byters : their wooll or their
wealth they make no other use of but to snarle and
enwrappe men with. The law (which was instituted
to redresse wrongs and oppressions) they wrest
contrarily, to oppresse and to wrong with. And yet
thats not so much wonder, for Law, Logique, and
the Swizers, may be hir'd to fight for any body ; and
so may an Usurer (for a halfepeny gaine) be hyred
to bite any body. For as the Beare cannot drinke
but he must byte the water, so cannot hee coole his
avaritious thirst, but he must plucke and bite out
hys Neighbors throate.

From ' The Martin Marprelate Tractates' [1589].

MARTINS MONTHS MINDE.[1]

AND therewithal, lifting up himselfe on his pillowe, [Olde Martin][2] commanded the elder *Martin* to go into his studie, and to fetch his Will, that lay sealed in his deske, and bound fast with an hempen string: which when he had brought, he commanded to be broken up, and to be read in their hearing; which was as followeth.

After he had begun with the usual stile; next touching his bodie (for it should seeme he had forgotten his soule: for the partie that heard it told me, he heard no word of it), he would, should not be buried in any *Church* (especiallie *Cathedrall,* which ever he detested), *Chappell,* nor *Churchyard,* for that they had been prophaned with superstition: but in some barne, outhowse or field (yea, rather then faile, dunghill), where their prime prophecyings had been used; without bell, pompe, or any solemnitie; save that his friends should mourne for him in gownes, and whoods, of a bright yellowe :. the whoods made of a strawnge fashion, for no ordinarie thing contented him (belike with a crest after *Hoydens cut*), and Minstrells going before him; wherein hee would have a Hornpipe at any hand, because he loved that instrument above measure : the rest he referred to their discretion; but a *Rebuke, and a Shame,* in my opinion, were the fittest fiddles for him.

Minister he would have none to burie him, but his sonne, or some one of his lay brethren, to tumble him into the pit. He would not be laid East and West (for hee ever went against the haire), but North, and South : I think because *ab aquilone*

---

[1] Longing.　　　[2] Martin = the Puritans.

omne malum; and the South wind ever brings corruption with it : tombe he would have none (for feare belike that his disciples finding the monument, would commit some Idolatrie to it), nor *Epitaph* upon his grave, but on some post, or tree, not farre from it, he would have onelie engraven : M. M. M.

Whereby his sonnes say, he meant ; *Memoriæ Martini magni.*

But I thinke rather this : *Monstrum Mundi Martinus.*

From ' Have with you to Saffron Walden ' [1596].

DR. GABRIEL HARVEY'S HEXAMETERS.

WERE he as he hath been (I can assure thee) he would clothe and adorne thee with manie gracious gallant complements, and not a rotten tooth that hangs out at thy shop window, but should cost him an indefinite Turkish armie of English Hexameters. O, he hath been olde dogge at that drunken, staggering kinde of verse, which is all up hill and downe hill, like the way betwixt Stamford and Beechfield, and goes like a horse plunging through the myre in the deep of winter, now soust up to the saddle, and straight aloft on his tiptoes. Indeed in old King Harrie sinceritie, a kind of verse it is hee hath been enfeoft in from his minoritie, for as I have bin faithfully informed, hee first cryde in that verse in the verie moment of his birth, and when he was but yet a fresh-man in Cambridge he set up *Siquisses*[1] and sent his accounts to his father in those joulting Heroicks. . . . But though he be in none of your Courts Licentiate, and a Courtier otherwise hee is never like to be ; one of the Emperour

[1] Bills for anything lost.

Justinians Courtiers (the civill Lawes chiefe Founder)
malgre he will name himselfe : and a quarter of a
yeare since, I was advertised, that aswell his workes,
as the whole body of that Law compleat (having no
other employment in his Facultie), hee was in hand
to tourne into English Hexameters ; and if he
might have had his will, whiles he was yet resident
in *Cambridge*, it should have been severely enacted
throghout the Universitie, that none should speake
or ordinarily converse, but in that cue. For himselfe, hee verie religiously observ'd it, never meeting
anie Doctor or frend of his, but he would salute
him, or give him the time of the day in it most
heroically, even as hee saluted a Phisition of speciall
account in these tearmes,

> ' *Nere can I meet you, sir, but needs must I veile my
> bonnetto.*'

Which he (loth to be behinde with him in curtesie)
thus turned upon him againe,

> ' *Nere can I meet you, sir, but needs must I call ye
> knavetto.*'

Once hee had made an Hexameter verse of seaven
feete, whereas it would lawfully beare but sixe ;
which fault a pleasant Gentleman having found him
with, wrapt the said verse in a peece of paper, and
sent a lowse with it, inserting vnderneath, *This verse
hath more feet than a lowse.* But to so Dictionarie a
custome it was grown with him, that after supper if
he chaunst to play at Cards, and had but one Queen
of Harts light in his hand, he would *extempore*, in
that kinde of verse, runne uppon mens hearts and
womens hearts all the night long, as,

> ' *Stout heart and sweet hart, yet stoutest hart to be
> stooped.*'

No may-pole in the streete, no wether-cocke on anie Church steeple, no garden, no arbour, no lawrell, no ewe tree, that he would overslip without haylsing after the same methode. His braynes, his time, all hys maintenance and exhibition vpon it he hath consumed, and never intermitted, till such time as he beganne to Epistle it against mee, since which I have kept him a work indifferently.

THOMAS LODGE [1558-1625].

From 'A Fig for Momus' [1595], Satire I.

TELL pursie Rollus lusking in his bed
That humors by excessive ease are bred,
That sloth corrupts, and choakes the vital sprights,
And kils the memorie, and hurts the lights;
He will not sticke (after a cup of sacke)
To flout his counsellor behind his backe,
For with a world of mischiefes and offence
Unbridled will rebelles against the sence,
And thinketh it no little prejudice,
To be reproov'd though by good advice:
For wicked men repine their sinnes to heare,
And folly flings, if counsaile tuch him neare. . . .
Find me a niggard that doth want the shift
To call his cursed avarice good thrift?
A rakehell, sworne to prodigalitie,
That dares not terme it liberalitie?
A letcher, that hath lost both flesh and fame,
That holds not letcherie a pleasant game?
And why? because they cloake their shame by this,
And will not see the horror what it is.
And cunning sinne being clad in Vertues shape

Flies much reproofe, and many scornes doth
  scape. . . .
Thus with the world, the world dissembles still,
And to their own confusions follow will;
Holding it true felicitie to flie
Not from the sinne, but from the seeing eie,
Then in this world who winks at each estate
Hath found the means to make him fortunate;
To colour hate with kindness, to defraud
In private, those in publique we applaud;
To keep this rule, kaw me and I kaw thee;
To play the Saints, whereas we divels bee.
Whate'er men doe, let them not reprehend;
For cunning knaves will cunning knaves defend.

From Satire IV.

THE MISER.

MARKE me a miserable mysing wretch,
That lives by others losse, and subtle fetch,
He is not onely plagu'd with heavines,
For that which other happie men possesse,
But takes no tast of that himselfe partakes,
And sooner life, then miserie forsakes;
And what in most aboundance he retaines
In seeming little doth augment his paines;
His travailes are suspitions backt by feare,
His thoughts distraught incessant troubles leare,
He doubts the raine, for feare it raise a floud
And beare away his houses, and his good,
He dreads his neighbours cattle as they pass,
For feare they stay and feed upon his grasse,
He hides his treasures under locke and kay,

Lest theeves break in, and beare his bags away ;
Onely unto himselfe, for whom he spares,
His eie disdaines his hungrie bellie meate,
Himselfe repines, at that himselfe doth eate,
Though rents increase, he lets his body lacke,
And neither spares his bellie nor his backe :
What on himselfe he laies, he houlds it lost,
What on his wife, he deemes unthriftie cost,
What on his heires, his miserie and misse ;
What on his servantes, ryotting it is. . . .
So lives he to the wretched world alone,
Lothsome to all that long to see him gone.

JOHN DONNE, D.D. [1573-1631].

From Satire I. [1593].

AWAY, thou changeling motley humourist,
Leave me, and in this standing wooden chest,
Consorted with these few books, let me lie
In prison, and here be coffin'd when I die.
Here are God's conduits, grave divines, and here
Nature's secretary, the philosopher,
And wily statesmen, which teach how to tie
The sinews of a city's mystic body ;
Here gathering chroniclers, and by them stand
Giddy fantastic poets of each land.
Shall I leave all this constant company,
And follow headlong wild, uncertain thee ?
First, swear by thy best love, here, in earnest
—If thou, which lovest all, canst love any best—
Thou wilt not leave me in the middle street,
Though some more spruce companion thou dost
  meet,
Not though a captain do come in thy way

Bright parcel-gilt, with forty dead men's pay;
Not though a brisk perfumid pert courtier
Deign with a nod thy courtesy to answer;
Nor come a velvet justice with a long
Great train of blue coats, twelve or fourteen strong,
Wilt thou grin, or fawn on him, or prepare
A speech to court his beauteous son and heir?
For better or worse take me, or leave me;
To take and leave me is adultery.
O monstrous, superstitious puritan,
Of refined manners, yet ceremonial man,
That when thou meet'st one, with enquiring eyes
Doth search, and, like a needy broker, prize
The silk and gold he wears, and to that rate,
So high or low, dost raise thy formal hat;
That wilt consort none, until thou have known
What lands he hath in hope, or of his own,
As though all thy companions should make thee
Jointures, and marry thy dear company.

From Satire II.

SIR, though—I thank God for it—I do hate
Perfectly all this town, yet there's one state
In all ill things so excellently best,
That hate toward them breeds pity towards the
  rest.
Though poetry indeed be such a sin
As I think that brings dearth and Spaniards in;
Though like the pestilence and old-fashion'd love
Riddlingly it catch men, and doth remove
Never, till it be starved out, yet their state
Is poor, disarm'd, like Papists, not worth hate.
One—like a wretch, which at bar judged as dead

Yet prompts him which stands next and cannot
    read,
And saves his life—gives idiot actors means,
Starving himself, to live by his labour'd scenes.
As in some organ, puppets dance above
And bellows pant below, which them do move,
One would move love by rhythms; but witchcraft's
    charms
Bring not now their old fears, nor their old harms.
Rams and slings now are silly battery;
Pistolets are the best artillery.
And they who write to lords, rewards to get,
Are they not like singers at doors for meat?
And they who write, because all write, have still
That excuse for writing, and for writing ill.

        *   *   *   *   *

But these do me no harm, nor they which use
To out-do ——, and out-usure Jews,
To out-drink the sea, to out-swear the ——;
Who with sins of all kinds as familiar be
As confessors, and for whose sinful sake
School-men new tenements in hell must make;
Whose strange sins canonists could hardly tell
In which commandment's large receipt they dwell;
But these punish themselves.

From Satire III.

KIND pity chokes my spleen; brave scorn forbids
Those tears to issue, which swell my eyelids.
I must not laugh, nor weep sins, but be wise.
Can railing, then, cure these worn maladies?
Is not our mistress, fair Religion,
As worthy of all our soul's devotion,

As virtue was in the first blinded age ?
Are not heaven's joys as valiant to assuage
Lusts, as earth's honour was to them ?   Alas,
As we do them in means, shall they surpass
Us in the end ? and shall thy father's spirit
Meet blind philosophers in heaven, whose merit
Of strict life may be imputed faith, and hear
Thee, whom he taught so easy ways, and near
To follow, damn'd ?   Oh ! if thou darest, fear this ;
This fear great courage and high valour is.

From Satire IV.

WELL ; I may now receive and die.   My sin
Indeed is great, but yet I have been in
A purgatory, such as fear'd hell is
A recreation and scant map of this.
My mind, nor with pride's itch, nor yet hath been
Poison'd with love to see, or to be seen.
I had no suit there, nor new suit to show,
Yet went to court ; but as Glaze which did go
To mass in jest, catch'd, was fain to disburse
The hundred marks, which is the statute's curse ;
Before he 'scaped ; so 't pleased my destiny—
Guilty of my sin in going—to think me
As prone to all ill, and of good as forget—
Full, as proud, lustful, and as much in debt,
As vain, as witless, and as false as they
Which dwell in court, for once going that way.
Therefore I suffer'd this ; towards me did run
A thing more strange than on Nile's slime the sun
E'er bred, or all which into Noah's ark came ;
A thing which would have posed Adam to name ;
Stranger than seven antiquaries' studies ;

Than Afric's monsters, Guiana's rarities;
Stranger than strangers; one, who for a Dane
In the Danes' massacre had sure been slain,
If he had lived then; and without help dies,
When next the 'prentices 'gainst strangers rise;
One, whom the watch, at noon, let scarce go by;
One to whom th' examining justice sure would cry,
'Sir, by your priesthood, tell me what you are.'
His clothes were strange, though coarse, and black,
   though bare,
Sleeveless his jerkin was, and it had been
Velvet, but 'twas now—so much ground was seen—
Become tufftaffaty; and our children shall
See it plain rash awhile, then nought at all.
The thing hath travell'd, and, faith, speaks all
   tongues,
And only knoweth what to all states belongs.
Made of th' accents and best phrase of all these,
He speaks one language. If strange meats dis-
   please,
Art can deceive, or hunger force my taste,
But pedant's motley tongue, soldier's bombast,
Mountebanks' drug-tongue, nor terms of law
Are strong enough preparatives to draw
Me to bear this, yet I must be content
With his tongue, in his tongue called compliment.

        *   *   *   *   *

He names me, and comes to me; I whisper, 'God!
How have I sinn'd, that Thy wrath's furious rod,
This fellow, chooseth me?' He saith, 'Sir,
I love your judgment; whom do you prefer,
For the best linguist?' And I sillily
Said, that I thought Calepine's dictionary.
'Nay, but of men, most sweet Sir?' Beza then,
Some Jesuits, and two reverend men
Of our two Academies I named. Here

He stopped me, and said : 'Nay, your apostles were
Good pretty linguists, and so Panurge was ;
Yet a poor gentleman all these may pass
By travel.'   Then, as if he would have sold
His tongue, he praised it, and such wonders told,
That I was fain to say, 'If you'd lived, sir,
Time enough to have been interpreter
To Babel's bricklayers, sure the tower had stood.'
He adds, ' If of court life you knew the good,
You would leave loneness.'   I said, 'Not alone
My loneness is ; but Spartan's fashion,
To teach by painting drunkards, doth not last
Now ; Aretine's pictures have made few chaste ;
No more can princes' court—though there be few
Better pictures of vice—teach me virtue.'
He, like a high-stretch'd lute-string, squeak'd, ' O sir,
' Tis sweet to talk of kings.'   ' At Westminster,'
Said I, 'the man that keeps the abbey tombs,
And for his price doth with whoever comes
Of all our Harrys and our Edwards talk,
From king to king, and all their kin can walk.
Your ears shall hear nought but kings ; your eyes meet
Kings only ; the way to it is King's Street.'
He smack'd and cried, ' He's base, mechanic, coarse,
So are all your Englishmen in their discourse.
Are not your Frenchmen neat ?' . . .

From Satire V.

O AGE of rusty iron !—some better wit
Call it some worse name, if aught equal it—

Th' iron age that was, when justice was sold—now
Injustice is sold dearer—did allow
All claimed fees and duties. Gamesters, anon,
The money which you sweat and swear for is gone
Into other hands. So controverted lands
'Scape, like Angelica, the striver's hands.
If law be in the judge's heart, and he
Have no heart to resist letter, or fee,
Where wilt thou appeal? Power of the courts below
Flows from the first main head, and these can throw
Thee, if they suck thee in, to misery,
To fetters, halters. But if the injury
Steel thee to dare complain ; alas, thou goest
Against the stream, upwards, when thou art most
Heavy and most faint; and in these labours they,
'Gainst whom thou shouldst complain, will in thy
    way
Become great seas, o'er which, when thou shalt be
Forced to make golden bridges, thou shalt see
That all thy gold was drown'd in them before.
All things follow their like; only who have, may
    have more.

JOSEPH HALL, D.D., BISHOP OF EXETER AND NORWICH [1574-1656].

From Book I., Satire III. [1597-1598].

WITH some pot-fury, ravish'd from their wit,
They sit and muse on some no-vulgar writ :
As frozen dung-hills in a winter's morn,
That void of vapours seemed all beforn,
Soon as the sun sends out his piercing beams,
Exhale out filthy smoke and stinking steams.
So doth the base, and the fore-barren brain,

Soon as the raging wine begins to reign.
One higher pitched doth set his soaring thought
On crowned kings, that fortune hath low brought :
Or some upreared high-aspiring swain,
As it might be the Turkish Tamberlain ;[1]
Then weeneth he his base drink-drowned spright,
Rapt to the threefold loft of heaven hight,
When he conceives upon his feigned stage
The stalking steps of his great personage,
Graced with huff-cap terms and thund'ring threats,
That his poor hearers' hair quite upright sets.
Such soon as some brave-minded hungry youth
Sees fitly frame to his wide-strained mouth,
He vaunts his voice upon an hired stage,
With high-set steps and princely carriage ;
Now swooping in side-robes of royalty,
That erst did scrub in lowsy brokery,
There if he can with terms Italianate,
Big-sounding sentences and words of state,
Fair patch me up his pure iambic verse,
He ravishes the gazing scaffolders :[2]
Then certes was the famous Corduban,[3]
Never but half so high tragedian.
Now, lest such frightful shows of Fortune's fall,
And bloody tyrants' rage, should chance appall
The dead-struck audience, midst the silent rout,
Comes leaping in a self-misformed lout,
And laughs, and grins, and frames his mimic face,
And justles straight into the prince's place ;
Then doth the theatre echo all aloud,
With gladsome noise of that applauding crowd.
A goodly hotch-potch ! when vile russetings[4]
Are match'd with monarchs, and with mighty kings.
A goodly grace to sober tragic muse,
When each base clown his clumsy fist doth bruise,[5]

---

[1] This is an attack upon Marlowe.   [2] The gallery.
[3] Seneca.   [4] Clowns.   [5] With applause.

And show his teeth in double rotten row,
For laughter at his self-resembled show.

From Book II., Satire II.

HAVE not I lands of fair inheritance,
Deriv'd by right of long continuance,
To firstborn males, so list the law to grace,
Nature's first fruits in an eternal race?
Let second brothers, and poor nestlings,
Whom more injurious nature later brings
Iuto the naked world; let them assaine
To get hard pennyworths with so bootless pain.
Tush! what care I to be Arcesilas,
Or some sad Solon, whose deed-furrowed face,
And sullen head, and yellow-clouded sight,
Still on the steadfast earth are musing pight;[1]
Mutt'ring what censures their destracted mind
Of brainsick paradoxes deeply hath defin'd:
Or of Parmenides, or of dark Heraclite,
Whether all be one, or ought be infinite?
Long would it be ere thou hast purchase[2] bought,
Or wealthier wexen by such idle thought.
Fond fool! six feet shall serve for all thy store;
And he that cares for most shall find no more.
We scorn that wealth should be the final end,
Whereto the heavenly Muse her course doth bend;
And rather had be pale with learned cares,
Than paunched[3] with thy choice of changed fares.
Or doth thy glory stand in outward glee?
A lave-ear'd[4] ass with gold may trapped be.

---

[1] Fixed.   [2] Profit.
[3] Stuffed.   [4] *I.e.*, long-eared.

Or if in pleasure? live we as we may,
Let swinish Grill delight in dunghill clay.

From Book II., Satire III.

THE crouching client, with low-bended knee,
And many worships, and fair flattery,
Tells on his tale as smoothly as him list,
But still the lawyer's eye squints on his fist;
If that seem lined with a larger fee,
Doubt not the suit, the law is plain for thee.
Tho must he buy his vainer hope with price,
Disclout his crowns, and thank him for advice.
So have I seen in a tempestuous stowre
Some brier-brush showing shelter from the show'r
Unto the hopeful sheep, that fain would hide
His fleecy coat from that same angry tide:
The ruthless brier, regardless of his plight,
Lays hold upon the fleece he would acquite,
And takes advantage of the careless prey,
That thought she in securer shelter lay.
The day is fair, the sheep would far to feed,
The tyrant brier holds fast his shelter's meed,
And claims it for the fee of his defence:
So robs the sheep, in favour's fair pretence.

Book II., Satire VI.

A GENTLE squire would gladly entertain
Into his house some trencher-chappelain;
Some willing man that might instruct his sons,
And that would stand to good conditions.
First, that he lie upon the truckle-bed,
Whiles his young master lieth o'er his head.

10

Second, that he do, on no default,
Ever presume to sit above the salt.
Third that he never change his trencher twice.
Fourth, that he use all common courtesies,
Sit bare at meals, and one half rise and wait.
Last, that he never his young master beat,
But he must ask his mother to define
How many jerks she would his breech should line.
All these observed, he could contented be,
To give five marks and winter livery.

From Book III., Satire I.

TIME was, and that was term'd the time of gold,
When world and time were young that now are old.
(When quiet Saturn swayed the mace of lead,
And pride was yet unborn, and yet unbred).
Time was, that whiles the autumn-fall did last,
Our hungry sires gap'd for the falling mast
                    Of the Dodonian oaks.
Could no unhusked acorn leave the tree,
But there was challenge made whose it might be.
And if some nice and licorous appetite
Desir'd more dainty dish of rare delight,
They scal'd the stored crab with clasped knee,
Till they had sated their delicious eye;
Or search'd the hopeful thicks of hedgy rows,
For briery berries, or haws or sourer sloes:
Or when they meant to fare the fin'st of all,
They lick'd oak-leaves besprent with honey-fall.
As for the thrice three-angled beech nut-shell,
Or chesnuts armed husk and hid kernell,
No squire durst touch, the law would not afford,
Kept for the court, and for the king's own board.

Their royal plate was clay, or wood, or stone,
The vulgar, save his hand, else he had none.
Their only cellar was the neighbour brook :
None did for better care, for better look.
Was then no plaining of the brewer's scape,[1]
Nor greedy vintner mix'd the strained grape,
The king's pavilion was the grassy green,
Under safe shelter of the shady treen.
Under each bank men laid their limbs along,
Not wishing any ease, not fearing wrong ;
Clad with their own, as they were made of old,
Not fearing shame, not feeling any cold.
But when by Ceres' huswifery and pain,
Men learn'd to bury the reviving grain,
And father Janus taught the new-found vine
Rise on the elm, with many a friendly twine :
And bare desire bade men to delven low,
For needless metals, then gan mischief grow.
Then farewell, fairest age, the world's best days:
Thriving in ill as it in age decays.

From Book III., Satire V.

LATE travelling along in London way,
We met, as seem'd by his disguised array,
A lusty courtier, whose curled head
With abron locks was fairly furnished.
I him saluted in our lavish wise :
He answers my untimely courtesies.
His bonnet vail'd, ere ever he could think,
The unruly wind blows off his periwinke.
He lights and runs, and quickly hath him sped,
To overtake his overrunning head.

[1] Tricks.

The sportful wind, to mock the headless man,
Tosses apace his pitch'd Rogerian:
And straight it to a deeper ditch hath blown;
There must my yonker fetch his waxen crown.
I look'd and laugh'd, whiles in his raging mind
He curs'd all court'sy and unruly wind.

I look'd and laugh'd and much I marvelled,
To see so large a causeway in his head,
And me bethought, that when it first begon,
'Twas some shrewd autumn that so bar'd the bone.
Is't not sweet pride, when men their crowns must
    shade,
With that which jerks the hams of every jade,
Or floor-strew'd locks from off the barber's shears?
But waxen crowns well 'gree with borrow'd hairs.

From Book V., Satire III.

THE satire should be like the porcupine,
That shoots sharp quilles out in each angry line,
And wounds the blushing cheek and fiery eye
Of him that hears, and readeth guiltily.
Ye antique satires, how I bless your days,
That brook'd your bolder style, their own dispraise,
And well near wish, yet joy[1] my wish is vain,
I had been then, or they were now again!
For now our ears been of more brittle mould,
Than those dull earthen ears that were of old:
Sith[2] theirs, like anvils, bore the hammer's head,
Our glass can never touch unshivered.
But from the ashes of my quiet style
Henceforth may rise some raging rough Lucille,

[1] Rejoice.   [2] Since.

That may with Æschylus both find and leese[1]
The snaky tresses of th' Eumenides :
Meanwhile, sufficeth me, the world may say
That I these vices loath'd another day.

JOHN MARSTON [1575-1634].

From Satire I.

BUT see—who's yonder ?   True Humility,
The perfect image of faire Curtisie ;
See—he doth daine to be in servitude
Where he hath no promotions livelihood !
Marke, he doth curtsie, and salutes a block,
Will seeme to wonder at a weathercock ;
Trenchmore with apes, play musicke to an owle,
Blesse his sweet honours running brasell bowle ;
Cries ' Brauly broake' when that his lordship mist,
And is of all the thrunged scaffold hist ;
O is not this a curteous-minded man !
No foole, no, a damn'd Machevelian.
Holds candle to the devill for a while,
That he the better may the world beguile
Thats fed with shows.   He hopes, thogh som repine,
When sunne is set the lesser starres will shine ;
He is within a haughty malecontent,
Though he doe use such humble blandishment.
But, bold-fac'd Satyre, straine not over hie,
But laugh and chuck at meaner gullery.

¹ Lose.

From Satire III.

BEDLAME, Frenzie, Madnes, Lunacie,
I challenge all your moody empery
Once to produce a more distracted man
Than is inamorato Lucian !
For when my eares receav'd a fearfull sound
That he was sicke, I went, and there I found
Him layde of love, and newly brought to bed
Of monstrous folly and a franticke head.
His chamber hang'd about with elegies,
With sad complaints of his loves miseries ;
His windows strow'd with sonnets, and the glasse
Drawne full of love-knots.   I approacht the asse,
And straight he weepes, and signes some sonnet out
To his faire love ! And then he goes about
For to perfume her rare perfection
With some sweet-smelling pinck epitheton ;
Then with a melting looke he writhes his head,
And straight in passion riseth in his bed ;
And having kist his hand, stroke up his haire,
Made a French conge, cryes, ' O cruell feare '
To the antique bed-post.   I laught a maine,
That down my cheeks the mirthfull drops did raine.
Well, he's no Janus, but substantiall,
In show and essence a good naturall ;
When as thou hear'st me aske spruce Duceus
From whence he comes; and he straight answers us,
From Lady Lilla ; and is going straight
To the Countess of (   ), for she doth waite
His comming, and will surely send her coach,
Unlesse he make the speedier approach.
Art not thou ready for to break thy spleen
At laughing at the fondness thou hast seene
In this vain-glorious foole, when thou dost know
He never durst unto these ladies show
His pippin face ?

From Satire V.

FIE, fie ! I am deceived all thys while,
A mist of errors doth my sense beguile ;
I have beene long of all my wits bereaven
Heaven for hell taking, taking hell for heaven ;
Vertue for vice, and vice for vertue still ;
Sower for sweet, and good for passing ill.
If not, would vice and odious villanie
Be still rewarded with high dignity ?
Would damned Jovians be of all men praised,
And with high honors unto heaven raised ?
   Tis so, tis so ; riot and luxurie
Are vertuous, meritorious chastitie :
That which I thought to be damn'd hel-borne pride,
Is humble modestie, and nought beside ;
That which I deemed Bacchus surquedry,
Is grave and staied, civill sobrietie.
O then, thrice holy age, thrice sacred men,
Mong whom no vice a Satyre can discerne,
Since lust is turned into chastitie,
And riot into sad sobrietie,
Nothing but goodness raigneth in our age,
And vertues all are joyn'd in marriage !
Heere is no dwelling for impiety,
No habitation for vile villanie ;
Heere are no subject for Reproofes sharpe vaine ;
Then hence, rude Satyre, make away amaine,
And seeke a seate where more impuritie
Doth lye and lurke in still securitie !

To Everlasting Oblivion.

Epilogue to 'The Scourge of Villainie.'

Thou mightie gulfe, insatiat cormorant !
Deride me not, though I seeme petulant
To fall into thy chops.   Let others pray
For ever their faire poem flourish may ;
But as for mee, hungry Oblivion
Devour me quick, accept my orizon :
My earnest prayers, which doe importune thee
With gloomy shade of thy still emperie,
To vaile both me and my rude poesie,
Farre worthier lines, in silence of thy state,
Doe sleep securely, free from love or hate ;
From which this living nere can be exempt,
But whilst it breathes will hate and furie tempt,
Then close his eyes with thy all-dimming hand,
Which not right glorious actions can with-stand ;
Peace hatefull tongues, I now in silence pace,
Unlesse some hownde doe wake me from my place.
   I with this sharpe, yet well-meant poesie,
   Will sleep secure, right free from injuric
   Of cancred hate, or rankest villanie.

JOHN DAY.

From ' Peregrinatio Scholastica ' [1607 ?].

Philosophos, glad to be out of the reach of the
sworde of Justice, presentlie inquires for this honest
Vicker (and here by the way let me tell you, this
new Vicker was made out of an olde ffrier that had
beene twice turnd at a Religion-dressers) ; and him
he fownde with two or thre of the best men in his

parish goeing to take in fresh water at the Barlie-Island (Alehouse). Who (Philosophos having saluted him and told him his busines) tooke him into the harbour with him and, while their vessels were a fillinge, returnd him this short, but nothing sweete answere: Sir, you are very wellcome and, could my poore livinge afford it, I would make you better wellcome. I love and honour schollers, haveinge a full prentishipp to the trade myselfe: but, as my honest neighbours here knowe, I have but a poore vicoridge which one Mr. Symon-Monye, or more familiarlie sym-monie, helpt me to. And though I have noe great store of Lerneinge lieing by me (for, as you know, *omnia mea mecum porto* is the old worde amongst schollers), yet I have enough to read a marriadge and buriall, and, if neede be, to saye a homelie of a hollidaie. And thats as much as my honest parishioners desire, more a great deale then manie of them deserve; for these honnest men, know they are a companie of turbulent mechanickes, and yet so prowd in their owne conceits I have much adoe to please them; for, but for readeing one Latin worde in an homely (and that was out afore I was aware to), some of them call me papist and shonn me as a puritan would doe a crosse, and never dronke above twice or thrice in my companie since. And therefore haveinge neither occasion to use lerneinge nor meanes to maintaine it if I had it, heares the tother halfe cann and so I take my leave of you.

GEORGE WITHER [1588-1677].

From 'Abuses Stript and Whipt' [1613].

HATE many times from wrongs receiv'd hath grown:
Envy is seen where injuries are none.
Her malice also is more general;
For hate to some extends, and she to all.
Yet envious men do least spite such as he
Of ill-report, or of a low degree.
But rather they do take aim at such
Who either well-beloved are or rich;
And therefore some do fitly liken these
Unto those flies we call cantharides;
Since for the most part they alight on none
But on the flowers that are fairest blown;
Or to the boisterous wind, which sooner grubs
The stately cedar than the humble shrubs.
Yet I have known it shake the bush below,
And move the leaf that's wither'd long ago;
As if it had not shown sufficient spite
Unless it also could o'erwhelm it quite,
Or bury it in earth. Yea, I have found
The blast of envy fly as low's the ground.
And when it hath already brought a man
Even to the very meanest state it can,
Yet 'tis not satisfi'd, but still devising
Which way it also may disturb his rising.

REVENGE.

ROOM for Revenge, he's no comedian
That acts for pleasure, but a grim tragedian:
A foul, stern monster, which if we displease him,
Death, wounds, and blood, or nothing, can appease
    him.

This most inhuman passion, now and then,
With violence and fury hurries man
So far from that sweet mildness, wherewith he,
Being himself, should ever temper'd be ;
That man nor devil can we term him well,
For part he hath of earth, and part of hell,
Yet this (so much of all good men disdain'd)
Many there are have rashly entertain'd,
And hugg'd as a sweet contenting passion,
Though in a various and unlikely fashion.

Some are so staid they can their purpose keep
Long time conceal'd, to make the wound more deep;
And these it is not heat of blood that blind,
But rather the fell canker of the mind.
Some by respect to time and place are staid,
And some again by nothing are allay'd ;
But them mad rage oft furiously will carry,
Without respect of friends or sanctuary.
Then some of them are fearful, some are bolder,
Some are too hot, and some again are colder.
O, I have seen and laugh'd at heart to see 't,
Some of our hot spurs drawing in the street,
As though they could not passion's rage withstand,
But must betake them to it out of hand.
But why i' th' street ?   Oh, comp'ny doth heart
    them,
And men may see their valorous acts, and part them.

JEALOUSY.

SOMETIMES this passion, as it may appear,
Proceeds out of a too much love, with fear ;

It is sent
Of God, as a peculiar punishment
To those who do the creature so affect,
As thereby their Creator they neglect.
Love is the highest and the noblest bliss
That for mankind on earth ordained is ;
But when true measure it exceeds, and gets
Beyond the decent bounds that reason sets,
God turns it to a plague, whereby He will
Show them their folly, and correct the ill.
He adds a fear of losing of their joy
In that they love, which quickly doth destroy
All their delight, and strewing good with ill,
Makes things seem lost though they are with them
    still.

ADDRESS TO THE KING (WRITTEN IN PRISON,
1614 ?).

IN this poore state I can as well content me,
As if that I had Wealth and Honours lent me ;
Nor for my owne sake doe I seeke to shunne
This thraldome, wherein now I seeme undone :
For though I prize my freedome more then golde
And use the meanes to free myself from hold,
Yet with a minde (I hope) unchang'd and free,
Here can I live and play with miserie,
Yea in despight of want and slavery,
Laugh at the world in all her bravery,
Here have I learn'd to make my greatest wrongs
Matter for mirth, and subjects but for songs.
Here can I smile to see my selfe neglected,
And how the meane man's sute is disrespected,
Whilst those that are more rich and better friended,
Can have twice greater faults thrice sooner ended.

RICHARD CORBET, BISHOP OF OXFORD AND NORWICH [1582-1635].

From the ' Journey into France.'

I WENT from England into France
Nor yet to learn to cringe nor dance,
  Nor yet to ride or fence ;
Nor did I go like one of those
That do returne with half a nose
  They carried from hence.

But I to Paris rode along
Much like John Dory in the song,
  Upon a holy tide.
I on an ambling nag did jet,
I trust he is not paid for yet,
  And spur'd him on each side.

And to St. Dennis fast we came,
To see the sights of Nostre Dame,
  The man that shows them snaffles ;
Where who is apt for to beleeve
May see our Ladie's right-arm sleeve,
  And eke her old pantofles ;

Her breast, her milk, her very gown
That she did wear in Bethlehem town
  When in the inn she lay.
Yet all the world knows that's a fable,
For so good clothes ne'er lay in stable
  Upon a lock of hay.

No carpenter could by his trade
Gain so much coyn as to have made
  A gown of so rich stuff.
Yet they, poor fools, think, for their credit,
They may believe old Joseph did it,
  'Cause he deserv'd enough.

There is one of the crosse's nails,
Which whoso sees his bonnet vails,
    And, if he will, may kneel.
Some say 'twas false, 'twas never so,
Yet, feeling it, thus much I know,
    It is as true as steel.

There is a lanthorn which the Jews,
When Judas led them forth, did use,
    It weighs my weight downright :
But to believe it, you must think
The Jews did put a candle in't,
    And then 'twas very light.

There's one saint there has lost his nose :
Another's head, but not his toes,
    His elbow and his thumb.
But when that we had seen the rags
We went to th' inn and took our nags,
    And so away did come.

We came to Paris on the Seine,
'Tis wondrous fair, 'tis nothing clean,
    'Tis Europe's greatest town.
How strong it is I need not tell it,
For all the world may easily smell it,
    That walk it up and down.

There many strange things are to see,
The palace and great gallery,
    The Place Royal doth excel :
The new bridge and the statues there,
At Nostre Dame, Saint Q. Peter,
    The steeple bears the bell.

The Bastile and Saint Dennis-Street,
The Shafflenist, like London-Fleet,

The Arsenal, no toy.
But if you'll see the prettiest thing,
Go to the court and see the king,
    O 'tis a hopeful boy.

He is of all his dukes and peers
Reverenc'd for much wit at 's years,
    Nor must you think it much ;
For he with little switch doth play,
And make fine dirty pyes of clay,
    O never king made such !

JOHN CLEVELAND [1613-1658].

From ' The Rebel Scot.'

HE that saw Hell in's melancholy Dream,
And in the Twy-light of his Phancie's Theme
Scar'd from his Sins, repented in a fright,
Had he view'd *Scotland* had turn'd Proselite,
A Land where one may pray with curst intent,
O may they never suffer Banishment !
Had *Cain* been *Scot*, God would have chang'd his
    Doom,
Not forc'd him wander, but confin'd him home ;
Like *Jews* they spread, and as Infection fly,
As if the Devil had Ubiquity.
Hence 'tis they live as Rovers and defie
This, or that place, Rags of Geography.
They're Citizens o' th' World, they'r all in all,
Scotland's a Nation Epidemical.

    *   *   *   *   *

Lord ! what a godly thing is want of Shirts !
How a Scotch Stomach and no Meat converts !

They wanted Food and Rayment; so they took
Religion for their Seamstress, and their Cook.
Unmask them well, their Honours and Estate
As well as Conscience are Sophisticate.
Shrive but their Title and their Moneys poize,
A Laird and twenty pence pronounc'd with noise,
When constru'd but for a plain Yeoman go,
And a good sober two pence, and well so.
Hence then you proud Impostors, get you gone,
You *Picts* in Gentry and Devotion.
You Scandal to the Stock of Verse, a Race
Able to bring the Gibbet in disgrace.
Hyperbolus by suffering did traduce
The Ostracism, and sham'd it out of use.
The *Indian* that Heaven did forswear,
Because he heard some *Spaniards* were there;
Had he but known what *Scots* in Hell had been,
He would *Erasmus*-like have hung between.

From ' *The Puritan.*'

WITH Face and Fashion to be known,
For one of sure Election,
With Eyes all white, and many a Groan,
With Neck aside to draw in Tone,
With Harp in 's Nose, or he is none.
  See a new Teacher of the Town,
  O the Town, O the Town's new Teacher.

With Pate cut shorter than the Brow,
With little Ruff starch'd you know how,
With Cloak like *Paul* no Cape I trow,
With Surplice none; but lately now,
With Hands to thump, no Knees to bow.
  See a new Teacher, etc.

With coz'ning Cough, and hollow Cheek,
To get new Gatherings every Week,
With Paltry Change of *and* to *eke*,
With some small Hebrew, and no Greek,
To find out Words, when stuff's to seek,
  See a new Teacher, etc.

With Speech unthought, quick Revelation,
With boldness in Predestination,
With threats of absolute Damnation,
For *Yea* and *Nay* hath some Salvation
For his own Tribe, not every Nation,
  See a new Teacher, etc.

ANDREW MARVELL [1621-1678].

From ' The Rehearsal Transprosed ' [1672].

BUT is it not a great pity to see a man in the flower
of his age and the vigor of his studies, to fall into
such a distraction, that his head runs upon nothing
but ' Roman Empire ' and ' Ecclesiastical Policy ' ?
This happens by his growing too early acquainted
with Don Quixot, and reading the Bible too late ;
so that the first impressions being most strong, and
mixing with the last, as more novel, have made
such a medley in his brain-pan that he is become a
mad priest, which of all the sorts is the most incur-
able.   Hence it is that you shall hear him anon
instructing princes, like Sancho, how to govern his
island : as he is busied at present in vanquishing
the Calvinists of Germany and Geneva.   Had he no
friends to have given him good counsel before his
understanding were quite unsettled ? or if there was
none near, why did not men call in the neighbours,

and send for the parson of the parish, to perswade with him in time, but let it run on thus till he is fit for nothing but Bedlam or Hogsdon? However, though it be a particular damage, it may tend to a general advantage; and young students will, I hope, by this example learn to beware henceforward of overweening presumption and preposterous am - bition. For this gentleman, as I have heard, after he had read Don Quixot and the Bible, besides such school-books as were necessary for his age, was sent early to the University; and there studied hard, and in a short time became a competent rhetorician, and no ill disputant. He had learnt how to erect a thesis, and to defend it pro or con with a serviceable distinction; while the truth (as his camarade Mr. Bayes hath it on another occasion),

> ' Before a full pot of ale you can swallow,
>   Was here with a whoop and gone with a holla.'

And so thinking himself so ripe and qualified for the greatest undertakings and highest fortune, he there- fore exchanged the narrowness of the university for the town; but coming out of the confinement of the square-cap and the quadrangle into the open air, the world began to turn round with him, which he imagined, though it were his own giddiness, to be nothing less than the quadrature of the circle. This accident concurring so happily to increase the good opinion which he naturally had of himself, he thence- forward applied to gain a like reputation with others. He follow'd the town life, haunted the best com- panies, and, to polish himself from any pedantick roughness, he read and saw the Plaies, with much care and more proficiency than most auditory. But all this while he forgot not the main chance, but hearing of a vacancy with a nobleman, he clap'd in, and easily obtain'd to be his chaplain. From that day you may take the date of his preferments and his ruine. For having soon wrought himself dexteriously into his patron's favour, by short graces and sermons, and a mimical way of drolling upon the Puritans, which he knew take both at chappel and table; he gained great authority likewise among all the domesticks. They all listened to him as an oracle; and they allowed him by common consent to have not onely all the divinity, but more wit too than all the rest of the family put together. This alone elevated him exceedingly in his own conceit, and raised him hypochondria into the region of the brain, that his head swell'd like any bladder with wind and vapour. But after he was stretch'd to such an height in his own fancy, that he could not look down from top to toe but his eyes dazzled at the precipice of his stature, there fell out, or in, another natural chance which push'd him headlong; for being of an amorous complexion, and finding himself (as I told you) the cock-divine and the cock-wit of the family, he took the privilege to walk among the hens: and thought it was not impolitick to establish his new acquired reputation upon the gentlewomen's side. And they that perceived he was a rising man, and of pleasant conversation, dividing his day among them into canonical hours, of reading now the Common Prayer, and now the Romances, were very much taken with him. The sympathy of silk began to stir and attract the tippet to the pettycoat, and the pettycoat toward the tippet. The innocent ladies found a strange unquietness in their minds, and could not distinguish whether it were love and devotion. Neither was he wanting on his part to carry on the work; but shifted himself every day with a clean surplice, and, as oft as he had occasion to bow, he directed his reverence towards the gentlewomen's pew. Till, having before had enough of the libertine, and undertaken his calling only for preferment, he was transported now with the sanctity of his office, even to extasy : and like the Bishop over Maudlin College altar, or like Maudlin de la Croix, he was seen in his prayers to be lifted up sometimes in the air, and once particularly so high that he cracked his skull against the chappel ceiling. I do not hear, for all this, that he had ever practised upon the honour of the ladies, but that he preserved always the civility of a Platonick knight-errant. For all this courtship had no other operation than to make him still more in love with himself; and if he frequented their company, it was only to speculate his own baby in their eyes. But being thus, without competitor or rival, the darling of both sexes in the family, and his own minion, he grew beyond all measure elated, and that crack of his skull, as in broken looking-glasses, multiplied him in self-conceit and imagination. Having fixed his center in this nobleman's house, he thought he could now move and govern the whole earth with the same facility. Nothing now would serve him but he must be a madman in print, and write a book of Ecclesiastical Policy. There he distributes all the 'territories of Conscience' into the Prince's province, and makes the Hierarchy to be but Bishops of the air: and talks at such an extravagant rate in things of higher concernment, that the Reader will avow that in the whole discourse he had not one lucid interval. This book he was so bent upon that he sate up late at nights, and wanting sleep, and drinking sometimes wine to animate his fancy, it increas'd his distemper. Beside that, too, he had the misfortune to have two friends, who being both also out of their wits, and of the same, though something a calmer, phrensy, spurr'd him on perpetually with commendation.

And when his Book was once come out, and he saw himself an Author; that some of the gallants of the town layd by the new tune, and the 'tay, tay, tarree,' to quote some of his impertinencies; that his title-page was posted and pasted up at every avenue next under the Play for that afternoon at the King's or the Duke's house: the vain-glory of this totally confounded him. He lost all the little remains of his understanding, and his *cerebellum* was so dryed up that there was more brains in a walnut, and both their shells were alike thin and brittle.

From ' The Character of Holland' [1672].

HOLLAND,[1] that scarce deserves the name of land,
As but th' off-scouring of the British sand,
And so much earth as was contributed
By British pilots when they heav'd the lead,
Or what by the ocean's slow alluvion fell
Of shipwrackt cockle and the music-shell:
This indigested vomit of the sea
Fell to the Dutch by just propriety.
  Glad then, as miners who have found the oar,
They, with mad labour, fish'd the land to shoar;
And div'd as desperately for each piece
Of earth, as if't had been of ambergreece;
Collecting anxiously small loads of clay,
Less than what building swallows bear away;
Or than those pills which sordid beetles roul,
Transfusing into them their dunghill soul.
  How did they rivet with gigantick piles,
Thorough the centre their new-catchèd miles;
And to the stake a struggling country bound,
Where barking waves still bait the forcèd ground;

---

[1] Cf. Butler's poem on the same subject.

Building their wat'ry Babel far more high
To reach the sea, then those to scale the sky !
 Yet still his claim the injur'd ocean laid,
And oft at leap-frog ore their steeples plaid ;
As if on purpose it on land had come
To show them what's their mare liberum.
A daily deluge over them does boyl ;
The earth and water play at level-coyl.
The fish ofttimes the burger dispossest,
And sat, not as a meat, but as a guest,
And oft the Tritons and the sea-nymphs saw
Whole sholes of Dutch serv'd up for Cabillau ;
Or, as they over the new level rang'd
For pickled herring, pickled heeren chang'd.
Nature, it seem'd, asham'd of her mistake,
Would throw their land away at duck and drake.
 Therefore Necessity, that first made kings,
Something like government among them brings ;
For, as with pygmies, who best kills the crane,
Among the hungry, he that treasures grain,
Among the blind, the one-ey'd blinkard reigns,
So rules among the drownèd he that draines ;
Not who first see the rising sun commands,
But who could first discern the rising lands ;
Who best could know to pump an earth so leak,
Him they their Lord, and Country's Father, speak ;
To make a bank, was a great Plot of State ;
Invent a shov'l and be a magistrate.
Hence some small dyke-grave, unperceiv'd, invades
The pow'r, and grows as 'twere a King of Spades,
But, for less envy, some joynt States endures,
Who look like a commission of the Sewers :
For these Half-anders, half wet, and half dry,
Nor bear strict service, nor pure liberty.

From ' *The Last Instructions to a Painter about the Dutch Wars* ' [1667].

PAINT last the King, and a dead shade of night,
Only disperst by a weak taper's light,
And those bright gleams that dart along and glare
From his clear eyes (yet those too dart with care) ;
There, as in the calm horror all alone,
He wakes and muses of th' uneasy throne ;
Raise up a sudden shape with virgin's face,
Tho' ill agree her posture, hour or place ;
Naked as born, and her round arms behind,
With her own tresses interwove and twined ;
Her mouth lockt up, a blind before her eyes,
Yet from beneath her veil her blushes rise,
And silent tears her secret anguish speak,
Her heart throbs, and with very shame would break.
The object strange in him no terror mov'd,
He wondred first, then pitied, then he lov'd ;
And with kind hand does the coy vision press,
Whose beauty greater seem'd by her distress ;
But soon shrunk back, chill'd with a touch so cold,
And the airy picture vanisht from his hold.
In his deep thoughts the wonder did increase,
And he divin'd 'twas England, or the Peace.
    Express him startling next, with list'ning ear,
As one that some unusual noise doth hear ;
With cannons, trumpets, drums, his door surround,
But let some other Painter draw the sound.
Thrice he did rise, thrice the vain tumult fled,
But again thunders when he lies in bed.
His mind secure does the vain stroke repeat,
And finds the drums Lewis's march did beat.
    Shake then the room, and all his curtains tear,
And with blue streaks infect the taper clear,

While the pale ghost his eyes doth fixed admire
Of grandsire Harry, and of Charles his sire.
Harry sits down and in his open side
The grisly wound reveals of which he dy'd;
And ghastly Charles, turning his coller low,
The purple thred about his neck does show;
Then whisp'ring to his son in words unheard,
Through the lock't door both of them disappear'd.
The wondrous night the pensive King revolves,
And rising straight on Hyde's disgrace resolves.

From ' *Advice to a Painter.*'

NEXT, Painter, draw the rabble of the plot:
German, FitzGerald, Loftus, Porter, Scot:
These are fit heads indeed to turn a State,
And change the order of a nation's fate;
Ten thousand such as these shall ne'er control
The smallest atom of an English soul.
Old England on its strong foundation stands
Defying all their heads and all their hands;
Its steady basis never could be shook
When wiser men her ruin undertook;
And can her guardian angel let her stoop
At last to madmen, fools, and to the Pope?
No, Painter, no! close up the piece and see
This crowd of traytors hang'd in effigie.

From ' *Britannia and Raleigh.*'

RAWLEIGH, no more! for long in vain I've try'd
The Stewart from the tyrant to divide.
As easily learn'd virtuosos may
With the dog's blood his gentle kind convey

Into the wolf, and make him guardian turn
To th' bleating flock, by him so lately torn.
If this imperial juice once taint his blood,
'Tis by no potent antidote withstood.
Tyrants, like lep'rous kings, for public weal
Should be immur'd, lest the contagion steal
Over the whole.   Th' elect of the Jessean line
To this firm law their sceptre did resign ;
And shall this base tyrannick brood invade
Eternal laws, by God for mankind made ?

From 'An Historical Poem.'

PRIESTS were the first deluders of mankind,
Who with vain Faith made all their Reason blind ;
Not Lucifer himself more proud than they,
And yet persuade the world they must obey,
'Gainst avarice and luxury complain,
And practise all the vices they arraign.
Riches and honour they from laymen reap,
And with dull crambo feed the silly sheep.
As Killigrew buffoons his master, they
Droll on their God, but a much duller way.
With hocus-pocus and their heavenly slight,
They gain on tender consciences at night.
Whoever hath an over-zealous wife
Becomes the priest's Amphitrio during life.
Who would such men heaven's messengers believe,
Who from the sacred pulpit dare deceive ?
Baal's wretched curates legerdemain'd it so,
And never durst their tricks above-board show.

My Muse presum'd a little to digress,
And touch their holy function with my verse.

Now to the State again she tends direct,
And does on giant Lauderdale reflect.
This haughty monster, with his ugly claws,
First temper'd poison to destroy our laws ;
Declares the Council's Edicts are beyond
The most authentick statutes of the Land ;
Sets up in Scotland *à la mode de France*—
Taxes, Excise, and Armies does advance.
This Saracen his Country's freedom broke,
To bring upon their necks the heavier yoke.
This is the savage pimp, without dispute,
First brought his mother for a prostitute.
Of all the miscreants e'er went to hell,
This villain rampant bears away the bell.

JOHN WILMOT, EARL OF ROCHESTER
[1647-1680].

From ' The History of Insipids ' [1676].

CHAST, pious, prudent, Charles the Second,
    The Miracle of thy Restoration,
May like to that of Quails be reckon'd
    Rain'd on the *Israelitish* Nation ;
The wish'd for Blessing from Heav'n sent,
Became their Curse and Punishment.

His Father's Foes he doth reward,
    Preserving those that cut off 's Head ;
Old Cavaliers, the Crown's best Guard,
    He lets them starve for want of Bread.
Never was any King endow'd
With so much Grace and Gratitude.

A Parliament of Knaves and Sots,
   Members by name you must not mention,
He keeps in Pay, and buys their Votes ;
   Here with a Place, there with a Pension.
When to give Money he can't cologue 'um,
He doth with Scorn prorogue, prorogue 'um.

But they long since, by too much giving,
   Undid, betray'd and sold the Nation ;
Making their Memberships a Living,
   Better than e'er was Sequestration.
God give thee, Charles, a Resolution
To damn the Knaves by Dissolution.

Fame is not grounded on Success,
   Tho' Victories were *Cæsar's* Glory ;
Lost Battels make not *Pompey* less,
   But left them stiled great in Story.
Malicious Fate doth oft devise
To beat the Brave, and Fool the Wise.

Charles in the first *Dutch* War stood fair
   To have been Sovereign of the Deep,
When *Opdam* blew up in the Air,
   Had not his Highness gone to sleep ;
Our Fleet slack'd Sails, fearing his waking,
The *Dutch* else had been in sad taking.

Mists, Storms, short Victuals, adverse Winds,
   And once the Natives wise Division,
Defeated *Charles* his best designs,
   Till he became his Foes Derision.
But he had swing'd the *Dutch* at *Chatham,*
Had he had Ships but to come at 'em. . . .

If of all Christian Blood the guilt
   Cry loud for Vengeance unto Heaven,
That Sea by treacherous *Lewis* spilt
   Can never be by God forgiven.

Worse Scourge unto his Subjects, Lord,
Than Pest'lence, Famine, Fire or Sword.

That false rapacious Wolf of *France*,
  The Scourge of *Europe*, and its Curse,
Who at his Subject's cry does dance,
  And studies how to make them worse.
To say such Kings, Lord, rule by thee,
Were most prodigious Blasphemy.

Such know no Laws but their own Lust,
  Their Subjects Substance, and their Blood,
They count it Tribute due and just,
  Still spent and spilt for Subjects good.
If such Kings are by God appointed,
The Devil may be the Lord's Anointed.

Epigram on Charles II.

HERE lies our Sovereign Lord the King,
  Whose word no man relies on,
Who never said a foolish thing,
  Nor ever did a wise one.

SAMUEL BUTLER [1612-1680].

From 'Hudibras' [1662-1678]. *Part I., Canto I.*

WHEN civil fury first grew high,
And men fell out, they knew not why;
When hard words, jealousies, and fears,
Set folks together by the ears,

And made them fight, like mad or drunk,
For Dame Religion, as for punk ;
Whose honesty they all durst swear for,
Though not a man of them knew wherefore :
When Gospel-Trumpeter, surrounded
With long-eared rout, to battle sounded
And pulpit, drum ecclesiastic
Was beat with fist instead of a stick ;
Then did Sir Knight abandon dwelling,
And out he rode a colonelling.

  * * * * *

He was in logic a great critic,
Profoundly skilled in analytic ;
He could distinguish, and divide
A hair 'twixt south, and south-west side ;
On either which he would dispute,
Confute, change hands, and still confute ;
He'd undertake to prove, by force
Of argument, a man's no horse ;
He'd prove a buzzard is no fowl,
And that a lord may be an owl,
A calf an alderman, a goose a justice,
And rooks Committee-men and Trustees.
He'd run in debt by disputation,
And pay with ratiocination.
All this by syllogism, true
In mood and figure, he would do.
 For rhetoric, he could not ope
His mouth, but out there flew a trope ;
And when he happened to break off
I' th' middle of his speech, or cough,
H' had hard words ready to show why,
And tell what rules he did it by ;
Else, when with greatest art he spoke,
You'd think he talked like other folk.
For all a rhetorician's rules
Teach nothing but to name his tools. . . .

In mathematics he was greater
Than Tycho Brahe, or Erra Pater :
For he, by geometric scale,
Could take the size of pots of ale ;
Resolve, by sines and tangents straight,
If bread or butter wanted weight ;
And wisely tell, what hour o' th' day
The clock does strike, by algebra.
   Beside, he was a shrewd philosopher,
And had read every text and gloss over ;
Whate'er the crabbed'st author hath,
He understood b' implicit faith :
Whatever sceptic could inquire for,
For ev'ry why he had a wherefore ;
Knew more than forty of them do,
As far as words and terms could go.
All which he understood by rote,
And, as occasion served, would quote ;
No matter whether right or wrong,
They might be either said or sung.
His notions fitted things so well,
That which was which he could not tell ;
But oftentimes mistook the one
For th' other, as great clerks have done. . . .
He could raise scruples dark and nice,
And after solve 'em in a trice ;
As if Divinity had catched
The itch on purpose to be scratched ;
Or, like a mountebank, did wound
And stab herself with doubts profound,
Only to show with how small pain
The sores of Faith are cured again ;
Although by woful proof we find
They always leave a scar behind. . . .
For his Religion, it was fit
To match his learning and his wit ;
'Twas Presbyterian, true blue ;

For he was of that stubborn crew
Of errant saints, whom all men grant
To be the true Church Militant ;
Such as do build their faith upon
The holy text of pike and gun ;
Decide all controversies by
Infallible artillery ;
And prove their doctrine orthodox
By apostolic blows and knocks ;
Call fire, and sword, and desolation,
A godly, thorough Reformation,
Which always must be carried on,
And, still be doing, never done ;
As if Religion were intended
For nothing else but to be mended.
A sect, whose chief devotion lies
In odd perverse antipathies ;
In falling out with that or this,
And finding somewhat still amiss ;
More peevish, cross, or splenetic,
Than dog distract or monkey sick.
That with more care keep holy-day
The wrong, than others the right way ;
Compound for sins they are inclined to,
By damning those they have no mind to ;
Still so perverse and opposite,
As if they worshipped God for spite.
The self-same thing they will abhor
One way, and long another for.
Free-will they one way disavow,
Another, nothing else allow.
All piety consists therein
In them, in other men all sin.
Rather than fail, they will defy
That which they love most tenderly ;
Quarrel with minced-pies, and disparage
Their best and dearest friend—plum-porridge ;

Fat pig and goose itself oppose,
And blaspheme custard through the nose. . . .
   Thus clad and fortified, Sir Knight,
From peaceful home set forth to fight.
But first, with nimble, active force,
He got on th' outside of his horse :
For having but one stirrup tied
T' his saddle on the further side,
It was so short, h' had much ado
To reach it with his desperate toe.
But after many strains and heaves,
He got up to the saddle-eaves,
From whence he vaulted into th' seat,
With so much vigour, strength, and heat,
That he had almost tumbled over
With his own weight, but did recover,
By laying hold on tail and mane,
Which oft he used instead of rein. . . .
   A Squire he had, whose name was Ralph,
That in th' adventure went his half,
Though writers, for more stately tone,
Do call him Ralpho, 'tis all one ;
And when we can, with metre safe,
We'll call him so, if not, plain Ralph ;
For rhyme the rudder is of verses,
With which, like ships, they steer their courses.
An equal stock of wit and valour
He had laid in ; by birth a tailor. . . .
His knowledge was not far behind
The knight's, but of another kind,
And he another way came by 't ;
Some call it Gifts, and some New-light ;
A liberal art that costs no pains
Of study, industry, or brains.
His wits were sent him for a token,
But in the carriage cracked and broken ;

Like commendation nine-pence crooked
With—To and from my love—it looked.
He ne'er considered it, as loth
To look a gift-horse in the mouth ;
And very wisely would lay forth
No more upon it than 'twas worth ;
But as he got it freely, so
He spent it frank and freely too :
For saints themselves will sometimes be,
Of gifts that cost them nothing, free.
By means of this, with hem and cough,
Prolongers to enlighten snuff,
He could deep mysteries unriddle,
As easily as thread a needle :
For as of vagabonds we say,
That they are ne'er beside their way :
Whate'er men speak by this new light,
Still they are sure to be i' th' right.
'Tis a dark-lantern of the spirit,
Which none can see but those that bear it ;
A light that falls down from on high,
For spiritual trades to cozen by ;
An *ignis fatuus*, that bewitches,
And leads men into pools and ditches,
To make them dip themselves, and sound
For Christendom in dirty pond ;
To dive, like wild-fowl, for salvation,
And fish to catch regeneration.
This light inspires, and plays upon
The nose of saint, like bag-pipe drone,
And speaks, through hollow empty soul,
As through a trunk, or whispering hole,
Such language as no mortal ear
But spirit'al eaves-droppers can hear.
So Phœbus, or some friendly muse,
Into small poets song infuse ;

12

Which they at second-hand rehearse,
Through reed or bagpipe, verse for verse.

  *   *   *   *   *

Thou that with ale or viler liquors
Didst inspire Withers, Prynne, and Vickars,
And force them, though it was in spite
Of Nature, and their stars, to write ;
Who, as we find in sullen writs
And cross-grained works of modern wits,
With vanity, opinion, want,
The wonder of the ignorant,
The praises of the author, penned
By himself, or wit-insuring friend ;
The itch of picture in the front,
With bays, and wicked rhyme upon 't,
All that is left o' th' forked hill
To make men scribble without skill ;
Canst make a poet, spite of fate,
And teach all people to translate,
Though out of languages, in which
They understand no part of speech ;
Assist me but this once, I'mplore,
And I shall trouble thee no more.

From Canto II.

FOR if bear-baiting we allow,
What good can reformation do ?
The blood and treasure that's laid out
Is thrown away, and goes for nought.
Are these the fruits o' th' protestation,
The prototype of reformation,
Which all the saints, and some, since martyrs,
Wore in their hats like wedding garters,
When 'twas resolvèd by their house

Six members' quarrel to espouse?
Did they for this draw down the rabble,
With zeal, and noises formidable;
And make all cries about the town
Join throats to cry the bishops down?
Who having round begirt the palace,
As once a month they do the gallows,
As members gave the sign about,
Set up their throats with hideous shout.
When tinkers bawled aloud to settle
Church-discipline, for patching kettle,
No sow-gelder did blow his horn
To geld a cat, but cried Reform;
The oyster-women locked their fish up,
And trudged away to cry, No Bishop;
The mouse-trap men laid save-alls by
And 'gainst ev'l counsellors did cry;
Botchers left old clothes in the lurch,
And fell to turn and patch the church;
Some cried The Covenant, instead
Of pudding-pies and ginger-bread;
And some for brooms, old boots, and shoes,
Bawled out to purge the Commons house;
Instead of kitchen-stuff, some cry
A gospel-preaching ministry;
And some for old suits, coats, or cloak,
No Surplices nor Service-book;
A strange harmonious inclination
Of all degrees to reformation.
And is this all? Is this the end
To which these carr'ings on did tend? . . .
So say the wicked—and will you
Make that sarcasmus scandal true,
By running after dogs and bears,
Beasts more unclean than calves or steers?
Have powerful preachers plied their tongues,
And laid themselves out, and their lungs;

12—2

Used all means, both direct and sin'ster,
I' th' pow'r of gospel-preaching min'ster?
Have they invented tones, to win
The women, and make them draw in
The men, as Indians with a female
Tame elephant inveigle the male?
Have they told Prov'dence what it must do,
Whom to avoid, and whom to trust to;
Discovered th' Enemy's design,
And which way best to countermine;
Prescribed what ways he hath to work,
Or it will ne'er advance the kirk?
Told it the news o' th' last express,
And after good or bad success
Made prayers, not so like petitions,
As overtures and propositions,
Such as the army did present
To their creator, the parliament;
In which they freely will confess,
They will not, cannot acquiesce,
Unless the work be carried on
In the same way they have begun,
By setting church and common-weal
All on a flame, bright as their zeal,
On which the saints were all a-gog,
And all this for a bear and dog?

From Part II., Canto I.

'I GRANT,' quoth he, ' wealth is a great
Provocative to amorous heat:
It is all philtres and high diet
That makes love rampant, and to fly out:
'Tis beauty always in the flower,
That buds and blossoms at fourscore:

'Tis that by which the sun and moon,
At their own weapons, are out-done :
That makes knights-errant fall in trances,
And lay about 'em in romances.
'Tis virtue, wit, and worth, and all
That men divine and sacred call :
For what is worth in any thing,
But so much money as 'twill bring ?'

From Part II., Canto II.

'TIS strange how some men's tempers suit,
Like bet and brandy, with dispute,
That for their own opinions stand fast,
Only to have them clawed and canvast ;
That keep their consciences in cases,
As fiddlers do their crowds and bases,
Ne'er to be used, but when they're bent
To play a fit for argument ;
Make true and false, unjust and just,
Of no use but to be discussed ;
Dispute and set a paradox,
Like a strait boot, upon the stocks,
And stretch it more unmercifully
Than Helmont, Montaigne, White, or Tully.
So th' ancient Stoics, in their porch,
With fierce dispute maintained their church,
Beat out their brains in fight and study,
To prove that virtue is a body :
That *bonum* is an animal,
Made good with stout polemic brawl ;
In which some hundreds on the place
Were slain outright, and many a face
Retrenched of nose, and eyes, and beard,
To maintain what their sect averred. . . .

'Why should not conscience have vacation
As well as other courts o' th' nation ?
Have equal power to adjourn,
Appoint appearance and return ?
And make as nice distinctions serve
To split a case, as those that carve,
Invoking cuckolds' names, hit joints ?
Why should not tricks as slight, do points ?
Is not th' high-court of justice sworn
To judge that law that serves their turn ?
Make their own jealousies high-treason,
And fix them whomso'er they please on ?
Cannot the learned counsel there
Make laws in any shape appear ?
Mould 'em as witches do their clay,
When they make pictures to destroy ?
And vex them into any form
That fits their purpose to do harm ?
Rack 'em until they do confess,
Impeach of treason whom they please,
And most perfidiously condemn
Those that engaged their lives for them ?
And yet do nothing in their own sense,
But what they ought by oath and conscience.
Can they not juggle, and with slight
Conveyance play with wrong and right ;
And sell their blasts of wind as dear,
As Lapland witches bottled air ?
Will not fear, favour, bribe, and grudge,
The same case several ways adjudge ?
As seamen with the self-same gale
Will several different courses sail ;
As when the sea breaks o'er its bounds,
And overflows the level grounds,
Those banks and dams, that, like a screen,
Did keep it out, now keep it in ;
So when tyrannical usurpation

Invades the freedom of a nation,
The laws o' th' land, that were intended
To keep it out, are made defend it.
Does not in chancery every man swear
What makes best for him in his answer?
Is not the winding up of witnesses
And nicking more than half the business?
For witnesses, like watches, go
Just as they're set, too fast or slow;
And where in conscience they're strait-laced,
'Tis ten to one that side is cast.
Do not your juries give their verdict
As if they felt the cause, not heard it?
And as they please, make matter o' fact
Run all on one side, as they're packed?
Nature has made man's breast no windores,
To publish what he does within doors;
Nor what dark secrets there inhabit,
Unless his own rash folly blab it.
If oaths can do a man no good
In his own business, why they should
In other matters do him hurt
I think there's little reason for 't.
He that imposes an oath makes it,
Not he that for convenience takes it:
Then how can any man be said
To break an oath he never made?
These reasons may perhaps look oddly
To th' wicked, though they evince the godly;
But if they will not serve to clear
My honour, I am ne'er the near.
Honour is like that glassy bubble
That finds philosophers such trouble;
Whose least part cracked, the whole does fly,
And wits are cracked to find out why!'
　Quoth Ralpho, ' Honour's but a word
To swear by only, in a lord:

In other men 'tis but a huff
To vapour with, instead of proof :
That, like a wen, looks big and swells,
Insenseless, and just nothing else.'

From Part III., Canto I.

WHILE thus the lady talked, the knight
Turned th' outside of his eyes to white,
As men of inward light are wont
To turn their optics in upon 't. . . .
Quoth she, ' There are no bargains driven,
Nor marriages clapped up in heaven ;
And that's the reason, as some guess,
There is no heaven in marriages—
Two things that naturally press
Too narrowly, to be at ease.
Their business there is only love,
Which marriage is not like t' improve.
Love, that's too gen'rous t'abide
To be against its nature tied :
For where 'tis of itself inclined,
It breaks loose when it is confined,
And, like the soul, its harbourer,
Debarred the freedom of the air,
Disdains against its will to stay,
But struggles out, and flies away,
And therefore never can comply
T' endure the matrimonial tie,
That binds the female and the male,
Where the one is but the other's bail—
Like Roman gaolers, when they slept
Chained to the prisoners they kept ;
Of which the true and faithfull'st lover
Gives best security to suffer.

Marriage is but a beast, some say,
That carries double in foul way,
And therefore 'tis not to b' admired,
It should so suddenly be tired ;
A bargain at a venture made
Between two partners in a trade,
For what's inferred by t'have and t'hold,
But something past away, and sold ?
That, as it makes but one of two,
Reduces all things else as low,
And at the best is but a mart
Between the one and th' other part,
That on the marriage-day is paid,
Or hour of death, the bet is laid.

*From the 'Satire Upon the Weakness and Misery of
Man.'*

OUR pains are real things, and all
Our pleasures but fantastical ;
Diseases of their own accord,
But cures come difficult and hard.
Our noblest piles and stateliest rooms
Are but outhouses to our tombs ;
Cities, though e'er so great and brave,
But mere warehouses to the grave.
Our bravery's but a vain disguise
To hide us from the world's dull eyes,
The remedy of a defect
With which our nakedness is deckt ;
Yet makes us swell with pride, and boast
As if we'd gain'd by being lost.

JOHN OLDHAM [1653-1683].

From Satire II. upon the Jesuits [1679].

THESE are the Janizaries of the Cause,
The Life-Guard of the Roman Sultan, chose
To break the Force of Huguenots and Foes.
The Churche's Hawkers in Divinity,
Who, 'stead of Lace and Ribbons, Doctrine cry:
Rome's Strollers, who survey each Continent,
Its Trinkets and Commodities do vent,
Export the Gospel, like mere Ware for Sale,
And truck'd for Indigo and Cochineal,
As the known Factors here, the Brethren, once
Swopt Christ about for Bodkins, Rings, and Spoons.
  * * * * *
It pitied holy Mother Church to see
A world so drown'd in gross Idolatry;
It griev'd to see such goodly Nations hold
Bad Errors and unpardonable gold.
Strange, what a fervent *Z*eal can Coin infuse—
What Charity Pieces of Eight[1] produce!
So you were chosen the fittest to reclaim
The Pagan World, and giv't a Christian Name,
And great was the Success; whole Myriads stood
At Font, and were baptiz'd in their own Blood.
Millions of Souls were hurl'd from hence to burn
Before their Time, be damn'd before their Turn.
 Yet these were in Compassion sent to Hell,
The rest reserv'd in Spite, and worse to feel,
Compell'd, instead of Fiends, to worship you,
The more inhuman Devils of the two.
Rare way, and Method of Conversion this,
To make your Votaries your Sacrifice.
If to destroy be Reformation thought,

[1] Dollars.

A Plague as well might the good Work have
    wrought.
  Now see we why your Founder, weary grown,
Would lay his former trade of Killing down;
He found 'twas dull, he found a Crown would be
A fitter Case and Badge of Cruelty.
Each snivling Hero Seas of Blood can spill,
When Wrongs provoke, and Honour bids him Kill.
Give me your through-pac'd Rogue, who scorns to be
Prompted by poor Revenge, or Injury,
But does it of true inbred Cruelty;
Your cool and sober Murderer, who prays
And stabs at the same time, who one hand has
Stretch'd up to Heaven, t'other to make the pass.
  So the late Saints of blessed Memory,
Cut Throats in godly pure Sincerity,
And with uplifted Hands and Eyes devout,
Said Grace and carv'd a slaughter'd Monarch out.

From Satire III. upon the Jesuits.

NEXT for Religion, learn what's fit to take,
How small a Dram does the just Compound make,
As much as is by the crafty Statesmen worn
For Fashion only, or to serve a Turn:
To bigot Fools its idle Practice leave,
Think it enough the empty Form to have;
The outward Show is seemly, cheap, and light,
The Substance cumbersome, of Cost, and Weight:
The Rabble judge by what appears to th' Eye,
None, or but few, the Thoughts within descry,
Make't you an Engine to ambitious Pow'r
To stalk behind, and hit your Mark moie sure.
A Cloak to cover well-hid Knavery,
Like it, when us'd, to be with Ease thrown by.

A shifting Card, by which your Course to steer,
And taught with every changing Wind to veer,
Let no nice, holy, conscientious Ass
Amongst your better Company find Place,
Me, and your whole Foundation to disgrace ;
Let Truth be banish'd, ragged Virtue fly,
And poor, unprofitable Honesty ;
Weak Idols, who their wretched Slaves betray :
To every Rook and every Knave a Prey.

From Satire IV. upon the Jesuits.

ONE undertakes by Scale of miles to tell
The Bounds, Dimensions, and Extent of Hell ;
How far and wide th' Infernal Monarch reigns,
How many German Leagues his Realm contains ;
Who are his Ministers, pretends to know,
And all their several Offices below ;
How many Chaldrons he each Year expends
In Coals for roasting Huguenots and Fiends,
And with as much Exactness states the Case,
As if he 'ad been Surveyor of the Place.

From ' A Satire addressed to a Friend that is about to leave the University.'

SOME think themselves exalted to the Sky,
If they light in some noble Family :
Diet, an Horse, and thirty Pounds a Year,
Besides th' Advantage of his Lordship's Ear,
The Credit of the Business and the State,
Are things, that in a Youngster's Sense, sound great.

Little th' unexperienc'd Wretch does know,
What Slavery he oft must undergo :
Who, tho' in silken Scarf and Cassock drest,
Wears but a gayer Livery at best ;
When Dinner calls, the Implement must wait
With holy Words, to consecrate the Meat :
But hold it for a Favour seldom known,
If he be deign'd the Honour to sit down.
Soon as the Tarts appear, Sir Crape withdraw!
Those Dainties are not for a spiritual Maw :
Observe your Distance, and be sure to stand
Hard by the Cistern, with your Cap in Hand ;
There for Diversion you may pick your Teeth,
Till the kind Voider[1] comes for your Relief :
For meer Board-wages, such their Freedom sell
Slaves to an Hour, and Vassals to a Bell :
And if th' Enjoyment of one Day be stole,
They are but Pris'ners out upon Parole :
Always the Marks of Slavery remain,
And they, tho' loose, still drag about their Chain.
And where's the mighty Prospect, after all,
A Chaplainship serv'd up, and seven Years Thrall ?
The menial Thing, perhaps, for a Reward,
Is to some slender Benefice preferr'd,
With this Proviso bound, that he must wed
My Lady's antiquated Waiting-maid,
In Dressing only skill'd, and Marmalade.
Let others who such Meannesses can brook,
Strike Countenance to ev'ry great Man's Look :
Let those that have a Mind, turn Slaves to eat,
And live contented by another's Plate :
I rate my Freedom higher, nor will I
For Food and Rayment truck my Liberty.
But if I must to my last Shifts be put,
To fill a Bladder, and twelve Yards of Gut ;
Rather with counterfeited wooden Leg,

[1] Basket.

And my right Arm ty'd up, I'll chuse to beg:
I'll rather chuse to starve at large, than be
The gawdiest Vassal to Dependency.
'T has ever been the Top of my Desires,
The utmost Height to which my Wish aspires,
That Heav'n would bless me with a small Estate,
Where I might find a close obscure Retreat ;
There, free from Noise and all ambitious Ends,
Enjoy a few choice Books, and fewer Friends.
Lord of myself, accountable to none,
But to my Conscience, and my God alone :
There live unthought of, and unheard of die,
And grudge Mankind my very Memory.
And since the Blessing is (I find) too great
For me to wish for, and expect of Fate :
Yet maugre all the Spite of Destiny,
My Thoughts and Actions are, and shall be free.

JOHN DRYDEN [1631-1700].

From the ' Satire on the Dutch ' [1662].

As needy gallants, in the scrivener's hands,
Court the rich knaves that gripe their mortgag'd
    lands;
The first fat buck of all the season's sent,
And keeper takes no fee in compliment ;
The dotage of some Englishmen is such,
To fawn on those who ruin them, the Dutch.
They shall have all, rather than make a war
With those, who of the same religion are.
The Straits, the Guiney-trade, the herrings too ;
Nay, to keep friendship, they shall pickle you.
Some are resolved not to find out the cheat,
But, cuckold-like, love them that do the feat.

What injuries soc'er upon us fall,
Yet still the same religion answers all.
Religion wheedled us to civil war,
Drew English blood, and Dutchmen's now would
        spare.
Be gull'd no longer ; for you'll find it true,
They have no more religion, faith ! than you.
Interest's the god they worship in their state,
And we, I take it, have not much of that.
Well monarchies may own religion's name,
But states are atheists in their very frame.
They share a sin ; and such proportions fall,
That, like a stink, 'tis nothing to them all.
Think on their rapine, falsehood, cruelty,
And that what once they were, they still would be.
To one well born th' affront is worse and more,
When he's abus'd and baffled by a boor.
With an ill grace the Dutch their mischiefs do ;
They've both ill nature and ill manners too.
Well may they boast themselves an ancient nation ;
For they were bred ere manners were in fashion :
And their new commonwealth has set them free
Only from honour and civility.

From ' An Essay on Satire' [1669].

ROCHESTER I despise for want of wit,
Though thought to have a tail and cloven feet ;
For while he mischief means to all mankind,
Himself alone the ill effects does find :
And so like witches justly suffers shame,
Whose harmless malice is so much the same.
False are his words, affected is his wit ;
So often he does aim, so seldom hit ;

To every face he cringes while he speaks,
But when the back is turn'd the head he breaks ;
Mean in each action, lewd in every limb,
Manners themselves are mischievous in him :
A proof that chance alone makes every creature
A very Killigrew without good nature.
For what a Bessus has he always liv'd,
And his own kickings notably contriv'd ?
For there's the folly that's still mix'd with fear,
Cowards more blows than any hero bear ;
Of fighting sparks some may their pleasures say,
But 'tis a bolder thing to run away :
The world may well forgive him all his ill,
For every fault does prove his penance still :
Falsely he falls into some dangerous noose,
And then as meanly labours to get loose ;
A life so infamous is better quitting,
Spent in base injury and low submitting.
I'd like to have left out his poetry;
Forgot by all almost as well as me.
Sometimes he has some humour, never wit,
And if it rarely, very rarely, hit,
'Tis under so much nasty rubbish laid,
To find it out's the cinder woman's trade ;
Who for the wretched remnants of a fire
Must toil all day in ashes and in mire.
So lewdly dull his idle works appear,
The wretched texts deserve no comment here ;
Where one poor thought sometimes left all alone,
For a whole page of dulness must atone.[1]

---

[1] The publication of this satire probably occasioned the
beating of Dryden in Rose Street, Covent Garden, by ruffians
hired by Rochester. Mulgrave says that Dryden 'was praised
and beaten for another's rhymes.'

From ' *Absalom and Achitophel* ' [1681],¹ *Part I.*

So several factions from this first ferment
Work up to foam, and threat the government.²
Some by their friends, more by themselves thought
    wise,
Oppos'd the power to which they could not rise.
Some had in courts been great, and thrown from
    thence,
Like fiends were harden'd in impenitence.
Some by their monarch's fatal mercy, grown
From pardon'd rebels kinsmen to the throne,
Were raised in power and public office high ;
Strong bands, if bands ungrateful men could tie.
Of these the false Achitophel was first ;
A name to all succeeding ages curst :
For close designs, and crooked councils fit ;
Sagacious, bold, and turbulent of wit ; ∠
Restless, unfix'd in principles and place ;
In power unpleas'd, impatient of disgrace ;
A fiery soul, which, working out its way,
Fretted the pigmy-body to decay,
And o'er-inform'd the tenement of clay.
A daring pilot in extremity ;
Pleas'd with the danger, when the waves went high
He sought the storms : but for a calm unfit,
Would steer too nigh the sands to boast his wit.
Great wits are sure to madness near allied,
And thin partitions do their bounds divide ;
Else why should he, with wealth and honour blest,
Refuse his age the needful hours of rest ?

---

¹ A satire, under Biblical names, upon the intrigues of
Shaftesbury (Achitophel) and Monmouth (Absalom) against
the Catholic and Court interest.
² The Popish Plot, as disclosed by the infamous Titus Oates.

Punish a body which he could not please ;
Bankrupt of life, yet prodigal of ease ?
And all to leave what with his toil he won,
To that unfeather'd two-legg'd thing, a son ;
Got, while his soul did huddled notions try ;
And born a shapeless lump, like anarchy.
In friendship false, implacable in hate ;
Resolv'd to ruin or to rule the State.
To compass this the triple bond he broke ;[1]
The pillars of the public safety shook ;
And fitted Israel for a foreign yoke :
Then seized with fear, yet still affecting fame,
Usurp'd a patriot's all-atoning name.
So easy still it proves in factious times,
With public zeal to cancel private crimes.
How safe is treason, and how sacred ill,
Where none can sin against the people's will,
Where crowds can wink, and no offence be known,
Since in another's guilt they find their own !
Yet fame deserv'd no enemy can grudge ;
The statesman we abhor, but praise the judge.
In Israel's court ne'er sat an Abethdin
With more discerning eyes, or hands more clean,
Unbrib'd, unsought, the wretched to redress.
Swift of dispatch, and easy of access,
Oh ! had he been content to serve the crown,
With virtues only proper to the gown ;
Or had the rankness of the soil been freed
From cockle, that oppress'd the noble seed ;
David for him his tuneful harp had strung,
And heaven had wanted one immortal song.

*   *   *   *   *

To further this,[2] Achitophel unites
The malcontents of all the Israelites :
Whose differing parties he could wisely join,
For several ends, to serve the same design.

[1] Triple Alliance of 1667.   [2] The plot.

The best, and of the princes some were such,
Who thought the power of monarchy too much ;
Mistaken men, and patriots in their hearts ;
Not wicked, but seduc'd by impious arts.
By these the springs of property were bent,
And wound so high, they cracked the government.
The next for interest sought to embroil the state,
To sell their duty at a dearer rate ;
And make their Jewish markets of the throne ;
Pretending public good to serve their own.
Others thought kings a useless heavy load,
Who cost too much, and did too little good.
These were for laying honest David by,
On principles of pure good husbandry.
With them join'd all the haranguers of the throng,
That thought to get preferment by the tongue.
Who follow next a double danger bring,
Not only hating David,[1] but the king ;
The Solymæan rout,[2] well vers'd of old,
In godly faction, and in treason bold ;
Cowering and quaking at a conqueror's sword ;
But lofty to a lawful prince restored ;
Saw with disdain an Ethnic[3] plot begun,
And scorn'd the Jebusites[4] to be outdone.
Hot Levites headed these ; who pull'd before
From the ark, which in the Judges' day they bore,
Resum'd their cant, and with a zealous cry
Pursued their old beloved Theocracy :
Where Sanhedrin and priest enslav'd the nation,
And justified their spoils by inspiration :
For who so fit to reign as Aaron's race,
If once dominion they could found in grace !
These led the pack ; though not of surest scent,
Yet deepest mouth'd against the government.
A numerous host of dreaming saints succeed,

[1] Charles II.   [2] London rebels.
[3] Popish plot.   [4] Papists.

Of the true old enthusiastic breed :
'Gainst form and order they their power employ,
Nothing to build, and all things to destroy.
But far more numerous was the herd of such,
Who think too little, and who talk too much.
These out of mere instinct, they knew not why,
Ador'd their fathers' God and property ;
And by the same blind benefit of fate
The devil and the Jebusite did hate :
Born to be sav'd, even in their own despite,
Because they could not help believing right.
Such were the tools : but a whole Hydra more
Remains of sprouting heads too long to score.
Some of their chiefs were princes of the land ;
In the first rank of these did Zimri[1] stand ;
A man so various, that he seem'd to be
Not one, but all mankind's epitome :
Stiff in opinions, always in the wrong ;
Was every thing by starts, and nothing long ;
But, in the course of one revolving moon,
Was chymist, fiddler, statesman, and buffoon ;
Then all for women, painting, rhyming, drinking,
Besides ten thousand freaks that died in thinking.
Blest madman, who could every hour employ,
With something new to wish, or to enjoy !
Railing and praising were his usual themes ;
And both, to show his judgment, in extremes :
So over violent, or over civil,
That every man with him was God or Devil.
In squandering wealth was his peculiar art ;
Nothing went unrewarded but desert.
Beggar'd by fools, whom still he found too late ;
He had his jest, and they had his estate.
He laugh'd himself from court ; then sought relief
By forming parties, but could ne'er be chief :
For, spite of him, the weight of business fell

[1] Buckingham.

On Absalom and wise Achitophel ;
Thus, wicked but in will, of means bereft,
He left not faction, but of that was left.

  *   *   *   *   *

Shimei,[1] whose youth did early promise bring
Of zeal to God, and hatred to his king,
Did wisely from expensive sins refrain,
And never broke the sabbath, but for gain ;
Nor was he ever known an oath to vent,
Or curse, unless against the government.
Thus reaping wealth, by the most ready way
Among the Jews,[2] which was to cheat and pray ;
The city, to reward his pious hate
Against his master, chose him magistrate.
His hand a vare of justice did uphold ;
His neck was loaded with a chain of gold.
During his office treason was no crime ;
The sons of Belial had a glorious time :
For Shimei, though not prodigal of pelf,
Yet lov'd his wicked neighbour as himself.
When two or three were gather'd to declaim
Against the monarch of Jerusalem,
Shimei was always in the midst of them :
And if they curs'd the king when he was by,
Would rather curse than break good company.
If any durst his factious friends accuse,
He pack'd a jury of dissenting Jews ;
Whose fellow-feeling in the godly cause
Would free the suffering saint from human laws.
For laws are only made to punish those
Who serve the king, and to protect his foes.
If any leisure time he had from power,
(Because 'tis sin to misemploy an hour),
His business was, by writing to persuade,
That kings were useless, and a clog to trade ;

[1] Slingsby Bethel, a Sheriff of the City of London.
[2] English.

And that his noble style he might refine,
No Rechabite more shunn'd the fumes of wine.
Chaste were his cellars, and his shrival board
The grossness of a city feast abhorr'd:
His cooks with long disuse their trade forgot;
Cool was his kitchen, though his brains were hot.
Such frugal virtue malice may accuse;
But sure 'twas necessary to the Jews:
For towns, once burnt, such magistrates require
As dare not tempt God's providence by fire.
With spiritual food he fed his servants well,
But free from flesh that made the Jews rebel:
And Moses' Laws he held in more account,
For forty days of fasting in the mount.
To speak the rest who better are forgot
Would tire a well-breath'd witness of the plot.
Yet, Corah,[1] thou shalt from oblivion pass;
Erect thyself, thou monumental brass,
High as the serpent of thy metal made,
While nations stand secure beneath thy shade.
What, though his birth was base, yet comets rise
From earthly vapours, ere they shine in skies.
Prodigious actions may as well be done
By weavers' issue, as by prince's son.
This arch-attestor for the public good
By that one deed ennobles all his blood.
Who ever ask'd the witness's high race,
Whose oath with martyrdom did Stephen grace?
Ours was a Levite, and as times went then,
His tribe were God Almighty's gentlemen.
Sunk were his eyes, his voice was harsh and loud,
Sure signs he neither choleric was nor proud:
His long chin prov'd his wit; his saint-like grace
A church vermilion, and a Moses' face.
His memory, miraculously great,
Could plots, exceeding man's belief, repeat;

[1] Dr. Oates.

Which therefore cannot be accounted lies,
For human wit could never such devise.
Some future truths are mingled in his book;
But where the witness fail'd, the prophet spoke:
Some things like visionary flights appear;
The spirit caught him up the Lord knows where:
And gave him his rabbinical degree,
Unknown to foreign university.
His judgment yet his memory did excel;
Which piec'd his wondrous evidence so well,
And suited to the temper of the times,
Then groaning under Jebusitic crimes.
Let Israel's foes suspect his heavenly call,
And rashly judge his writ apocryphal;
Our laws for such affronts have forfeits made:
He takes his life who takes away his trade.
Were I myself in witness Corah's place,
The wretch who did me such a dire disgrace
Should whet my memory, though once forgot,
To make him an appendix of my plot.
His zeal to heaven made him his prince despise
And load his person with indignities.
But zeal peculiar privilege affords,
Indulging latitude to deeds and words:
And Corah might for Agag's[1] murder call,
In terms as coarse as Samuel us'd to Saul.
What others in his evidence did join,
The best that could be had for love or coin,
In Corah's own predicament will fall:
For witness is a common name to all.

[1] Sir E. Godfrey.

From Part II. [1682].

DOEG,[1] though without knowing how and why,
Made still a blundering kind of melody;
Spur'd boldly on, and dash'd through thick and thin,
Through sense and nonsense, never out nor in;
Free from all meaning, whether good or bad,
And, in one word, heroically mad:
He was too warm on picking-work to dwell,
But fagotted his notions as they fell,
And if they rhym'd and rattled, all was well.
Spiteful he is not, though he wrote a satire,
For still there goes some thinking to ill-nature:
He needs no more than birds and beasts to think,
All his occasions are to eat and drink.
If he call rogue and rascal from a garret,
He means you no more mischief than a parrot,
The words for friend and foe alike were made,
To fetter 'em in verse is all his trade.
Let him be gallows free by my consent,
And nothing suffer since he nothing meant;
Hanging supposes human soul and reason,
This animal's below committing treason;
Shall he be hang'd who never could rebel?
That's a preferment for Achitophel.
Railing in other men may be a crime,
But ought to pass as mere instinct in him:
Instinct he follows, and no farther knows,
For to write verse with him is to transprose.
'Twere pity treason at his door to lay,
Who makes heaven's gate a lock to its own key:
Let him rail on, let his invective muse
Have four-and-twenty letters to abuse,
Which if he jumbles to one line of sense,
Indict him of a capital offence.

[1] Elkanah Settle. He had replied to Part I. with the ' Achitophel Transprosed,' referred to below.

In fireworks give him leave to vent his spite,
Those are the only serpents he can write;
The height of his ambition is, we know,
But to be master of a puppet-show.
On that one stage his works may yet appear,
And a month's harvest keeps him all the year.
   Now stop your noses, readers, all and some,
For here's a tun of midnight work to come,
Og,[1] from a treason-tavern rolling home.
Round as a globe, and liquor'd every chink,
Goodly and great he sails behind the link;
With all this bulk there's nothing lost in Og,
For every inch that is not fool is rogue;
A monstrous mass of foul corrupted matter,
As all the devils had spew'd to make the batter.
When wine has giv'n him courage to blaspheme,
He curses God, but God before curst him;
And if man could have reason, none has more,
That made his paunch so rich, and him so poor.
With wealth he was not trusted, for heaven knew
What 'twas of old to pamper up a Jew;
To what would he on quail and pheasant swell,
That e'en on tripe and carrion could rebel?
But though Heaven made him poor (with reverence
     speaking),
He never was a poet of God's making;
The midwife laid her hand on his thick skull,
With this prophetic blessing—Be thou dull;
Drink, swear, and roar, forbear no lewd delight
Fit for thy bulk, do anything but write:
Thou art of lasting make, like thoughtless men,
A strong nativity—but for the pen;
Eat opium, mingle arsenic in thy drink,
Still thou mayst live, avoiding pen and ink.
I see, I see, 'tis counsel given in vain,
For treason botch'd in rhyme will be thy bane,

       [1] Shadwell.

Rhyme is the rock on which thou art to wreck,
'Tis fatal to thy fame and to thy neck :
Why should thy metre good king David blast ?
A psalm of his will surely be thy last.
Dar'st thou presume in verse to meet thy foes,
Thou whom the penny pamphlet foil'd in prose ?
Doeg, whom God for mankind's mirth has made,
O'ertops thy talent in thy very trade ;
Doeg to thee, thy paintings are so coarse,
A poet is, though he's the poet's horse.
A double noose thou on thy neck dost pull,
For writing treason, and for writing dull ;
To die for faction is a common evil,
But to be hang'd for nonsense is the devil :
Hadst thou the glories of thy king express'd,
Thy praises had been satire at the best ;
But thou in clumsy verse, unlick'd, unpointed,
Hast shamefully defied the Lord's anointed :
I will not rake the dunghill of thy crimes,
For who would read thy life that reads thy rhymes ?
But of King David's foes, be this the doom,
May all be like the young man Absalom ;
And, for my foes, may this their blessing be,
To talk like Doeg, and to write like thee.

From ' The Medal.'

OF all our antic sights and pageantry,
Which English idiots run in crowds to see,
The Polish Medal bears the prize alone :
A monster, more the favourite of the town
Than either fairs or theatres have shown.
Never did art so well with nature strive ;
Nor ever idol seem'd so much alive :
So like the man[1]; so golden to the sight,

[1] Shaftesbury.

So base within, so counterfeit and light.
One side is fill'd with title and with face ;
And, lest the king should want a regal place,
On the reverse, a tower the town surveys ;
O'er which our mounting Sun his beams displays.
The word, pronounc'd aloud by shrieval voice,
Laetamur, which, in Polish, is rejoice.
The day, month, year, to the great act are join'd,
And a new canting holiday design'd.
Five days he sat for every cast and look,
Four more than God to finish Adam took.
But who can tell what essence angels are,
Or how long Heaven was making Lucifer ?
Oh ! could the style that copied every grace,
And plough'd such furrows for a eunuch face—
Could it have form'd his ever-changing will,
The various piece had tir'd the graver's skill !
A martial hero first, with early care,
Blown, like a pigmy by the winds, to war.
A beardless chief, a rebel, ere a man :
So young his hatred to his prince began.
Next this (how wildly will ambition steer !),
A vermin wriggling in the Usurper's ear,
Bartering his venal wit for sums of gold,
He cast himself into the saint-like mould ;
Groan'd, sigh'd, and pray'd while godliness was gain,
The loudest bagpipe of the squeaking train.
But, as 'tis hard to cheat a juggler's eyes,
His open lewdness he could ne'er disguise.
There split the saint : for hypocritic zeal
Allows no sins but those it can conceal.
Whoring to scandal gives too large a scope :
Saints must not trade, but they may interlope.
The ungodly principle was all the same ;
But a gross cheat betrays his partner's game.
Beside, their pace was formal, grave, and slack ;
His nimble wit outran the heavy pack.

Yet still he found his fortune at a stay,
Whole droves of blockheads choking up his way;
They took, but not rewarded, his advice :
Villain and wit exact a double price.
Power was his aim; but, thrown from that pretence,
The wretch turn'd loyal in his own defence,
And malice reconcil'd him to his prince.
Him, in the anguish of his soul, he serv'd,
Rewarded faster still than he deserv'd.
Behold him now exalted into trust,
His counsel's oft convenient, seldom just.
E'en in the most sincere advice he gave,
He had a grudging still to be a knave.
The frauds he learn'd in his fanatic years
Made him uneasy in his lawful gears.
At best as little honest as he could,
And, like white witches, mischievously good.
To his first bias longingly he leans,
And rather would be great by wicked means.

     *   *   *   *   *

He preaches to the crowd that power is lent,
But not convey'd to kingly government ;
That claims successive bear no binding force,
That coronation oaths are things of course ;
Maintains the multitude can never err,
And sets the people in the Papal chair.
The reason's obvious, interest never lies—
The most have still their interest in their eyes :
The power is always theirs, and power is ever wise.
Almighty crowd, thou shortenest all dispute,
Power is thy essence, wit thy attribute !
Nor faith nor reason make thee at a stay,
That leap'st o'er all eternal truths in thy Pindaric
    way !
Athens, no doubt, did righteously decide,
When Phocion and when Socrates were tried ;
As righteously they did those dooms repent ;

Still they were wise whatever way they went.
Crowds err not, though to both extremes they run :
To kill the father and recall the son.
Some think the fools were most as times went then,
But now the world's o'erstock'd with prudent men.
The common cry is e'en religion's test :
The Turk's is at Constantinople best ;
Idols in India ; Popery at Rome ;
And our own worship only true at home :
And true but for the time : 'tis hard to know
How long we please it shall continue so.
This side to-day, and that to-morrow burns ;
So all are God-a'mighties in their turns.
A tempting doctrine, plausible and new.
What fools our fathers were, if this be true !

From 'The Hind and the Panther.'

BISHOP BURNET.

A PORTLY prince, and goodly to the sight,
He seem'd a son of Anak for his height,
Like those whom stature did to crowns prefer—
Black-brow'd, and bluff, like Homer's Jupiter,
Broad-back'd, and brawny-built for love's delight :
A prophet form'd to make a female proselyte.
A theologue more by need than genial bent,
By breeding sharp, by nature confident.
Interest in all his actions was discern'd ;
More learn'd than honest, more a wit than learn'd ;
Or forc'd by fear, or by his profit led,
Or both conjoin'd, his native clime he fled ;
But brought the virtues of his heaven along :
A fair behaviour, and a fluent tongue.
And yet with all his arts he could not thrive—

The most unlucky parasite alive.
Loud praises to prepare his paths he sent,
And then himself pursued his compliment ;
But by reverse of fortune chas'd away,
His gifts no longer than their author stay.
He shakes the dust against the ungrateful race,
And leaves the stench of ordures in the place.
Oft has he flatter'd and blasphem'd the same ;
For in his rage he spares no Sovereign's name.
The hero and the tyrant change their style
By the same measure that they frown or smile.
When well receiv'd by hospitable foes,
The kindness he returns is to expose ;
For courtesies, though undeserv'd and great,
No gratitude in felon-minds beget ;
As tribute to his wit, the churl receives the treat.
His praise of foes is venomously nice—
So touch'd, it turns a virtue to a vice ;
A Greek, and bountiful, forewarns us twice.
Seven sacraments he wisely does disown,
Because he knows Confession stands for one ;
Where sins to sacred silence are convey'd,
And not for fear, or love, to be betray'd.
But he, uncall'd, his patron to control,
Divulg'd the secret whispers of his soul ;
Stood forth the accusing Satan of his crimes,
And offer'd to the Moloch of the times,
Prompt to assail, and careless of defence,
Invulnerable in his impudence,
He dares the world ; and, eager of a name,
He thrusts about, and justles into fame.
Frontless, and satire-proof, he scours the streets,
And runs an Indian-muck at all he meets.
So fond of loud report, that, not to miss
Of being known (his last and utmost bliss),
He rather would be known for what he is.

From ' MacFlecknoe.'

ALL things human are subject to decay,
And when fate summons, monarchs must obey.
This Flecknoe[1] found, who, like Augustus, young
Was call'd to empire, and had governed long ;
In prose and verse, was own'd without dispute,
Through all the realms of Nonsense, absolute.
This aged prince, now flourishing in peace,
And bless'd with issue of a large increase ;
Worn out with business did at length debate
To settle the succession of the state :
And, pondering which of all his sons was fit
To reign, and wage immortal war with wit,
Cried, ' 'Tis resolv'd ; for nature pleads, that he
Should only rule who most resembles me.
Shadwell alone my perfect image bears,
Mature in dulness from his tender years ;
Shadwell alone, of all my sons, is he
Who stands confirm'd in full stupidity.
The rest to some faint meaning make pretence,
But Shadwell never deviates into sense .
Some beams of wit on other souls may fall,
Strike through, and make a lucid interval ;
But Shadwell's genuine night admits no ray,
His rising fogs prevail upon the day.
Beside, his goodly fabric fills the eye,
And seems design'd for thoughtless majesty :
Thoughtless as monarch oaks, that shade the plain
And spread in solemn state, supinely reign.
Heywood and Shirley were but types of thee,
Thou last great prophet of tautology.
Even I, a dunce of more renown than they,
Was sent before but to prepare thy way ;
And, coarsely clad in Norwich drugget, came
To teach the nations in thy greater name.'
      *   *   *   *   *

[1] An Irish priest and poet.

The hoary prince in majesty appear'd,
High on a throne of his own labours rear'd.
At his right hand our young Ascanius sate,
Rome's other hope, and pillar of the state.
His brows thick fogs, instead of glories, grace,
And lambent dulness play'd around his face.
As Hannibal did to the altars come,
Swore by his sire, a mortal foe to Rome;
So Shadwell swore, nor should his vow be vain,
That he till death true dulness would maintain:
And, in his father's right, and realm's defence,
Ne'er to have peace with art, nor truce with sense.

ALEXANDER POPE [1688-1744].

From ' An Essay on Criticism ' [1709].

'Tis hard to say, if greater want of skill
Appear in writing or in judging ill;
But of the two, less dangerous is the offence
To tire our patience than mislead our sense.
Some few in that, but numbers err in this,
Ten censure wrong for one who writes amiss;
A fool might once himself alone expose,
Now one in verse makes many more in prose.
    'Tis with our judgments as our watches, none
Go just alike, yet each believes his own.
In poets as true genius is but rare,
True taste as seldom is the critic's share;
Both must alike from Heaven derive their light,
These born to judge, as well as those to write.
Let such teach others who themselves excel,
And censure freely who have written well.

Authors are partial to their wit, 'tis true,
But are not critics to their judgment too ?

*   *   *   *   *

Of all the causes which conspire to blind
Man's erring judgment, and misguide the mind,
What the weak head with strongest bias rules,
Is pride, the never-failing vice of fools.
Whatever nature has in worth denied,
She gives in large recruits of needful pride ;
For as in bodies, thus in souls, we find
What wants in blood and spirits, swell'd with wind :
Pride, where wit fails, steps in to our defence,
And fills up all the mighty void of sense.
If once right reason drives that cloud away,
Truth breaks upon us with resistless day.
Trust not yourself; but your defects to know
Make use of every friend—and every foe.
A little learning is a dangerous thing :
Drink deep, or taste not the Pierian spring :
There shallow draughts intoxicate the brain,
And drinking largely sobers us again.
Fired at first sight with what the muse imparts,
In fearless youth we tempt the heights of art,
While from the bounded level of our mind,
Short views we take, nor see the lengths behind ;
But more advanced, behold with strange surprise
New distant scenes of endless science rise !
So pleased at first the towering Alps we try,
Mount o'er the vales, and seem to tread the sky,
The eternal snows appear already pass'd,
And the first clouds and mountains seem the last :
But, those attain'd, we tremble to survey
The growing labours of the lengthen'd way,
The increasing prospe t tires our wandering eyes,
Hills peep o'er hills and Alps on Alps arise !

*   *   *   *   *

But most by numbers judge a poet's song,
And smooth or rough, with them, is right or wrong :
In the bright Muse, though thousand charms con-
    spire,
Her voice is all these tuneful fools admire ;
Who haunt Parnassus but to please their ear,
Not mend their minds ; as some to church repair,
Not for the doctrine, but the music there.
These equal syllables alone require,
Though oft the ear the open vowels tire ;
While expletives their feeble aid do join ;
And ten low words oft creep in one dull line :
While they ring round the same unvaried chimes,
With sure returns of still expected rhymes ;
Where'er you find ' the cooling western breeze,'
In the next line, it ' whispers through the trees ' :
If crystal streams ' with pleasing murmurs creep,'
The reader's threaten'd (not in vain) with ' sleep ' :
Then, at the last and only couplet fraught
With some unmeaning thing they call a thought,
A needless Alexandrine ends the song,
That, like a wounded snake, drags its slow length
    along.
   *   *   *   *   *

'Tis best sometimes your censure to restrain,
And charitably let the dull be vain :
Your silence there is better than your spite,
For who can rail so long as they can write ?
Still humming on, their drowsy course they keep
And lash'd so long, like tops, are lash'd asleep.
False steps but help them to renew the race,
As, after stumbling, jades will mend their pace.
What crowds of these, impenitently bold,
In sounds and jingling syllables grown old,
Still run on poets in a raging vein,
Even to the dregs and squeezing of the brain,
Strain out the last dull droppings of their sense,

And rhyme with all the rage of impotence.
Such shameless bards we have; and yet 'tis true,
There are as mad, abandon'd critics too,
The bookful blockhead ignorantly read,
With loads of learned lumber in his head,
With his own tongue still edifies his ears,
And always listening to himself appears.
All books he reads, and all he reads assails,
From Dryden's Fables down to Durfey's Tales.
With him most authors steal their works, or buy;
Garth did not write his own Dispensary.
Name a new play, and he's the poet's friend,
Nay show'd his faults—but when would poets
    mend?
No place so sacred from such fops is barr'd,
Nor is Paul's church more safe than Paul's church-
    yard:
Nay, fly to altars; there they'll talk you dead;
For fools rush in where angels fear to tread.
Distrustful sense with modest caution speaks,
It still looks home, and short excursions makes;
But rattling nonsense in full volleys breaks,
And never shock'd, and never turn'd aside,
Bursts out, resistless, with a thundering tide.

From 'The Rape of the Lock' [1712].

THE SYLPHS.

OUR humbler province is to tend the fair,
Not a less pleasing, though less glorious care;
To save the powder from too rude a gale,
Nor let the imprison'd essences exhale;
To draw fresh colours from the vernal flowers;

14—2

To steal from rainbows ere they drop in showers
A brighter wash ; to curl their waving hairs,
Assist their blushes, and inspire their airs ;
Nay, oft, in dreams, invention we bestow,
To change a flounce, or add a furbelow.
  This day, black omens threat the brightest fair
That e'er deserved a watchful spirit's care ;
Some dire disaster, or by force or slight ;
But what, or where, the fates have wrapt in night.
Whether the nymph shall break Diana's law,
Or some frail China jar receive a flaw ;
Or stain her honour, or her new brocade ;
Forget her prayers, or miss a masquerade ;
Or lose her heart, or necklace, at a ball ;
Or whether Heaven has doom'd that Shock must
    fall.
Haste then, ye Spirits ! to your charge repair :
The fluttering fan be Zephyretta's care ;
The drops to thee, Brillante, we consign ;
And Momentilla, let the watch be thine ;
Do thou, Crispissa, tend her favourite Lock ;
Ariel himself shall be the guard of Shock.
  To fifty chosen sylphs, of special note,
We trust the important charge, the petticoat :
Oft have we known that sevenfold fence to fail,
Though stiff with hoops and arm'd with ribs of
    whale ;
Form a strong line about the silver bound,
And guard the wide circumference around.

From 'An Essay on Man' [1732-34], *Epistle II.*

KNOW thou thyself, presume not God to scan,
The proper study of Mankind is Man.
Placed on this isthmus of a middle state,

A being darkly wise, and rudely great ;
With too much knowledge for the sceptic side,
With too much weakness for the stoic's pride,
He hangs between ; in doubt to act or rest ;
In doubt to deem himself a god or beast ;
In doubt his mind or body to prefer ;
Born but to die, and reasoning but to err ;
Alike in ignorance, his reason such,
Whether he thinks too little or too much ;
Chaos of thought and passion all confused ;
Still by himself abused, or disabused ;
Created half to rise and half to fall ;
Great lord of all things, yet a prey to all ;
Sole judge of truth, in endless error hurled ;
The glory, jest, and riddle of the world !
　Go, wondrous creature ! mount where science guides,
Go, measure earth, weigh air, and state the tides ;
Instruct the planets in what orbs to run,
Correct old Time, and regulate the sun ;
Go, soar with Plato to the empyreal sphere,
To the first good, first perfect, and first fair ;
Or tread the mazy round his followers trod,
And quitting sense call imitating God ;
As Eastern priests in giddy circles run,
And turn their heads to imitate the sun.
Go, teach Eternal Wisdom how to rule,
Then drop into thyself, and be a fool !

From 'Moral Essays' [1732-35], *Epistle II.*

BUT what are these to great Atossa's mind ?
Scarce once herself, by turns all womankind !
Who, with herself, or others, from her birth
Finds all her life one warfare upon earth :
Shines in exposing knaves, and painting fools,

Yet is whate'er she hates and ridicules.
No thought advances, but her eddy brain
Whisks it about, and down it goes again.
Full sixty years the world has been her trade,
The wisest fool much time has ever made.
From loveless youth to unrespected age,
No passion gratified except her rage.
So much the fury still outran the wit,
The pleasure miss'd her, and the scandal hit.
Who breaks with her provokes revenge from hell,
But he's a bolder man who dares be well.
Her every turn with violence pursued,
No more a storm her hate than gratitude :
To that each passion turns, or soon or late ;
Love, if it makes her yield, must make her hate :
Superiors ? death ! and equals ? what a curse !
But an inferior not dependent ? worse.
Offend her, and she knows not to forgive ;
Oblige her, and she'll hate you while you live ;
But die, and she'll adore you—then the bust
And temple rise—then fall again to dust.
Last night her lord was all that's good and great ;
A knave this morning, and his will a cheat.
Strange ! by the means defeated of the ends,
By spirit robb'd of power, by warmth of friends,
By wealth of followers ! without one distress,
Sick of herself through very selfishness !
Atossa, cursed with every granted prayer,
Childless with all her children, wants an heir.
To heirs unknown descends the unguarded store,
Or wanders, heaven directed, to the poor.

     *   *   *   *   *

  Men, some to business, some to pleasure take ;
But every woman is at heart a rake ;
Men, some to quiet, some to public strife ;
But every lady would be queen for life.
  Yet mark the fate of a whole sex of queens !

Power all their end, but beauty all the means :
In youth they conquer with so wild a rage,
As leaves them scarce a subject in their age :
For foreign glory, foreign joy, they roam ;
No thought of peace or happiness at home.
But wisdom's triumph is well-timed retreat,
As hard a science to the fair as great !
Beauties, like tyrants, old and friendless grown,
Yet hate repose, and dread to be alone,
Worn out in public, weary every eye,
Nor leave one sigh behind them when they die.

   *   *   *   *   *

Oh! blest with temper, whose unclouded ray
Can make to-morrow cheerful as to-day ;
She who can love a sister's charms, or hear
Sighs for a daughter with unwounded ear ;
She who ne'er answers till a husband cools,
Or, if she rules him, never shows she rules.
Charms by accepting, by submitting sways,
Yet has her humour most when she obeys ;
Let fops or fortune fly which way they will ;
Disdains all loss of tickets, or codille ;
Spleen, vapours or small-pox, above them all,
And mistress of herself, though china fall.

From ' Moral Essays,' Epistle III.

TO LORD BATHURST.

P. WHO shall decide, when doctors disagree,
And soundest casuists doubt, like you and me ?
You hold the word, from Jove to Momus given,
That man was made the standing jest of Heaven ;
And gold but sent to keep the fools in play,
For some to heap and some to throw away.

But I, who think more highly of our kind,
(And surely Heaven and I are of a mind),
Opine, that Nature, as in duty bound,
Deep hid the shining mischief under ground.
But when by man's audacious labour won,
Flamed forth this rival to its sire, the sun,
Then careful Heaven supplied two sorts of men,
To squander these, and those to hide again.
Like doctors thus, when much dispute has past,
We find our tenets just the same at last.
Both fairly owning, riches, in effect,
No grace of Heaven, or token of the elect ;
Given to the fool, the mad, the vain, the evil,
To Ward, to Waters, Chartres, and the Devil.
    B. What nature wants, commodious gold bestows,
'Tis thus we eat the bread another sows.
    P. But how unequal it bestows, observe,
'Tis thus we riot, while, who sow it, starve :
What nature wants (a phrase I much distrust)
Extends to luxury, extends to lust :
Useful, I grant, it serves what life requires,
But dreadful too, the dark assassin hires.
    B. Trade it may help, society extend.
    P. But lures the pirate, and corrupts the friend.
    B. It raises armies in a nation's aid.
    P. But bribes a senate, and the land's betray'd.
In vain may heroes fight and patriots rave;
If secret gold sap on from knave to knave.
Once, we confess, beneath the patriot's cloak,
From the crack'd bag the dropping guinea spoke,
And jingling down the back stairs, told the crew,
' Old Cato is as great a rogue as you.'
Blest paper-credit ! last and best supply !
That lends corruption lighter wings to fly.
Gold imp'd by thee, can compass hardest things,
Can pocket states, can fetch or carry kings ;
A single leaf shall waft an army o'er,

Or ship off senates to a distant shore ;
A leaf, like Sibyl's, scatter to and fro
Our fates and fortunes, as the winds shall blow :
Pregnant with thousands flits the scrap unseen,
And silent sells a king or buys a queen.

*From 'The Prologue to the Satires,' Epistle to Dr.
Arbuthnot.*

ADDISON.

PEACE to all such ! but were there one whose fires
True genius kindles, and fair fame inspires ;
Blest with each talent and each art to please,
And born to write, converse, and live with ease ;
Should such a man, too fond to rule alone,
Bear, like the Turk, no brother near the throne,
View him with scornful, yet with jealous eyes,
And hate for arts that caused himself to rise ;
Damn with faint praise, assent with civil leer,
And without sneering, teach the rest to sneer ;
Willing to wound, and yet afraid to strike,
Just hint a fault, and hesitate dislike ;
Alike reserved to blame, or to commend,
A timorous foe, and a suspicious friend ;
Dreading even fools, by flatterers besieged,
And so obliging, that he ne'er obliged ;
Like *Cato*, give his little senate laws,
And sit attentive to his own applause ;
While wits and templars every sentence raise,
And wonder with a foolish face of praise—
Who but must laugh, if such a man there be ?
Who would not weep, if Atticus were he ?

*   *   *   *   *

SPORUS (LORD HERVEY).

LET Sporus tremble— *A*. What? that thing of
    silk,
Sporus, that mere white curd of ass's milk ?
Satire or sense, alas! can Sporus feel ?
Who breaks a butterfly upon a wheel ?
  P. Yet let me flap this bug with gilded wings,
This painted child of dirt, that stinks and stings ;
Whose buz the witty and the fair annoys,
Yet wit ne'er tastes, and beauty ne'er enjoys ;
So well-bred spaniels civilly delight
In mumbling of the game they dare not bite.
Eternal smiles his emptiness betray,
As shallow streams run dimpling all the way.
Whether in florid impotence he speaks,
And, as the prompter breathes, the puppet squeaks,
Or at the ear of Eve, familiar toad,
Half froth, half venom, spits himself abroad,
In puns, or politics, or tales or lies,
Or spite, or smut, or rhymes, or blasphemies :
His wit all see-saw, between that and this,
Now high, now low, now master up, now miss ;
And he himself one vile antithesis.
Amphibious thing! that acting either part,
The trifling head, or the corrupted heart,
Fop at the toilet, flatterer at the board,
Now trips a lady, and now struts a lord.
Eve's tempter thus the Rabbins have exprest,
A cherub's face, a reptile all the rest,
Beauty that shocks you, parts that none will trust,
Wit that can creep, and pride that licks the dust.

From 'Imitations of Horace' [1734].

To Mr. Murray.

' Not to admire, is all the art I know,
To make men happy, and to keep them so.'
(Plain truth, dear Murray, needs no flowers of speech,
So take it in the very words of Creech.[1])
   This vault of air, this congregated ball,
Self-centred sun, and stars that rise and fall,
There are, my friend ! whose philosophic eyes
Look through, and trust the ruler with his skies,
To him commit the hour, the day, the year,
And view this dreadful All without a fear.
Admire we then what earth's low entrails hold,
Arabian shores, or Indian seas infold ;
All the mad trade of fools and slaves for gold ?
Or popularity ? or stars and strings ?
The mob's applauses, or the gifts of kings ?
Say with what eyes we ought at courts to gaze,
And pay the great our homage of amaze ?
   If weak the pleasure that from these can spring,
The fear to want them is as weak a thing ;
Whether we dread, or whether we desire,
In either case, believe me, we admire ;
Whether we joy or grieve, the same the curse,
Surprised at better, or surprised at worse.
Thus good or bad, to one extreme betray
The unbalanced mind, and snatch the man away ;
For virtue's self may too much zeal be had ;
The worst of madmen is a saint run mad.

   [1] The two first lines are quoted from Creech's translation of Horace.

From 'The Dunciad' [1728-1742], Book I.

THE mighty mother, and her son who brings
The Smithfield muses to the ear of kings,
I sing.   Say you, her instruments, the great !
Call'd to this work by Dulness, Jove, and Fate ;
You by whose care, in vain decried and curst,
Still Dunce the second reigns like Dunce the first ;
Say how the goddess bade Britannia sleep,
And pour'd her spirit o'er the land and deep.

   In eldest time, ere mortals writ or read,
Ere Pallas issued from the Thunderer's head,
Dulness o'er all possess'd her ancient right,
Daughter of Chaos and eternal Night :
Fate in their dotage this fair idiot gave,
Gross as her sire, and as her mother grave,
Laborious, heavy, busy, bold, and blind,
She ruled, in native anarchy, the mind.

   Still her old empire to restore she tries,
For, born a goddess, Dulness never dies.

   O thou ! whatever title please thine ear,
Dean, Drapier, Bickerstaff or Gulliver !
Whether thou choose Cervantes' serious air,
Or laugh and shake in Rabelais' easy chair,
Or praise the court, or magnify mankind,
Or thy grieved country's copper chains unbind ;
From thy Bœotia though her power retires
Mourn not, my Swift, at aught our realm acquires,
Here pleased behold her mighty wings outspread
To hatch a new Saturnian age of lead.

   Close to those walls where Folly holds her throne,
And laughs to think Monroe would take her down,
Where o'er the gates, by his famed father's hand
Great Cibber's brazen, brainless brothers stand ;
One cell there is, conceal'd from vulgar eye,
The cave of Poverty and Poetry.

Keen hollow winds howl thro' the bleak recess,
Emblem of music caus'd by emptiness.
Hence bards, like Proteus, long in vain tied down,
Escape in monsters, and amaze the town.
Hence Miscellanies spring, the weekly boast
Of Curll's chaste press, and Lintot's rubric post ;
Hence hymning Tyburn's elegiac lines,
Hence Journals, Medleys, Merc'ries, Magazines ;
Sepulchral lies, our holy wars to grace,
And new-year odes, and all the Grub-street race.
   In clouded majesty here Dulness shone ;
Four guardian Virtues, round, support her throne :
Fierce champion Fortitude, that knows no fears
Of hisses, blows, or want, or loss of ears :
Calm Temperance, whose blessings those partake
Who hunger and who thirst for scribbling' sake :
Prudence, whose glass presents the approaching jail ;
Poetic Justice, with her lifted scale,
Where, in nice balance, truth with gold she weighs,
And solid pudding against empty praise.
   Here she beholds the chaos dark and deep,
Where nameless somethings in their causes sleep,
'Till genial Jacob, or a warm third day,
Call forth each mass, a poem, or a play ;
How hints, like spawn, scarce quick in embryo lie,
How new-born nonsense first is taught to cry ;
Maggots half-form'd in rhyme exactly meet,
And learn to crawl upon poetic feet.
Here one poor word an hundred clenches makes,
And ductile Dulness new meanders takes ;
There motley images her fancy strike,
Figures ill pair'd, and similes unlike,
She sees a mob of metaphors advance,
Pleased with the madness of the mazy dance :
How Tragedy and Comedy embrace ;
How Farce and Epic get a jumbled race ;
How Time himself stands still at her command,

Realms shift their place, and ocean turns to land.
Here gay Description Ægypt glads with showers,
Or gives to Zembla fruits, to Barca flowers ;
Glittering with ice here hoary hills are seen,
There painted valleys of eternal green,
In cold December fragrant chaplets blow,
And heavy harvests nod beneath the snow.
  All these, and more, the cloud-compelling queen
Beholds through fogs, that magnify the scene :
She, tinsel'd o'er in robes of varying hues,
With self-applause her wild creation views ;
Sees momentary monsters rise and fall,
And with her own fools-colours gilds them all.

From Book II.

AND now the Queen, to glad her sons, proclaims
By herald hawkers, high heroic games. . . .
With authors, stationers obey'd the call
(The field of glory is a field for all).
Glory and gain, the industrious tribe provoke ;
And gentle Dulness ever loves a joke.
A poet's form she placed before their eyes,
And bade the nimblest racer seize the prize ;
No meagre, muse-rid mope, adust and thin,
In a dun night-gown of his own loose skin ;
But such a bulk as no twelve bards could raise,
Twelve starveling bards of these degenerate days,
All as a partridge plump, full-fed and fair,
She form'd this image of well-bodied air ;
With pert flat eyes she window'd well its head ;
A brain of feathers and a heart of lead ;
And empty words she gave, and sounding strain,
But senseless, lifeless ! idol void and vain !

Never was dash'd out, at one lucky hit,
A fool, so just a copy of a wit;
So like, that critics said, and courtiers swore,
A wit it was, and call'd the phantom More.

From Book IV.

DR. BENTLEY.

NOR wert thou, Isis! wanting to the day,
(Tho' Christchurch long kept prudishly away.)
Each staunch polemic, stubborn as a rock,
Each fierce logician, still expelling Locke,
Came whip and spur, and dash'd through thin and
    thick
On German Crouzaz and Dutch Burgersdyck.
As many quit the streams that murmuring fall
To lull the sons of Margaret and Clare-hall,
Where Bentley late tempestuous wont to sport
In troubled waters, but now sleeps in port.
Before them march'd that awful Aristarch;
Plough'd was his front with many a deep remark:
His hat, which never vail'd to human pride,
Walker with reverence took, and laid aside,
Low bow'd the rest: he, kingly, did but nod;
So upright Quakers please both man and God.
' Mistress! dismiss that rabble from your throne:
Avaunt —— is Aristarchus yet unknown?
Thy mighty scholiast, whose unwearied pains
Made Horace dull, and humbled Milton's strains.
Turn what they will to verse, their toil is vain,
Critics like me shall make it prose again.
Roman and Greek grammarians! know your better:
Author of something yet more great than letter;

While towering o'er your alphabet, like Saul,
Stands our Digamma, and o'ertops them all.
'Tis true, on words is still our whole debate,
Disputes of *me* or *te*, of *aut* or *at*,
To sound or sink in *cano*, O or A,
Or give up Cicero to C or K.
Let Freind affect to speak as Terence spoke,
And Alsop never but like Horace joke :
For me, what Virgil, Pliny may deny,
Manilius or Solinus shall supply :
For Attic phrase in Plato let them seek,
I poach in Suidas for unlicensed Greek.
In ancient sense if any needs will deal,
Be sure I give them fragments, not a meal ;
What Gellius or Stobæus hash'd before,
Or chew'd by blind old scholiasts o'er and o'er,
The critic eye, that microscope of wit,
Sees hairs and pores, examines bit by bit :
How parts relate to parts, or they to whole,
The body's harmony, the beaming soul,
Are things which Kuster, Burman, Wasse shall see,
When man's whole frame is obvious to a *flea*.'

THE TRIUMPH OF DULNESS.

SHE comes! she comes! the sable throne behold
Of *Night* primeval, and of Chaos old !
Before her Fancy's gilded clouds decay,
And all its varying rainbows die away.
Wit shoots in vain its momentary fires,
The meteor drops, and in a flash expires.
As one by one, at dread Medea's strain,
The sickening stars fade off the ethereal plain ;
As Argus' eyes by Hermes' wand opprest,
Closed one by one to everlasting rest ;

Thus at her felt approach, and secret might,
Art after art goes out and all is night.
See skulking Truth to her old cavern fled,
Mountains of casuistry heap'd o'er her head.
Philosophy, that lean'd on Heaven before,
Shrinks to her second cause, and is no more.
Physic of Metaphysic begs defence
And Metaphysic calls for aid on Sense !
See Mystery to Mathematics fly :
In vain ! they gaze, turn giddy, rave, and die.
Religion blushing veils her sacred fires,
And unawares Morality expires.
Nor public flame, nor private, dares to shine ;
Nor human spark is left, nor glimpse divine !
Lo ! thy dread empire, Chaos ! is restored ;
Light dies before thy uncreating word :
Thy hand, great anarch ! lets the curtain fall ;
And universal darkness buries all.

JONATHAN SWIFT [1667-1745].

From the Preface to ' The Tale of a Tub ' [published 1704].

IT is a great ease to my conscience, that I have written so elaborate and useful a discourse, without one grain of satire intermixed; which is the sole point wherein I have taken leave to dissent from the famous originals of our age and country. I have observed some satirists to use the publick much at the rate that pedants do a naughty boy, ready horsed for discipline : first, expostulate the case, then plead the necessity of the rod from great provocations, and conclude every period with a lash.

Now if I know anything of mankind these gentlemen might very well spare their reproof and correction ; for there is not, through all nature, another so callous and insensible a member, as the world's posteriors, whether you apply to it the toe or the birch.   Besides, most of our late satirists seem to lie under a sort of mistake, that because nettles have the prerogative to sting, therefore all other weeds must do so too.   I make not this comparison out of the least design to detract from these worthy writers ; for it is well known among mythologists that weeds have the pre-eminence ₍over all other vegetables ; and therefore the first monarch of this island, whose taste and judgement were so acute and refined, did very wisely root out the roses from the collar of the order, and plant the thistles in their stead, as the nobler flower of the two.   For which reason it is conjectured by profounder antiquaries that the satirical itch, so prevalent in this part of our island, was first brought among us from beyond the Tweed.   Here may it long flourish and abound : may it survive and neglect the scorn of the world, with as much ease and contempt as the world is insensible to the lashes of it.   May their own dulness, or that of their party, be no discouragement for the authors to proceed ; but let them remember, it is with wits as with razors, which are never so apt to cut those they are employed on, as when they have lost their edge.

  *   *   *   *   *

But though the matter for panegyrick were as fruitful as the topicks of satire, yet would it not be hard to find out a sufficient reason, why the latter will be always better received than the first.   For, this being bestowed only upon one, or a few persons at a time, is sure to raise envy, and consequently ill words from the rest, who have no share in the blessing :

but satire, being levelled at all, is never resented for an offence by any, since every individual person makes bold to understand it of others, and very wisely removes his particular part of the burden upon the shoulders of the world, which are broad enough, and able to bear it. To this purpose I have sometimes reflected upon the difference between Athens and England, with respect to the point before us. In the Attick commonwealth, it was the privilege and birthright of every citizen and poet to rail aloud, and in publick, or to expose upon the stage, by name, any person they pleased, though of the greatest figure, whether a Creon, an Hyperbolus, an Alcibiades, or a Demosthenes: but, on the other side, the least reflecting word let fall against the people in general, was immediately caught up, and revenged upon the authors, however considerable for their quality or their merits. Whereas in England it is just the reverse of all this. Here, you may securely display your utmost rhetorick against mankind, in the face of the world; tell them, 'That all are gone astray; that there is none that doth good, no not one; that we live in the very dregs of time; that knavery and atheism are epidemick as the pox; that honesty is fled with Astræa;' with any other common places, equally new and eloquent, which are furnished by the *splendida bilis*. And when you have done, the whole audience, far from being offended, shall return you thanks, as a deliverer of precious and useful truths. Nay, farther; it is but to venture your lungs, and you may preach in Covent-Garden against foppery and fornication, and something else: against pride, and dissimulation, and bribery, at White-hall: you may expose rapine and injustice in the inns of court chapel; and in a city pulpit be as fierce as you please against avarice, hypocrisy, and extortion. 'Tis but a ball bandied to and fro, and

15—2

every man carries a racket about him to strike it
from himself, among the rest of the company. But,
on the other side, whoever should mistake the nature
of things so far, as to drop him but a single hint in
publick, how such a one starved half the fleet, and
half poisoned the rest: how such a one, from a true
principle of love and honour, pays no debts but for
wenches and play: how such a one has got a ——,
and runs out of his estate: how Paris, bribed by
Juno and Venus, loth to offend either party, slept out
the whole cause on the bench: or, how such an orator
makes long speeches in the senate with much thought,
little sense, and to no purpose; whoever, I say,
should venture to be thus particular, must expect to
be imprisoned for scandalum magnatum; to have
challenges sent him; to be sued for defamation; and
to be brought before the bar of the house.

But I forget that I am expatiating on a subject
wherein I have no concern, having neither a talent
nor an inclination for satire. On the other side, I
am so entirely satisfied with the whole present pro-
cedure of human things, that I have been some
years preparing materials towards A Panegyrick
upon the World; to which I intended to add a
second part, entitled, A modest Defence of the Pro-
ceedings of the Rabble in all Ages. Both these I
had thoughts to publish, by way of Appendix to the
following treatise; but finding my commonplace
book fill much slower than I had reason to expect,
I have chosen to defer them to another occasion.
Besides, I have been unhappily prevented in that
design by a certain domestick misfortune, in the
particulars whereof, though it would be very seasonable, and much in the modern way, to inform the
gentle reader, and would also be of great assistance
towards extending this Preface into the size now in
vogue, which by rule ought to be large in proportion

as the subsequent volume is small; yet I shall now dismiss our impatient ·reader from any further attendance at the porch; and having duly prepared his mind by a preliminary discourse, shall gladly introduce him to the sublime mysteries that ensue.

From '*The Tale of a Tub.*'

THE worshippers of this deity (the Tailor-God) had also a system of their belief, which seemed to turn upon the following fundamentals. They held the universe to be a large suit of clothes, which invests every thing: that the earth is invested by the air; the air is invested by the stars; and the stars are invested by the *primum mobile.* Look on this globe of earth, you will find it to be a very complete and fashionable dress. What is that which some call land, but a fine coat faced with green? or the sea, but a waistcoat of water-tabby? Proceed to the particular works of the creation, you will find how curious journeyman nature has been, to trim up the vegetable beaux; observe how sparkish a periwig adorns the head of a beech, and what a fine doublet of white sattin is worn by the birch. To conclude from all, what is man himself but a micro-coat, or rather a complete suit of clothes with all its trimmings? As to his body, there can be no dispute: but examine even the acquirements of his mind, you will find them all contribute in their order towards furnishing out an exact dress; to instance no more; is not religion a cloak; honesty a pair of shoes worn out in the dirt; self-love a surtout; vanity a shirt; and conscience a pair of breeches?

These *postulata* being admitted, it will follow in

due course of reasoning, that those beings, which the world calls improperly suits of clothes are in reality the most refined species of animals; or to proceed higher, that they are rational creatures, or men. For, is it not manifest, that they live, and move, and talk, and perform all other offices of human life? are not beauty, and wit, and mien, and breeding, their inseparable proprieties? in short, we see nothing but them, hear nothing but them. Is it not they who walk in the streets, fill up parliament-, coffee-, play-, bawdy-houses? It is true, indeed, that these animals, which are vulgarly called suits of clothes, or dresses, do according to certain compositions receive different appellations. If one of them be trimmed with a gold chain, and a red gown, and a white rod, and a great horse, it is called a lord-mayor: if certain ermines and furs be placed in a certain position, we style them a judge; and so an apt conjunction of lawn and black sattin we intitle a bishop.

Others of these professors, though agreeing in the main system, were yet more refined upon certain branches of it; and held that man was an animal compounded of two dresses, the natural and celestial suit, which were the body and the soul: that the soul was the outward, and the body the inward clothing; that the latter was *ex traduce;* but the former of daily creation and circumfusion. This last they proved by Scripture, because, in them we live, and move, and have our being; as likewise by philosophy, because they are all in all, and all in every part. Besides, said they, separate these two, and you will find the body to be only a senseless unsavoury carcase. By all which it is manifest, that the outward dress must needs be the soul.

To this system of religion were tagged several subaltern doctrines, which were entertained with great vogue; as particularly, the faculties of the mind were deduced by the learned among them in this manner: embroidery was sheer wit; gold fringe was agreeable conversation; gold lace was repartee; a huge long periwig was humour; and a coat full of powder was very good raillery: all which required abundance of *finesse* and *delicatesse* to manage with advantage, as well as a strict observance after times and fashions.

From 'The Battle of the Books' [published 1704].

DAY being far spent, and the numerous forces of the moderns half inclining to a retreat, there issued forth from a squadron of their heavy-armed foot, a captain, whose name was Bentley, the most deformed of all moderns; tall, but without shape or comeliness; large, but without strength or proportion. . . . Thus completely armed, he advanced with a slow and heavy pace, where the modern chiefs were holding a consult upon the sum of things; who, as he came onwards, laughed to behold his crooked leg, and hump shoulder, which his boot and armour vainly endeavouring to hide, were forced to comply with, and expose. The generals made use of him for his talent of railing; which, kept within government, proved frequently of great service to their cause, but at other times did more mischief than good; for at the least touch of offence, and often without any at all, he would, like a wounded elephant, convert it against his leaders. Such at this juncture was the disposition of Bentley, grieved to see the enemy prevail, and dissatisfied with everybody's conduct but his own. He humbly gave the modern generals to understand, 'that he conceived, with great submission, they were all a pack of rogues, and fools, and sons of ——, and d——n'd cowards, and confounded loggerheads, and illiterate whelps, and nonsensical scoundrels; that if himself had been constituted general, these presumptuous dogs, the ancients, would long before this have been beaten out of the field. You,' said he, 'sit here idle; but when I, or any other valiant modern kill an enemy, you are sure to seize the spoil. But I will not march one foot against the foe, till you all swear to me, that whomever I take or kill, his arms I shall quietly possess.' Bentley having spoken thus, Scaliger, bestowing him a sour look, 'Miscreant prater,' said he, 'eloquent only in thine own eyes, thou railest without wit, or truth, or discretion. The malignity of thy temper perverteth nature, thy learning makes thee more barbarous, thy study of humanity more inhuman; thy converse among poets more groveling, miry, and dull. All arts of civilizing others render thee rude and untractable; courts have taught thee ill manners, and polite conversation has finished thee a pedant. Besides, a greater coward burdeneth not the army. But never despond; I pass my word, whatever spoil thou takest, shall certainly be thy own; though, I hope, that vile carcase will first become a prey to kites and worms.'

Bentley durst not reply; but, half choked with spleen and rage, withdrew in full resolution of performing some great achievement. With him, for his aid and companion, he took his beloved Wotton; resolving, by policy or surprize, to attempt some neglected quarter of the ancients' army. They began their march over carcases of their slaughtered friends; then to the right of their own forces; then wheeled northward, till they came to Aldrovandus's tomb, which they passed on the side of the declining

sun. And now they arrived with fear towards the
enemy's out-guards ; looking about, if haply they
might spy the quarters of the wounded, or some
struggling sleepers, unarmed, and remote from the
rest. As when two mongrel curs, whom native
greediness and domestick want provoke and join
in partnership, though fearful, nightly to invade the
folds of some rich grazier, they, with tails depressed,
and lolling tongues, creep soft and slow : meanwhile
the conscious moon, now in her zenith, on their
guilty heads darts perpendicular rays ; nor dare they
bark though much provoked at her refulgent visage,
whether seen in puddle by reflection, or in sphere
direct ; but one surveys the region round, while the
other scouts the plain, if haply to discover, at
distance from the flock, some carcase half devoured,
the refuse of gorged wolves, or ominous ravens. So
marched this lovely, loving pair of friends, nor with
less fear and circumspection ; when, at distance,
they might perceive two shining suits of armour,
hanging upon an oak, and the owners not far off in
a profound sleep. The two friends drew lots, and
the pursuing of this adventure fell to Bentley ; on
he went, and in his van, Confusion and Amaze ;
while Horrour and Affright brought up the rear.
As he came near, behold two heroes of the ancients'
army, Phalaris and Æsop, lay fast asleep ; Bentley
would fain have dispatched them both, and, stealing
close, aimed his flail at Phalaris's breast. But then
the goddess Affright interposing, caught the modern
in her icy arms, and dragged him from the danger
she foresaw ; both the dormant heroes happened to
turn at the same instant, though soundly sleeping,
and busy in a dream. For Phalaris was just that
minute dreaming how a most vile poetaster had
lampooned him, and how he had got him roaring in
his bull. And Æsop dreamed that, as he and the

ancient chiefs were lying on the ground, a wild ass broke loose, ran about trampling and kicking and dunging in their faces. Bentley, leaving the two heroes asleep, seized on both their armours, and withdrew in quest of his darling Wotton.

From " An Argument against abolishing Christianity"
[1708].

ANOTHER advantage proposed by the abolishing of Christianity is the clear gain of one day in seven, which is now entirely lost, and consequently the kingdom one-seventh less considerable in trade, business, and pleasure ; beside the loss to the publick of so many stately structures, now in the hands of the clergy, which might be converted into play-houses, market-houses, exchanges, common dormitories, and other publick edifices.

I hope I shall be forgiven a hard word, if I call this a perfect cavil. I readily own there has been an old custom, time out of mind, for people to assemble in the churches every Sunday, and that shops are still frequently shut, in order, as it is conceived, to pre-serve the memory of that ancient practice ; but how this can prove a hindrance to business or pleasure is hard to imagine. What if the men of pleasure are forced, one day in the week, to game at home instead of the chocolate-houses? are not the taverns and coffee-houses open ? can there be a more con-venient season for taking a dose of physick ? Is not that the chief day for traders to sum up the accounts of the week, and for lawyers to prepare their briefs ? But I would fain know how it can be pretended that the churches are misapplied ? where are more appointments and rendezvouses of gallantry ? where more care to appear in the foremost box, with greater advantage of dress? where more meetings for business? where more bargains driven of all sorts? and where so many conveniencies or incitements to sleep?

*   *   *   *   *

And to urge another argument of a parallel nature : if Christianity were once abolished, how could the freethinkers, the strong reasoners, and the men of profound learning be able to find another subject, so calculated in all points whereon to display their abilities? what wonderful productions of wit should we be deprived of, from those whose genius, by continual practice, has been wholly turned upon raillery and invectives against religion, and would therefore never be able to shine or distinguish themselves upon any other subject! We are daily complaining of the great decline of wit among us, and would we take the greatest, perhaps the only topick we have left? who would have ever suspected Asgyll for a wit, or Toland for a philosopher, if the inexhaustible stock of Christianity had not been at hand, to provide them with materials? what other subject through all art or nature could have produced Tindal for a profound author, or furnished him with readers? It is the wise choice of the subject that alone adorns and distinguishes the writer. For, had a hundred such pens as these been employed on the side of religion, they would have immediately sunk into silence and oblivion.

To conclude: whatever some may think of the great advantages to trade by this favourite scheme, I do very much apprehend that in six months' time after the act is passed for the extirpation of the Gospel, the Bank and East-India stock may fall at least one per cent. And since that is fifty times more than ever the wisdom of our age thought fit to venture for the preservation of Christianity, there is no reason we should be at so great a loss, merely for the sake of destroying it.

From 'Gulliver's Travels' [1726-1727].

THE Emperor of the Lilliputians is taller, by almost the breadth of my nail, than any of his court; which alone is enough to strike an awe into the beholders. His features are strong and masculine, with an Austrian lip and arched nose, his complexion olive, his countenance erect, his body and limbs well proportioned, all his motions graceful, and his deportment majestic. He was then past his prime, being twenty-eight years and three quarters old, of which he had reigned about seven in great felicity, and generally victorious. For the better convenience of beholding him, I lay on my side, so that my face was parallel to his, and he stood but three yards off: however, I have had him since many times in my hand, and therefore cannot be deceived in the description. His dress was very plain and simple, and the fashion of it between the Asiatic and the European: but he had on his head a light helmet of gold, adorned with jewels, and a plume on the crest. He held his sword drawn in his hand to defend himself, if I should happen to break loose; it was almost three inches long; the hilt and the scabbard were gold enriched with diamonds. His voice was shrill, but very clear and articulate; and I could distinctly hear it when I stood up. . . .

The Emperor had a mind one day to entertain me with several of the country shows, wherein they exceed all nations I have known, both for dexterity and magnificence. I was diverted with none so much as that of the rope-dancers, performed upon a slender white thread, extended about two feet, and twelve inches from the ground. Upon which I shall desire liberty, with the reader's patience, to enlarge a little.

This diversion is only practised by those persons who are candidates for great employments, and high favour at court. They are trained in this art from their youth, and are not always of noble birth, or liberal education. When a great office is vacant, either by death or disgrace (which often happens), five or six of those candidates petition the emperor to entertain his majesty and the court with a dance on the rope ; and whoever jumps the highest, without falling, succeeds in the office. Very often the chief ministers themselves are commanded to show their skill, and to convince the emperor that they have not lost their faculty. Flimnap, the treasurer, is allowed to cut a caper on the straight rope at least an inch higher than any other lord in the whole empire. I have seen him do the summer-set several times together, upon a trencher fixed on a rope which is no thicker than a common pack-thread in England. My friend Reldresal, principal secretary for private affairs, is, in my opinion, if I am not partial, the second after the treasurer ; the rest of the great officers are much upon a par.

These diversions are often attended with fatal accidents, whereof great numbers are on record. I myself have seen two or three candidates break a limb. But the danger is much greater, when the ministers themselves are commanded to show their dexterity ; for, by contending to excel themselves and their fellows, they strain so far that there is hardly one of them who has not received a fall, and some of them two or three. I was assured that, a year or two before my arrival, Flimnap would in-fallibly have broke his neck, if one of the king's cushions, that accidentally lay on the ground, had not weakened the force of his fall.

There is likewise another diversion, which is only shown before the emperor and empress, and first minister, upon particular occasions.

The emperor lays on the table three fine silken threads of six inches long; one is blue, the other red, and the third green. These threads are pro-posed as prizes for those persons whom the emperor has a mind to distinguish by a peculiar mark of his favour. The ceremony is performed in his majesty's great chamber of state, where the candidates are to undergo a trial of dexterity, very different from the former, and such as I have not observed the least resemblance of in any other country of the new or old world. The emperor holds a stick in his hands, both ends parallel to the horizon, while the candi-dates advancing, one by one, sometimes leap over the stick, sometimes creep under it, backward and forward, several times, according as the stick is advanced or depressed. Sometimes the emperor holds one end of the stick, and his first minister the other; sometimes the minister has it entirely to himself. Whoever performs his part with most agility, and holds out the longest in leaping and creeping, is rewarded with the blue coloured silk; the red is given to the next, and the green to the third, which they all wear girt round about the middle; and you see few great persons about this court who are not adorned with one of these girdles.

*   *   *   *   *

One morning, about a fortnight after I had obtained my liberty, Reldresal, principal secretary (as they style him) for private affairs, came to my house attended only by one servant. He ordered his coach to wait at a distance, and desired that I would give him an hour's audience ; which I readily consented to, on account of his quality and personal merits, as well as of the many good offices he had done me during my solicitations at court. I offered to lie down, that he might the more conveniently reach my ear ; but he chose rather to let me hold him in my hand during our conversation. He began with compliments on my liberty ; said, 'he might pretend to some merit in it ;' but however added, ' that if it had not been for the present situation of things at court, perhaps I might not have obtained it so soon. For,' said he, ' as flourishing a condition as we may appear to be in to foreigners, we labour under two mighty evils : a violent faction at home, and the danger of an invasion, by a most potent enemy, from abroad. As to the first, you are to understand that for above seventy moons past there have been two struggling parties in this empire, under the names of Tramecksan and Slamecksan,[1] from the high and low heels of their shoes, by which they distinguish themselves. It is alleged, indeed, that the high heels are most agreeable to our ancient constitution ; but, however this be, his majesty has determined to make use only of low heels in the administration of the government, and all offices in the gift of the crown, as you cannot but observe ; and particularly that his majesty's imperial heels are lower at least by a *drurr*, than any of his court : *drurr* is a measure about the fourteenth part of an inch. The animosities between these two parties run so high, that they will neither eat, nor drink, nor talk with each other. We compute the Tramecksan, or high heels, to exceed us in number ; but the power is wholly on our side. We apprehend his imperial highness, the heir to the crown, to have some

[1] High Church and Low Church, or Whigs and Tories.

tendency towards the high heels; at least, we can plainly discover that one of his heels is higher than the other, which gives him a hobble in his gait. Now, in the midst of these intestine disquiets, we are threatened with an invasion from the Island of Blefuscu, which is the other great empire of the universe, almost as large and powerful as this of his majesty.

'For as to what we heard you affirm, that there are other states and kingdoms in the world, inhabited by human creatures as large as yourself, our philosophers are in much doubt, and would rather conjecture that you dropped from the moon, or one of the stars; because it is certain, that a hundred mortals of your bulk would in a short time destroy all the fruits and cattle of his majesty's dominions: besides, our histories of six thousand moons make no mention of any other regions than the two great empires of Lilliput and Blefuscu. Which two mighty powers have, as I was going to tell you, been engaged in a most obstinate war for six-and-thirty moons past. It began upon the following occasion: it is allowed on all hands, that the primitive way of breaking eggs, before we eat them, was upon the larger end; but his present majesty's grandfather, while he was a boy, going to eat an egg, and breaking it according to the ancient practice, happened to cut one of his fingers. Whereupon, the emperor his father published an edict, commanding all his subjects, upon great penalties, to break the smaller end of their eggs. The people so highly resented this law, that our histories tell us there have been six rebellions raised on that account; wherein one emperor lost his life, and another his crown. These civil commotions were constantly fomented by the monarchs of Blefuscu; and when they were quelled, the exiles always fled for refuge to that empire. It is computed that eleven thousand persons have at several times suffered death, rather than submit to break their eggs at the smaller end. Many hundred large volumes have been published upon this controversy; but the books of the Big-endians have been long forbidden, and the whole party rendered incapable by law of holding employments. During the course of these troubles, the emperors of Blefuscu did frequently expostulate by their ambassadors, accusing us of making a schism in religion, by offending against a fundamental doctrine of our great prophet Lustrog, in the fifty-fourth chapter of the Blundecral, which is their Alcoran. This however is thought to be a mere strain upon the text; for the words are these : that all true believers break their eggs at the convenient end. And which is the convenient end, seems, in my humble opinion, to be left to every man's conscience, or at least in the power of the chief magistrate to determine. Now, the Big-endian exiles have found so much credit in the emperor of Blefuscu's court, and so much private assistance and encouragement from the party here at home, that a bloody war has been carried on between the two empires for six and thirty moons with various success : during which time we have lost forty capital ships, and a much great number of smaller vessels, together with thirty thousand of our best seamen and soldiers; and the damage received by the enemy is reckoned to be somewhat greater than ours. However, they have now equipped a numerous fleet, and are just preparing to make a descent upon us ; and his imperial majesty, placing great confidence in your valour and strength, has commanded me to lay this account of his affairs before you.'

I desired the secretary to present my humble duty to the emperor ; and to let him know, 'that I thought it would not become me, who was a foreigner, to

16

interfere with parties ; but I was ready, with the hazard of my life, to defend his person and the state against all invaders.'

From ' The Voyage to Laputa.'

AFTER this preface, he gave me a particular account of the *struldbrugs*[1] among them. He said, ' they commonly acted like mortals, till about thirty years old ; after which, by degrees, they grew melancholy and dejected, increasing in both till they came to fourscore. This he learned from their own confession : for otherwise, there not being above two or three of that species born in an age, they were too few to form a general observation by. When they came to fourscore years, which is reckoned the extremity of living in this country, they had not only all the follies and infirmities of other old men, but many more which arose from the dreadful prospect of never dying. They were not only opinionative, peevish, covetous, morose, vain, talkative ; but incapable of friendship, and dead to all natural affection, which never descended below their grandchildren. Envy, and impotent desires, are their prevailing passions. But those objects against which their envy seems principally directed, are the vices of the younger sort, and the deaths of the old. By reflecting on the former, they find themselves cut off from all possibility of pleasure ; and whenever they see a funeral, they lament and repine that others are gone to a harbour of rest to which they themselves never can hope to arrive. They have no remembrance of anything, but what they learned and observed in their youth and middle age, and even that is very imperfect. And for the truth or

[1] Immortals.

particulars of any fact, it is safer to depend on common tradition, than upon their best recollections. The least miserable among them, appear to be those who turn to dotage, and entirely lose their memories; these meet with more pity and assistance, because they want many bad qualities, which abound in others.

'If a *struldbrug* happen to marry one of his own kind, the marriage is dissolved of course, by the courtesy of the kingdom, as soon as the younger of the two comes to be fourscore. For the law thinks it a reasonable indulgence, that those who are condemned, without any fault of their own, to a perpetual continuance in the world, should not have their misery doubled by the load of a wife.

'As soon as they have completed the term of eighty years, they are looked on as dead in law; their heirs immediately succeed to their estates, only a small pittance is reserved for their support; and the poor ones are maintained at the public charge. After that period, they are held incapable of any employment of trust or profit; they cannot purchase lands, or take leases; neither are they allowed to be witnesses in any cause, either civil or criminal, not even for the decision of meers and bounds.

'At ninety, they loose their teeth and hair; they have at that age no distinction of taste, but eat and drink whatever they can get, without relish or appetite. The diseases they were subject to still continue, without increasing or diminishing. In talking, they forget the common appellation of things, and the names of persons, even of those who are their nearest friends and relations. For the same reason, they never can amuse themselves with reading, because their memory will not serve to carry them from the beginning of a sentence to the end; and by this defect, they are deprived of the

16—2

only entertainment, whereof they might otherwise be capable.

'The language of this country being always upon the flux, the *struldbrugs* of one age do not understand those of another; neither are they able, after two hundred years, to hold any conversation (farther than by a few general words) with their neighbours the mortals; and thus they lie under the disadvantage of living like foreigners, in their own country.'

This was the account given me of the *struldbrugs*, as near as I can remember. I afterwards saw five or six of different ages, the youngest not above two hundred years old, who were brought to me at several times by some of my friends; but although they were told 'that I was a great traveller, and had seen all the world,' they had not the least curiosity to ask me a question; only desired 'I would give them *slumskudask*, or a token of remembrance'; which is a modest way of begging, to avoid the law, that strictly forbids it, because they are provided for by the public, although indeed with a very scanty allowance.

They are despised and hated by all sorts of people. When one of them is born, it is reckoned ominous, and their birth is recorded very particularly: so that you may know their age by consulting the register, which, however, has not been kept above a thousand years past, or at least has been destroyed by time or public disturbances. But the usual way of computing how old they are is by asking them what kings or great persons they can remember, and then consulting history; for infallibly the last prince in their mind did not begin his reign after they were fourscore years old.

They were the most mortifying sight I ever beheld; and the women more horrible than the men. Beside the usual deformities in extreme old age, they acquired an additional ghastliness, in proportion to their number of years, which is not to be described; and among half a dozen, I soon distinguished which was the eldest, although there was not above a century or two between them.

From ' A Rhapsody on Poetry ' [1733].

FAIR Britain, in thy monarch blest,
Whose virtues bear the strictest test ;
Whom never faction could bespatter,
Nor minister nor poet flatter ;
What justice in rewarding merit !
What magnanimity of spirit ;
What lineaments divine we trace
Through all his figure, mien, and face !
Though peace with olive bind his hands,
Confess'd the conquering hero stands.
Hydaspes, Indus, and the Ganges,
Dread from his hand impending changes.
From him the Tartar and Chinese,
Short by the knees, entreat for peace.
The consort of his throne and bed,
A perfect goddess born and bred,
Appointed sovereign judge to sit
On learning, eloquence, and wit.
Our eldest hope, divine Iulus,
(Late, very late, O may he rule us !)
What early manhood has he shown,
Before his downy beard was grown !
Then think, what wonders will be done
By going on as he begun,
An heir for Britain to secure
As long as sun and moon endure.

The remnant of the royal blood
Comes pouring on me like a flood.
Bright goddesses, in number five ;
Duke William, sweetest prince alive.
  Say poet, in what other nation
Shone ever such a constellation !
Attend, ye Popes, and Youngs, and Gays,
And tune your harps, and strow your bays :
Your panegyrics here provide ;
You cannot err on flattery's side.
Above the stars exalt your style,
You still are low ten thousand mile.
On Lewis all his bards bestow'd
Of incense many a thousand load ;
But Europe mortified his pride,
And swore the fawning rascals lied.
Yet what the world refus'd to Lewis,
Apply'd to George, exactly true is.
Exactly true ! invidious poet !
'Tis fifty thousand times below it.

From ' The Beasts' Confession ' [1732].

THE Statesman tells you, with a sneer,
His fault is to be too sincere ;
And having no sinister ends,
Is apt to disoblige his friends.
The nation's good, his master's glory,
Without regard to Whig or Tory,
Were all the schemes he had in view,
Yet he was seconded by few :
Though some had spread a thousand lies,
'Twas he defeated the excise.
'Twas known, though he had borne aspersion,
That standing troops were his aversion :

His practice was, in every station,
To serve the king, and please the nation.
Though hard to find in every case
The fittest man to fill a place:
His promises he ne'er forgot,
But took memorials on the spot;
His enemies, for want of charity,
Said, he affected popularity:
'Tis true, the people understood,
That all he did was for their good;
Their kind affections he has tried;
No love is lost on either side.
He came to court with fortune clear,
Which now he runs out every year;
Must, at the rate that he goes on,
Inevitably be undone:
O! if his majesty would please
To give him but a writ of ease,
Would grant him license to retire,
As it has long been his desire,
By fair accounts it would be found,
He's poorer by ten thousand pound.
He owns, and hopes it is no sin,
He ne'er was partial to his kin;
He thought it base for men in stations
To crowd the court with their relations:
His country was his dearest mother,
And every virtuous man his brother;
Through modesty or awkward shame
(For which he owns himself to blame),
He found the wisest man he could,
Without respect to friends or blood;
Nor ever acts on private views,
When he has liberty to choose.

JOSEPH ADDISON [1672-1719].

From 'The Spectator,' No. 105 [1711].

A MAN who has been brought up among books, and is able to talk of nothing else, is a very indifferent companion, and what we call a Pedant. But, methinks, we should enlarge the title, and give it every one that does not know how to think out of his profession and particular way of life.

What is a greater Pedant than a meer man of the town? Barr him the play-houses, a catalogue of the reigning beauties, and an account of a few fashionable distempers that have befallen him, and you strike him dumb.

How many a pretty Gentleman's knowledge lies all within the verge of the Court? He will tell you the names of the principal favourites, repeat the shrewd sayings of a man of quality, whisper an intreague that is not yet blown upon by common fame; or, if the sphere of his observations is a little larger than ordinary, will perhaps enter into all the incidents, turns, and revolutions in a game of Ombre. When he has gone thus far, he has shown you the whole circle of his accomplishments, his parts are drained, and he is disabled from any further conversation. What are these but rank Pedants? and yet these are the men who value themselves most on their exemption from the pedantry of Colleges. I might here mention the Military Pedant, who always talks in a camp and is storming towns, making lodgments and fighting battles from one end of the year to the other. Every thing he speaks smells of gunpowder; if you take away his artillery from him, he has not a word to say for himself. I might likewise mention the Law Pedant, that is perpetually putting cases, repeating the transactions of Westminster Hall, wrangling with you upon the most indifferent circumstances of life, and not to be convinced of the distance of a place or of a most trivial point in conversation, but by dint of argument. The State Pedant is wrapt up in news, and lost in politicks. If you mention either of the kings of Spain or Poland he talks very notably; but if you go out of the *Gazette*, you drop him. In short, a meer Courtier, a meer Soldier, a meer Scholar, a meer anything, is an insipid, pedantick character, and equally ridiculous.

Of all the species of Pedants which I have mentioned, the Book-pedant is much the most supportable: he has at least an exercised understanding, and a head which is full though confused, so that a man who converses with him may often receive from him hints of things that are worth knowing, and what he may possibly turn to his own advantage, though they are of little use to the owner. The worst kind of Pedants among learned men are such as are naturally endued with a very small share of common sense, and have read a great number of books without taste or distinction.

The truth of it is, Learning, like travelling and all other methods of improvement, as it finishes good sense, so it makes a silly man ten thousand times more insufferable, by supplying variety of matter to his impertinence, and giving him an opportunity of abounding in absurdities. Shallow Pedants cry up one another much more than men of solid and useful learning. To read the titles they give an editor, or collator of a manuscript, you would take him for the glory of the common-wealth of letters, and the wonder of his age; when perhaps upon examination you find that he has only rectified a Greek particle, or laid out a whole sentence in proper commas. They are obliged to be thus lavish of their praises, that they may keep one another in countenance; and it is no wonder if a great deal of knowledge, which is not capable of making a man wise, has a natural tendency to make him vain and arrogant.

SAMUEL JOHNSON, D.D. [1709-1784].

From 'London' [1738].

By numbers here from shame or censure free,
All crimes are safe but hated poverty.
This, only this, the rigid law pursues,
This, only this, provokes the snarling Muse.
The sober trader at a tatter'd cloak
Wakes from his dream, and labours for a joke;
With brisker air the silken courtiers gaze,
And turn the varied taunt a thousand ways.
  Of all the griefs that harass the distress'd,
Sure the most bitter is a scornful jest;
Fate never wounds more deep the gen'rous heart,
Than when a blockhead's insult points the dart.
  Has Heaven reserv'd, in pity to the poor,
No pathless waste, or undiscovered shore?
No secret island in the boundless main?
No peaceful desert yet unclaim'd by Spain?
Quick let us rise, the happy seats explore,
And bear oppression's insolence no more.
This mournful truth is every where confess'd,
Slow rises worth by poverty depress'd:
But here more slow, where all are slaves to gold,
Where looks are merchandise, and smiles are sold:
Where won by bribes, by flatteries implor'd,
The groom retails the favours of his lord.

From '*The Vanity of Human Wishes*' [1749].

BUT, scarce observ'd, the knowing and the bold
Fall in the gen'ral massacre of gold ;
Wide wasting pest ! that rages unconfin'd,
And crowds with crimes the records of mankind ;
For gold his sword the hireling ruffian draws,
For gold the hireling judge distorts the laws ;
Wealth heap'd on wealth, nor truth nor safety buys,
The dangers gather as the treasures rise.
Let hist'ry tell where rival kings command,
And dubious title shakes the madded land,
When statutes glean the refuse of the sword,
How much more safe the vassal than the lord ;
Low skulks the hind beneath the rage of power,
And leaves the wealthy traitor in the Tower,
Untouch'd his cottage, and his slumbers sound,
Tho' confiscation's vultures hover round.

    *   *   *   *   *

Yet still one gen'ral cry the skies assails,
And gain and grandeur load the tainted gales ;
Few know the toiling statesman's fear or care,
Th' insidious rival and the gaping heir.
Once more, Democritus, arise on Earth,
With cheerful wisdom and instructive mirth,
See motley life in modern trappings dress'd,
And feed with varied fools th' eternal jest :
Thou who could'st laugh, where want enchain'd
    caprice,
Toil crush'd conceit, and man was of a piece ;
Where wealth, unlov'd, without a mourner dy'd ;
And scarce a sycophant was fed by pride ;
Where ne'er was known the form of mock debate,
Or seen a new-made mayor's unwieldy state ;
Where change of fav'rites made no change of laws,
And senates heard before they judg'd a cause ;

How would'st thou shake at Briton's modish tribe,
Dart the quick taunt, and edge the piercing gibe ?
Attentive truth and nature to descry,
And pierce each scene with philosophic eye,
To thee were solemn toys, or empty show,
The robes of pleasure, and the veils of woe :
All aid the farce, and all thy mirth maintain,
Whose joys are causeless, or whose griefs are vain.

Letter to the Earl of Chesterfield [1775].

MY LORD,
I have been lately informed by the proprietor
of the *World* that two papers, in which my dictionary
is recommended to the publick, were written by
your Lordship.   To be so distinguished is a honour,
which, being very little accustomed to favours from
the great, I know not well how to receive, or in what
terms to acknowledge.

When, upon some slight encouragement, I first
visited your Lordship, I was overpowered, like the
rest of mankind, by the enchantment of your address ;
and could not forbear to wish that I might boast
myself *Le vainqueur du vainqueur de la terre ;* that I
might obtain that regard for which I saw the world
contending ; but I found my attendance so little
encouraged that neither pride nor modesty would
suffer me to continue it.   When I had once addressed
your Lordship in publick, I had exhausted all the art
of pleasing which a retired and uncourtly scholar can
possess.   I had done all I could ; and no man is
well pleased to have his all neglected, be it ever so
little.

Seven years, my Lord, have now past, since I

waited in your outward rooms, or was repulsed from your door ; during which time I have been pushing on my work through difficulties, of which it is useless to complain, and have brought it at last to the verge of publication, without one act of assistance, one word of encouragement, or one smile of favour. Such treatment I did not expect, for I never had a Patron before. The shepherd in Virgil grew at last acquainted with Love, and found him a native of the rocks.

Is not a Patron, my Lord, one who looks with unconcern on a man struggling for life in the water, and when he has reached ground, encumbers him with help? The notice which you have been pleased to take of my labours, had it been early, had been kind; but it has been delayed till I am indifferent, and cannot enjoy it; till I am solitary and cannot impart it ; till I am known, and do not want it. I hope it is no very cynical asperity not to confess obligations where no benefit has been received, or to be unwilling that the publick should consider me as owing that to a Patron, which Providence has enabled me to do for myself.

Having carried on my work thus far with so little obligation to any favourer of learning, I shall not be disappointed though I shall conclude it, if less be possible, with less; for I have been long wakened from that dream of hope, in which I once boasted myself with so much exultation,

My Lord,
Your Lordship's most humble,
Most obedient servant,
SAM. JOHNSON.

BERNARD MANDEVILLE [1670-1733].

From 'The Fable of the Bees' [1706].

VAST numbers throng'd the fruitful Hive;
Yet those vast Numbers made 'em thrive;
Millions endeavouring to supply
Each other's Lust and Vanity;
Whilst other Millions were employ'd,
To see their Handy-works destroy'd;
They furnish'd half the Universe;
Yet had more Work than Labourers.
Some with vast Stocks and little Pains
Jumped into Business of great gains;
And some were damn'd to Sythes and Spades,
And all those hard laborious Trades;
Where willing Wretches daily sweat,
And wear out Strength and Limbs to eat:
Whilst others follow'd Misteries,
To which few Folks bind 'Prentices;
That want no Stock, but that of Brass,
And may set up without a Cross;
As Sharpers, Parasites, Pimps, Players,
Pick-Pockets, Coiners, Quacks, South-Sayers,
And all those that in Enmity,
With downright Working, cunningly
Convert to their own Use the Labour
Of their good-Natur'd heedless Neighbour.
These were called Knaves, but bar the Name
The grave Industrious were the same:
All Trades and Places knew some Cheat,
No calling was without Deceit.

From ' An Enquiry into the Origin of Moral Virtue.'

IT is common among cunning Men, that understand
the Power which Flattery has upon Pride, when they
are afraid they shall be impos'd upon, to enlarge,
tho' much against their Conscience, upon the
Honour, fair Dealing, and Integrity of the Family,
Country, or sometimes the Profession of him they
suspect ; because they know that Men often will
change their Resolution, and act against their Inclination, that they may have the Pleasure of con-
tinuing to appear in the Opinion of somewhat they
are conscious not to be in reality. Thus Sagacious
Moralists draw Men like Angels, in hopes that the
Pride, at least, of some, will put 'em upon copying
after the beautiful originals which they are represented to be.

From ' Remarks on the Fable of the Bees.'

THUS I have prov'd, that the Real Pleasures of all
Men in Nature are worldly and sensual, if we judge
from their Practice. I say, all Men in Nature,
because Devout Christians, who alone are to be
excepted here, being regenerated, and preternaturally
assisted by the Divine Grace, cannot be said to be
in Nature. How strange it is that they should all
so unanimously deny it ! Ask not only the Divines
and Moralists of every Nation, but likewise all that
are rich and powerful, about real Pleasure, and
they'll tell you, with the Stoicks, that there can be
no true Felicity in Things Mundane and Corruptible ;
but then look upon their Lives, and you will find
they take delight in no other.

What must we do in this Dilemma ?

There is nothing left us than to say what Mr. Bayle

has endeavour'd to prove at large in his Reflections on Comets: That Man is so unaccountable a Creature as to act most commonly against his Principle; and this is so far from being injurious, that it is a Compliment to Human Nature, for we must say either this or worse.

This Contradiction in the Frame of Man is the Reason that the Theory of Virtue is so well understood, and the Practice of it so rarely to be met with. If you ask me where to look for those beautiful shining Qualities of Prime Ministers, and the great Favourites of Princes that are so finely painted in Dedications, Addresses, Epitaphs, Funeral Sermons and Inscriptions, I answer, There, and no where else. Where would you look for the Excellency of a Statue, but in that part which you see of it? 'Tis the Polish'd outside only that has the Skill and Labour of the Sculptor to boast of; what's out of sight is untouch'd. Would you break the Head, or cut open the Breast to look for the Brains or the Heart, you'd only shew your Ignorance and destroy the Workmanship. This has often made me compare the Virtues of great Men to your large China Jars; they make a fine Shew, and are ornamental even to a Chimney; one would by the Bulk they appear in, and the Value that is set upon them, think they might be very useful, but look into a thousand of them, and you'll find nothing in them but Dust and Cobwebs.

DR. JOHN ARBUTHNOT [1667-1735].

From 'The History of John Bull' [1711-1712].

BULL, in the main, was an honest, plain-dealing fellow, choleric, bold, and of a very unconstant temper ; he dreaded not old Lewis, either at back-sword, single falchion, or cudgel-play; but then he was very apt to quarrel with his best friends, especially if they pretended to govern him; if you flattered him, you might lead him like a child. John's temper depended very much upon the air; his spirits rose and fell with the weather-glass. John was quick, and understood his business very well; but no man alive was more careless in looking into his accounts, or more cheated by partners, apprentices, and servants. This was occasioned by his being a boon companion, loving his bottle and his diversion, for, to say truth, no man kept a better house than John, nor spent his money more generously.

*   *   *   *   *

John had a sister,[1] a poor girl that had been starved at nurse ; any body would have guessed miss to have been bred up under the influence of a cruel step-dame, and John to be the fondling of a tender mother. John looked ruddy and plump, with a pair of cheeks like a trumpeter; miss looked pale and wan, as if she had the green sickness : and no wonder, for John was the darling, he had all the good bits, was crammed with good pullet, chicken, pig, goose, and capon, while miss had only a little oatmeal and water, or a dry crust without butter. John had his golden pippins, peaches, and nectarines; poor miss a crab-apple, sloe, or a blackberry. Master

---

[1] The nation and Church of Scotland.

lay in the best apartment, with his bedchamber toward the south sun. Miss lodged in a garret, exposed to the north wind, which shrivelled her countenance ; however, this usage, though it stunted the girl in her growth, gave her a hardy constitution ; she had life and spirit in abundance, and knew when she was ill-used : now and then she would seize upon John's commons, snatch a leg of pullet, or a bit of good beef, for which they were sure to go to fisty-cuffs. Master was indeed too strong for her ; but miss would not yield in the least point; but even when master had got her down, she would scratch and bite like a tiger ; when he gave her a cuff on the ear, she would prick him with her knitting needle. John brought a great chain one day to tie her to the bedpost, for which affront miss aimed a penknife at his heart. In short, these quarrels grew up to rooted aversions; they gave one another nicknames : she called him Gundyguts, and he called her Lousy Peg ; though the girl was a tight clever wench as any was, and through her pale looks you might discern spirit and vivacity, which made her not, indeed, a perfect beauty, but something that was agreeable. It was barbarous in parents not to take notice of these early quarrels, and make them live better together, such domestic feuds proving afterward the occasion of misfortunes to them both. Peg had, indeed, some odd humours and comical antipathies, for which John would jeer her. 'What think you of my sister Peg,' says he, 'that faints at the sound of an organ, and yet will dance and frisk at the noise of a bagpipe?' 'What's that to you, Gundyguts (quoth Peg), every body's to choose their own music.' Then Peg had taken a fancy not to say her Pater-noster, which made people imagine strange things of her.

From '*The Art of Political Lying*' [1712].

HERE the author makes a digression in praise of the whig party for the right understanding and use of proof-lies. A proof-lie is like a proof-charge for a piece of ordnance, to try a standard credulity. Of such a nature he takes transubstantiation to be in the church of Rome—a proof-article, which, if any-one swallows, they are sure he will digest everything else. Therefore, the whig party do wisely to try the credulity of the people sometimes by swingers, that they may be able to judge to what height they may charge them afterward. Toward the end of this chapter he warns the heads of parties against be-lieving their own lies, which has proved of pernicious consequences of late, both a wise party and a wise nation having regulated their affairs upon lies of their own invention. The causes of this he supposes to be too great a zeal and intenseness in the practise of this art, and a vehement heat in mutual conversa-tion, whereby they persuade one another that what they wish, and report to be true, is really so : that all parties have been subject to this misfortune. The jacobites have been constantly infested with it ; but the whigs of late seemed even to exceed them in this ill habit and weakness. To this chapter the author subjoins a calendar of lies, proper for the several months of the year.

The ninth chapter treats of the celerity and dura-tion of lies. As to the celerity of their motion, the author says it is almost incredible. He gives several instances of lies that have gone faster than a man can ride post. 'Your terrifying lies travel at a pro-digious rate, above ten miles an hour; your whispers move in a narrow vortex, but very swiftly.' The author says it is impossible to explain several pheno-

17—2

mena in relation to the celerity of lies, without the
supposition of synchronism and combination.

As to the duration of lies, he says there are of all
sorts, from hours and days, to ages ; that there are
some which, like insects, die and revive again in a
different form ; that good artists, like people who
build upon a short lease, will calculate the duration
of a lie surely to answer their purpose ; to last just
as long, and no longer, than the turn is served.

MATTHEW PRIOR [1664-1721].

A Simile.

DEAR Thomas, didst thou ever pop
Thy head into a tinman's shop ?
There, Thomas, didst thou never see
('Tis but by way of simile)
A squirrel spend his little rage
In jumping round a rolling cage ;
The cage, as either side turn'd up,
Striking a ring of bells at top ?
Mov'd in the orb, pleas'd with the chimes.
The foolish creature thinks he climbs :
But here or there, turn wood or wire,
He never gets two inches higher.
    So fares it with those merry blades,
That frisk it under Pindus' shades.
In noble song and lofty odes,
They tread on stars and talk with gods ;
Still dancing in an airy round,
Still pleas'd with their own verses' sound—
Brought back, how fast soe'er they go,
Always aspiring, always low.

Epigrams.

I.

To John I ow'd great obligation;
  But John unhappily thought fit
To publish it to all the nation:
  Sure John and I are more than quit.

II.

YES, every poet is a fool,
  By demonstration Ned can show it,
Happy, could Ned's inverted rule
  Prove every fool to be a poet.

Alma.

From Canto III.

' THAT old philosopher grew cross,
Who could not tell what motion was;
Because he walk'd against his will,
He fac'd men down that he stood still.
And he who, reading on the heart
(When all his *quodlibets* of art
Could not expound its pulse and heat),
Swore he had never felt it beat;
Chrysippus, foil'd by Epicurus,
Makes bold (Jove bless him!) to assure us
That all things which our mind can view
May be at once both false and true;
And Malebranch has an odd conceit
As ever enter'd Frenchman's pate:
Says he, " So little can our mind
Of matter or of spirit find,

That we by guess at least may gather
Something, which may be both, or neither."
Faith, Dick, I must confess, 'tis true
(But this is only *entre nous*)
That many knotty points there are,
Which all discuss, but few can clear.
As nature slily had thought fit,
For some by-ends, to cross-bite wit :
Circles to square, and cubes to double,
Would give a man excessive trouble.
The longitude uncertain roams,
In spite of Whiston and his bombs.
What *system*, Dick, has right averr'd
The cause why woman has no beard ?
Or why, as years our frame attack,
Our hairs grow white, our teeth grow black ?
In points like these, we must agree,
Our barbers know as much as we.
Yet still, unable to explain,
We must persist the best we can ;
With care our *system* still renew,
And prove things likely, though not true

JOHN GAY [1685-1732].

Fable II.

The Spaniel and the Cameleon.

A SPANIEL, bred with all the care
That waits upon a favourite heir,
Ne'er felt Correction's rigid hand ;
Indulg'd to disobey command,
In pamper'd ease his hours were spent—
He never knew what learning meant.
Such forward airs—so pert, so smart !—
Were sure to win his lady's heart.

Each little mischief gain'd him praise ;
How pretty were his fawning ways !
   The wind was south, the morning fair,
He ventures forth to take the air.
He ranges all the meadow round,
And rolls upon the softest ground ;
When near him a Cameleon seen,
Was scarce distinguish'd from the green.
   ' Dear emblem of the flattering host,
What ! live with clowns ?—a genius lost !
To cities and the court repair,
A fortune cannot fail thee there.
Preferments shall thy talents crown ;
Believe me, friend, I know the town.'
   ' Sir,' says the sycophant, ' like you,
Of old, politer life I knew ;
Like you, a courtier born and bred,
Kings lean'd their ear to what I said.
My whisper always met success ;
The ladies prais'd me for address.
I knew to hit each courtier's passion,
And flatter'd every vice in fashion.
But Jove, who hates the liar's ways,
At once cut short my prosperous days,
And, sentenc'd to retain my nature,
Transform'd me to this crawling creature.
Doom'd to a life obscure and mean,
I wander in the sylvan scene ;
For Jove the heart alone regards—
He punishes what man rewards.
How different is thy case and mine !
With men, at least, you sup and dine,
While I, condemn'd to thinnest fare,
Like those I flatter'd, feed on air.'

MATTHEW GREEN [1696-1737].

From ' The Spleen.'

To cure the mind's wrong bias, Spleen,
Some recommend the bowling-green ;
Some, hilly walks; all, exercise ;
Fling but a stone, the giant dies ;
Laugh and be well. Monkeys have been
Extreme good doctors for the Spleen ;
And kitten, if the humour hit,
Has harlequin'd away the fit.
Since mirth is good in this behalf,
At some partic'lars let us laugh.
Witlings, brisk fools, curs'd with half sense,
That stimulates their impotence ;
Who buzz in rhymes, and, like blind flies,
Err with their wings for want of eyes.
Poor authors worshipping a calf,
Deep tragedies that make us laugh,
A strict dissenter saying grace,
A lect'rer preaching for a place,
Disdainful prudes, who ceaseless ply
The superb muscle of the eye,
And fops in military show,
Are sov'reign for the case in view.
 * * * * *
I never am at meeting seen,
Meeting, that region of the Spleen ;
The broken heart, the busy fiend,
The inward call, on Spleen depend.
Law, licens'd breaking of the peace,
To which vacation is disease :
A gipsy diction scarce known well
By th' magi, who law-fortunes tell,
I shun ; nor let it breed within
Anxiety, and that the Spleen ;
Law, grown a forest, where perplex

The mazes, and the brambles vex;
Where its twelve verd'rers every day
Are changing still the public way:
Yet if we miss our path and err,
We grievous penalties incur;
And wand'rers tire, and tear their skin,
And then get out where they went in.

* * * * *

Passion, as frequently is seen,
Subsiding settles into Spleen.
Hence, as the plague of happy life,
I run away from party-strife.
A prince's cause, a church's claim,
I've known to raise a mighty flame,
And priest, as stoker, very free
To throw in peace and charity.
 That tribe, whose practicals decree
Small beer the deadliest heresy;
Who own wine's old prophetic aid,
And love the mitre Bacchus made,
Forbid the faithful to depend
On half-pint drinkers for a friend,
And in whose gay red-letter'd face
We read good-living more than grace:
Nor they so pure, and so precise,
Immac'late as their white of eyes,
Who for the spirit hug the Spleen,
Phylacter'd throughout all their mien,
Who their ill-tasted home-brew'd pray'r
To the state's mellow forms prefer;
Who doctrines, as infectious, fear,
Which are not steep'd in vinegar,
And samples of heart-chested-grace
Expose in show-glass of the face,
Did never me as yet provoke
Either to honour band and cloak,
Or deck my hat with leaves of oak.

EDWARD YOUNG [1681-1765].

'LOVE OF FAME THE UNIVERSAL PASSION.'

From Satire I.

MY lord comes forward; forward let him come !
Ye vulgar ! at your peril, give him room :
He stands for fame on his forefathers' feet,
By heraldry, prov'd valiant or discreet.
With what a decent pride he throws his eyes
Above the man by three descents less wise ?
If virtues at his noble hands you crave,
You bid him raise his father's from the grave.
Men should press forward in fame's glorious chace ;
Nobles look backward, and so lose the race.
Let high birth triumph !   What can be more great ?
Nothing—but merit in a low estate.
To virtue's humblest son let none prefer
Vice, though descended from the Conqueror.
Shall men, like figures, pass for high, or base,
Slight or important, only by their place ?
Titles are marks of honest men, and wise ;
The fool, or knave, that wears a title, lyes.
They that on glorious ancestors enlarge,
Produce their debt, instead of their discharge.

From Satire II.

WHILE I a moment name, a moment's past,
I'm nearer death in *this* verse, than the *last* :
What, then, is to be done ?   Be wise with speed ;
A fool at forty is a fool indeed.
And what so foolish as the chace of fame ?
How vain the prize ! how impotent our aim !

For what are men who grasp at praise sublime,
But bubbles on the rapid stream of time,
That rise, and fall, that swell, and are no more,
Born and forgot, ten thousand in an hour ?

From Satire V.

'But adoration ! give me something more,'
Cries Lyce on the borders of three-score :
Nought treads so silent as the foot of Time ;
Hence we mistake our autumn for our prime ;
'Tis greatly wise to know before we're told
The melancholy news that we grow old.
Autumnal Lyce carries in her face
Memento mori to each public place.
O how your beating breast a mistress warms
Who looks through spectacles to see your charms !
While rival undertakers hover round,
And with his spade the sexton marks the ground,
Intent not on her own, but others' doom,
She plans new conquests and defrauds the tomb.
In vain the cock has summon'd sprites away,
She walks at noon and blasts the bloom of day.
Gay rainbow silks her mellow charms infold,
And nought of Lyce but herself is old.
Her grizzled locks assume a smirking grace,
And art has levelled her deep furrow'd face.
Her strange demand no mortal can approve,
We'll ask her blessing, but can't ask her love.
She grants, indeed, a lady *may* decline
(All ladies but herself) at ninety-nine.

From Satire VI.

JULIA's a manager; she's born for rule;
And knows her wiser husband is a fool;
Assemblies holds, and spins the subtle thread
That guides the lover to his fair one's bed :
For difficult amours can smooth the way,
And tender letters dictate, or convey.
But if depriv'd of such important cares,
Her wisdom condescends to less affairs,
For her own breakfast she'll project a scheme,
Nor take her tea without a stratagem,
Presides o'er trifles with a serious face;
Important, by the virtue of grimace.
Ladies supreme among amusements reign;
By nature born to soothe, and entertain.
Their prudence in a share of folly lies:
Why will they be so weak as to be wise?
Syrena is for ever in extremes,
And with a vengeance she commends or blames,
Conscious of her discernment, which is good,
She strains too much to make it understood.
Her judgment just, her sentence is too strong;
Because she's right, she's ever in the wrong.

DANIEL DEFOE [1661-1731].

From 'The True-Born Englishman' [1701].

WHEREVER God erects a House of Prayer,
The Devil always builds a Chapel there;
And 'twill be found, upon examination,
The latter has the largest congregation.
For ever since he first debauched the mind,
He made a perfect conquest of mankind.

With uniformity of service he
Reigns with a general aristocracy.
No nonconforming sects disturb his reign ;
For of his yoke there's very few complain !
He knows the genius and the inclination,
And matches proper sins for every nation.
He needs no Standing Army Government,
He always rules us by our own consent !
His laws are easy, and his gentle sway
Makes it exceeding pleasant to obey.
The list of his Viceregents and Commanders
Outdoes your Cæsars or your Alexanders :
They never fail of his infernal aid,
And he's as certain ne'er to be betrayed.
Through all the world they spread his vast command,
And Death's eternal empire is maintained.
They rule so politicly and so well,
As if there were Lords Justices of Hell !
Duly divided to debauch mankind,
And plant infernal dictates in their mind.

From the ' Hymn to the Pillory.'[1]

HAIL ! hieroglyphic State Machine,
Contrived to punish Fancy in !
Men that are men in thee can feel no pain ;
And all thy insignificants disdain !
Contempt, that false new word for shame,
Is, without crime an empty name !
A shadow to amuse mankind :
But never frights the wise or well-fixed mind !

[1] Defoe stood in the pillory, July 29-31, 1703, for writing and publishing 'The Shortest Way with the Dissenters,' in which famous piece of irony he had burlesqued the intolerance of the Nonjuring party.

Virtue despises human scorn!
And scandals Innocence adorn.
Exalted on thy stool of State,
What prospect do I see of sovereign fate!
How the inscrutables of Providence
Differ from our contracted sense!
Here, by the errors of the Town
The fools look out! the knaves look on!
Persons or Crimes find here the same respect;
And Vice does Virtue oft correct!
The undistinguished fury of the street
With mob and malice mankind greet!
No bias can the rabble draw;
But dirt throws dirt, without respect to Merit or to
    Law.

     *   *   *   *   *

Thou Bugbear of the Law! stand up and speak!
Thy long misconstrued silence break!
Tell us, Who 'tis, upon thy Ridge stands there,
So full of fault, and yet so void of fear?
And from the Paper in his hat
Let all mankind be told for what!
Tell them, It was because he was too bold,
And told those truths which should not have been
    told!
Extol the Justice of the Land;
Who punish what they will not understand.
Tell them, He stands exalted there
For speaking what we would not hear.
And yet he might have been secure,
Had he said less or would he have said more!
Tell them that, This is his reward,
And worse is yet for him prepared;
Because his foolish virtue was so nice,
As not to sell his friends, according to his friends'
    advice.
And thus he's an example made,

To make men of their honesty afraid;
That for the Time to come they may
More willingly their friends betray!
Tell them, The men that placed him here
Are scandals to the Times!
Are at a loss to find his guilt
And can't commit his crimes!

CHRISTOPHER ANSTEY [1766].

From the 'New Bath Guide,' Letter VIII.

FROM the earliest ages, dear mother, until now,
All statesmen and great politicians allow
That nothing advances the good of a nation,
Like giving all money a free circulation:
What thanks to the city of Bath then are due
From all who this patriot maxim pursue!
For in no place whatever that national good
Is practis'd so well, and so well understood.
What infinite merit and praise does she claim in
Her ways and her means for promoting of gaming!
And gaming, no doubt, is of infinite use
That same circulation of cash to produce.
What true public-spirited people are here,
Who for that very purpose come every year!
All eminent men, who no trade ever knew
But gaming, the only good trade to pursue:
All other professions are subject to fail,
But gaming's a bus'ness will ever prevail;
Besides, 'tis the only good way to commence
An acquaintance with all men of spirit and sense;
We may grub on without it thro' life, I suppose,
But then 'tis with people—that nobody knows.

We ne'er can expect to be rich, wise, or great,
Or look'd upon fit for employments of state :
'Tis your men of fine heads, and of nice calculations,
That afford so much service to administrations,
Who by frequent experience know how to devise
The speediest methods of raising supplies :
'Tis such men as these, men of honour and worth,
That challenge respect from all persons of birth ;
And is it not right they should all be carest
When they're all so polite, and so very well drest,
When they circulate freely the money they've won,
And wear a lac'd coat, tho' their fathers wore none ?

From Letter VII.

I'M sorry to find at the city of Bath,
Many folks are uneasy concerning their faith :
Nicodemus, the preacher, strives all he can do
To quiet the conscience of good sister Prue ;
But Tabby from scruples of mind is releas'd
Since she met with a learned Moravian priest,
Who says, There is neither transgression nor sin ;
A doctrine that brings many customers in.

HENRY FIELDING [1707-1754].

From 'The Life of Jonathan Wild.'

JONATHAN WILD had every qualification necessary
to form a great man. As his most powerful and
predominating passion was ambition, so nature had,
with consummate propriety, adapted all his faculties
to the attaining those glorious ends to which this

passion directed him. He was extremely ingenious
in inventing designs, artful in contriving the means
to accomplish his purposes, and resolute in executing
them; for as the most exquisite cunning and most
undaunted boldness qualified him for any undertaking,
so was he not restrained by any of those weaknesses
which disappoint the views of mean and vulgar
souls, and which are comprehended in one general
term of honesty, which is a corruption of HONOSTY,
a word derived from what the Greeks call an ass.
He was entirely free from those low vices of modesty
and good-nature, which, as he said, implied a total
negation of human greatness, and were the only
qualities which absolutely rendered a man incapable
of making a considerable figure in the world. His
lust was inferior only to his ambition; but, as for
what simple people call love, he knew not what it
was. His avarice was immense, but it was of the
rapacious, not of the tenacious kind; his rapacious-
ness was indeed so violent that nothing ever contented him but the whole; for, however considerable
the share was which his coadjutors allowed him of a
booty, he was restless in inventing means to make
himself master of the smallest pittance reserved by
them.

He said laws were made for the use of *prigs*[1] only,
and to secure their property; they were never, therefore, more perverted than when their edge was
turned against these; but that this generally
happened through their want of sufficient dexterity.
The character which he most valued himself upon,
and which he principally honoured in others, was
that of hypocrisy. His opinion was that no one
could carry *priggism* very far without it; for which
reason, he said, there was little greatness to be
expected in a man who acknowledged his vices, but

[1] Thieves.

always much to be hoped from him who professed
great virtues; wherefore, though he would always
shun the person whom he discovered guilty of a
good action, yet he was never deterred by a good
character, which was more commonly the effect of
profession than of action; for which reason he himself was always very liberal of honest professions, and
had as much virtue and goodness in his mouth as a
saint, never in the least scrupling to swear by his
honour, even to those who knew him the best. Nay,
though he held good-nature and modesty in the
highest contempt, he constantly practised the affectation of both, and recommended this to others,
whose welfare, on his own account, he wished well
to. He laid down several maxims as the certain
methods of attaining greatness, to which, in his own
pursuit of it, he constantly adhered. As:

1. Never to do more mischief to another than was
necessary to the effecting his purpose; for that
mischief was too precious a thing to be thrown
away.

2. To know no distinction of men from affection;
but to sacrifice all with equal readiness to his
interest.

3. Never to communicate more of an affair than
was necessary to the person who was to execute it.

4. Not to trust him who hath deceived you, nor
who knows he hath been deceived by you.

5. To forgive no enemy; but to be cautious and
often dilatory in revenge.

6. To shun poverty and distress, and to ally himself as close as possible to power and riches.

7. To maintain a constant gravity in his countenance and behaviour, and to affect wisdom on all
occasions.

8. To foment eternal jealousies in his gang, one
of another.

9. Never to reward anyone equal to his merit; but always to insinuate that the reward was above it.

10. That all men were knaves or fools, and much the greater number a composition of both.

11. That a good name, like money, must be parted with, or at least greatly risqued, in order to bring the owner any advantage.

12. That virtues, like precious stones, were easily counterfeited; that the counterfeits in both cases adorned the wearer equally, and that very few had knowledge or discernment sufficient to distinguish the counterfeit jewel from the real.

13. That many men were undone by not going deep enough in roguery; as in gaming, any man may be a loser who doth not play the whole game.

14. That men proclaim their own virtues, as shopkeepers expose their goods, in order to profit by them.

15. That the heart was the proper seat of hatred, and the countenance of affection and friendship.

He had many more of the same kind, all equally good with these, and which were after his decease found in his study, as the twelve excellent and celebrated rules were in that of king Charles the first; for he never promulgated them in his lifetime, not having them constantly in his mouth, as some grave persons have the rules of virtue and morality, without paying the least regard to them in their actions; whereas our hero, by a constant and steady adherence to his rules in conforming everything he did to them, acquired at length a settled habit of walking by them, till at last he was in no danger of inadvertently going out of the way; and by these means he arrived at that degree of greatness which few have equalled; none, we may say, have exceeded; for, though it must be allowed that there have been

some few heroes, who have done some greater mischiefs to mankind, such as those who have betrayed
the liberty of their country to others, or have under-
mined and overpowered it themselves ; or conquerors
who have impoverished, pillaged, sacked, burnt, and
destroyed the countries and cities of their fellow-
creatures, from no other provocation than that of
glory, *i.e.*, as the tragic poet calls it,

> ' A privilege to kill,
> A strong temptation to do bravely ill.'

Yet, if we consider it in the light wherein actions are
placed in this line,

> ' Lætius est, quoties magno tibi constat honestum ;'

when we see our hero, without the least assistance
or pretence, setting himself at the head of a gang
which he had not any shadow of right to govern ;
if we view him maintaining absolute power, and
exercising tyranny over a lawless crew, contrary to
all law but that of his own will ; if we consider him
setting up an open trade publickly, in defiance not
only of the laws of his country but of the common
sense of his countrymen ; if we see him first contriving the robbery of others, and again the defraud-
ing the very robbers of that booty which they had
ventured their necks to acquire, and which, without
any hazard, they might have retained ; here sure he
must appear admirable, and we may challenge not
only the truth of history, but almost the latitude of
fiction to equal his glory.

*　　*　　*　　*　　*

Indeed, while greatness consists in power, pride,
insolence, and doing mischief to mankind—to speak
out—while a great man and a great rogue are synonymous terms, so long shall Wild stand unrivalled on

the pinnacle of GREATNESS. Nor must we omit here, as the finishing of his character, what indeed ought to be remembered on his tomb or his statue, the conformity above-mentioned of his death to his life; and that Jonathan Wild the Great, after all his mighty exploits, was, what so few GREAT men can accomplish—hanged by the neck till he was dead.

OLIVER GOLDSMITH [1728-1774].

From ' The Citizen of the World' [1760-1762].

THE Republic of Letters is a very common expression among the Europeans; and yet when applied to the learned of Europe is the most absurd that can be imagined; since nothing is more unlike a republic than the society which goes by that name. From this expression one would be apt to imagine that the learned were united into a single body, joining their interests and concurring in the same design. From this one might be apt to compare them to our literary society in China, where each acknowledges a just subordination, and all contribute to build the temple of science, without attempting, from ignorance or envy, to obstruct each other.

But very different is the state of learning here; every member of this fancied republic is desirous of governing, and none willing to obey; each looks upon his fellow as a rival, but not an assistant in the same pursuit. They calumniate, they injure, they despise, they ridicule, each other; if one man writes a book that pleases, others shall write books to show that he might have given still greater pleasure, or should not have pleased. If one happens to hit upon something new, there are numbers ready to assure the public that all this was no novelty to them or the learned; that Cardanus, or Brunus, or some other author too dull to be generally read, had anticipated the discovery. Thus, instead of uniting like the members of a commonwealth, they are divided into almost as many factions as there are men; and their jarring constitution, instead of being styled a republic of letters, should be entitled an anarchy of literature.

It is true there are some of superior abilities, who reverence and esteem each other; but their mutual admiration is not sufficient to shield off the contempt of the crowd. The wise are but few, and they praise with a feeble voice; the vulgar are many, and roar in reproaches. The truly great seldom unite in societies, have few meetings, no cabals; the dunces hunt in full cry, till they have run down a reputation, and then snarl and fight with each other about dividing the spoil. Here you may see the compilers and the book-answerers of every month, when they have got up some respectable name, most frequently reproaching each other with stupidity and dulness; resembling the wolves of the Russian forest, who prey upon venison, or horseflesh when they can get it; but in cases of necessity, lying in wait to devour each other. While they have new books to cut up they make a hearty meal; but if this resource should unhappily fail, then it is that critics eat up critics, and compilers rob from compilations.

*   *   *   *   *

To make a fine gentleman several trades are required, but chiefly a barber. You have undoubtedly heard of the Jewish champion, whose strength lay in his hair. One would think that the English were for placing all wisdom there. To appear wise, nothing more is requisite here than for

a man to borrow hair from the heads of all his neighbours, and clap it like a bush on his own. The dis-
tributors of law and physic stick on such quantities
that it is almost impossible, even in idea, to distinguish between the head and the hair.

Those whom I have now been describing affect
the gravity of the lion ; those I am going to describe more resemble the pert vivacity of smaller
animals. The barber, who is still master of the
ceremonies, cuts their hair close to the crown, and
then, with a composition of meal and hog's-lard,
plasters the whole in such a manner as to make it
impossible to distinguish whether the patient wears
a cap or a plaster ; but, to make the picture more
perfectly striking, conceive the tail of some beast—a
greyhound's tail, or a pig's tail, for instance—
appended to the back of the head, and reaching
down to the place where tails in other animals are
generally seen to begin. Thus be-tailed and be-
powdered, the man of taste fancies he improves in
beauty, dresses up his hard-featured face in smiles,
and attempts to look hideously tender. Thus
equipped, he is qualified to make love, and hopes for
success more from the powder on the outside of his
head than the sentiments within.

From ' *The Traveller* ' [1764].

THINE, Freedom, thine the blessings pictur'd here,
Thine are those charms that dazzle and endear ;
Too blest, indeed, were such without alloy ;
But foster'd e'en by Freedom, ills annoy ;
That independence Britons prize too high,
Keeps man from man, and breaks the social tie ;

The self-dependent lordlings stand alone,
All claims that bind and sweeten life unknown;
Here, by the bonds of nature feebly held,
Minds combat minds, repelling and repell'd;
Ferments arise, imprison'd factions roar,
Represt ambition struggles round her shore;
Till over-wrought, the general system feels
Its motions stop, or phrenzy fire the wheels.

*　　　*　　　*　　　*　　　*

Oh, then how blind to all that truth requires,
Who think it freedom when a part aspires!
Calm is my soul, nor apt to rise in arms,
Except when fast approaching danger warms:
But when contending chiefs blockade the throne,
Contracting regal pow'r to stretch their own;
When I behold a factious band agree
To call it freedom when themselves are free;
Each wanton judge new penal statutes draw,
Laws grind the poor, and rich men rule the law;
The wealth of climes where savage nations roam,
Pillag'd from slaves to purchase slaves at home;
Fear, pity, justice, indignation, start,
Tear off reserve, and bare my swelling heart;
Till half a patriot, half a coward grown,
I fly from petty tyrants to the throne.

From ' The Deserted Village' [1770].

Ill fares the land, to hastening ills a prey,
Where wealth accumulates, and men decay;
Princes and lords may flourish, or may fade;
A breath can make them, as a breath has made:
But a bold peasantry, their country's pride,
When once destroyed, can never be supplied.

A time there was, ere England's griefs began,
When every rood of ground maintained its man ;
For him light labour spread her wholesome store,
Just gave what life required, but gave no more :
His best companions, innocence and health ;
And his best riches, ignorance of wealth.
　　But times are altered ; trade's unfeeling train
Usurp the land and dispossess the swain ;
Along the lawn, where scattered hamlets rose,
Unwieldy wealth and cumbrous pomp repose,
And every want to opulence allied,
And every pang that folly pays to pride.
Those gentle hours that plenty bade to bloom,
Those calm desires that asked but little room,
Those healthful sports that graced the peaceful scene,
Lived in each look, and brightened all the green ;
These, far departing, seek a kinder shore,
And rural mirth and manners are no more.

＊　　　＊　　　＊　　　＊　　　＊

　　Beside yon straggling fence that skirts the way
With blossom'd furze, unprofitably gay,
There, in his noisy mansion, skill'd to rule,
The village master taught his little school :
A man severe he was, and stern to view,
I knew him well, and every truant knew ;
Well had the boding tremblers learned to trace
The day's disasters in his morning face ;
Full well they laughed with counterfeited glee
At all his jokes, for many a joke had he ;
Full well the busy whisper, circling round,
Convey'd the dismal tidings when he frown'd ;
Yet he was kind, or if severe in aught,
The love he bore to learning was in fault ;
The village all declar'd how much he knew ;
'Twas certain he could write and cipher too ;

Lands he could measure, terms and tides presage,
And ev'n the story ran that he could gauge.
In arguing, too, the parson own'd his skill,
For ev'n though vanquish'd he could argue still;
While words of learned length, and thund'ring sound,
Amaz'd the gazing rustics rang'd around;
And still they gaz'd, and still the wonder grew
That one small head should carry all he knew.

From 'The Retaliation' [1774].

HERE lies our good Edmund,[1] whose genius was
  such,
We scarcely can praise it or blame it too much;
Who, born for the universe, narrowed his mind,
And to party gave up what was meant for mankind;
Though fraught with all learning, yet straining his
  throat
To persuade Tommy Townshend to lend him a
  vote;
Who, too deep for his hearers, still went on refining,
And thought of convincing, while they thought of
  dining;
Though equal to all things, for all things unfit;
Too nice for a statesman, too proud for a wit,
For a patriot too cool, for a drudge disobedient,
And too fond of the right to pursue the expedient.
In short, 'twas his fate, unemployed, or in place, sir,
To eat mutton cold, and cut blocks with a razor.

Here lies David Garrick, describe me who can;
An abridgement of all that was pleasant in man,
As an actor, confessed without rival to shine:
As a wit, if not first, in the very first line:

[1] Burke.

Yet, with talents like these, and an excellent heart,
The man had his failings, a dupe to his art.
Like an ill-judging beauty, his colours he spread,
And beplastered with rouge his own natural red.
On the stage he was natural, simple, affecting ;
'Twas only that, when he was off, he was acting.
With no reason on earth to go out of his way,
He turned and he varied full ten times a day :
Though secure of our hearts, yet confoundedly sick
If they were not his own by finessing and trick :
He cast off his friends, as a huntsman his pack,
For he knew when he pleased he could whistle them
    back.
Of praise a mere glutton, he swallowed what came ;
And the puff of a dunce, he mistook it for fame ;
Till his relish grown callous, almost to disease,
Who peppered the highest was surest to please.
But let us be candid, and speak out our mind :
If dunces applauded, he paid them in kind.
Ye Kenricks, ye Kellys and Woodfalls so grave,
What a commerce was yours, while you got and you
    gave !
How did Grub-street re-echo the shouts that you
    raised,
While he was be-Rosciused, and you were bepraised.
But peace to his spirit, wherever it flies,
To act as an angel and mix with the skies :
Those poets who owe their best fame to his skill
Shall still be his flatterers, go where he will ;
Old Shakespeare receive him with praise and with
    love,
And Beaumonts and Bens be his Kellys above.

Here Reynolds is laid, and, to tell you my mind,
He has not left a wiser or better behind.
His pencil was striking, resistless, and grand ;
His manners were gentle, complying, and bland :

Still born to improve us in every part,
His pencil our faces, his manners our heart.
To coxcombs averse, yet more civilly steering :
When they judged without skill, he was still hard of
    hearing ;
When they talk'd of their Raphaels, Corregios, and
    stuff,
He shifted his trumpet, and only took snuff.

CHARLES CHURCHILL [1731-1764].

From 'The Rosciad' [1761].

FITZPATRICK.

WITH that low cunning, which in fools supplies,
And amply too, the place of being wise,
Which Nature, kind, indulgent parent! gave
To qualify the blockhead for a knave ;
With that smooth falsehood, whose appearance
    charms,
And reason of each wholesome doubt disarms ;
Which to the lowest depths of guilt descends,
By vilest means pursues the vilest ends,
Wears Friendship's mask for purposes of spite,
Fawns in the day, and butchers in the night ;
With that malignant envy which turns pale
And sickens, even if a friend prevail,
Which merit and success pursues with hate,
And damns the worth it cannot imitate ;
With the cold caution of a coward's spleen,
Which fears not guilt, but always seeks a screen,
Which keeps this maxim ever in her view—
What's barely done, should be done safely too,
With that dull, rooted, callous impudence
Which, dead to shame and every nicer sense,

Ne'er blush'd, unless, in spreading vice's snares,
She blundered on some virtue unawares ;
With all these blessings, which we seldom find
Lavish'd by Nature on one happy mind,
A motley figure, of the Fribble tribe,
Which heart can scarce conceive or pen describe,
Came simpering on . . . .
A six-foot suckling, mincing in its gait,
Affected, peevish, prim and delicate ;
Fearful it seem'd, though of athletic make,
Lest brutal breezes should too roughly shake
Its tender form, and savage motion spread
O'er its pale cheeks the horrid, manly red.

Much did it talk, in its own pretty phrase,
Of genius and of taste, of players and plays ;
Much too of writings, which itself had wrote,
Of special merit, though of little note ;
For Fate, in a strange humour, had decreed
That what it wrote, none but itself should read.

QUIN.

His eyes in gloomy socket taught to roll,
Proclaimed the sullen habit of the soul.
Heavy and phlegmatic he trod the stage,
Too proud for tenderness, too dull for rage. . . .
In fancied scenes, as in life's real plan,
He could not, for a moment, sink the man.
In whate'er cast his character was laid,
Self still, like oil, upon the surface played :
Nature, in spite of all his skill, crept in,
Horatio, Dorax, Falstaff—still 'twas Quin.

*   *   *   *   *

MURPHY.

As one with various disappointments sad,
Whom dulness only kept from being mad,
Apart from all the rest great Murphy came—
Common to fools and wits the rage of fame.
What though the sons of Nonsense hail him Sire,
Auditor, Author, Manager, and Squire !
His restless soul's ambition stops not there ;
To make his triumphs perfect dub him Player.
  In person tall, a figure form'd to please,
If symmetry could charm deprived of ease ;
When motionless he stands, we all approve ;
What pity 'tis the thing was made to move !
  His voice, in one dull, deep, unvaried sound,
Seems to break forth from caverns under ground ;
From hollow chest the low, sepulchral note
Unwilling heaves, and struggles in his throat.
  Could authors butcher'd give an actor grace,
All must to him resign the foremost place.
When he attempts, in some one favourite part,
To ape the feelings of a manly heart,
His honest features the disguise defy,
And his face loudly gives his tongue the lie.

From ' The Ghost.'

DR. JOHNSON.

POMPOSO, insolent and loud,
Vain idol of a scribbling crowd,
Whose very name inspires an awe,
Whose every word is sense and law ;
(For what his greatness hath decreed,
Like laws of Persia and of Mede,

Sacred through all the realms of Wit
Must never of repeal admit) ;
Who, cursing flattery, is the fool
Of every fawning, flattering fool ;
Who wit with jealous eye surveys,
And sickens at another's praise :
Who, proudly seiz'd of learning's throne,
Now damns all learning but his own :
Who scorns those common wares to trade in,
Reas'ning, convincing, and persuading,
But makes each sentence current pass
With ' puppy,' ' coxcomb,' ' scoundrel,' ' ass ' :
(For 'tis with him a certain rule
That folly's proved when he calls ' Fool !') ;
Who to increase his native strength
Draws words six syllables in length,
With which, assisted with a frown
By way of club, he knocks us down.

From ' The Duellist,' Book III.

BISHOP WARBURTON.

THE first (entitled to the place
Of honour both by gown and grace,
Who never let occasion slip
To take right hand of fellowship,
And was so proud, that should he meet
The Twelve Apostles in the street,
He'd turn his nose up at them all,
And shove his Saviour from the wall ;
Who was so mean (Meanness and Pride
Still go together side by side)
That he would cringe, and creep, be civil,
And hold a stirrup for the devil,

If in a journey to his mind,
He'd let him mount and ride behind ;
Who basely fawned through all his life,
For patrons first, then for a wife ;
Wrote Dedications which must make
The heart of every Christian quake ;
Made one man equal to, or more
Than God, then left him, as before
His God he left, and, drawn by pride,
Shifted about to t'other side ;)
Was by his sire a parson made,
Merely to give the boy a trade ;
But he himself was thereto drawn
By some faint omens of the lawn,
And on the truly Christian plan
To make himself a gentleman,
A title in which form arrayed him,
Though Fate ne'er thought on't when she made
    him.
   The oaths he took, 'tis very true,
But took them as all wise men do,
With an intent, if things should turn,
Rather to temporize than burn.
Gospel and loyalty were made
To serve the purposes of trade :
Religion's are but paper ties,
Which bind the fool, but which the wise,
Such idle notions far above,
Draw on and off, just like a glove :
All Gods, all kings (let his great aim
Be answered) were to him the same.

JUNIUS.

From ' The Letters of Junius ' [1769-1772].

LETTER XII.—TO THE DUKE OF GRAFTON.

RELINQUISHING, therefore, all idle views of amendment to your Grace, or of benefit to the public, let me be permitted to consider your character and conduct, merely as a subject of curious speculation. There is something in both which distinguishes you, not only from other Ministers, but all other men. It is not that you do wrong by design, but that you should never do right by mistake. It is not that your indolence and your activity have been equally misapplied, but that the first uniform principle, or, if I may call it, the genius of your life, should have carried you through every possible change and contradiction of conduct, without the momentary imputation or colour of a virtue; and that the wildest spirit of inconsistency should never have once betrayed you into a wise or honourable action. This, I own, gives an air of singularity to your fortune, as well as to your disposition. Let us look back, together, to a scene in which a mind like yours will find nothing to repent of. Let us try, my Lord, how well you have supported the various relations in which you stood to your Sovereign, your country, your friends, and yourself. Give us, if it be possible, some excuse to posterity, and to ourselves, for submitting to your administration. If not the abilities of a great minister, if not the integrity of a patriot, or the fidelity of a friend, show us, at least, the firmness of a man. For the sake of your mistress, the lover shall be spared. I will not lead her into public, as you have done; nor will I insult the memory of departed beauty. Her sex, which alone made her amiable in your eyes, makes her respectable in mine.

The character of the reputed ancestors of some men has made it possible for their descendants to be vicious in the extreme, without being degenerate. Those of your Grace, for instance, left no distressing examples of virtue even to their legitimate posterity; and you may look back with pleasure to an illustrious pedigree, in which heraldry has not left a single good quality upon record to insult or upbraid you. You have better proofs of your descent, my Lord, than the register of a marriage, or any troublesome inheritance of reputation. There are some hereditary strokes of character by which a family may be clearly distinguished, as by the blackest features of the human face. Charles the First lived and died a hypocrite. Charles the Second was a hypocrite of another sort, and should have died upon the same scaffold. At the distance of a century we see their different characters happily revived and blended in your Grace. Sullen and severe without religion, profligate without gaiety, you live like Charles the Second, without being an amiable companion; and, for aught I know, may die, as his father did, without the reputation of a martyr.

LETTER XV.—TO THE SAME.

MY LORD, If nature had given you an understanding qualified to keep pace with the wishes and principles of your heart, she would have made you, perhaps, the most formidable minister that was ever employed under a limited monarch, to accomplish the ruin of a free people. When neither the feelings of shame, the reproaches of conscience, nor the dread of punishment, form any bar to the designs of a minister, the people would have too much reason to lament their condition, if they did not find some resource in the weakness of his understanding. We owe it to the bounty of Providence, that the completest depravity of the heart is sometimes strangely united with a confusion of the mind, which counteracts the most favourite principles, and makes the same man treacherous without art, and a hypocrite without deceiving. The measures, for instance, in which your Grace's activity has been chiefly exerted, as they were adopted without skill, should have been conducted with more than common dexterity. But truly, my Lord, the execution has been as gross as the design. . . .

Whether you have talents to support you, at a crisis of such difficulty and danger, should long since have been considered. Judging truly of your disposition, you have, perhaps, mistaken the extent of your capacity. Good faith and folly have so long been received as synonymous terms, that the reverse of the proposition has grown into credit, and every villain fancies himself a man of abilities. It is the apprehension of your friends, my Lord, that you have drawn some hasty conclusion of this sort, and that a partial reliance upon your moral character has betrayed you beyond the depth of your understanding. You have now carried things too far to retreat. You have plainly declared to the people what they are to expect from the continuance of your administration. It is time for your Grace to consider what you also may expect in return from their spirit and their resentment.

JOHN WOLCOT (PETER PINDAR) [1738-1819].

Conversation on Johnson between Mrs. Piozzi (Thrale) and Mr. Boswell.

Bozzy. WHEN Foote his leg, by some misfortune, broke,
Says I to Johnson, all by way of joke,
' Sam, sir, in paragraph will soon be clever,
And take off Peter better now than ever.'
On which says Johnson without hesitation,
' George will rejoice at Foote's depeditation.'
On which says I, a penetrating elf,
' Doctor, I'm sure you coin'd that word yourself.'
The Doctor owned to me I had divin'd it,
For, bona fide, he had really coin'd it.
' And yet, of all the words I've coin'd,' says he,
' My Dictionary, sir, contains but three.'
Mdme. Piozzi. The Doctor said, ' In literary matters,
A Frenchman goes not deep,—he only smatters;'
Then ask'd, what could be hoped for from the dogs,—
Fellows that liv'd eternally on frogs ?
Bozzy. In grave procession to St. Leonard's College,
Well stuff'd with every sort of useful knowledge,
We stately walked as soon as supper ended ;
The landlord and the waiter both attended ;
The landlord, skill'd a piece of grease to handle,
Before us marched, and held a tallow candle ;
A lantern (some famed Scotsman its creator)
With equal grace was carried by the waiter.
Next morning from our beds we took a leap,
And found ourselves much better for our sleep.

Mdme. Piozzi. In Lincolnshire, a lady show'd our friend
A grotto which she wished him to commend.
Quoth she, ' How cool in summer this abode !'
' Yes, madam (answered Johnson), *for a toad.*'

WILLIAM COWPER [1731-1800].

From 'Conversation.'

DUBIUS is such a scrupulous good man—
Yes—you may catch him tripping if you can.
He would not, with a peremptory tone,
Assert the nose upon his face his own ;
With hesitation admirably slow
He humbly hopes—presumes—it may be so.
His evidence, if he were call'd by law
To swear to some enormity he saw,
For want of prominence and just relief,
Would hang an honest man, and save a thief.
Through constant dread of giving truth offence,
He ties up all his hearers in suspense ;
Knows what he knows, as if he knew it not ;
What he remembers seems to have forgot ;
His sole opinion, whatsoe'er befall,
Centring at last in having none at all.
Yet, though he tease and balk your list'ning ear,
He makes one useful point exceeding clear,
Howe'er ingenious on his darling theme
A sceptic in philosophy may seem,
Reduc'd to practice, his beloved rule
Would only prove him a consummate fool ;
Useless in him alike both brain and speech,
Fate having placed all truth above his reach,
His ambiguities his total sum,
He might as well be blind, and deaf, and dumb.

Where men of judgment creep and feel their way,
The positive pronounce without dismay;
Their want of life and intellect supplied
By sparks absurdity strikes out of pride.
Without the means of knowing right from wrong,
They always are decisive, clear and strong;
Where others toil with philosophic force,
Their nimble nonsense takes a shorter course;
Flings at your head conviction in the lump,
And gains remote conclusions in a jump :
Their own defect, invisible to them,
Seen in another, they at once condemn;
And, though self-idolized in every case,
Hail their own likeness in a brother's face.
The cause is plain, and not to be denied,
The proud are always most provok'd by pride,
Few competitions but engender spite;
And those the most where neither has the right.

From ' The Task.'

GOD made the country, and man made the town,
What wonder then that health and virtue, gifts
That can alone make sweet the bitter draught
That life holds out to all, should most abound
And least be threatened in the fields and groves?
Possess ye therefore, ye who, borne about
In chariots and sedans, know no fatigue
But that of idleness, and taste no scenes
But such as art contrives, possess ye still
Your element ; there only can ye shine.
There only minds like yours can do no harm.
Our groves were planted to console at noon
The pensive wand'rer in their shades. At eve
The moon-beam, sliding softly in between

The sleeping leaves, is all the light they wish,
Birds warbling all the music.   We can spare
The splendour of your lamps ; they but eclipse
Our softer satellite.   Your songs confound
Our more harmonious notes : the thrush departs
Scar'd, and th' offended nightingale is mute.
There is a public mischief in your mirth ;
It plagues your country.   Folly such as yours
Grac'd with a sword, and worthier of a fan,
Has made, what enemies could ne'er have done,
Our arch of empire, stedfast but for you,
A mutilated structure, soon to fall.

WILLIAM GIFFORD [1757-1826].

From ' The Baviad' [1794].

Lo, Della Crusca !   In his closet pent
He toils to give the crude conception vent.
Abortive thoughts that right and wrong confound,
Truth sacrificed to letters, sense to sound,
False glare, incongruous images, combine ;
And noise and nonsense clatter through the line.
'Tis done.   Her house the generous Piozzi lends,
And thither summons her blue-stocking friends ;
The summons her blue-stocking friends obey,
Lured by the love of Poetry—and Tea.
   The Bard steps forth, in birth-day splendour
      dress'd,
His right hand graceful waving o'er his breast ;
His left extending, so that all may see,
A roll inscribed ' The Wreath of Liberty.'
So forth he steps, and, with complacent air
Bows round the circle, and assumes the chair ;

With lemonade he gargles next his throat,
Then sweetly preludes to the liquid note :
And now 'tis silence all. ' Genius or Muse '—
Thus while the flowery subject he pursues,
A wild delirium round the assembly flies ;
Unusual lustre shoots from Emma's eyes,
Luxurious Arno drivels as he stands,
And Anna frisks, and Laura claps her hands.
  O wretched man ! And dost thou toil to please,
At this late hour such prurient ears as these ?
Is thy poor pride contented to receive
Such transitory fame as fools can give ?
Fools, who, unconscious of the critic's laws,
Rain in such showers their indistinct applause.
That Thou, even Thou, who liv'st upon renown,
And, with eternal puffs, insult'st the town,
Art forced at length to check the idiot roar,
And cry, ' For Heaven's sweet sake, no more, no
      more !'

GEORGE CRABBE [1754-1832].

From ' The Library.'

But here the dormant fury rests unsought,
And Zeal sleeps soundly by the foes she fought.
Here all the rage of controversy ends,
And rival zealots rest like bosom-friends ;
An Athanasian here, in deep repose,
Sleeps with the fiercest of his Arian foes ;
Socinians here with Calvinists abide,
And thin partitions angry chiefs divide ;
Here wily Jesuits simple Quakers meet,
And Bellarmine has rest at Luther's feet.
Great authors, for the Church's glory fired,
Are, for the Church's peace, to rest retired ;

And close beside, a mystic, maudlin race,
Lie 'Crumbs of Comfort for the Babes of Grace.'
Against her foes Religion well defends
Her sacred truths, but often fears her friends ;
If learn'd, their pride, if weak their zeal she dreads,
And their hearts' weakness, who have soundest
   heads ;
But most she fears the controversial pen,
The holy strife of disputatious men,
Who the blest Gospel's peaceful page explore,
Only to fight against its precepts more.

From 'The Village' [1783].

FLED are those times when, in harmonious strains,
The rustic poet praised his native plains ;
No shepherds now, in smooth, alternate verse,
Their country's beauty or their nymphs' rehearse ;
Yet still for these we frame the tender strain,
Still in our lays fond Corydons complain,
And shepherds' boys their amorous pains reveal—
The only pains, alas ! they never feel.
On Mincio's banks, in Cæsar's bounteous reign,
If Tityrus found the Golden Age again,
Must sleepy bards the flattering dream prolong,
Mechanic echoes of the Mantuan song ?
From Truth and Nature shall we widely stray,
Where Virgil, not where Fancy, leads the way ? . . .
Lo ! where the heath, with withering brake grown
   o'er,
Lends the light turf that warms the neighbouring
   poor ;
From thence a length of burning sand appears,
Where the thin harvest waves its wither'd ears.

Rank weeds, that every art and care defy,
Reign o'er the land, and rob the blighted rye ;
There thistles stretch their prickly arms afar,
And to the ragged infant threaten war ;
There poppies nodding, mock the hope of toil ;
There the blue bugloss paints the sterile soil.
Hardy and high, above the slender sheaf,
The slimy mallow waves her silky leaf.
O'er the young shoot the charlock throws a shade,
And clasping tares cling round the sickly blade ;
With mingled tints the rocky coasts abound,
And a sad splendour vainly shines around. . . .
Here, wand'ring long, amid these frowning fields,
I sought the simple life that Nature yields ;
Rapine, and Wrong, and Fear usurp'd her place,
And a bold, artful, surly, savage race,
Who, only skill'd to take the finny tribe
The yearly dinner, or septennial bribe,
Wait on the shore, and, as the waves run high,
On the lost vessel bend their eager eye,
Which to their coast directs its vent'rous way,
Theirs, or the ocean's miserable prey.
    As on their neighbouring beach yon swallows
        stand,
And wait for favouring winds to leave the land,
While still for flight the ready wing is spread,
So waited I the favouring hour, and fled—
Fled from these shores where guilt and famine reign,
And cried, ' Ah ! hapless they who still remain—
Who still remain to hear the ocean roar,
Whose greedy waves devour the lessening shore,
Till some fierce tide, with more imperious sway,
Sweeps the low hut, and all it holds, away ;
When the sad tenant weeps from door to door,
And begs a poor protection from the poor ! . . .
    Theirs is yon House that holds the parish poor,
Whose walls of mud scarce bear the broken door ;

There, where the putrid vapours, flagging, play,
And the dull wheel hums doleful through the day—
There children dwell who know no parents' care ;
Parents who know no children's love dwell there !
Heart-broken matrons on their joyless bed,
Forsaken wives, and mothers never wed ;
Dejected widows with unheeded tears,
And crippled age with more than childhood fears.
The lame, the blind, and, far the happiest they !
The moping idiot, and the madman gay.
  Here, too, the sick their final doom receive,
Here brought, amid the scenes of grief, to grieve,
Where the loud groans from some sad chamber flow,
Mixt with the clamours of the crowd below.
Here, sorrowing, they each kindred sorrow scan,
And the cold charities of man to man,
Whose laws indeed for ruin'd age provide,
And strong compulsion plucks the scrap from pride ;
But still that scrap is bought with many a sigh,
And pride embitters what it can't deny.

From 'The Newspaper' [1785].

WE, who for longer fame with labour strive,
Are pain'd to keep our sickly works alive ;
Studious we toil, with patient care refine,
Nor let our love protect one languid line.
Severe ourselves, at last our works appear,
When, ah ! we find our readers more severe,
For, after all our care and pains, how few
Acquire applause, or keep it if they do !
Not so these sheets, ordain'd to happier fate,
Praised through their day, and but that day their
    date ;

Their careless authors only strive to join
As many words as make an even line ;
As many lines as fill a row complete,
As many rows as furnish up a sheet.
From side to side, with ready types they run,
The measure's ended, and the work is done.
Oh, born with ease, how envied and how blest
Your fate to-day and your to-morrow's rest !
To you all readers turn, and they can look
Pleased on a paper, who abhor a book.
Those who ne'er deign'd their Bible to peruse
Would think it hard to be denied their news.
Sinners and saints, the wisest with the weak,
Here mingle tastes, and one amusement seek ;
This, like the public inn, provides a treat,
Where each promiscuous guest sits down to eat ;
And such this mental food as we may call
Something to all men, and to some men all.

From ' The Parish Register,' Part III. — Burials
[1807].

WITH Andrew Collett we the year begin,
The blind, fat landlord of the Old Crown Inn.
Big as his butt, and, for the self-same use,
To take in stores of strong fermenting juice.
On his huge chair beside the fire he sate,
In revel chief, and umpire in debate.
Each night his string of vulgar tales he told,
When ale was cheap, and bachelors were bold.
His heroes all were famous in their days ;
Cheats were his boast, and drunkards had his
    praise.
' One, in three draughts, three mugs of ale took
    down,
As mugs were then—the champion of the Crown.

For thrice three days another lived on ale,
And knew no change but that of mild and stale ;
Two thirsty soakers watch'd a vessel's side,
When he the tap, with dext'rous hand, applied ;
Nor from their seats departed till they found
That butt was out, and heard the mournful sound.'

He praised a poacher—precious child of fun !—
Who shot the keeper with his own spring-gun ;
Nor less the smuggler who the exciseman tied,
And left him hanging at the birch-wood side,
There to expire ; but one who saw him hang
Cut the good cord—a traitor of the gang.

His own exploits with boastful glee he told,
What ponds he emptied, and what pikes he sold ;
And how, when blest with sight alert and gay,
The night's amusements kept him through the day.

He sang the praises of those times when all
' For cards and dice, as for their drink, might call ;
When Justice wink'd on every jovial crew,
And ten-pins tumbled in the parson's view.'

He told, when angry wives, provoked to rail,
Or drive a third-day drunkard from his ale,
What were his triumphs, and how great the skill
That won the vex'd virago to his will,
Who raving came ; then talk'd in milder strain,
Then wept, then drank, and pledg'd her spouse
    again.

Such were his themes : how knaves o'er laws
    prevail,
Or, when made captives, how they fly from jail.
The young, how brave !—how subtle were the old !
And oaths attested all that Folly told.

On death like his what name shall we bestow,
So very sudden, yet so very slow ?
'Twas slow. Disease, augmenting year by year,
Show'd the grim king by gradual steps brought
    near.

'Twas not less sudden. In the night he died,
He drank, he swore, he jested, and he lied ;
Thus aiding folly with departing breath :
' Beware, Lorenzo, the slow-sudden death.'

From ' The Borough.'

THE VICAR.

ALL things new
He deem'd superfluous, useless, or untrue ;
To all beside indifferent, easy, cold,
Here the fire kindled, and the wo was told.
Habit with him was all the test of truth,
' It must be right : I've done it from my youth.'
Questions he answer'd in as brief a way,
' It must be wrong—it was of yesterday.'
Though mild benevolence our Priest possess'd,
'Twas but by wishes or by words express'd,
Circles in water, as they wider flow,
The less conspicuous in their progress grow,
And when at last they touch upon the shore,
Distinction ceases, and they're view'd no more.
His love, like that last circle, all embraced,
But with effect that never could be traced.

ROBERT BURNS [1759-1796].

ADDRESS TO THE UNCO GUID, OR THE RIGIDLY
RIGHTEOUS.

O YE wha are sae guid yoursel',
   Sae pious and sae holy,
Ye've nought to do but mark and tell
   Your neibours' fauts and folly !

Whase life is like a weel-gaun mill
Supply'd wi' store o' water,
The heapet happer's ebbing still,
And still the clap plays clatter.

Hear me, ye venerable core,
As counsel for poor mortals,
That frequent pass douce Wisdom's door
For glaikit[1] Folly's portals ;
I, for their thoughtless, careless sakes,
Would here propone defences,
Their donsie[2] tricks, their black mistakes,
Their failings and mischances.

Ye see your state wi' theirs compar'd,
And shudder at the niffer,[3]
But cast a moment's fair regard,
What maks the mighty differ ?
Discount what scant occasion gave
That purity ye pride in,
And (what's aft mair than a' the lave[4])
Your better art o' hidin'.

Think, when your castigated pulse
Gi'es now and then a wallop,
What ragings must his veins convulse,
That still eternal gallop :
Wi' wind and tide fair i' your tail,
Right on ye scud your sea-way ;
But in the teeth o' baith to sail,
It maks an unco lee-way.

See social life and glee sit down,
All joyous and unthinking,
Till, quite transmogrify'd they're grown,
Debauchery and drinking :

[1] Foolish.　[2] Unlucky.　[3] Exchange.　[4] The rest.

O would they stay to calculate
　Th' eternal consequences ;
Or your more dreaded hell to state
　D-mnation of expenses !

Ye high, exalted, virtuous dames,
　Tied up in godly laces,
Before ye gie poor frailty names
　Suppose a change o' cases :
A dear lov'd lad, convenience snug,
　A treacherous inclination—
But, let me whisper i' your lug,
　Ye're aiblins nae temptation.

Then gently scan your brother man,
　Still gentler sister woman ;
Though they may gang a kennin'[1] wrang,
　To step aside is human :
One point must still be greatly dark,
　The moving *why* they do it :
And just as lamely can ye mark
　How far, perhaps, they rue it.

Who made the heart, 'tis He alone
　Decidedly can try us ;
He knows each chord—its various tone,
　Each spring—its various bias :
Then at the balance let's be mute,
　We never can adjust it :
What's done we partly may compute,
　But know not what's resisted.

[1] A little.

GEORGE CANNING [1770-1827].

The Friend of Humanity and the Knife-grinder.

' NEEDY Knife-grinder! whither are you going?
Rough is the road, your wheel is out of order—
Bleak blows the blast—your hat has got a hole in't,
        So have your breeches!

' Weary Knife-grinder! little think the proud ones,
Who in their coaches roll along the turnpike
Road, what hard work 'tis crying all day "Knives and
        Scissars to grind O!"

' Tell me, Knife-grinder, how came you to grind
    knives?
Did some rich man tyrannically use you?
Was it the squire? or parson of the parish?
        Or the attorney?

' Was it the squire, for killing of his game? or
Covetous parson, for his tithes distraining?
Or roguish lawyer, made you lose your little
        All in a lawsuit?

'(Have you not read the Rights of Man, by Tom
    Paine?)
Drops of compassion tremble on my eyelids,
Ready to fall, as soon as you have told your
        Pitiful story.'

' Story! God bless you! I have none to tell, sir,
Only last night a-drinking at the Chequers,
This poor old hat and breeches, as you see, were
        Torn in a scuffle.
          20

' Constables came up for to take me into
Custody ; they took me before the justice ;
Justice Oldmixon put me in the parish
      Stocks for a vagrant.

' I should be glad to drink your Honour's health in
A pot of beer, if you will give me sixpence ;
But for my part, I never love to meddle
      With politics, sir.'

' I give thee sixpence! I will see thee damn'd
  first—
Wretch ! whom no sense of wrongs can rouse to
  vengeance—
Sordid, unfeeling, reprobate, degraded,
      Spiritless outcast !'

 (Kicks the Knife-grinder, overturns his wheel, and
exit in a transport of Republican enthusiasm and
universal philanthropy.)

From the ' New Morality.'

FIRST, stern Philanthropy : not she, who dries
The orphan's tears, and wipes the widow's eyes ;
Not she, who, sainted Charity her guide,
Of British bounty pours the annual tide :
But *French* Philanthropy ; whose boundless mind
Glows with the general love of all mankind ;
Philanthropy, beneath whose baneful sway
Each patriot passion sinks, and dies away.
 Taught in her school to imbibe thy mawkish strain,
Condorcet, filter'd through the dregs of Paine,
Each pert adept disowns a Briton's part,
And plucks the name of England from his heart.
 What, shall a name, a word, a sound control
The aspiring thought, and cramp the expansive soul?

Shall one half-peopled Island's rocky round
A love, that glows for all creation, bound ?
And social charities contract the plan
Framed for thy Freedom, universal man ?
—No—through the extended globe his feelings run
As broad and general as the unbounded sun !
No narrow bigot *he; his* reason'd view
Thy interests, England, ranks with thine, Peru !
France at our doors, *he* sees no danger nigh,
But heaves for Turkey's woes the impartial sigh ;
A steady Patriot of the World alone,
The Friend of every Country—but his own.

     *   *   *   *   *

' Much may be said on both sides.'   Hark ! I hear
A well-known voice that murmurs in my ear—
The voice of Candour.   Hail ! most solemn sage,
Thou drivelling virtue of this moral age,
Candour, which softens party's headlong rage.
Candour, which spares its foes ; nor e'er descends
With bigot zeal to combat for its friends.
Candour, which loves in see-saw strain to tell
Of *acting foolishly* but *meaning well ;*
Too nice to praise by wholesale, or to blame,
Convinced that *all* men's *motives* are the same ;
And finds, with keen discriminating sight,
Black's not *so* black ; nor white *so very* white. . . .
  Give me the avow'd, the erect, the manly foe,
Bold I can meet—perhaps may turn his blow ;
But of all plagues, good Heaven, thy wrath can send,
Save, save, oh ! save me from the *Candid Friend !*

LORD BYRON [1788-1824].

From 'English Bards and Scotch Reviewers' [1809].

STILL must I hear? shall hoarse Fitzgerald bawl
His creaking couplets in a tavern hall,
And I not sing, lest, haply, Scotch reviews
Should dub me scribbler, and denounce my muse?
Prepare for rhyme—I'll publish, right or wrong:
Fools are my theme, let satire be my song.
*   *   *   *   *
A man must serve his time to every trade
Save censure—critics all are ready made.
Take hackney'd jokes from Miller, got by rote,
With just enough of learning to misquote;
A mind well skill'd to find or forge a fault;
A turn for punning, call it Attic salt;
To Jeffrey go, be silent and discreet,
His pay is just ten sterling pounds per sheet:
Fear not to lie, 'twill seem a sharper hit;
Shrink not from blasphemy, 'twill pass for wit;
Care not for feeling—pass your proper jest,
And stand a critic, hated yet caress'd.
And shall we own such judgment? No: as soon
Seek roses in December—ice in June;
Hope constancy in wind, or corn in chaff;
Believe a woman or an epitaph,
Or any other thing that's false, before
You trust in critics, who themselves are sore;
Or yield one single thought to be misled
By Jeffrey's heart, or Lambe's Bœotian head.
To these young tyrants, by themselves misplaced,
Combined usurpers on the throne of taste;
To these, when authors bend in humble awe,
And hail their voice as truth, their word as law—

While these are censors, 'twould be sin to spare,
While such are critics, why should I forbear?
But yet, so near all modern worthies run,
'Tis doubtful whom to seek, or whom to shun;
Nor know we when to spare, or where to strike,
Our bards and censors are so much alike.

Then should you ask me, why I venture o'er
The path that Pope and Gifford trod before;
If not yet sicken'd, you can still proceed:
Go on; my rhyme will tell you as you read.
'But hold!' exclaims a friend, 'here's some neglect:
This—that—and t'other line seem incorrect.'
What then? the self-same blunder Pope has got,
And careless Dryden—'Ay, but Pye has not.'—
Indeed!—'tis granted, faith!—but what care I?
Better to err with Pope, than shine with Pye.

Next comes the dull disciple of thy school,
That mild apostate from poetic rule,
The simple Wordsworth, framer of a lay
As soft as evening in his favourite May,
Who warns his friend 'to shake off toil and trouble,
And quit his books, for fear of growing double;'
Who, both by precept and example, shows
That prose is verse, and verse is merely prose;
Convincing all, by demonstration plain,
Poetic souls delight in prose insane;
And Christmas stories tortured into rhyme
Contain the essence of the true sublime.
Thus, when he tells the tale of Betty Foy,
The idiot mother of 'an idiot boy;'
A moon-struck, silly lad, who lost his way,
And, like his bard, confounded night with day;
So close on each pathetic part he dwells,
And each adventure so sublimely tells,

That all who view the ' idiot in his glory,'
Conceive the bard the hero of the story.

Shall gentle Coleridge pass unnoticed here,
To turgid ode and tumid stanza dear ?
Though themes of innocence amuse him best,
Yet still obscurity's a welcome guest.
If Inspiration should her aid refuse
To him who takes a pixy for a muse,
Yet none in lofty numbers can surpass
The bard who soars to elegise an ass.
So well the subject suits his noble mind,
He brays the laureat of the long-ear'd tribe.

   *   *   *   *   *

Health to immortal Jeffrey ! once, in name
England could boast a judge almost the same ;
In soul so like, so merciful, yet just,
Some think that Satan has resign'd his trust,
And given the spirit to the world again,
To sentence letters as he sentenced men.
With hand less mighty, but with heart as black,
With voice as willing to decree the rack ;
Bred in the courts betimes, though all that law
As yet hath taught him is to find a flaw ;
Since well instructed in the patriot school
To rail at party, though a party tool,
Who knows, if chance his patrons should restore
Back to the sway they forfeited before,
His scribbling toils some recompense may meet,
And raise this Daniel to the judgment-seat ?
Let Jeffreys' shade indulge the pious hope,
And greeting thus, present him with a rope :
' Heir to my virtues ! man of equal mind !
Skill'd to condemn as to traduce mankind,
This cord receive, for thee reserved with care,
To wield in judgment, and at length to wear.'

Health to great Jeffrey ! Heaven preserve his life
To flourish on the fertile shores of Fife,
And guard it sacred in its future wars,
Since authors sometimes seek the field of Mars !
Can none remember that eventful day,
That ever-glorious, almost fatal fray,
When Little's leadless pistol met his eye,
And Bow-Street myrmidons stood laughing by ?
Oh, day disastrous ! on her firm-set rock,
Dunedin's castle felt a secret shock ;
Dark rolled the sympathetic waves of Forth,
Low groan'd the startled whirlwinds of the north ;
Tweed ruffled half his waves to form a tear,
The other half pursued his calm career ;
Arthur's steep summit nodded to its base,
The surly Tolbooth scarcely kept her place.
The Tolbooth felt—for marble sometimes can,
On such occasions, feel as much as man—
The Tolbooth felt defrauded of his charms,
If Jeffrey died, except within her arms :
Nay, last, not least, on that portentous morn,
The sixteenth storey, where himself was born,
His patrimonial garret, fell to ground,
And pale Edina shudder'd at the sound ;
Strew'd were the streets around with milk-white
    reams,
Flow'd all the Canongate with inky streams ;
This of his candour seem'd the sable dew,
That of his valour show'd the bloodless hue ;
And all with justice deem'd the two combined
The mingled emblems of this mighty mind.
But Caledonia's goddess hover'd o'er
The field, and saved him from the wrath of Moore ;
From either pistol snatch'd the vengeful lead,
And straight restor'd it to her favourite's head ;
That head, with greater than magnetic power,
Caught it, as Danaë caught the golden shower,

And, though the thickening dross will scarce refine,
Augments its ore, and is itself a mine.

From ' The Waltz' [1813].

IMPERIAL Waltz ! imported from the Rhine
(Famed for the growth of pedigree and wine),
Long be thine import from all duty free,
And hock itself be less esteem'd than thee ;
In some few qualities alike—for hock
Improves our cellar—thou our living stock.
The head to hock belongs—thy subtler art
Intoxicates alone the heedless heart.
Through the full veins thy gentler poison swims,
And wakes to wantonness the willing limbs.
O Germany ! how much to thee we owe,
As heaven-born Pitt can testify below,
Ere cursed confederation made thee France's,
And only left us thy d——d debts and dances!
Of subsidies and Hanover bereft,
We bless thee still—for George the Third is left !
Of kings the best, and last not least in worth,
For graciously begetting George the Fourth.
To Germany, and highnesses serene,
Who owe us millions—don't we owe the Queen ?
To Germany, what owe we not besides ?
So oft bestowing Brunswickers and brides :
Who paid for vulgar, with her royal blood,
Drawn from the stem of each Teutonic stud ;
Who sent us—so be pardon'd all our faults—
A dozen dukes, some kings, a queen—and Waltz.

From 'Don Juan' [1819-1823].

THE portion of this world which I at present
Have taken up, to fill the following sermon,
Is one of which there's no description recent :
The reason why is easy to determine ;
Although it seems both prominent and pleasant,
There is a sameness in its gems and ermine,
A dull and family likeness through all ages,
Of no great promise for poetic pages.

With much to excite, there's little to exalt ;
Nothing that speaks to all men and all times ;
A sort of varnish over every fault,
A kind of commonplace, even in their crimes ;
Factitious passion, wit without much salt,
A want of that true nature which sublimes
Whate'er it shows with truth ; a smooth monotony
Of character, in those at least who've got any.

Sometimes indeed like soldiers off parade
They break their ranks and gladly leave the drill ;
But then the roll-call draws them back afraid,
And they must be or seem what they were : still
Doubtless it is a brilliant masquerade.
But when of the first sight you've had your fill,
It palls : at least it did so upon me,
This paradise of pleasure and *ennui*.

When we have made our love and gained our gaming,
Drest, voted, shone, and, maybe, something more :
With dandies dined ; heard senators declaiming ;
Seen beauties brought to market by the score,
Sad rakes to sadder husbands chastely taming ;
There's little left but to be bored and bore.
Witness those *ci-devant jeunes hommes* who stem
The stream, nor leave the world which leaveth them.

'Tis said—indeed, a general complaint—
    That no one has succeeded in describing
The *monde* exactly as they ought to paint :
    Some say that authors only snatch, by bribing
The porter, some slight scandals strange and quaint,
    To furnish matter for their moral gibing ;
And that their books have but one style in common—
My lady's prattle, filtered through her woman.

But this can't well be true just now ; for writers
    Are grown of the *beau monde* a part potential :
I've seen them balance even the scale with fighters,
    Especially when young, for that's essential.
Why do their sketches fail them as inditers
    Of what they deem themselves most consequential,
The real portrait of the highest tribe ?
'Tis that, in fact, they've little to describe.

WILLIAM MACKWORTH PRAED
[1802-1839].

*From 'A Letter of Advice from Miss Medora Trevilian,
at Padua, to Miss Araminta Vavasour, in London.'*

If he wears a top-boot in his wooing,
    If he comes to you riding a cob,
If he talks of his baking or brewing,
    If he puts up his feet on the hob,
If he ever drinks port after dinner,
    If his brow or his breeding is low,
If he calls himself ' Thomson ' or ' Skinner,'
    My own Araminta, say ' No !'

If he studies the news in the papers
    While you are preparing the tea,
If he talks of the damps or the vapours,
    While moonlight lies soft on the sea,

If he's sleepy while you are capricious,
　If he has not a musical ' Oh !'
If he does not call Werther delicious,
　My own Araminta, say ' No !'

If he ever sets foot in the City,
　Among the stockbrokers and Jews,
If he has not a heart full of pity,
　If he don't stand six feet in his shoes,
If his lips are not redder than roses,
　If his hands are not whiter than snow,
If he has not the model of noses,
　My own Araminta, say ' No !'

If he speaks of a tax or a duty,
　If he does not look grand on his knees,
If he's blind to a landscape of beauty—
　Hills, valleys, rocks, waters and trees,
If he dotes not on desolate towers,
　If he likes not to hear the blast blow,
If he knows not the language of flowers,
　My own Araminta, say ' No !'

He must walk like a god of old story
　Come down from the home of his rest ;
He must smile like the sun in his glory
　On the buds he loves ever the best ;
And oh ! from its ivory portal
　Like music his soft speech must flow ;
If he speak, smile, or walk like a mortal,
　My own Araminta, say ' No !'

Don't listen to tales of his bounty,
　Don't hear what they say of his birth,
Don't look at his seat in the county,
　Don't calculate what he is worth ;

But give him a theme to write verse on,
And see if he turns out his toe ;
If he's only an excellent person,
My own Araminta, say ' No !'

THOMAS CARLYLE [1795-1881].

From ' Sartor Resartus ' [1831].

' STRANGE enough how creatures of the human-kind
shut their eyes to plainest facts, and, by the mere
inertia of Oblivion and Stupidity, live at ease in the
midst of Wonders and Terrors. But, indeed, man
is, and was always, a blockhead and dullard, much
readier to feel and digest than to think and consider.
Prejudice, which he pretends to hate, is his absolute
lawgiver—mere use-and-wont everywhere leads him
by the nose. Thus, let but a Rising of the Sun, let
but a Creation of the World happen twice, and it
ceases to be marvellous, to be noteworthy, or notice-
able. Perhaps not once in a lifetime does it occur
to your ordinary biped, of any country or generation,
be he gold-mantled Prince or russet-jerkined Peasant,
that his Vestments and his Self are not one and indi-
visible, that he is naked, without vestments, till he
buy or steal such, and by forethought sew and button
them.

' For my own part, these considerations of our
Clothes-thatch, and how, reaching inwards even to
our heart of hearts, it tailorises and demoralises us,
fill me with a certain horror at myself and mankind
—almost as one feels at those Dutch Cows which,
during the wet season, you see grazing deliberately
with jackets and petticoats (of striped sacking) in the

meadows of Gouda. Nevertheless, there is something great in the moment when a man first strips himself of adventitious wrappages, and sees indeed that he is naked, and, as Swift has it, "a forked, straddling animal with bandy legs," yet also a Spirit, and unutterable Mystery of Mysteries.'

THE DANDIACAL BODY.

FIRST, touching Dandies, let us consider, with some scientific strictness, what a Dandy specially is. A Dandy is a Clothes-wearing Man, a Man whose trade, office and existence consist in the wearing of Clothes. Every faculty of his soul, spirit, purse and person is heroically consecrated to this one object : the wearing of Clothes wisely and well, so that, as others dress to live, he lives to dress. The all-importance of Clothes, which a German Professor, of unequalled learning and acumen, writes his enormous Volume to demonstrate, has sprung up in the intellect of the Dandy without effort, like an instinct of genius. He is inspired with Cloth, a Poet of Cloth. What Teufelsdröckh would call a 'Divine Idea of Cloth' is born with him; and this, like other such Ideas, will express itself outwardly, or wring his heart asunder with unutterable throes. But, like a generous, creative enthusiast, he fearlessly makes his Idea an Action, shows himself in peculiar guise to mankind ; walks forth a witness and living martyr to the eternal worth of Clothes. We called him a Poet: is not his body the (stuffed) parchment-skin whereon he writes, with cunning Huddersfield dies, a Sonnet to his mistress' eyebrow? Say, rather, an Epos, and Clotha Virumque cano, to the whole world, in Macaronic verses, which he that runs may read. Nay, if you grant what seems to be admissible, that the Dandy has a thinking-principle in him, and some notions of Time and Space, is there not in this Life-devotedness to Cloth, in this so-willing sacrifice of the Immortal to the Perishable, something (though in reverse order) of that blending and identification of Eternity with Time, which, as we have seen, constitutes the Prophetic character? And now, for all this perennial Martyrdom, and Poesy, and even Prophecy, what is it that the Dandy asks in return? Solely, we may say, that you would recognise his existence, would admit him to be a living object, or, even failing this, a visual object, or thing that will reflect rays of light. Your silver or your gold (beyond what the niggardly Law has already secured him) he solicits not—simply the glance of your eyes. Understand his mystic significance, or altogether miss and misinterpret it. Do but look at him, and he is contented. May we not well cry ' Shame !' on an ungrateful world which refuses even this poor boon, which will waste its optic faculty on dried Crocodiles and Siamese Twins, and over the domestic, wonderful wonder of wonders, a live Dandy, glance with hasty indifference and a scarcely concealed contempt! Him no Zoologist classes among the Mammalia, no Anatomist dissects with care. When did we see any injected Preparation of the Dandy in our Museums?—any specimen of him preserved in spirits? Lord Herringbone may dress himself in a snuff-brown suit, with snuff-brown shirt and shoes: it skills not. The undiscerning public, occupied with grosser wants, passes by regardless on the other side. The age of Curiosity, like that of Chivalry, is indeed, properly speaking, gone. Yet, perhaps, only gone to sleep, for here arises the Clothes-Philosophy to resuscitate, strangely enough, both the one and the other ! Should sound views of this Science come to prevail, the essential nature of the British Dandy, and the mystic signifi-cance that lies in him, cannot always remain hidden under laughable and lamentable hallucination. . . . The sect of the Dandies have their Temples, whereof the chief, as the Jewish Temple did, stands in their metropolis, and is named Almack's, a word of un-certain etymology. They worship principally by night, and have their High-priests and High-priestesses, who, however, do not continue for life. The rites, by some supposed to be of the Menadic sort, or perhaps with an Eleusinian or Cabiric char-acter, are held strictly secret. Nor are Sacred Books wanting to the Sect : these they call Fashionable Novels. However, the Canon is not completed, and some are canonical, and others not. . . .

ARTICLES OF FAITH.

' 1. COATS should have nothing of the triangle about them; at the same time, wrinkles behind should be carefully avoided.

' 2. The collar is a very important point : it should be low behind, and slightly rolled.

' 3. No license of fashion can allow a man of delicate taste to adopt the posterial luxuriance of a Hottentot.

' 4. There is safety in a swallow-tail.

' 5. The good sense of a gentleman is nowhere more finely developed than in his rings.

' 6. It is permitted to mankind, under certain re-strictions, to wear white waistcoats.

' 7. The trousers must be exceedingly tight across the hips.'

All which Propositions I, for the present, content myself with modestly but peremptorily and irrevoc-ably denying.

THOMAS LOVE PEACOCK [1785-1866].

RICH AND POOR, OR SAINT OR SINNER.

THE poor man's sins are glaring;
In the face of ghostly warning
He is caught in the fact, of an overt act,
Buying greens on Sunday morning.

The rich man's sins are hidden
In the pomp of wealth and station;
And escape the sight of the children of light,
Who are wise in their generation.

The rich man has a cellar,
And a ready butler by him;
The poor must steer for his pint of beer
Where the saint can't choose but spy him.

The rich man's painted windows
Hide the concerts of the quality;
The poor can but share a crack'd fiddle in the air,
Which offends all sound morality.

The rich man is invisible
In the crowd of his gay society;
But the poor man's delight is a sore in the sight
And a stench in the nose of piety.

The rich man has a carriage
Where no rude eye can flout him;
The poor man's bane is a third class train,
With the daylight all about him.

The rich man goes out yachting,
Where society can't pursue him;
The poor goes afloat in a fourpenny boat,
Where the bishop groans to view him.

WILLIAM MAKEPEACE THACKERAY.

From 'The Book of Snobs.'

ABOVE all, I never knew a man of letters *ashamed of his profession.*

Those who know us, know what an affectionate and brotherly spirit there is among us all. Sometimes one of us rises in the world : we never attack him or sneer at him under those circumstances, but rejoice to a man at his success.

If Jones dines with a lord, Smith never says Jones is a courtier and cringer. Nor, on the other hand, does Jones, who is in the habit of frequenting the society of great people, give himself any airs on account of the company he keeps ; but will leave a duke's arm in Pall Mall to come over and speak to poor Brown, the young penny-a-liner.

That sense of equality and fraternity amongst authors has always struck me as one of the most amiable characteristics of the class. It is because we know and respect each other, that the world respects us so much ; that we hold such a good position in society, and demean ourselves so irreproachably when there.

Literary persons are held in such esteem by the nation, that about two of them have been absolutely invited to Court during the present reign ; and it is probable that, towards the end of the season, one or two will be asked to dinner by Sir Robert Peel. They are such favourites with the public that they are continually obliged to have their pictures taken and published ; and one or two could be pointed out, of whom the nation insists upon having a fresh portrait every year. Nothing can be more gratifying than this proof of the affectionate regard which the

21

people has for its instructors. Literature is held in such honour in England that there is a sum of nearly twelve hundred pounds per annum set apart to pension deserving persons following that profession. And a great compliment this is, too, to the professors, and a proof of their generally prosperous and flourishing condition. They are generally so rich and thrifty, that scarcely any money is wanted to help them.

It seems to me that all English society is cursed by this mammoniacal superstition; and that we are sneaking and bowing and cringing on the one hand, or bullying and scorning on the other, from the lowest to the highest. My wife speaks with great circumspection—'proper pride' she calls it—to our neighbour the tradesman's lady: and she, I mean Mrs. Snob—Eliza—would give one of her eyes to go to Court, as her cousin, the Captain's wife, did. She, again, is a good soul, but it costs her agonies to be obliged to confess that we live in Upper Thompson Street, Somers Town. And though I believe in her heart Mrs. Whiskerington is fonder of us than of her cousins, the Smigsmags, you should hear how she goes on prattling about Lady Smigsmag—and 'I said to Sir John, my dear John'; and about the Smigsmags' house and parties in Hyde Park Terrace.

Lady Smigsmag, when she meets Eliza—who is a sort of a kind of a species of a connection of the family, pokes out one finger, which my wife is at liberty to embrace in the most cordial manner she can devise. But oh, you should see her ladyship's behaviour on her first-chop dinner-party days, when Lord and Lady Longears come!

I can bear it no longer—this diabolical invention of gentility which kills natural kindliness and honest friendship. Proper pride, indeed! Rank and precedence, forsooth! The table of ranks and degrees is a lie, and should be flung into the fire. Organize rank and precedence! that was well for the masters of ceremonies of former ages. Come forward, some great marshal, and organize Equality in society, and your rod shall swallow up all the juggling old Court gold-sticks. If this is not gospel-truth—if the world does not tend to this—if hereditary-great-man worship is not a humbug and an idolatry—let us have the Stuarts back again, and crop the Free Press's ears in the Pillory.

THE END.

INDEX OF AUTHORS.

INDEX OF SUBJECTS.

BILLING AND SONS, PRINTERS, GUILDFORD.

www.ingramcontent.com/pod-product-compliance
Lightning Source LLC
Chambersburg PA
CBHW020937030726
47496CB00005B/1236